REQUIEM OF SIN

ZAKREVSKY BRATVA
BOOK 1

NICOLE FOX

ALSO BY NICOLE FOX

Zhukova Bratva

Tarnished Tyrant

Tarnished Queen

Stepanov Bratva

Satin Sinner

Satin Princess

Makarova Bratva

Shattered Altar

Shattered Cradle

Solovev Bratva

Ravaged Crown

Ravaged Throne

Vorobev Bratva

Velvet Devil

Velvet Angel

Romanoff Bratva

Immaculate Deception

Immaculate Corruption

Kovalyov Bratva

Gilded Cage

Gilded Tears

Jaded Soul

Jaded Devil

Ripped Veil

Ripped Lace

Mazzeo Mafia Duet

Liar's Lullaby (Book 1)

Sinner's Lullaby (Book 2)

Bratva Crime Syndicate

Can be read in any order!

Lies He Told Me

Scars He Gave Me

Sins He Taught Me

Belluci Mafia Trilogy

Corrupted Angel (Book 1)

Corrupted Queen (Book 2)

Corrupted Empire (Book 3)

De Maggio Mafia Duet

Devil in a Suit (Book 1)

Devil at the Altar (Book 2)

Kornilov Bratva Duet

Married to the Don (Book 1)

Til Death Do Us Part (Book 2)

Heirs to the Bratva Empire

Can be read in any order!

Kostya

Maksim

Andrei

Princes of Ravenlake Academy (Bully Romance)

Can be read as standalones!

Cruel Prep

Cruel Academy

Cruel Elite

Tsezar Bratva

Nightfall (Book 1)

Daybreak (Book 2)

Russian Crime Brotherhood

Can be read in any order!

Owned by the Mob Boss

Unprotected with the Mob Boss

Knocked Up by the Mob Boss

Sold to the Mob Boss

Stolen by the Mob Boss

Trapped with the Mob Boss

Volkov Bratva

Broken Vows (Book 1)

Broken Hope (Book 2)

Broken Sins *(standalone)*

Other Standalones

Vin: A Mafia Romance

Box Sets

Bratva Mob Bosses (Russian Crime Brotherhood Books 1-6)

Tsezar Bratva (Tsezar Bratva Duet Books 1-2)

Heirs to the Bratva Empire

The Mafia Dons Collection

The Don's Corruption

MAILING LIST

REQUIEM OF SIN

What happens when there's a gorgeous naked man in your hotel room?

That sounds like the setup to a joke, but I promise it's not.

It's the setup to a nightmare.

Here's what happened:

On the worst day of my life, I hit the jackpot.

The literal, actual, million-dollar jackpot at Las Vegas's Meridian casino.

The pit boss gave me a free night's stay in the Sapphire Suite.

I went upstairs, giddy in disbelief, opened the door to my lavish new digs…

And promptly collided with the most beautiful man I've ever seen.

Demyen Zakrevsky is the growly, chiseled, unfairly beautiful billionaire owner of the casino.

He's also completely and totally **naked**.

One thing leads to another, and my perfect night ends in fireworks.

But when the afterglow fades, reality slaps me in the face.

I know this man.

And he definitely knows me.

Fifteen years ago, my testimony put Demyen's older brother in jail for life.

He's been hunting for me ever since.

And now, he's found me… in his bed, no less.

When Demyen figures out who I am, he locks me in a cage and throws away the key.

I'm his now.

His plaything.

His pet.

His perfect little monster.

Here's the other problem, though:

I'm also pregnant with his baby.

REQUIEM OF SIN is Book 1 of the Zakrevsky Bratva

trilogy. Demyen and Clara's continues in Book 2, SONATA OF LIES.

1

CLARA

This cannot be happening.

I must've suddenly gone insane, because there's no way in hell I'm seeing this machine flash that giant word in front of me.

Jackpot.

The slot machine is blaring happy-but-loud alarms to celebrate; that explains why so many heads have turned my way to stare. Some look excited for me; some look frustrated.

Most look *pissed*.

One in particular, an older lady in a tracksuit and fanny pack, is mouthing curses so intense her dentures nearly fall out. I can't really blame her—she'd just moved from this exact seat moments ago.

But I don't hear any of it.

Not Grandma's cussing, not the whispers, not the bells and whistles announcing the lucky break I've been begging my whole life to receive. I'm a little busy trying to retrace my steps to make sure this isn't some fever dream I'm having in a ditch somewhere.

Here's the thing: I don't gamble. Gambling is for people who have nothing to lose, and I—

Wait. I take that back.

I never gambled *before*, because gambling is for people who have nothing to lose, and I've always had far too much at stake.

That changed tonight.

Tonight, as I limped my way to a night shift at my second job slinging drinks as a cocktail waitress for one of Las Vegas's most exclusive nightclubs, I realized that I literally had nothing to lose.

Nothing tangible, anyway.

I've always been broke. I work long hours and sleep short ones just so I can scrape together enough money and time for my daughter. Willow is only five, and she deserves to have her mother present and active in her daily life. It's why I started taking night shifts as often as possible—so I could be there for her, providing for her emotional needs, even if I could barely afford to provide for her practical ones.

Martin promised to take care of us. He promised to take care of me even before I got pregnant, actually, and his pretty song only grew louder as my stomach grew larger. When he held our newborn in his arms for the first time, tears streamed down his face as he swore to take care of us for the rest of our lives.

Of course, I believed him. Who wouldn't? He wasn't just my boyfriend and my kinda-sorta, we'll-get–to-it-eventually-fiancé; he's an officer with the Las Vegas Police Department.

Which is why I grew suspicious when his promises fell flat only a few short months after the birth.

I was supposed to stay at home, which was something we both agreed on. He doesn't earn six figures by any stretch of the imagination, but he's on the cusp of making detective and the bonuses he's gotten have been enough to keep our heads above water.

At least, I thought they were.

Until all of a sudden, I felt like I was drowning.

The first time he hit me was when I asked why he only gave me thirty dollars for grocery shopping.

The second time was when I asked him about the vague, ominous "Final Notices" appearing in the mailbox like clockwork.

The third time he slapped me across the face happened in the dark, because the electricity had been shut off.

I've been able to brush it off each time because of his job. The stress he's under, and in *this* city? It's enough to make Mother Teresa lose her shit. He was always mortified at what he'd done and would spend the days after worshiping me like a goddess. He gave me a little more for groceries, and the Final Notices disappeared. He figured out that the electricity issue was a simple misunderstanding, something in their billing office that was misfiled.

Or so he said.

But none of that ever lasted for long.

The fourth time he hit me was when I told him I got a job. He took it as an affront to his identity as the provider, a sign that I didn't trust him. An "underhanded, bullshit, feminist move to emasculate me, to cut my fuckin' balls off" were his exact words.

The truth is, I was tired of Googling eighty different ways to cook potatoes. I was tired of pretending like I don't eat breakfast just so I could ration out enough oatmeal for Willow. I was tired of being tired of being too poor to be a mother.

I started off waitressing at the kind of big chain where they make all the servers sing a goofy rendition of *"Happy Birthday,"* but I quickly figured out that the real money was in the night scene. I will never set foot inside a strip club, don't get me wrong, but cocktail waitresses still make way more money than pancake house servers.

I eventually convinced Martin that it was a good idea. More money, fewer questions.

That didn't mean he's stopped smacking me around.

He doesn't like how I spray perfume in my long hair to coax bigger tips from the drunk executives who breathe it in whenever I lean over the leather couches to serve their cocktails. He doesn't like the way the polyester uniforms hug my curves, or show off my legs, or put my cleavage on display for any jackass with a five-dollar bill burning a hole in his pocket.

If it's something he feels will tempt men to ogle me, Martin hates it.

And he's very efficient about letting me know.

The nightclub I work at recently updated their wardrobe and my new uniform arrived yesterday. It's sequined, champagne-colored fabric with ruched sides, a plunging neckline to show off the tatas, and toga-like straps on each shoulder to keep it all in place.

On someone less voluptuous, it might go to just above the knee. But on me, it stops at the middle of my thigh. There's a pair of matching heels we're expected to wear while on the floor, but management encouraged us to bring flats for our breaks and commutes. How kind of them.

Martin let me know exactly what he thought about my new look when he got home and found me trying on the shoes. This time, he didn't care that Willow was right there next to me.

But *I* cared.

So when he slapped me so hard across the face I almost fell off the couch—when I heard Willow's terrified screams—I decided right then and there that enough was enough.

"What are you gonna do, huh? What the fuck are you gonna do?" He laughed at me.

He didn't care that I was seething.

He didn't care that I was glaring up at him with murderous rage in my eyes or that our daughter was sobbing and cowering away from him.

"You're not leaving this house looking like some two-dollar whore!" When he saw my tears, Martin tilted his head to one side in mocking sympathy. "Awww, did that hurt? I'm sorry, baby…"

Willow hiccupped between her sobs and peeked up at him. "Daddy?"

"*Shut up!*" he roared at her.

I don't know what came over me, other than pure maternal instinct. I just know that one moment, I was on the couch, my face burning from the slap...

And the next, I was flying through the air at him.

I slammed into Martin so hard that he stumbled over the recliner and we both toppled to the floor into a painful heap of limbs.

I didn't waste time to check and see if he was hurt. I sprung up to my feet, whirled around, grabbed Willow, and ran with her to her bedroom. Once I made sure the door was locked, I wrapped her up in my arms and we rocked together on her tiny bed.

You're probably asking, why didn't I call the police?

Answer: *Because Martin* is *the police.*

I held my daughter close as his fists banged against her door. Loud. Furious. *Violent.* I kissed her tears away as they continued to flow. I needed her to know that I'm here. I'll always be here. I'll never let her grow up in the hell that *I* had to endure.

Eventually, she was able to stop hiccupping enough to sing our favorite song together, about rainbows and daydreams and bluebirds flying to places we can only imagine.

Eventually, the banging slowed into a persistent knock.

Eventually, his shouts melted into apologies and pleas.

And eventually, finally, he was gone.

I waited until I heard the front door slam shut and the sound of his car vanished down the road before I dared move from the bed. Then, once I knew for sure he was gone, I threw a few changes of clothes for Willow into her backpack and called my best friend to let her know it was finally happening.

We were leaving.

Roxy peeled into the driveway less than ten minutes later. I'd bet everything I've ever owned that she blew through every red light on her way over.

She greeted Willow the same as always, hiding the worry in her eyes behind a brilliant smile. "Hey, pretty lady! Wanna have a girls' night? I got pizza and ice cream and three kinds of soda!"

"Yeah!" Still puffy-eyed, Willow practically threw herself into Roxy's SUV.

I'd usually scold my best friend for poisoning my child with junk food, but not tonight. Willow needed to forget what we just went through, and Roxy knew exactly how to make that happen. She's been making it happen for me since we were kids.

"You okay?" Roxy lowered her voice as she glanced around for my bags. "You should call in. Pack your things and come with us."

I shook my head. "I need the money. I know Martin wasn't holding his end well, but it was still more than I can do on my own. Plus… I could use the distraction. The normalcy."

"Right."

Reluctant as she was, Roxy respected my decision to go to work as if everything was normal. I made sure to grab the old, dented coffee can Martin never paid attention to before I locked up the house and tucked it under my arm as we made our way to the SUV.

She cocked a brow at my choice of luggage. "Isn't that a bit small for a weekender bag?"

I managed a genuine, albeit small, laugh. "It's enough to *buy* me a weekender bag."

Her eyes widened when I opened the lid once we were safely buckled inside her car. "Holy freaking shit."

"Language!" Willow scolded from her booster in the backseat.

Roxy snorted. "Sorry, Wills. But really, Clara… what…?"

I shrugged and pulled a few bills from the thick wad nestled inside the can. "I may have only told Martin about… *half* of my tips."

Which is how I ended up walking The Strip to work in a sexy cocktail dress with almost every penny I had tucked inside my strapless bra.

I left the rest with Roxy in case she needed anything for Willow, despite her protests and reassurances that there's no way a tiny girl could rack up a huge pizza bill. I knew that, but what I didn't know was how Martin would react when he returned home to find it empty. I left my car there, my things there, but it wouldn't take long for him to figure out we were gone.

And if anything happens to me, I need to know Willow is going to be okay.

Which brought me to the front of the casino.

I've walked past The Meridian a dozen times since taking on this second night job, but this was the first time I'd ever paused to actually look at it. I don't know why I did this time. Maybe it was fate. Maybe it was foolishness.

Maybe it was simply because the golden lights matched my dress.

The Meridian Casino & Hotel is one of those places that makes it clear that it caters to an elite clientele—crystal chandeliers, marble balustrades, and amber lights enveloping every square inch of Strip-facing architecture in a way that manages to pull you in without blinding you. It's open to anyone who wants to try their luck at the slots and tables, but I've always dismissed it as one of those places a peasant like me would never be able to afford to even breathe in.

Nothing had changed about my financial situation, that was certain.

What changed was the fact that I literally had nothing to lose.

A handsome executive in a sharply tailored tuxedo stepped out of a car behind me, nearly clipping me with his door. He didn't seem to notice—he certainly didn't bother apologizing —but he was very attentive to the gorgeous woman who draped herself on his arm the second she slid out of the vehicle. They looked like celebrities walking the red carpet as they made their way into the casino.

Something tugged me in their slipstream, down that same rich carpet leading to the front doors of The Meridian. I watched the couple nod to the attendants who scurried to open the doors for them.

And as I watched, something in my heart ached.

I've never desired wealth or status, but in that moment, I wanted so much for a taste of that world. Just a taste.

And tonight, I could afford it, because I had nothing to lose.

I quickly changed from my flats to my heels and tried my best to make my bag look like it was part of my ensemble. The attendants smiled, nodded, greeted me with "good evenings," and opened the doors for me just as they had for the couple before me.

I felt like Dorothy entering the Emerald City for the very first time. Everything shimmered and glowed and dinged and tinkled. Even the staff had an inner shine. As if they were part of the architecture, brought to life by the setting sun and the neon lights, their veins flush with absinthe and dreams.

Table games scared me. The leers, the scowls, the desperate men hunched over hands of cards with menace in their eyes. I don't know much about slots, either, but they seemed easier to handle. Push a button and pray—that was more my style.

I don't remember walking across the floor, through the pit, or really moving anywhere at all. But I must have, because I somehow found myself at a cluster of slot machines tucked into a corner.

An older woman in a garish pink tracksuit huffed in frustration and stood from her stool at the machine closest to the pit. She grumbled something about "gone cold" and shuffled her way over to a different row of the same game.

I stared at that stool.

Why not?

That was the question burning on my mind as I sat down and pulled out a hundred-dollar bill from my bra.

2

DEMYEN

TWENTY MINUTES EARLIER

"Don't forget, you have a 10 A.M. tomorrow with Stevenson."

I don't bother tearing my gaze from the window. "Postpone it."

I was bored the moment I stepped into the town car, and I'm not going to pretend I'm interested in anything now. Certainly not meeting with Edwin fucking Stevenson, the most boring man in Las Vegas.

Bambi arches an elegant brow but doesn't look up from her tablet. It's her quietly respectful way of questioning my judgment. "This will be the third time we've rescheduled, Demyen."

"Fine." I lean back in the leather seat with a sigh and a matching grimace. "Order a spread for brunch. I don't care as long as I can kick him out once my hangover outweighs my patience."

Her other brow joins the first. "Anticipating an exciting night? Or a rough one?"

Champagne drips from his nose and hair. He's gorgeous; there's no denying that. I don't know if he's an avenging angel or a fallen one, but he's carved from the same marble as this palatial room and he's breathtaking.

And all I can think is, … *Jackpot?*

So mundane.

Like my whole damn life didn't just change.

My lungs are finally working again, though, and they suck in a deep breath. Then I cry out as loud as I can, "*YES!*"

I leap to my feet with victory fists punching the air. I've escaped hell and won my way into heaven. Roxy, Willow, and I are going to take the first private jet out of Nevada. We're going to find somewhere warm and quiet and we're going to wear matching coconut bikinis and drink mocktails on the beach. We're going to be okay.

We're going to be okay.

But, as I realize a moment too late, my victory fist is on a crash course with a nearby server just as she rounds the corner bearing an overloaded tray of hot coffees and watered-down vodka cranberries.

I turn in horror. It's too late to stop it. My hand keeps going. Up and up, until it collides with the waitress's tray…

Everything after that happens in slow motion.

First, I see the girl's mascara-encrusted eyes go wide as saucers. I'm sure mine are doing the same.

Then the tray tips. Coffee sloshes over the rim of the highest mug in the stack. It becomes a murky brown waterfall, then intermingles with the vodka crans until it all looks like sewage. The whole nasty mess flies through the air, a tidal wave of the stuff, and sends it surging down…

All over a gorgeous man in a sharply tailored tuxedo.

Glass shatters. People scream. The man, though, just turns to glare at me full-on.

This is insane.

I need this money.

But my hands moved like they couldn't hear what I was thinking.

I didn't know how the game played, or what it paid out, or what all the connecting arrows on a super complicated chart meant. I just watched a few people nearby feed their money to their machine, press the big, glowing button, and wait.

So I fed this machine my hundred-dollar bill, pressed the big, glowing button, and waited.

Things spun. Lights flashed. Buttons whirred. And then, a seven-letter word popped up to change the course of my life.

Jackpot.

~

The sound comes rushing back in now. The vacuum punctures and the world hammers at my eardrums.

Which means I can very clearly hear the bells and whistles screaming at me that I've won.

A small slip of paper spits out of the machine, and I take it. It's oddly underwhelming. I thought it would start spewing gold coins and I could dive into my newfound money jacuzzi like Scrooge McDuck, but I guess not. Nothing but a small little ticket, single ply paper, fading ink. *"SEE CASHIER FOR WINNINGS"* is printed in bold across the top.

So neat.

So simple.

Maybe it's more accurate to say that I'm not bored as much as I'm drained. Thoroughly and irrevocably drained. What I need is a drink, so I can scrub the day's events from memory.

Today was my older brother Tolya's scheduled appearance at the Court of Appeals to plead new developments in his case. New witnesses are willing to come forward and testify, and we're getting closer to tracking down the location of the false witness whose testimony condemned him to a life sentence. I hired the best legal defense team in the state of Nevada, a squad of fucking sharks with J.D.s, and we marched into that courtroom with a bulletproof case for appeal.

It was denied.

It seems the opinion of Judge Andrew Cartwell is that, without the retraction of the key eyewitness's testimony, my brother will spend the rest of his life behind bars for a murder he didn't commit.

Too bad the key eyewitness is nowhere to be found.

The hard part wasn't facing down the judge, or forcing myself to remain calm when the idiot banged the gavel against the blatantly obvious, or keeping my hands in my pockets so I didn't strangle every last one of those preening motherfuckers.

The hard part was watching Tolya get dragged away, yet again, bound in cuffs and reassuring me over his shoulder that it's okay. *It's all going to be okay.*

I was a helpless teenager all over again. Unable to protect my own brother. Unable to stand up for him.

I waited until I returned to my penthouse and stepped into the private gym, before I let the rage and despair loose. I didn't even bother changing out of the suit and into workout gear. I needed to punch things, to throw things. Feeling priceless seams rip only added to the rush.

Bambi offered to send in some "extra relief," but I turned her down. I don't believe in dipping one's pen inside the company's ink. And with the way I'm feeling, it's better for women to stay out of my way *and* out of my bed.

Now, I'm drained, and yet the night's just begun. I tried sleeping through the afternoon to get some of my energy back, but I just need something to jumpstart my willpower.

Nothing a few shots of bourbon and a successful night of burying myself in work can't fix.

The town car pulls to a stop in front of the casino. Even through the tinted windows, The Meridian's lights sparkle over my arm in a twinkling promise of guaranteed good fortune to come.

Well… good fortune for me, at least. Seeing as how I own the place.

"What's the headcount for tonight?"

She taps the screen of her tablet and puckers her lips as she runs through a few calculations. "Twenty-one escorts working the Main Floor, seven men and fourteen women. Although we do have a few from the new pool of recruits waiting in the wings. Would you like me to—"

"Just one. Add them to the Main Floor and make sure we incorporate more tomorrow. For tonight, I like the numbers as they are."

I tell the press I'm not a superstitious person, but that's a boldfaced lie.

I don't fuck with Lady Luck.

The giveaway is the elegant statue of the goddess herself carved over the archway of The Meridian, welcoming gamblers to my establishment. I prefer the high rollers. Nothing like a rich fool with money to lose. But I do take a certain sort of secret delight at seeing the average Joe rejoice in a win now and then.

Bambi's roster of escorts isn't simply an additional service we offer. It's also our way of keeping tabs. When you know what your big spenders like, it becomes very easy to tempt them into doing it on camera. And when they know that you know... well, safe to say their business will remain ours for as long as they live.

It's almost shocking how many powerful men have very particular tastes they'd never breathe to their closest friends or, heaven forbid, their innocent wives.

And not just corrupt politicians—athletes, too, and tech whizzes, and bad men with businesses almost as depraved as mine.

Also—federal judges.

Now, *that* was an unexpected surprise.

"Add a few more security personnel to the High Roller Lounge." I tap a finger on my chin as I think. "Make sure they're wired. And let's extend VIP hospitality to Mr. Cartwell. Keep him happy and keep him rolling. Just make sure every word he breathes is recorded and transcribed."

I open the door and step out onto the plush crimson carpet of The Meridian's main entrance. It's a bit of an old Hollywood touch I wasn't sure about at first, but after seeing people stop and take selfies and follow it inside to try their luck at the slots, I decided to keep it. I did make sure the material wouldn't catch on any stiletto heels—the last thing I need is a personal injury lawsuit splashed all over the headlines.

Good thing, too, because I don't see the woman standing next to the car. The door nearly slams into her, but she manages to stumble backward without falling.

I ignore her. No harm, no foul, and not my fault or my problem.

But I do catch a glimpse of her in the corner of my eye. As I do, some faint spark of recognition ignites in the back of my mind.

"Is she one of ours?" I murmur to Bambi as I help her out of the car.

Bambi steals a quick glance and shakes her head. "Not on our roster."

"Hm."

"Want me to look into it?" She loops her arm through mine and leans in close so it looks like we're sharing an intimate secret.

"Don't bother. Just thought I recognized her."

Bambi looks like she wants to press further, but she lets it go. Instead, she smiles cordially at the attendants as they open the glass doors for us and smooths a hand over her silk jumpsuit with a sigh. "Ready?"

I don't answer. I simply lead us into the Main Floor and let the cacophony of the casino envelop us.

Time to get to work.

3

DEMYEN

It's a busy night—as it should be, given that it's Friday. Payday for the rank-and-file means the slots are fuller and the money is flowing from their hands to the machines to my pocket. Just the way I like it.

"Mr. Zakrevsky."

"Good evening, Mr. Zakrevsky."

"Good evening, sir."

My name fills the air as I meander through the casino. My payroll is rife with people in every line of work imaginable. Not just escorts, but cocktail waitresses, bartenders, attendants, concierges, and the like. People who know better than to ask questions.

People who have nothing to do with the Zakrevsky Bratva.

"What can I start you off with tonight, Mr. Zakrevsky?" The bartender, Mike, flashes me a genuine smile and preps a tumbler with ice. He already knows what I'm about to order, but he always gives me the chance to surprise him.

I don't. "Bourbon. On the rocks. Make it a double."

The drink is already in my hand before I finish the sentence.

Bambi scrunches her freckled nose as I toss it back and savor the syrupy burn down my throat. "I'll take mine neat," she tells Mike. "Room temp. Like a normal person."

I chuckle and set the empty tumbler down. "Judge me all you want. We live in a fucking desert. Ice is a blessing."

As I wait for her to finish her drink, I take the moment to lean back and scan the room. I'm not looking for anything or anyone in particular. Sometimes, it's just nice to enjoy the sights and sounds of the empire I rule over.

The same empire that should have been my brother's.

We're about to leave the bar and head for the office suite when a woman's voice reaches my ears. "… No, thanks. Really."

It's the way her words tremble that pulls my attention.

"C'mon, baby." Some guy in a dark leather jacket with too much gel in his hair rubs her waist as she tries to slide off the stool. When she leans away, his fingers tighten. "I got a room upstairs. We can have a real nice time—"

She musters a quivering smile and tries to maneuver from his grasp. "Really. It's okay. I'm good."

"But I bought you that drink!"

"I didn't ask you to." There's fear in her eyes, but she's trying so hard to be polite.

The bartender starts to move in their direction, but I give him a subtle signal to back down.

I'll handle this.

Bambi sits back and orders another drink, this time something pink with a fancy straw. She knows how I operate. She's ready to enjoy the show.

"Good evening." I saunter up to the tangled pair, my most brilliant host's smile plastered on my face. "How are you two doing tonight?"

"We're fine, man. Everything's fine." The man waves me off with an irritated flick of his hand.

I loft a brow. "Is it?" My gaze slides to the woman. She looks shaken, but she forces a smile of her own.

"I was just leaving," she mumbles, grabbing her clutch.

"Please—stay." I gesture to her barstool but still give her wide enough berth to run if she feels the need. She doesn't know who I am, but her eyes do a quick once-over and something eases just a bit in her posture.

Before she does decide to run, I gesture for the bartender. "Mike."

He slides over, his face serious even as his eyes glint with mischief. We love this game. "Yeah, boss?"

"What is this beautiful young lady drinking?"

Mike cocks his head at the empty glass on the countertop. "Well rum and coke."

I click my tongue in mock admonishment. "Oh, no, no, no. We can do better than that."

The gropey man huffs and holds a hand up to interrupt me, but I ignore it. Right now, he doesn't exist. And when I do decide to turn my attention to him, he'll long for the days when I didn't know him from a fucking hole in the ground.

I lean against the counter and focus my attention on the woman. "What's your poison? Anything under the sun. Name it and it's yours."

"Listen, buddy—" The man grabs my arm. And then he yelps when he's immediately ripped away by my security.

I stay focused on the woman. She blushes and settles back onto the stool. She is pretty, I'll give her that. Definitely a tourist, and given the tan line on her ring finger, I'd guess a recent divorcee.

"Um, I don't know…" She tucks a strand of hair behind her ear. The ends are frayed and her roots haven't been touched in months. It doesn't take long for me to piece together the story of someone scrimping by just to survive an ordeal. This is probably her one chance at a break before she's back to cold, hard reality. "Vodka? Maybe?"

My smile broadens. "Have you ever tasted Russo-Baltique vodka?"

The man stiffens behind me. He instantly stops struggling with my guards when he hears my native accent slip out.

She blushes more and shakes her head. "Hell no. That stuff is… No, safe to say I have never, ever tried million-dollar vodka. As you can tell, my luck here hasn't been that great."

I nod to Mike, who is already pouring a shot glass from the diamond-encrusted bottle we keep in the refrigerated safe under the bar.

"Are… are you serious?" she balks.

I nod. "On the house."

Mike slides me another shot glass, and I hold it up for her to clink. "To new beginnings."

Again, her eyes widen, but she tosses it back at the same time I do. We both hiss at the afterburn. It's like drinking glacier water.

I glance over to Bambi. She's wearing her amused smile. "Let's get our beautiful guest set up with some VIP treatment, hm?"

"On it." Bambi taps a few things on her phone, a smirk tugging at her lips. "Want me to include The Celestial?"

"Absolutely."

"Done."

It's not even a full minute before one of our concierges appears at the woman's elbow. He offers her a warm smile and a slight bow. "If you'll come with me, madam?"

She glances between the three of us, then settles her perplexed stare on me. "What's going on?"

I set my shot glass back on the counter. "I'm guessing your luck hasn't been great for a while. That's why you came out here, isn't it?"

Her eyes dart down and away. She nods mutely.

"Well, then, time for a change." I straighten my jacket, give her one final nod, then turn to deal with the other loose end.

Behind me, the concierge escorts the woman down a nearby side hall toward the spa. When she's out of sight, I signal for security to bring the man along.

He and I are going in a slightly different direction.

4

DEMYEN

The poor bastard tries to drag his feet on the carpet like he's hoping the earth will swallow him whole before we reach the private security room tucked behind the glass elevator. But my men are stronger than him, and they hoist him up so only his toes skate over the plush fibers.

I hear him mutter pleas, stammer promises to leave and never come back, but I ignore him.

It's too late for that.

Bambi bids us *adieu* at the door; she's never had much taste or patience for what comes next. It's just as well—she needs to go check in with all our escorts in the pit.

The man is firmly seated into one of the metal chairs. Two of my men keep a hand on each of his shoulders to make sure he doesn't think running is a good idea. The others lean in the corners, every bit the silent, violent sentinels they're trained to be.

Even before I speak, the message is clear.

And it's dripping down the man's face in rivulets.

"Listen, man," he stutters, "I meant you no disrespect—"

I hold up a hand and he falls silent. "Of course not." I flash him a charming smile, but my eyes are full of venom. "You came into *my* house, drank *my* liquor, and harassed *my* guests. But you meant no disrespect to me specifically."

His mouth snaps shut.

"Here's the thing…" I check the message from Bambi on my smartwatch. "… Mr. Nichols. Mr. *Josh* Nichols. From Los Angeles as well—how lovely. We're practically neighbors."

I meet his terrified gaze, my smile still perfectly in place. His throat bobs with a terrified swallow.

"Here's the thing," I repeat. "This is a business. This is *my* business. And what people do under *my* roof is *my* business. So when someone like you comes in here and threatens my guests, you threaten my business."

He gulps again. It's audible in the silent room.

"And I simply can't have you threatening my business, Mr. Nichols."

"I-I s-s-swear, man, I'll never—"

He grimaces in pain when both men bracing his shoulders squeeze tight. Any more pressure and they'll snap his collarbone.

"I swear, *Mr. Zakrevsky*! I'm out! I'll never come back!"

I steal a glance to the guard on my right, who immediately hands me the man's now-unlocked phone. I skim through the texts. Most of them are hookup requests and uncouth responses to various rejections on one dating app after another.

The truth is, this guy is hardly worth the time I'm giving him right now. The only reason why I'm even bothering is because reputation precedes performance, and the public currently milling around the Main Floor need to see the House keeps things safe and clean.

But there are far greater threats than Mr. Nichols out there. Truth is, this sad excuse for a man doesn't even register. So I do the next best thing and cut him some slack.

Notice I *didn't* say that I cut him loose.

"Sasha."

The guard to my left steps forward. He's intimidating with broad shoulders, a deep chest, and bald head tattooed with tribal flames near his ears. The very picture of *Do not fuck with me.*

"*Da, pakhan?*" he grunts in Russian.

I smirk. He knows the game well.

"Keep Mr. Nichols company while we decide what to do with him. And see what you can do about these dating profiles; they're atrocious."

Sasha nods and calmly sits in the chair opposite Nichols, taking the phone once I set it on the table. Nichols slumps in his chair, clearly on the verge of sobbing. He doesn't know what's about to happen to him. He doesn't know how Sasha is going to "keep him company." All his mind can do is run through the worst possible scenarios, and they're obviously terrible.

If he were anyone who mattered, they probably would be.

But I don't need the blood on my furniture, and besides—the nightmares he can conjure himself are worse than anything Sasha's brass knuckles could ever do to him. My men will make him shit his pants for an hour, then rough him up a bit, throw him into the back alley, and let him scurry back to whatever rat hole he calls home.

I give a curt nod. The rest of the men file behind each other and we exit the room together, leaving Josh Nichols to the worst hour of his life.

The curious gazes that skirt our way as we stride to the pit are exactly why I have this little protocol in place. No one knows what's going on in that room—only that Demyen Zakrevsky personally manhandled a serial sleaze who dared come into this House.

Bambi matches my smirk when she hands me her tablet at the edge of the pit. "Right on schedule."

The screen is lit with selfies and captions posted by the now-elated VIP guest as she tours her luxury suite and tries on the silk complimentary robes. Comments and likes continue to pour in as friends and family push the posts through the social media algorithms.

"And the bookings?" I accept a tumbler from a passing server and take a sip.

"Up by fifteen percent since it went viral. We'll have a busy weekend next week."

"Perfect."

Bambi flips the cover shut and tucks the tablet under her arm. "Tolya would be proud of you, you know."

The thought comes as a hard punch to my gut. My mood suddenly sours, and I resist shooting her a glare. I know she means it as a compliment. I hate how it feels more like a reminder that his empire fell into my lap through Fate's cruelest twist.

It doesn't matter that even Tolya insists I stole nothing from him. It still *feels* like I did.

"He'd have it twice as successful than it is now," I grumble. "With half as many idiots poisoning the bar."

Bambi rolls her eyes and makes no effort at all to hide it. "When are you going to take credit for your own success?"

I toss back the rest of the tumbler's contents and slam the glass down on a nearby table. "When I find that fucking 'key witness' and thank them myself for the opportunity."

Because that's what this all boils down to.

I have everything around me, this glittering empire of dreams and diamond dust, because some snot-nosed kid lied on the stand fifteen years ago.

I shake my head before I can sink into the usual storm of rage and angst over how it's been so long and I still haven't found her. "Give me the report," I order.

Bambi sighs and pulls out her tablet and flips to a screen where the Main Floor layout is outlined in blue. Every machine is labeled according to its placement, with a running tracker of wins and losses indicating whether it's "hot" or "cold" by the second. If a machine stays hot for too long, we're alerted of a glitch so we can pull it, fix it, and minimize our losses.

And if it's cold for too long…

"What's our coldest?" I peer at the screen.

Bambi taps on a section next to the pit, and an enlarged window zeroes in on the machines. "Looks like *Medusa's Wrath*. Only two payouts in the last hour. This one on the end has been cold for…" She frowns. "Six hours. That's odd. Want me to call in tech support?"

I shake my head. "Not yet. Funnel the wins to that machine and we'll pull later. No one's gonna touch something that icy."

Bambi nods her agreement and makes the necessary adjustments. She funnels additional funds to the glitched-up machine.

With that settled, I start another circuit of the casino floor. I'm only vaguely aware of Bambi rattling off a To-Do list as we wander. Bambi's intended praise still swirls in my head.

Tolya would be proud.

Would he, though? I have no idea how Tolya would have run things. He never got the chance to even try. Our old man was still around calling the shots and ruling with an iron fist when Tolya was arrested for a murder he never committed.

Everything hinged on the testimony of an eight-year-old little girl who swore she saw my brother gun down LVPD Detective Michael Little. To this day I can't shake the feeling that someone, somehow, skewed the facts so my brother would never see the light of day. But I can't put my finger on which one.

Fact: Michael Little was fatally shot inside a warehouse.

Fact: That warehouse, unfortunately, was owned by the Zakrevsky Corporation.

Fact: The key witness *was* there.

Fact: Tolya was nowhere near the warehouse when it all went down.

Today's failed appeal was to establish that last fact to an undeniable level. No fewer than eight witnesses prepared written and notarized testimonies to having either seen or been with Tolya that night, clear across the city and far away from the warehouse five miles east outside Vegas.

But Judge Cartwell simply stated that the little girl who "saw it all" held more validity than all those witnesses combined.

My fists clench. I need to get to my office before I punch something and start a scene we *don't* want splashed all over social media.

So I quicken my pace, Bambi close behind, her nose buried in whatever stats are rolling across her tablet screen.

My own stats are rolling in my head, alongside the list of facts that won't let me sleep. The number of innocent men incarcerated in the state of Nevada. The number of innocent men who never get exonerated.

The odds of me ever finding that witness.

I step out of the pit and turn toward the wall where the elevator to my office is hidden behind a camouflage panel. I make a mental note to check on the Medusa's Wrath slot machines—

And then, suddenly, I'm doused in coffee and champagne.

5

CLARA

I very, very slowly lower my victory fists.

The avenging angel flicks champagne off his arms as he stares at me. It's not quite a glare, but he's not laughing, either. Droplets cling to the perfectly manicured, just-this-side-of-shadow beard, and the way the light hits him makes them sparkle.

I should be apologizing, but I can't stop staring at how tragically beautiful he truly is.

I should really be apologizing.

"I-I am… *so* sorry!" I frantically glance around for napkins and only find a used wad of them on the machine next to mine. Ew, no. "Really, I—"

"Have no consideration for your surroundings?"

If I thought his face was gorgeous, his deep timbre has officially made my insides melt.

It takes me a moment to register the actual words he said. When they do, they hit deep and I flinch.

I muster an embarrassed little smile. Broken glass crunches under his feet when he steps to the side, and I flinch again.

He towers over me, a good head and a half taller at the very least. Even stained with bubbly, his expensive tuxedo screams "powerful," and the contours of the body beneath it underscore that word times a hundred. Dark hair falls into his eyes when he looks back at me again, and I suck in a breath at the way his smoky gray eyes seem to glow in the casino's lighting.

Those eyes flick to the paper clenched in my lowered fist. His brow arches as realization dawns on him. "Jackpot win?"

That vacuum on my lungs threatens to start up again as I slowly nod. "Yeah," comes out more like a squeak than an actual word.

"Congratulations." He chuckles. "Now, you can afford a new tux for me."

I blanch.

"Breathe. I'm kidding." He accepts a cloth napkin that a stunning woman with dark curls hands him and pats himself down. I instantly recognize her from the town car when I first came in.

Oh, good Lord. I've doused her husband in alcohol.

She's doing her absolute best to hold back the laughter as she nods to someone in the pit and helps my splash zone victim dab off the remaining liquid from his sleeve. I'm actually envious of her. I volunteer myself to be the one to feel his biceps through the fabric.

I give myself a subtle little shake. *Focus, Clara.*

"Really, is there anything I can do?" I ask. "I feel terrible."

He waves me off. "Don't worry about it. Just enjoy the rest of your evening, and try to aim your bubbly next time." His face grows suddenly serious. "Any more champagne showers in here, and I'll have to call Security."

I almost gasp—but then he winks at me.

Then he saunters off, gorgeous wife/girlfriend/escort/whoever trailing close behind him.

She suddenly stops. Turns around. And stares at me.

Her eyes flick to the flashing graphics on the slot machine I'm standing in front of. She glances down at a tablet tucked on her arm, then back up at me.

She looks shocked.

And then the most impish grin I've ever seen on a human being spreads across her face.

She wiggles her fingers at me in a playful "goodbye," and in a strange move, also blows me a kiss. Then she spins on her elegant stilettos and sashays away, albeit not exactly in the same direction as the Champagne Angel. Odd, but who am I to judge couples in Vegas?

Lord knows I've got my own relationship problems.

I uncrumple the paper from my death-grip and read the jackpot total again.

And again.

And again.

I may have a truckload of problems in my life right now, but money is no longer one of them.

I nearly trip over my own heels in my mad dash for the cashier's counter. A few curious people follow me with their eyes and I realize I need to be as minimally conspicuous as possible until I get out of this building. Hell, until I get it all deposited in the bank and take Willow far, far away from this place.

"I'd like to cash out, please." I smile at the middle-aged cashier wearing the casino's signature gold referee uniform and a matching gold chain on her reading glasses. She seems nice, trustworthy. She returns my smile warmly.

That smile immediately plummets into a look of pure shock when she scans the ticket. "I—ah… Are you sure?" she asks with a small, nervous laugh.

"I'm very sure." My fingers clutch my bag until my knuckles turn white.

She clicks a few things on her keyboard, glancing at me every five seconds. It's difficult to tell what she's thinking. Her face keeps switching between different expressions depending on what she's looking at—the computer screen, the ticket, or me.

"Okay, I'll just need to see your driver's license, and…" She turns and dips for something under the counter, then sets a stack of papers in front of me. "I'll need you to fill these forms out. Top to bottom, please. If you have any questions, just ask."

I try to not look or feel as overwhelmed as I suddenly feel. "All this?"

She snorts, but it's all in good nature. "All this for all *that*. You will also need to make sure you file a W2-G when tax season rolls around, and be aware that all winnings are typically subject to a twenty-five percent tax rate—"

"Twenty-five percent?" I blurt out.

A few people glance our way. I immediately duck my face behind my hand.

The cashier gives me a genuine little chuckle. "Honey, twenty-five percent taken from your winnings still leaves you a very wealthy woman. If I were in your shoes, I'd take the win."

"Right. You're right. Sorry."

Solid point, really.

I get to work filling out the forms, bubble by bubble and letter space by letter space. Who knew hitting it big time at the casino would be so... so... *boring*?

I slide the papers back to the cashier, and she gives them a thorough review before nodding her approval and scanning them into the system.

"You have a few options for your on-site payout." She slides a thick linen brochure to me. "But I will need to know if you would prefer a lump sum deposited into your bank account, or if you want it dispersed in an annuity—"

"Can't I have it in cash?"

She blinks at me.

Then she cackles.

"Sweetheart," the cashier coos once she can breathe again, "I *wish* you and I could see and feel what that amount of cash is like. Believe me. But to be honest, the house doesn't physically have enough cash to cover that amount up front."

"Oh."

There must be something in the way my face instantly falls that tugs at her. Maybe it's the tears brimming in my eyes. Or the hopelessness I suddenly feel.

Whatever it is, it makes her reach across the counter to pat the back of my hand. "I can, however, give you a nice chunk of change tonight. If that will help?"

"Yeah?" I sniff back the tears that thankfully didn't fall. Yet. "How much?"

She clicks a few keys on her keyboard. Scrunches her face in thought. Mutters a few things to herself, and it sounds like she's dancing through a few loopholes for my sake.

"How does... fifty thousand sound?"

I do a dry spit take, and then quickly wipe my mouth clean with an embarrassed blush. "Um, yeah! That... that will be great."

More than great. I made half that for the whole of last year.

I'm about to walk away with *two entire years'* worth of income in my hands.

Don't worry, Willow-tree. We'll go somewhere real nice and we'll never go hungry again.

The cashier slides the stacks of cash to me. I stuff them inside my bag next to my flats. They feel so heavy and yet so light. With every bound stack of hundred-dollar bills I tuck inside my purse, I count another dream on the verge of being fulfilled.

Get out of Las Vegas.

Get out of poverty.

Get away from him.

I almost jump for joy when I realize: I never have to go back to that shack of a house ever again. I don't need anything we left behind—I can simply buy replacements. New clothes, new toys, new furniture—heck, I can buy a whole new house!

"I'll take that lump sum for the rest of it, if that's okay," I whisper to the cashier. I don't know why I feel so embarrassed about it. Like I don't deserve it.

She smiles warmly at me and nods. "Absolutely, hon."

Maybe that's what it is. I'm embarrassed because I'm afraid this is all just a weird fever dream, and I'm about to wake up next to Martin. He'll ask me what the dream was about, then find some way to punish me for dumping champagne on a total stranger and winning more money than he'll ever see in a lifetime.

It won't matter that it's all a dream.

He'll find a way to punish me.

I'm going to wake up, and all this will be gone.

The cashier frowns with concern. "Honey… are you okay?"

I don't realize I've started to have a panic attack until she says something. I'm gripping the counter and breathing hard, and for a moment, I completely forgot where I was.

Slowly, I nod. "Uh-huh. Sorry. Just… wrapping my head…" I twirl a finger in the air.

She smirks. "It's real, hon. You are wide awake."

"I'm free."

I don't realize I said that out loud until our eyes meet. There's a sudden warmth of sympathy in her gaze, and I kind of want to hug her.

"Yeah, hon. You're free."

I swallow hard. Nod. Tighten the straps on my bag, make sure it's zipped, and hold it close to my chest. Then nod again. "I guess… I guess I'm doing this."

The cashier winks at me. "You're doing this. And you'll do just fine." She leans forward and drops her voice to a conspiratorial whisper. "May he choke on the dust of your tires."

When women know, we *know*.

Smiling in disbelief, I hug my bag and make my way to those ornate glass doors I'd walked through what now feels like a lifetime ago. They're only a few yards away. A few yards away, past the crystal fountain, and Willow and I are getting the hell outta—

"Miss?"

Two security guards suddenly approach me, then flank me. They're stone-faced and grim.

"Would you come with us, please?"

I was so close to freedom.

6

CLARA

Please, God. I don't even know what I'm praying for. Mercy, maybe?

I don't know what I've done, but it must be bad. We're joined by two more guards and now, I'm surrounded on all sides by armed men in uniform with badges and there's no escape and—

"Ah, there you are!"

An overly tanned man with silver hair and an impeccably white tuxedo greets me and my "entourage" with open arms and a beaming smile. "Miss Everett, yes?"

I nod. Slowly.

"My apologies for the scare. Seriously, gentlemen, can't you see she's terrified?" He shoos them away with a flick of his fingers. His million-watt smile returns, and he ushers me past another crystal fountain. "I was almost afraid we'd missed you. Right this way, Miss Everett."

I stop in my tracks, only because I'm struggling to process it all. "Where are we going?"

"Ah, right!" He claps his hands together. "Forgive me. It's been a busy night and there was a small disaster with the boss... Anyway. My name is Charles, and I am one of the floor managers here at The Meridian."

"You're..." I gulp. "You're a pit boss."

He scrunches his nose in distaste. "Only if you're a cheater. Which—not to worry, Miss Everett—we know you are not."

Well, that's good. At least, I think it is.

He sweeps an arm behind me to guide me forward without actually touching me. "You are quite the celebrity! Among those of us who know about your big win, that is. And it is my duty—nay, my *honor*, to grant you a complimentary stay in one of our most luxurious suites for the night. As congratulations for your obvious favor with Lady Luck."

For the night?

Oh, no...

"I'm so sorry." I'm stammering and I can't help it. But I'm also panicking. "I can't stay the night. I have to go get my—"

"Guests are welcome, of course. We must ask you to cap off at a maximum of four, for occupancy regulations and such."

I glance around the casino. I have no doubt the adjoining hotel is just as fancy, if not more. It definitely has a shower where I can rinse off all this sticky, dried bubbly from my skin.

And I know for a fact that Willow would go absolutely *nuts* to be able to live like a princess for a night.

At that, I manage to actually, genuinely smile.

"You know what? I think I'll take you up on that."

Charles smiles and offers me his arm. I still hug the bag to my chest, but I'm not as worried someone is going to steal it from me now. It occurs to me that that might be why so many guards flanked me just to get to Charles—they had to have known I was carrying a large amount of cash.

For the first time in my life, I actually feel somewhat *safe*.

The walk to my suite is a winding maze through crystal and diamonds, marble and gold. I have the presence of mind to ask for a map when Charles fetches me my card key.

He takes me as far as the elevator, but stops at the doors and encourages me to step inside. "Number 1702," he reminds me, pressing the button for the seventeenth floor. "And should you need anything, concierge is available at all hours, day and night. Just call the front desk for assistance."

I give Charles a small wave as the doors close.

Then I slump back against the wall and let out the giant breath I've been holding this whole time.

This is *real.*

This is *happening.*

The doors ding and slide open. I step out into a silent hallway lined with cream wallpaper and plush crimson carpet, peeking around to see if anyone else is wandering the halls. On a whim, I slip my heels off and let my toes sink into the soft carpet.

Yup. Even the floor feels expensive.

I tiptoe to Room 1702. It's at the end of another hallway and close to the fire escape stairwell. It's also the only door in this hall aside from Room 1701. I'm no expert in luxury suites, but something in my gut tells me that means this place is going to be *huge*.

I'm adding Roxy to the guest list. *Girl needs to experience this with me for* sure.

The light on the door lock turns green and I can hear the deadbolt slip back. I turn the handle and slowly step inside.

Whoa.

I was right: it's huge.

Huger than huge.

The Meridian's trademark golden flourishes decorate every inch of the palatial suite, but now, I can see more artistic patterns in the details I missed before in the casino. Everything has a bit of a constellation, Galileo, navigation "feel" to it. The wallpaper is brushed with faint script pulled from ancient maps and star charts. A globe with continents made from gemstones sits on the desk which is designed to look like a sea captain's study.

A king-sized bed made with the softest-looking white sheets takes up most of the space behind a room divider covered in shimmering tiles. Across the suite in a pseudo-living room is a full fireplace and a giant flat screen television mounted to the wall above it.

Plans confirmed: I'm definitely calling Roxy, and we are *definitely* having a girl's night tonight. No work, no sleep, no problems.

I dig in my bag for my phone.

The bathroom door opens. And out steps a dripping-wet man.

I suck in a gasp. *No. No way. No fucking way.*

It's him. The one I spilled on. The Champagne Angel.

And he's naked in my room.

7

CLARA

I scream.

He screams.

Everyone screams.

Okay, none of that actually happens. Real life isn't nearly so dramatic. But I do let out something that's a cross between a shriek and a yelp as I clap my hands over my mouth.

And he growls in surprise as well.

"What the fuck?" He ducks into the bathroom, then back out again, this time furiously tying a bath towel around his hips.

His eyes narrow when he gets a good look at me. "You. Again."

I'm very aware I'm getting a *very* good look at him. Every inch of him. His dark hair is wet and curled close against his forehead, but his eyes are glacially bright. Five o'clock shadow stubbles his cheeks and his lips have a cruel, beautiful sneer to them.

I was only kidding to myself when I compared his body to the marble statues adorning the exterior of The Meridian, but as he draws closer, I see maybe I wasn't so far off. I can see every muscle ripple and move like he's literally chiseled from the same hard rock.

In unrelated news, I've forgotten how to breathe.

"What are you doing here?"

He says it like a man who's used to getting immediate answers. And I want to answer, I do, I promise. I'm just... way too busy staring at his pecs to string together words.

I realize I'm supposed to be running the hell away from an abusive asshole. I know that.

But I'm not *dead*.

Or, y'know... *blind...*

"Hello?" He tips my gaze up to meet his with a finger under my chin. "What are you doing here?"

My trembling fingers hold up the keycard I have yet to put away. "Complimentary... suite..."

He eyes the black and gold card, then backs off. Only a little, though. At the very least, he's recognized that yes, I did get in here by legitimate means. It's not like anyone can just pick the lock and sneak in.

Wait...

"What are *you* doing here?"

Now, I want answers from the guy who's made himself at home in what's supposed to be *my* suite.

He waves a hand over himself with a look like the explanation is exceedingly obvious. "Taking a shower."

I palm my face with a groan. "No, I mean…"

Honestly, I'm too mortified to clarify.

He takes the liberty to do it for me. "Clearly, there's been a mix-up with the room listing in the system. I'll talk with my people to see where the glitch is. Now," he sweeps an arm toward the door, "kindly get the fuck out."

I narrow my eyes at him. This is supposed to be *my* room. But any and all bluster I would have had in a situation like this was completely drained from my body during the ordeal with Martin earlier tonight.

Good *Lord*, does that feel like centuries ago.

I rub the side of my face with a groan, then sigh. "Fine. You win. Whatever. Enjoy your palace."

Exhaustion suddenly settles into my bones. I sling my heels over my shoulder along with my bag and limp my way to the door.

I've been ignoring the soreness in my ankle this entire time, mainly because I had enough adrenaline pumping through my veins to numb it down. Between running from Martin, then doing something crazy and going into the casino, then *experiencing* something crazy by becoming an instant millionaire, that same adrenaline just kept pumping and pumping and pumping.

But now, I'm all tapped out, and I am feeling the painful twist that must have happened when I lunged at Martin to save Willow.

"What's wrong?"

I freeze at the door. He's right behind me, his voice low in my ear.

"I'm leaving. The room's yours."

His hands gently wrap around my waist. "No," he says, "I mean with your foot. You're limping."

The adrenaline is back. Centered solely on those strong, nimble fingers very faintly flexing against the sequins of my dress.

"Oh. I, uh, twisted my ankle. That's all."

I reach for the door, but those hands press just enough to stop me.

Just enough to want a bit more.

"How?"

I'm glad he's behind me so he can't see my eyes widen or my cheeks pinken. "Oh, um, I was just… running."

He lets out a soft snort. "From what?"

"Who."

The correction escapes me before I even realize I'm saying it. I don't even know this guy, and I'm already spilling my life's story to him. I need to shut up and leave. I'm sure I can find something nice somewhere else, like… a motel.

"From who?"

Something in my chest shudders. I do my best to shake it off. "My ex," I whisper hoarsely.

It's so still, so silent. One breath passes. Then two.

And then, suddenly, I'm swept off my feet and being carried back into the suite by this almost-naked, air-drying specimen of human perfection.

"What are you doing?" I half-gasp, half-shriek in shock and panic.

"You need to stay off your ankle." He says it like I asked him for a diagnosis. "Keep it elevated. The swelling will linger if you don't."

I glance at my throbbing ankle and wince. He's right—it's swollen, and painfully so. I can't believe I spent so much time in heels without even noticing until now.

He lays me down on the bed, making sure that I'm sufficiently propped up by the decorative pillows before he walks over to the coffee nook. When he returns, he's got a bag of ice in one hand. He uses his other to pick my feet up, sit down on the edge of the bed, and lower them back down on his lap.

I can't help the low moan of gratitude that rolls through me when he wraps the ice bag around my swollen ankle.

He clears his throat. "My name is Demyen."

"Clara."

Demyen grunts softly in acknowledgement, his head tilting in a slight nod. He's doing his best to focus on my ankle, but I catch his eyes skimming along my bare legs to where the dress is now bunched high around my thighs. I'm not sure if he notices his thumb tracing a slow, languid circle just above my ankle bone, but *I* sure as hell do.

"So… running from your ex?" His voice is calm on the surface, but there's definitely a faintly angry growl to the not-quite-a-question.

I don't know how to answer. I don't know if he's going to sell me out to the cops—to Martin, even if accidentally—so I hesitate.

But when his gaze meets mine, I'm suddenly captivated by the glinting intensity in his eyes. Like he's hypnotizing me. So I muster a small nod. "Yeah."

"He does shit like this often?"

I'm ashamed of the answer. Only because, now that I'm out of Martin's reach, I can't believe I actually stayed in that hellhole for as long as I did.

But I still manage another nod. "Often enough."

"Look." Demyen shifts my feet on his lap so he can press the ice to the other side of the swelling. "I'm not going to call the police. Unless you ask me to. But I—"

"No!" I blush under his hard stare. I didn't mean to shout so loud, but the panic took over my vocal cords.

"I prefer to keep things in-house," he slowly finishes. There's an amused smile tugging at the corner of his full mouth.

"Oh."

I'm not sure what to say to that. On one hand, I'm glad he's not going to run to the police with my domestic drama like some well-intentioned knight in shining armor.

On the other hand, my mind is racing to figure out what he means by "keep things in-house."

Until his fingers start massaging my foot, then my calf, sending a flood of relief through my body and straight to my brain. He's careful around the tender joint, and through my fluttering lashes, I can see that the swelling has gone down quite a bit.

No one has ever massaged my feet. Not like this.

"How does that feel?" Demyen's voice is a low murmur. It caresses my senses almost more than his fingers on my skin.

"So good…" I realize how I sound—desperate and desperately horny—but I don't mind.

Given what my other foot is feeling through the towel wrapped around his waist, it seems like he doesn't mind, either.

I loll my head back on the pillows and gaze up at the ornate ceiling. I'm about seventy percent certain this is all some lucid dream that I'm going to wake up from at any moment. There's no way in any universe that I, Clara Everett, have thousands of dollars in cash inside my bag which is sitting on a plush lounge chair inside a deluxe casino hotel suite while a gorgeous man wearing nothing but a white towel is massaging my feet.

I almost let out a delirious laugh, but then his thumb kneads a knot of tension from the arch of my foot. My back involuntarily arches and the sound emitting from my throat is pure pleasure.

"Oh, God… fuck…"

An appreciative growl rumbles low in his chest. His other hand joins the first, and he draws another writhe, another moan from me.

When I open my eyes to look at him, the whimper that slips from my lips has nothing to do with the way he's touching me...

And everything to do with the way he's *looking* at me.

Demyen rests my foot on his shoulder. His mouth is only inches from my skin, and his fingers lazily trace the curve of my calf.

Up and down.

Up and down.

But his gaze never leaves my face. His eyes flicker between mine and my mouth, and by the way the heat flares in those stormy irises as my dress pools around my hips...

I can only imagine what he's seeing.

I can only imagine what he's thinking.

And I *like* to imagine what he might be thinking about me as he turns his face and presses the softest of kisses to the side of my foot.

He still hasn't looked away from me, and I don't want him to. My heart is slamming against my ribcage, and I know I must be blushing fifty shades of shy insecurity, but I want him to see it. I want him to hear it.

Somehow, deep in my soul, I know that I'm safe. Here. With him.

And *that* feeling is entirely new.

His fingers slide up a bit more, closer to my knee, then stop. I feel the way my skin sticks to his at the same time his brow twitches with curiosity.

Ah, fuck. "Oh, umm... The, ah... champagne...thing..." I'm immediately humiliated all over again now that I realize I'm covered in dry bubbly. He's perfectly clean, and I'm a sticky mess of bundled nerves.

I try to slip my foot away, but he tightens his grip. Not hard, but just enough to let me know he's not letting me go any time soon.

Demyen leans forward, and I'm ready for him to scold me for my clumsiness.

He doesn't.

Instead, he glides his tongue over that sweet stickiness. Slow. Warm. Wet. Then finishes it off with a sucking kiss just behind my knee.

That right there is enough fantasy fuel to last the rest of my life.

Except he's not finished.

Not by a long shot.

Now, it's a game for him—finding where rivulets of expensive champagne have dried on my skin and licking each one up. He starts with a massaging press of his fingers and wherever he feels the stickiness, he dips his head to swipe his warm tongue across my flesh.

I'm trying my damned hardest to keep my breathing in check. To not squirm so wantonly on the bed, or let out so many breathless moans whenever he licks and kisses a sensitive spot.

But by the time he's "cleaned" both legs, his lips are caressing my thigh and I'm a quivering, simpering mess.

I've never been with any man save for Martin.

And Martin never, *ever* touched me like this.

Demyen rubs his hands over my hips in one smooth motion, pushing my dress up higher until he can see my panties. They're not sexy or seductive by any means. I'm almost too embarrassed by them to let him continue.

But then he rubs a thumb over the crease between my hip and my pelvis and I shiver with pleasure.

And I know he sees what he's doing to me.

He hooks his fingers in the waistband and pauses, lifting his gaze to mine. I know what he's asking. And I know, much to my surprise, what he's giving me.

I could walk away right now. I could get up, thank him for being so understanding, and walk out that door.

Instead, I nod.

Yes, I'm saying silently. *Destroy me.*

8

CLARA

A wicked smile curves Demyen's lips and he rips my panties apart like they're nothing more than a minor inconvenience.

I barely have enough time to register just how fucking *hot* that is when I'm suddenly spread wide, my legs hooked over his bare shoulders and his hungry gaze centered right on my aching core.

"Did any spill here?" he asks me, dragging a finger over my damp heat.

Words fly from my mind. The entire concept of spoken language goes right out the door with it.

But he waits for my answer, this cruel, teasing man, and I'm forced to whimper a pitiful "no" when he drags that finger back up and teases my clit with light little circles.

"Hmm. Shame." Demyen's grin spreads wide. "I should double-check."

I'm about to cry out "no" again—not because I don't want it, but because I'm afraid I'll literally crumble to pieces if he does what he's threatening.

But he's too fast. He dives down.

And when his tongue flattens and glides over my slit, I'm a goner.

My hips buck up involuntarily as a wordless cry rips out of my chest. He takes advantage of the moment by cupping my ass in his strong hands to pull me closer to him.

He's playing evil games.

I want more, so he teases.

I want faster, so he slows.

I need him to devour me like a starved man, but Demyen takes his time to taste every inch of me at his own leisurely pace.

"Demyen!" I cry out. My hips roll and his hands grip me, keeping me in place. I hate it. I love it. I want more of it.

His chuckle mixes with a growl of pride. I can feel it rumble from his lips straight to my core.

When he tugs again with that deliciously wicked mouth, it's perfectly timed with the press of his fingers inside me. My eyes roll back in my head as he presses and searches, then curls those fingers and begins to rub. I don't even know what magic button he's found inside me, but it's there and it's erasing every coherent thought from my brain.

My fingers thread through his hair and tug at the roots. I need something to grab or I'm going to skyrocket through the ceiling.

Hell, I might do that anyway. This pressure deep inside me is almost unbearable.

Demyen murmurs something against my skin, then presses a passionate kiss to my mound. That's all it takes.

Boom. Fireworks.

I'm shuddering. Sobbing. Drooling and riding out every single fucking second of euphoria on his hand like it's going to be my last.

He waits until I've calmed—or at least, until I'm only gasping for air and not actively hyperventilating—before he carefully pulls his fingers from me.

Then he looks me in the eyes.

And sucks each finger clean.

"You taste better than champagne." He says it like he's actually comparing vintages. Like it's an easy, factual statement and not something so salaciously naughty that I almost come again just from hearing it.

I lean up on my elbows right when he crawls over me. He's fully naked—his towel is long forgotten, dropped to the floor sometime between his "wine tasting" and making me see stars.

When his face is only inches away from mine, he pauses yet again.

And again, I know it without having to ask: I'm able to leave if I want to.

Not a single cell in my body wants to.

I lean up just a bit more and his mouth slants over mine. The kiss is tentative at first, searching, then quickly melts into something far more passionate. My lips part only a fraction and his tongue sweeps between them, seeking mine to tangle with and suckle. I can taste myself on his lips, on his tongue, and that alone makes my toes curl.

I'm not sure when or how he unzipped my dress. But it's completely open now, and Demyen is tugging it off my body. My bra quickly follows.

He pulls away just long enough to drink the sight of me in. I'm completely naked and spread wide, a feast for his hungry gaze.

"Demyen," I breathe. I want him. I *need* him. He lit this fire inside me and now, he needs to put it out or I'll die. Simple as that.

"You're so fucking beautiful." He rolls my nipple between his thumb and forefinger with just enough pressure to make my hips writhe. "You know that?"

Actually... No, I don't. I'm not allowed to be beautiful. Not if I want to avoid Martin's wrath.

I don't want *him* tainting this incredible moment, or this incredible night, without even being here. So I lean into Demyen's touch with a coy smile and smooth my hands over his washboard abs.

Fuck. So this *is what those feel like.*

I can feel him respond to my touch, and I'm loving the way his muscles twitch and tense under my fingertips.

When I glide my fingers over his length, he groans.

He's so warm. And bare.

And fucking *huge*.

I literally don't know how he's going to fit inside me—all I know is I need him and I need him right. Fucking. Now.

Demyen seems to have the exact same idea, because he captures my wrist and pins me down onto the mattress. His fingers find mine and they lace together while his other hand reaches down between us.

I'm spread open even wider than before. It makes it possible for him to work himself into me, solid inch by solid, throbbing, iron-hard inch.

In a lesser world, with a lesser man, it might hurt. But Demyen keeps my hand clutched close and takes his time and kisses the curve of my neck as he slowly pushes into me. And so there's no pain. I can feel nothing but pleasure.

Nothing but *him.*

He hooks my injured ankle over his shoulder, kissing my calf and gazing into my eyes as he continues to work himself inside me. I want so badly to touch the dark, silky strands of his hair as it falls into his eyes, but my free arm can't reach that far. He releases my other hand and I immediately grab for him, for any part of him I can caress...

But then I'm seeing stars again because his now-free hand has dipped down between us and strokes where we're joined.

I'm unraveling at the seams of my sanity.

The grin on his face tells me he knows.

I'm still shivering in the aftermath of the first explosive release when Demyen guides my leg to wrap around his waist, then the other, and leans down to cover me with his body. His lips devour mine, and we're a writhing, panting, groaning mass of tangled limbs and nipping teeth.

Demyen buries his face in my neck. I feel him suck on the curve, pressing with his teeth, and I want him to mark me. Mark me, claim me, make me his in every way he can.

My hands smooth over his back, gripping as he moves faster. But then he thrusts a bit harder, hits a new unfamiliar spot deep within me, and my fingernails drag over his shoulder blades.

And I'm suddenly back to that sweet edge of oblivion.

"Come with me," he breathes in my ear.

I don't know if I nod. I don't know if I even verbally respond. I'm checked out, on another planet entirely. All I know is that I can feel him thicken and pulse. My legs tighten around him, pulling him harder into me.

And then he's grunting, gasping, filling me with heat and taking me tumbling down with him into the sweet blackness of oblivion.

9

DEMYEN

Goddamn.

I have to take several long, slow, steadying breaths to regain any semblance of control over my own limbs. My heart rate, on the other hand, is a lost cause—it's pounding so fast I'm worried I might go into cardiac arrest.

The cause of my heart condition is barely conscious beneath me, smiling and glowing in the aftermath of our mutual—and mutually *mindblowing*—orgasm.

This was not on tonight's agenda.

She was not on tonight's agenda.

But the moment I saw her standing there, here in the hotel suite I randomly chose just to quickly rinse off the champagne she spilled all over me...

It was as if Lady Luck personally carried Clara straight into my arms.

Who am I to deny a gift from the goddess of fortune?

I ease myself off of her and roll to the side, but I tuck her into my arms as I settle into the bed with her. I make sure to drape her injured leg over my thighs so her ankle stays elevated. At least, that's what I'm telling myself. It might just be a convenient way to justify this need to caress the soft skin of her thigh.

She lays her head on my chest with a happy, purring sigh.

I wasn't just "in the moment" when I told her she's beautiful. She is, from the way her olive green eyes glow and her long lashes flutter when she's experiencing pleasure, to the deliciously supple curves of her body.

And the way she tastes... *fuck.* Every inch of her is exquisite.

It helps that she's in *my* arms, in *my* bed, in *my* hotel. Wearing my faint bite marks, her sweet honey scent mingling with my own all over her skin.

Like I said: exquisite.

But she hesitated when I asked her if she knew just how beautiful she is. I didn't miss the way she paused. The slight frown, the wrinkled brow.

It doesn't take much effort to put two and two together: she's running from her ex. There's no doubt he's fed her lie after lie just to keep her under his thumb.

She's free now, though.

His fucking loss.

An idea comes to me suddenly. I'm fully aware it's conceived from a combination of my own pride, possessiveness, and a craving for more of the shit we just did. But there's also an element of protectiveness swirling in the mix. Especially when I start to wonder what might happen should her ex find her here.

I don't have any idea who he is, or what he's done.

But I already know I'm going to make sure he has a hell of a time finding Clara.

"Come home with me." The sentence flies out of my mouth before I have time to really think it through.

She tenses. Then lifts her head to look at me. *My God*, the way her lips are swollen from my kisses... tangled hair framing her flushed face... I shift just enough so she doesn't feel the effect she has on me.

Not while we discuss this, at least.

"What?" She looks like she genuinely didn't hear my request.

So I repeat it. Even though it's not exactly a request. "Come home with me."

Clara squints at me, then laughs. "Right. Okay."

"I'm serious."

She must see that I mean it, because she sits up and self-consciously tucks a strand of hair behind her ear. "You don't even know me."

I sit up as well, leaning back against the pillows still propped against the headboard. "I know that you can't go home. Wherever 'home' used to be."

She doesn't respond.

"And I know that you didn't exactly plan your escape in advance, judging by what you were wearing, and the size of the bag you've been clinging to. Which means you don't actually know where to go, do you?"

Clara frowns, but she still avoids meeting my gaze. "I... might still need to figure out a few things."

"Like what?"

Now, she's more than nervous. Her bottom lip starts to tremble, and she bites it just hard enough to stop it. "I... I have a kid... waiting for me. A little girl."

Ah. That does make things interesting.

I tilt my head to one side and gently turn her face so she's forced to look me in the eyes. "Then bring her with you."

I'm not exactly leaping for joy at the prospect of playing host to a single mom and her snot-nosed carpet crawler. In fact, somewhere in the back of my mind, Normal Demyen is demanding to know what the actual fuck I'm doing.

If this was anyone else, I'd be telling her to kick bricks. Tough shit. *C'est la vie.*

But "anyone else" wouldn't be here with me, naked and warm and glistening in the soft light of the room as my fingers dance over her skin. I can't stop touching her.

And I can't stop the surge of aggression that keeps rising whenever I envision an alternative option. *Any* alternative option.

Letting her go means her ex will probably find her. It definitely means I'll never see her again.

I'm not okay with any of that. Not one fucking bit.

Clara looks unsure at first. Then a distinct sort of stubbornness settles into her expression and she straightens. "Thank you, really," she says, "but I'm good. We're good."

I loft a brow. "Really."

"School starts soon, and I'm going to go get Willow enrolled and all that parenting stuff, so…" She shrugs.

"I'm not joking, Clara. I'll send a car to get your daughter and—"

"Do you think you're the first white knight to come riding in to save the day?"

Her question stops me in my tracks. Not just the question itself, but the way she snaps it.

She sighs and sweeps her long hair over one shoulder. "Look, it's not that I'm not grateful. I appreciate the thought. But I've heard this song before." When her eyes meet mine again, they're filled with a deep sadness I suddenly have an urge to kiss away. "I just need to get out of Vegas and far away from him. I don't need a savior, or an avenging angel, or—"

I bark out a laugh. It startles her, and for a fleeting moment, she looks scared. But then she sees that I'm genuinely laughing and relaxes a little.

"I am no 'avenging angel'," I chuckle. "And I'm sure as fuck no one's savior."

It's her turn to arch a brow and stare at me with unabashed skepticism. "So then why take me home?"

I shrug. My hands smooth over her waist and lift her, pulling her to me until she's settled on my lap. "Because I'm selfish. Because I'm greedy. Because I always get what I want."

I love the way she spreads for me, even just to keep her balance as she straddles me. I can't resist caressing her thighs, then her hips... and then I tighten my grip just enough to make her rock on my length. Her eyes flutter close and her lips part, and I roll up into her to make my point.

"Wh... what..." Clara blinks and bites her lip. "What do you want?"

When I fist my hand in her hair at the nape of her neck, forcing her to look nowhere else but at me, I feel her shiver and hear the softest moan.

"You."

I don't give her time to respond. Or to argue.

The only reason why I don't kiss her right away is because I want to watch her take me. I want to see her lips part wider... her lashes flutter... her eyes roll back... and that blush spread from her neck to her cheeks when I guide her up and then pull her back down on me.

She's all velvet heat wrapped tightly around me, and it's fucking *heaven*.

"Demyen..." She gasps again. I can feel her start to tremble.

I hold her in place as I grind up into her, working every fucking inch of my cock inside her until my balls are nestled against her sweet ass.

Clara whimpers with pleasure. Her eyes flutter closed.

"Look at me." It's an order. She immediately obeys, and I want to reward her for being so good.

But first, I need her to agree to my terms.

"You're coming home with me."

She starts to whine, her hips writhing for relief. But I tighten my hold on her and she stills. Only her lips quiver, and it takes every ounce of self-control to stop myself from sucking on them.

"Okay," she finally whimpers.

"I will take care of you."

Her body is on the very edge of release, but I won't let her tumble over just yet. "O-okay."

I gaze into those enchanting green eyes a bit longer. And I realize... this is real. *She's* real. She's so sweetly responsive and none of it's rehearsed. None of it is a show for my benefit. Every shuddering gasp, every whimper and moan, is raw and pure and—

"*Mine.* You're mine."

I say it without thinking, but it feels right. Something snaps into place deep inside me, and it just feels so fucking *right*.

That same something snaps into place for her, too. I see it in her eyes. In the way her lips stop trembling as this new reality washes over both of us.

Clara nods. As much as my grasp on her will allow, anyway. "Yes."

That's when I kiss her.

That's when I release my grip, only to hold her close in my arms and guide her on me until we're both breathless and moaning and writhing uncontrollably.

I'm vaguely aware of my voice growling, then snarling her name. All I can hear is my heartbeat pounding in my ears, perfectly in time with my thrusts as I pour myself into her.

All I can think, as I hold her trembling body in my arms, as I breathe in her sweet honey hair…

… is that any motherfucker who comes for her will never get through me.

10

DEMYEN

Bambi pulled through with my early morning text for her to grab some clothes for Clara. As gorgeous as she looks in that sequined cocktail dress, it's not suited for breakfast. She'd only look like every other woman doing the Walk of Shame, and there is absolutely nothing for her to be ashamed of.

Not on my arm, anyway.

She's been pleasant all morning, and pleasantly surprised when the linen dress arrived for her to slip on. Paired, of course, with comfortable sandals that won't aggravate her ankle.

But Clara has also been quiet.

In the shower, she was quiet, at least until I made her cry out my name and spasm on my cock again. The beautiful afterglow spread across her delicate cheekbones and tinted the curve of her neck as I dried her off.

She was quiet while we dressed, except when she smiled at me and thanked me for everything.

Our walk to the car was quiet, too, save for the few required comments about checking out and giving my chauffeur the address to her friend's place. Once inside the car, Clara shifted her gaze out the window and hasn't spoken a word since.

It's been ten minutes.

I'm losing my goddamn mind.

I pretend to check something on my phone. As I do, I see a few missed text messages in the notifications. But before I can open the first one, Clara finally says something.

"If anything happens to my daughter... or me..." She sighs and slowly turns her gaze to me. "You'll have the Las Vegas Police Department to deal with."

I stifle a laugh. If only she knew how empty of a threat that really is to a man like me. "That's usually the case when things happen to people."

"No. I mean..." She shakes her head and rubs the bridge of her nose. "My ex. Willow's father. He's a detective on the force. And my dad is his boss."

I snort. "Wow. Okay. Tell me how you really feel."

"I don't know." Her voice takes on a new edge. There's a desperation in the corners of her eyes, almost like a panic. "I don't know how to feel," she says again. "Last night was..." Her mouth quirks in a wistful smile, then fades just as quickly as it appears. "I have a child. A *child*. And I don't know you, and—"

"You don't know if you can trust me."

I get it. I do, truly. The bruising around her ankle is a colorful reminder of what her trust in men she "knew" earned her; there's no telling what a man she doesn't know would do.

I'd applaud her instincts if I wasn't feeling so offended.

"It's nothing personal," she adds.

"It never is." I know I'm being abrupt, and I need to stop it. Especially if I need her to trust me to do the right thing by her and her kid. So I offer her a playful little smile and take her hand in mine. "Listen. LVPD will never darken the doors of my estate. They wouldn't dare. You're safe. Your daughter is safe. And I get the feeling that neither one of us wants to see that asshole's face any time soon."

That earns me a small laugh. Clara nods. "Thanks." She sniffs and sits up a bit straighter, confidence settling into her limbs. "Thank you, Demyen. Really. I don't know how to repay you."

I have several ideas. None of them involve clothing.

"We'll figure something out," I assure her with a coy wink. It takes a moment for the meaning to sink in, and when it does, that pretty blush pinks her skin.

I've never liked the color pink until I met this woman. Now, all I ever want to do is lick it.

She pulls her hand from mine to fiddle with the hem of her dress. I pretend like it doesn't suddenly bother me, because it shouldn't. But it does.

Distractions. I need distractions, and I need them right now. So I flip to the messages in my phone and do my best to focus on work.

It's not difficult, because the first message I open yanks my full attention.

CHARLES: *Medusa's Wrath jackpot winner tried cashing out. I caught up with her and comped her a high-roller suite.*

CHARLES: *Thought you should know—fingerprints pulled up a few records.*

The attachments show Clara's fingerprints and a scan of her I.D. on the payout forms that The Meridian requires from high rollers. But then there's another set of attachments that make me sit up straight. And my heart slams inside my ribcage.

There's another set of fingerprints. Confirmed match.. But this document is a court docket and a testimonial dossier from fifteen years ago...

... with a very young, very familiar face staring up at me.

No.

No.

I don't know what curdles first—my stomach or my blood.

I can't bring myself to look at her. I can't bring myself to read the name on the court documents despite knowing exactly what it says.

I can't force my mind to make sense of this.

"Clara—" I shut my mouth when I realize I can't stand the taste of her name on my tongue anymore.

"Yes?" She peers at me and must see the darkness clouding my face. "Is everything okay?"

No, it sure as fuck is not.

But I can't tell her yet. I can't let her know something is wrong; that everything is wrong. I have to play it cool, play it calm, and get her and her kid the fuck inside my house where security is strong and the deadbolts are stronger.

I've been looking for Clara Everett for fifteen years.

Through fate or sheer dumb luck, I finally have her.

There's no way in hell I'm going to let her slip through my fingers again.

11

CLARA

When we pull up into Roxy's driveway, I have to remind myself to wait for the car to stop before I leap out. I'm anxious to see Willow, and excited to get her to actual safety that won't put my best friend in danger.

Even though there's a sudden shadow over Demyen that he won't talk about, I can't help but feel like he's the genuine thing.

And I can't help but remind myself that that kind of thinking always lands me in trouble.

I shake it off and skip out of the car that's probably worth five years of my wages. I don't bother checking to see if he's behind me; the only thing I do check is to make sure my bag is on my shoulder as I walk up the wrought iron stairs of the adobe apartment building. All I can think about right now is seeing Willow. Making sure she's safe.

We're so close to our happily-ever-after.

Roxy meets me at the door to her tiny studio. Her eyes immediately narrow when she sees Demyen slowly emerge from the luxury sedan. "Clara…?"

I scrunch my nose and try to wave off the impending thousand questions. "He's a friend. Is Willow okay?"

"No, I fed her to a pool of sharks." Roxy rolls her eyes and ushers me inside. "Yes, of course she's okay. You think I'd let that jackass get to her?"

I let out a sigh of relief when I spot my sweet angel snoring on the couch, tucked beneath a light throw blanket and still clutching a bag of half-eaten popcorn.

"He has a gun," I gently remind my friend.

"Yeah. So do I."

I want to scold her for being so careless, but she's really not. Roxy Meir would absolutely go into battle with the entire Las Vegas PD if it meant protecting Willow.

"Don't worry," she calmly assures me as she picks up Willow's things around the room. "I made sure to fill her up with junk food and liquid sugar. All I need to do is give her a good shake and you'll have a blast the rest of the day."

Now, I do roll my eyes, but I can't hold back the laugh. "Gee, thanks bunches. You're a real friend."

Roxy smirks and tucks Willow's sweater inside her little backpack. "So… there's an insanely hot guy driving an equally smokin' car outside…"

Here we go. "He's just a friend, Rox."

"Mhm. And where has this 'friend' been up until now?"

I bite the inside of my cheek. She's got me there. I pick up one of Willow's toys she managed to slip in her bag and fiddle with it so I don't have to look at Roxy. "I just met him. Last night."

Her sharp intake of breath tells me all I need to know about *her* opinion. "Clara…"

"It's not what you think."

I'm suddenly very aware of the weight of the bag on my shoulder, and I steal a mischievous glance at my best friend. "I had a really great night. I mean… a *really* great night."

Roxy furrows her brow and sits on one of the bar stools at her kitchen island. "You didn't go to work?"

I grin. "I never have to go back to work again. Not for a very long time."

"Girl, if you're about to tell me you got yourself a sugar daddy—"

I unzip the bag. Then pull out stack… after stack… after stack… of cash and set them on the counter.

Roxy's eyes bug out of her head.

I nod giddily. "I know. Believe me… *I know.*"

She almost slides off her seat. Almost. But she catches herself and suddenly barks out a laugh, clapping her hand over her mouth before she wakes up Willow. "What the *fuck*?! Tell me that's not Sugar Daddy's—"

"God, no." I snort and shake my head. "He's not my sugar anything. And this is *my* money. Well, part of it."

"*Part—*?!"

"I had to get the rest in annuity, but I'm going to transfer it out once I can get a new bank account to handle the full amount."

Roxy leans back. "How much...?"

I almost stumble on the words. I've never actually spoken it out loud. "One..." I clear my throat. It's sticking to my tongue. "One million dollars."

She shrieks.

We quickly hush each other as I nearly shriek right along with her, and I take the opportunity to shove a few stacks of cash into her arms. She tries to shove them back at me, but I'm not going to let her refuse.

"Please, Roxy." I practically stuff a wad of cash down her shirt. "For me. Just take it."

"Bitch! What am I supposed to do with all this dough?!"

"I don't know!" I also don't know how else I could ever repay her for protecting my daughter and getting both of us out of that hellhole. "Keep it for me. Stash it in your bank; you can transfer it to me later. The less I have on hand, the harder it will be for me to lose it."

Realization dawns on Roxy's face. "Officer Asshole doesn't know."

"Not a fucking clue."

That seals the deal. "Done."

She's tucking the money into her cereal box when there's a knock at the door. We both jump, and for a moment, Willow whines in her sleep. My heart leaps into my throat.

Did he find us here?

"Clara."

Oh, thank God. It's Demyen.

Roxy's eyes bug out of her head and she mouths the question to me: *Sugar Daddy?* I roll my eyes, but nod. I'll make the introductions in a second.

I move to answer the door, but she blows past me and carefully peers at him through only a few inches of open space. I guess that's fair; it *is* her home. But I know her "ready for a fight" stance and she's absolutely in it, all tense and ready to pounce.

Demyen doesn't give her much of an expression, but he explains, "I heard shrieking." He tries to look inside over her head. "Everything okay?"

Roxy sizes him up, then opens the door wider to let him in. "You must be—"

"Demyen." I cut her off before she calls him any sort of name he might not find humor in. "This is Demyen. Demyen, this is my best friend, Roxy."

He gives her a polite nod, then looks to me. "I heard shrieking," he repeats.

I blush. "Yeah. Sorry. We just got excited and all."

He nods again. "Ready?"

Roxy tries to signal with her not-quite-blank expression that I don't have to go with him if I don't want to. But to be perfectly honest, I'm more on board with being surrounded by his security team and whatever cameras or alarms he has in place (because insanely wealthy guys like him *always* have all that).. .than with risking Roxy's safety against Martin.

"Yeah," I say, slipping my bag over my shoulder. "Lemme just grab Willow."

"I got her." Demyen moves to the couch and scoops her up in his arms like she doesn't weigh a single pound. She sniffles and shifts in his arms, but tucks her head in his shoulder and nestles into his warmth.

And just like that, my heart forgets to beat.

I've been wrestling with my logic, scolding myself for so quickly trusting a man I've just met—let alone sleeping with him the first night. (And the first morning. More than once.) But seeing him cradle my little girl in his arms, seeing her accept his embrace even in sleep... It's a snapshot of a life I've always wanted.

It's an image I've never seen before. Certainly not with Martin.

I feel Roxy nudge me as she passes to help with the door. She sees it, too. As detached as Demyen seems to look, there's no missing the way he's careful with Willow, or the twitch in the corner of his mouth when she wraps a small arm around his neck.

But then he gives Roxy one more nod and ducks out the door.

"I stand corrected," Roxy mutters when I hug her goodbye. "Emphasis on *daddy*, sugar!"

I roll my eyes and stifle my laugh. "You are going to get me in trouble!"

"Girl." She stops me from walking away to look me in the eye. "You're already in trouble. Because that man is sex on legs, and I'd bet every one of those dollars in your bra that he's going to be a better father in the next five minutes than Martin ever was in his whole miserable life put together."

There goes my heart again, forgetting how to operate.

This time, it's because I'm terrified that Roxy is right. It's not hard to be a better father than Martin—he was never much of a father at all. If Willow forms a bond with Demyen, it will shatter her heart when we leave.

And in the meantime, I don't know if I can resist temptation.

12

DEMYEN

This was not part of the plan.

None of this was.

But now, I'm wondering if I ever had a plan to begin with. I'm hating the fact that my brain keeps saying "no."

The kid is snuggled up under my arm, even though she's buckled in and the strap is digging into her shoulder. I wasn't planning on becoming a babysitter, so I don't have the necessary booster seat—and I'm realizing, as I adjust the seatbelt for her, that I'm going to have to make a shopping list for my staff.

That same list now scrolling through my head has me wondering how the hell I became an instant-father.

None of this was part of the plan.

I don't show any panic, though. I've trained myself over the years how to not give away any tells that my heart is pounding in my chest and my lungs are constricting.

Rule number one of any card game: never reveal your hand.

Clara must not know the rules. She's sitting in her seat, gazing out the tinted window, and doing nothing to hide her own worries.

I'd tried to get her to sit next to the kid once I got us all in, but Clara saw the way I've apparently become a human pillow and slid into a different seat so I could continue to perform that function.

I don't know what has me panicking more: the fact that Clara Everett's child seems to think I'm some sort of safety and comfort…

… or that I'm not exactly hating it.

When the car pulls up the long driveway, Clara's eyes widen. I'm not sure what she expected, but it clearly wasn't the vast estate we're now rolling into.

Even in the desert, the grass is lush and green. Where there isn't vibrant lawn, my landscapers have worked true artistry with desert foliage and colorful rocks to blend elegance with the arid climate.

I have a fleeting thought that the kid—Willow, I think?—will love running around the grass. Maybe get her a soccer ball, a jump rope, some toys…

And then I shake the thought away. None of that is my concern. I'm officially delegating all parental concerns to Clara and Bambi. Leave me the fuck out of it.

Willow wakes up when the car pulls to a stop. I swear, the kid could sleep through a full-on gun fight. That might not be a bad thing.

"Mommy?" she mumbles, rubbing her eyes.

Clara smiles and turns to her. "Hey, baby girl. We're going to stay with a friend for a while. This is Demyen."

I look down at Willow, who has to lean back just to see my face. Her eyes go wide. I smile, just so she's not terrified of me. It's easier to deal with kids when they're not kicking and screaming.

"Wow." She practically breathes the word. "You're... really, really big."

"Willow!" Clara starts to scold her, but my chuckle stops her.

"And you're really, really little," I observe, raising an eyebrow.

That seems to be satisfactory. Kid logic, I guess. She peers at me, and I'm struck by how much her eyes look like her mother's. "Are you my mommy's friend?"

"Yes, I am."

No, I'm not.

I bite my tongue. Mostly because I'm not exactly certain which one is the lie. I'm not liking this confusion when everything is supposed to be black and white, on and off, right and wrong.

I live in a clear-cut world.

This shit is a fucking mess I never wanted.

But as Willow smiles at me, her face full of sweet innocence, my gut says everything is incredibly blurry. It's gray, dim, and questionable.

No—it's fucking *irritating*, is what it is.

I push the door open, feeling like I could rip it off the hinges with the sheer energy crawling under my skin. I have to channel it all into that one emotion. Anger into irritation, fear into irritation, even affection and admiration and whatever the fuck kind of sensual magic this woman wove over me last night—it all goes into irritation.

But *fuck*, Clara looks beautiful just standing at the entrance of the main house, hand in hand with her daughter, a gentle breeze just barely teasing the skirt of her dress.

She looks like she belongs in my home.

She looks like she belongs in my bed.

She looks like she belongs in my life.

I shove all that deep down under the rage I've held for years and usher them inside. I do allow myself to enjoy the pride that comes with seeing a guest—in this case, *guests*—gasp in awe at the beauty of my home.

I'm not one for overtly extravagant decor. I've been to other homes where the dons and *pakhans* wasted money on marble statues and Renaissance oil paintings and bullshit like that. That shit has never been my style. I prefer clean edges, muted colors, open spaces.

I also prefer having water in the middle of a desert, which is why the foyer has a fountain. And why the main entry room has an even bigger fountain, and the living room is more like a courtyard with a fountain that's basically a pool.

Willow lights up and immediately asks her mother if she can go swimming. Clara hushes her, glancing at me apologetically.

Quite frankly, I don't care if the kid splashes her way through the entire house. I've got bigger things to worry about.

Bambi walks into the main entry room with a warm smile on her face and her trusty tablet tucked in her arm. "Welcome! You must be Clara." Her eyes shift to the kid, and her smile brightens. "And you," she says, crouching down to eye level, "must be Willow."

Willow nods, but retreats closer to Clara's leg.

"Sorry," Clara mutters. "She's shy."

Bambi giggles and winks at the kid, then straightens. I don't know if I've ever seen this side of her before. It's... weird. "I heard someone ask about swimming. We will definitely need to go do that later."

I clear my throat and scrub a hand over my jaw. Bambi gets the signal and nods, returning to her more professional demeanor.

"Your rooms are ready," she says. "I'll show you where—"

"Actually, why don't you go ahead and take Miss Willow here?" I interject. A sudden idea has struck, and it involves getting Clara alone. "I don't think we have enough toys yet, and the chef needs the recipe for chicken nuggets." I put on my best serious face and lean down a bit to wink at the kid. "Think you can help Bambi out here?"

Willow slowly smiles until it looks like her face will split. She nods and immediately takes Bambi's hand, following her down the wide hall toward the kitchen. I feel something strange in my chest—fondness, maybe?—as I watch them chatter and swing their clasped hands together playfully.

No, that can't be right. Demyen Zakrevsky does *not* grow fond of small children.

Especially not the small children of people I have a score to settle with.

Clara looks completely flabbergasted as she looks around now that her kid is elsewhere; she's practically spinning in place. When her eyes land on me once again, she sobers and clears her throat. "Sorry. Just… this place is amazing."

I nod. "It's comfortable. Speaking of which, let's find your room."

I hold a hand out to her, and she hesitates. But then she steps into the offered space and allows me to press my hand to the center of her back. I don't want her to feel threatened or scared; I don't want her to run away. I can't afford to scare her into running away.

Not when everything is *finally* falling into place.

Just a few more steps, and we can put a years-long plan into motion.

13

DEMYEN

The walk isn't too long. I'm grateful for it, though, because the silence is heavy between us. Clara seems uncertain but excited, self-conscious but relieved. Given what little I know of her ex, and the pitiful state of her friend's microscopic apartment, I can understand.

But a thousand questions and a thousand more demands are pressing on my tongue. I know that the moment I open my mouth, the flood will spill out.

So instead, I just open the door and let her gasp her way into the large guest room. It's more like a small apartment, complete with a walk-in closet, a full bathroom with a steam shower and separate jacuzzi tub, and a king-sized four-poster bed behind a privacy partition wall.

I have an image of tying Clara to the bed, one limb to each corner so she can only mewl her moans up to the ceiling as I devour her. The heat pools low as I wonder if we have enough time...

No. Not right now.

Business first.

"You'll be staying here," I inform her. My voice doesn't allow room for argument.

Of course, she tries anyway. "But Willow?" she immediately asks, spinning to face me with fear in her eyes. "I need to be near—"

I hold a hand up to stop whatever panic attack is about to ensue. "Willow will be fine, and right next door." I point to a door in the wall next to the lounge area. "That goes right into her playroom." Or really, what *will* be her playroom, once Bambi stocks up.

Clara visibly sags with relief and clasps a hand to her chest. "Oh. Wow." She gives herself a little shake. "I'm so sorry. I don't know what I assumed."

Oh, the irony. It makes me smirk and agree with her just a little bit. "That a wealthy and powerful man you've only just met might turn you into his prisoner?"

She blushes brightly. "Well, I mean…"

I chuckle, albeit darkly. It's not like the idea didn't flash through my mind on the way here. "If I wanted to do that, we'd be in *my* room."

Clara blanches.

I wave a hand and roll my eyes. "Relax. My room is on the other side of the house. This whole wing is just for you and your daughter, with Bambi nearby in case you need anything. There are call buttons under that panel over there, and the red button is to summon security. There's no cameras in any of the bedrooms, but there are in the hall. Just so you know."

It's not a complete lie. There really aren't any cameras in the bedrooms.

Yet.

I need to call my guy and get at least one installed inside Clara's room. There's no telling what she'll get up to, and I'm not taking any chances with her.

The kid, though… she needs the privacy. I'll make sure to increase security around the windows and doors, but otherwise, I've got no beef with a five-year-old.

It's her mother who has sins to pay for.

Clara runs a hand through her hair as she looks around her new room. "I… Shit, I don't have any clothes."

"We'll buy you some."

"My toothbrush—"

"Add it to the list."

She looks at me again, this time with eyes narrowed. "Why are you doing this?"

I sigh. That is the exact same question I've been wanting to ask her for years. But I know what she means, and I understand why she's asking. On the surface, this is all so random and unexpected.

Even deep beneath the surface, this is all random and unexpected.

So instead of answering, I open the door and gesture to the hall. "Let's go find your daughter. I'm pretty sure she's about to cannonball into one of my fountains."

Clara looks ready to apologize, but then she sees the humor in my eyes. I can't help it, and it's frustrating the fuck out of me. I'm supposed to be angry, or determined, or something devoid of happiness.

But every time she's near, I feel a surge of warmth that won't tamp the fuck down.

We walk through the house in search of Bambi and the kid. I'd give a more formal tour, but there will be plenty of time for that later. Right now, I need to make a dozen calls and set up half as many appointments. Time is ticking by every second I waste playing host to my Very Important Guests.

We find Bambi and Willow devouring towers of ice cream sundaes, giggling and playing in the mounds of whipped cream with their tiny spoons. It's very clear by the sheer amount of scoops, sprinkles, and sugar that I'm going to have to have a talk with my assistant about small children and cavities.

A sidelong glance at Clara tells me to calm down, at least for now—she looks like she's about to cry with joy.

Right. For a moment, I forgot: they probably don't even have the money for sugar, let alone ice cream.

So I ignore the dental nightmare and loft a brow at my giggling assistant. "Mind keeping these two company? I have a last-minute meeting I need to go take care of."

Bambi dabs her mouth with a napkin and switches back to her professional side again. "Yeah. No problem." She squints at me; it's not normal for me to attend meetings without her. "Everything okay?"

I nod. I realize, as I think of a response, that things are, in fact, more than okay. "All good. I'll fill you in later. Make yourselves at home." I glance at the girl and smirk. "I think you forgot the cookies in the cupboard."

Bambi snaps her fingers and rushes over to the hazelnut wafer cookies that will without a doubt be gone by the time I get back. I leave the women to it and make my way out of the kitchen to the garage, whistling a casual tune as I stuff my hands in my pockets.

The pair of dice I always keep on hand roll between my fingers. I don't know when I started the habit—I've just always kept this pair on me no matter which suit I'm wearing. The only thing I can remember about them is when Tolya used to teach me how to play craps when I was a kid.

I pause at the small table at the door to the garage. I pull the dice out, roll them in my hand, and tumble them onto the surface.

A pair of ones.

Snake eyes.

"Hudson." I don't give Tolya's lawyer time for small talk when I hit the speed dial. "We've got a situation. No, no, it's good. Very good. I'll see you in twenty."

Maybe Lady Luck is working in my favor after all.

14

CLARA

I can hear Willow squealing with laughter as she splashes in the pool outside. Bambi is with her, teaching her how to make even bigger waves with cupped hands, and their voices rise together with every loud *whoosh* of water.

I'd tried giving the poor woman a break; we've only just met but I understand her to be several pay grades above "nanny." But Bambi only laughed me off and insisted she's earned the day, as have I.

So here I am, wandering the huge house while my daughter and her new best friend wreak havoc in the courtyard.

Courtyard. This place has its own *courtyard.* I'm not even sure "house" is the right word to describe the huge layout of Demyen's home. There's more open space than a normal house, and it seems like half the ceilings are missing. On *purpose.*

One thing I'm noticing in every room is how it's all so... manicured. Perfect. Like no one actually lives here; it's more of a setup for a magazine photo shoot and guests who probably never intend to stay. There are no family photos, no personal details, no indication of personal taste. It's like Demyen hired someone to make it museum-worthy and just stopped there.

I stroll around a much smaller courtyard—or maybe it's meant to be a living room minus a rooftop, I dunno. There's a panel of buttons next to the light switch. I glance around before I flick the switch on. An array of golden wall lights glows to life, barely visible in the bright desert sunlight but undoubtedly enough to provide a warm shine after dark.

I spot a button that might be for the roof and press it. Sure enough, a faint whirring noise sounds as a dark panel of glass slowly slides from one end of the room to the other.

This guy is so rich, his ceilings are convertible.

I am *way* out of my league.

I press the button again and the giant sunroof whirrs back into wherever it's stored. For a moment, the kid in me wants to keep playing with all the ceilings around the place, but I quickly remind myself that I'm a grown woman. I don't want Demyen to catch me messing around with his smart home controls. God forbid I break something.

So I keep wandering, poking around where I probably don't belong. But that's just the thing: I feel like I *do* belong, and it's weird. I can easily imagine painting the walls of the smaller courtyard with desert murals... maybe a few more seating arrangements with throw pillows... and Willow, running around and playing with her siblings through the wide halls.

That makes me stop in my tracks.

I haven't even been here a full day, and I'm imagining myself making this my home... *with Demyen.*

Making more children… *with Demyen.*

And instead of fear or shame, all I feel is heat. Heat that coils low and settles between my legs, making me wish he was here so we could at least dance around the topic of repeating last night.

And this morning.

My god, this morning… I can still feel the way he impaled me on his cock and drove me to new heights of pleasure, all while the showerhead sprayed down on us. When I came, he didn't stop—only held himself deep inside me until I calmed enough for him to keep going.

I press my thighs together at the memory. And then I remember the jacuzzi tub back in my bedroom, and I turn to go get some relief for all this heat.

Desert heat, in case anyone asks.

It's just as well—I really shouldn't be sleeping with a guy I hardly know. We had a great time together, but that's all it was. A time. Singular. He doesn't deserve to be anchored down by some traumatized single mother, and Willow deserves far more stability than a mother who hops from one man's bed to the next.

The thought of Martin's bed is the bucket of ice water I needed.

I hated that bed. I hated what he'd do to me in it.

Our first time together was my first time, ever. He was gentle then, and diligent enough in his foreplay to make sure I was relaxed and ready. But it was still painful, and he didn't stop when I begged him to. He only pinned me down and pounded away until he emptied himself inside me.

Every time after, he only made sure to do the bare minimum so he could push easily enough into me to work out his stress. Or his anger. Or just to remind me, with words and with the pistoning of his hips, that I belonged to him. That no other man could ever replace him between my legs.

I snort out a laugh. Demyen more than replaced him in *that* department.

A set of double doors catches my eye. I think I'm on the other side of the house and that makes me realize, as I glance around, that this means I'm probably in Demyen's wing.

I should keep going to my room.

I shouldn't poke around his private quarters.

But he *did* say to make ourselves at home, right? And there's no sign on the door that says I *can't* go in and have a look around, is there?

I let out a low sigh of relief when I see that it's only a study. Like every other room I've seen so far, it's utterly devoid of any personal touches. So I have no hesitation over slipping inside and poking around.

I don't even know what I'm looking for. A pen? A notepad? Dirty secrets? Skeletons in the closet?

The desk chair is like an armchair on wheels, covered in dark brown leather, and it squeaks slightly when I sit in it. I giggle to myself as I spread my fingers on the huge desk's surface because my God, what on earth does he need all this space for? Does the president even have a desk this big?

One thing I'm also picking up about Demyen—everything matches. Nothing is disorganized. I notice the silver cup of pens and how they're all identical. So out of curiosity, I open the desk drawers to disprove my theory. But no, every pen is from the same pack. Black cartridges with gold accents. Even the stationary is the same soft linen with gold foil letterhead, stacked neatly and organized with all the precision of an office showroom display.

I think this guy might be a bit of a control freak.

With that thought firmly embedded in my brain, I decide it's time to officially return to my own room. Not even to take a bath; just to make sure I stay on my side of the house and Demyen stays in his.

I make my way to the door, but I stop when I see a small bookcase against the wall that I hadn't noticed when I came in. There's a set of photos arranged on the top shelf, the first personal touch I've seen in this whole house.

The first photo is of a smiling little boy holding a weathered soccer ball, his face streaked with dirt. Even with all the smudges and the years erased, I can see Demyen's eyes glittering on that sweet face. He looks so happy, so carefree.

Oh, Demyen. What happened to you?

Adulthood, probably. We all grow up and the smile fades. Even when Demyen smiles now, it seems like a stiff mask compared to the little boy's grin in the photo.

I set the frame down and pick up the next one. It's Demyen again, a few years older, but no less happy and playful. He looks like he's around sixteen, in the heart of adolescence, and my heart flutters. Had we been in the same school at the same time, I would have crushed *hard* on him. The way his hair falls into his eyes, the way his teeth sparkle behind that wide, boyish grin…

And again, I find myself wondering what our kids would look like.

Stupid. Stupid, stupid Clara.

I'm about to set this frame down, too, when I notice the guy next to him. They're arm-in-arm, laughing together, and clearly related.

And just like that, everything changes.

My blood runs cold.

Fuck.

Fuck.

Fuck.

I almost drop the photo, but I quickly catch it and set it back on the shelf.

Now, I don't just walk out of the study, I *run*.

I need to find Willow.

I need to grab what little belongings we have and get the hell out of here.

Maybe Bambi will take us back into town. Maybe she'll agree to take us shopping and I'll give her the slip once we're in a large enough crowd.

Or maybe I'll hotwire a car and crash my way out of here.

I don't know what the plan is going to be, but I know I have to settle on one before I reach Willow. She'll wonder what's wrong, and I don't want her to accidentally set off any alarms or let anyone know that… that *I* know.

Willow is with Bambi in her new room, towel-dried and wearing one of Bambi's tank tops tied at the back of her neck like a little sundress. They're laughing and playing a clapping game that keeps tangling after every few tries. I almost don't want to interrupt her fun. In a lifetime of violent chaos, she deserves this moment of happiness. Like a little oasis in the middle of endless desert.

But maybe that's just life, you know?

Maybe it's all just sun-beaten sand and jagged rocks and cacti that steal all the water away and stab you with their thorns if you get tangled up with them.

I shake my head and focus.

We need to get the fuck out of here.

"Hi, Mommy!" Willow grins at me and waves at where I'm standing in the doorway.

"She's quite the natural swimmer!" Bambi rubs her head and straightens, smiling at me. That smile fades when she sees my face. "Clara? What's wrong?"

Everything.

But I can't tell her that. So I think of the first excuse that sounds plausible. "I… er, nothing." I force a smile and return Willow's wave. "I'm just tired. I'll be next door if you need me."

"Okay, Mommy!"

Bambi doesn't buy my bullshit. I can see it in her eyes. But she doesn't stop me, either. She just smiles, nods, and assures me that they'll be fine.

I wish I could believe her.

But I know that I can't. I can't trust her, and I definitely can't trust Demyen. I realize, with an agony in my chest that threatens to turn into a sob, that I should have never trusted Demyen in the first place. If I'd been smart enough to be wary, I wouldn't ever have fallen into his trap.

This is all a trap. This home. His protection. His affection.

He's lured me into his prison, and it's only a matter of time before he reveals his true colors. His true intent. His true plans.

This is his prison, and I am his prisoner.

My daughter, my sweet innocent daughter, is caught up in his snare.

And it's all my fault.

15

DEMYEN

"Stop smiling. You're scaring me."

I roll my eyes at my sarcastic second-in-command, but I refuse to wipe the grin from my face. "I've got her," I explain. "I've finally found her."

Pavel slowly turns his swivel chair in place as he lets it sink in. Then he spins, sudden and swift, to gape at me. "Her? You mean…? No. No. No fucking way."

I nod. "She's at home. Right now."

"At home? *Your* home?" When he sees my nod, he claps a hand over his mouth and laughs. "This is huge!" He instantly sobers up and tilts his head to one side. "Did you tell Hudson?"

I snort and flip a pen between my fingers. "Of course I told Hudson. He's the first person I called, after I got her settled in."

Pavel rubs a hand over his face, then peers at me. "Does her father know?"

At the mention of that soulless bastard, my mood instantly sours. "No. I don't think he does."

"You don't 'think' he does?"

"Clara hasn't exactly been on speaking terms with her father, from what I gathered." I remember her mild threat this morning. She lobbed it at me like she really is Daddy's Precious Angel, but I knew better then and I know better now.

There's no way a doting father would allow his daughter to live in such a deplorable state. To be treated so terribly by any man, let alone one he works with.

That's one of the first things I did once I left the compound: I took Clara's threat to mind and ran background checks on both her ex, Martin, and her father, Detective Greg Everett.

The same Detective Greg Everett who arrested my brother.

He's high in the ranks now, calling the shots at LVPD and taking huge, all-cash salaries under the table from various crime families across the city. The Italian dons I spoke with estimated a good ten thousand dollars per overlooked hit was the going rate; even more for circumvention around the skin trade. His protégé and now-partner is none other than Martin Patterson—Clara's so-called "husband" and Willow's deadbeat father.

Everyone she knows is tied up in this shit.

I haven't met Patterson, but I already hate him. I *loathe* him when I think of that kid and the hell he must have put her through. I hated Greg Everett from the moment he slapped cuffs on Tolya, but now that I've confirmed that he probably knew about what Martin was doing to his own daughter and looked the other way…

They're scum, plain and simple. Both of them. Worthless fucking scum.

And when I'm done, they'll meet the same fate as every other cockroach to wander under my heel.

"Easy, brother," Pavel mutters. I follow his pointed gaze to where I've started to bend the pen in my fist.

I toss the pen onto the desk and sigh. "Even without Everett's knowledge that I have his daughter, there's still concern that his hold on her will prevent her from talking."

Pavel nods. "Makes sense. What did Hudson say about it?"

"Exactly that. And that, without Clara's retraction, there's no other evidence that can exonerate Tolya and end his sentence."

"So get her to recant."

"In front of her father?" I narrow my eyes. I've thought about it, sure, but it never plays out well in my head. "He won't let that happen. He won't even let her get on the stand. And any formal approach requires taking her into the police station to write an official statement. Which *definitely* won't happen."

The government wonders why organized crime is so romanticized. This is why. I have all the money and legal resources in the world, and I still can't get justice the "right" way.

It's my way or no way at all.

Pavel purses his lips as he thinks it over. "So..." He drums his fingers on the arm of his chair. "I'm guessing we're doing this the old-fashioned way."

"Everett and his daughter need to pay for what they've done." I stare out the floor-to-ceiling window of The Meridian's main office and mull over my options. "Everett will be easy, once we get the right distraction in place. Make him talk, make him confess, and then make him wish he was never born."

"And the girl?"

I glare at him. "No one touches the girl."

Pavel lifts his hands in surrender. "Got it. Got it. No one touches the girl. But I meant Clara," he adds with a sly smile.

Shit. Fucker's found me out.

"Don't read too much into it," I warn him. "I've got no beef with the kid. That's all."

"Uh-huh."

I stare hard at him. "I mean it. She's an innocent little girl who's done nothing wrong. I'm not going to traumatize her for something her parents did. Or her grandparent. I'm not a monster."

Pavel hasn't wiped that stupid grin off his face. "Whatever you say, boss."

I don't know why I feel the need to justify myself. I am the boss, the *pakhan* of our Bratva, as well as the owner and CEO of The Meridian Casino and Hotel. What I say goes, without question.

So why am I doing it anyway?

"Are you going to give the kid to her father?" Pavel asks.

I know he's thinking logically; I can't fault him for that. But I'm about to snap another fucking pen just from him mentioning it. "No. And he's not to get within fifty yards of her, either. I'm not about to tear a child away from her loving mother just to hand her over to some abusive excuse for a man."

Pavel's brow slowly creeps up his forehead. I have half a mind to smack it back down. "Okay. Protective detail on the kid. Got it." He leans back in his chair. "So what now?"

"Now..." I stare back out the window as the plan falls together in my head. I don't like it, but Pavel's voice reminds me of why I need to do it.

"She has to pay," he reminds me gently. "For what she did to your brother. So does Everett."

I nod. "I know. And I know exactly who to call to take care of Clara."

I hear Pavel gulp. "What about Everett?" he asks.

Despite his disregard for her safety, Everett *must* have some sort of pride in his daughter. I remember the way he kept encouraging her all those years ago, whispering in her ear to tell the truth, standing up for her at the risk of his own career when Tolya's lawyer intimidated her on the stand.

"Hit him where it hurts. Clara goes first, and he'll have to watch as I take his family away from him." I spin the pen in my fingers, then stab it into my desk. "Just like he took mine."

16

CLARA

I finish counting the money in my bag and tucking it inside all the inner pockets so no one sees it right away if anyone grabs it from me.

I know I'm being paranoid. But I can't afford not to be.

The door to Willow's room opens quietly. I tiptoe through the playroom, which is now full of stuffed toys and board games, dolls, and all sorts of things a little girl could ever want. Bambi even ordered her a coloring easel. It stands in the corner with a cheery blank canvas, waiting for her to add splashes of color.

My heart squeezes. I could never give Willow all this, and a part of me feels horribly guilty for taking her away from it.

But I have to keep her safe.

I have to keep her away from Demyen Zakrevsky.

Willow is sound asleep in her new canopy bed, surrounded by more stuffed animals and sunk deep into the softest pillows under a warm blanket. I might be able to fit one of the pillows into my bag, but I need to focus on getting her out.

"Willow, baby…" I gently nudge her arm and stroke her hair. "Sweetheart, wake up."

It's well past her bedtime. She groans softly and squints at me. "Mommy? What…?"

"Let's play a game." I try to keep my breath steady so she can't hear the fear dripping in my voice. "Let's play a fun game."

"But I'm sleepy, Mommy…"

"I know, baby girl." I stroke her hair back from her face. "I know. We'll go see Auntie Roxy and you can sleep there, okay?"

Willow slowly sits up, blinking away her sleep. "But why?"

We don't have time for this. "Sweetheart, don't you want to see Auntie Roxy?"

She frowns. "But I like it here. I don't wanna leave."

I try to guide her off the bed, but she yanks away from me and stamps her little foot. "No! No, Mommy!"

I quickly look around, my heart pounding in my ears and drowning out any possible warning of security running our way. The door doesn't slam open, and no one is crashing through the windows, so I know we still have some time.

Just not as much as we need if Willow doesn't stop throwing a tantrum.

Tears well up in her eyes. She's hugging a stuffed rabbit to her chest and dodging my attempts to grab her so we can run. "No, Mommy! Please! I wanna stay!"

Finally, I manage to grab her around the waist and lift her up so she has to look me in the eyes. "Willow, please!" When she hiccups and looks at me, I set her back down and stroked her hair. "I need you to listen to me. We're going to go see Auntie Roxy, and we're going to be very, very quiet so we don't wake up Miss Bambi, okay?"

Willow sniffles, but nods. "O-okay…"

"And we have to be super-duper fast, okay?"

"Okay."

"That's my girl."

I take a deep breath, then her hand. The one small comfort I have is knowing that everything we'll need can be paid for; the weight of the money strapped to my bag reminds me of that.

The house is quiet. I was counting on that, now that it's almost midnight. Bambi must be asleep, and Demyen never returned from his meeting—as far as I know.

The halls are empty. I don't see any guards, not even when we reach the front door.

I hesitate, hand over the handle.

Is this the right thing to do?

Then: "Mommy?"

Her little voice spurs me on.

I lead us through the front door and grip her hand tighter. The compound is illuminated by dozens of warm golden lights, and under any other circumstances, I would be in awe of how beautiful everything looks.

But I can only focus on one thing: those gates at the end. Climb them, squeeze through, dig a tunnel underneath... I don't care. Whatever it takes, just as long as I get Willow to safety.

"Run, run, run!" I whisper. I try to sound more excited than panicked. Willow, thankfully, obeys and starts running with me down the long driveway. She's still clutching the stuffed rabbit, and I worry about the fuss she'll make if I can't get it to fit through the gate.

Lights flicker on behind us.

Shouts echo across the compound.

"Run!"

Willow tries to run, but she trips over her bare feet and skids on the pavement. I quickly pick her up and carry her as I run. She's crying, and I'm trying so hard to hush her and comfort her as I run for our lives to those gates. I don't hear any engines rev or dogs bark, so I think we might actually have a chance.

I grab the bars.

We made it.

Except I realize, now that we're at the gate, that the bars are too close together for either of us to squeeze through. That damn rabbit has a better chance, but Willow clings to it as she hiccups and sobs into the soft fur.

There's nothing to hook my foot on so I can climb over. I move us to the stone wall the gates are connected to, then nearly scream in frustration when I realize it's not stone, but adobe. Smooth, flawless, gripless, unclimbable adobe.

"Willow, baby, listen to me." I try to swallow back my own tears as I wipe hers away. "I… I'm going to help you squeeze through."

She nods. Then eyes the bars with the same wariness I feel. Neither of us are sure if she actually will fit through, but I have to try.

Clicks sound next to my head.

I freeze.

"Don't give us reason to shoot."

Slowly, oh so slowly, I lift my hands in surrender. My fingers are trembling out of control, and tears stream down my face. Willow starts crying again, and now, I'm grateful she has that rabbit to hug.

One of Demyen's men steps in front of me, lowering his gun when he sees I'm not about to run.

I couldn't if I wanted to. I'm too terrified to move.

He holsters it and nods to the other men. I can't see how many there are, but by the sounds of them lowering and then holstering their own guns, at least four or five surround us. "We need to get you back to the house, ma'am," he explains gruffly.

The mother in me is struck by how gentle he's being. I know why he is—because his eyes keep flicking down to check on Willow. She only stares up at him, half-hidden by her stuffed animal, her sobs fading into hiccups again.

"Please," he adds. "For your kid."

I'm *doing this for my kid. That's the whole point.*

But I nod.

He holds a hand out. "I'm going to need to take your phone as well."

I just stare at his hand for a moment. Then back up to just below his face. I can't quite look him in the eyes; I'm starting to feel the same fear I had whenever Martin demanded something from me.

"I... I don't have a phone," I mutter.

The guard frowns. "Everyone has a phone."

I shake my head. Grab Willow's hand again. Take only a half a step back, enough to put distance between us but not enough to make them draw their guns again. The men do move to do exactly that, but he holds a hand up low with a quick nod and they back off.

I still can't meet his gaze. "Not me. I... I don't have a phone. He won't let me have a phone."

Willow peers up at me over her rabbit's floppy ears, and my tears flow again. I'm back there—in my head, I'm back there. I'm back in that house, in that kitchen with peeling linoleum floors, staring at the worn pattern while Martin berates me for doing something stupid. While he demands money from me that I don't have. While he questions every little thing I do and reminds me how lucky I am that he's wasting his time on me.

The guard's warm, strong hand rests on my shoulder.

I jump.

"Hey... hey." His voice is low, soft. "It's okay. Let's get back to the house. You'll be safe there."

He doesn't know.

But neither does Willow. And she's been terrified enough tonight.

So I give in and nod. He squeezes my shoulder and turns me around. I'm forced to look at the beautiful prison with the glowing lights and exotic flowers that's coming closer and closer with every step I take.

The guard scoops Willow up in his arms. Instead of the fear I expect from her, she nuzzles into him just like she did with Demyen. From the way he softly coos at her and makes her smile through her drying tears, I wonder if he has children of his own.

It's so wrong—how someone can be so gentle and so violent at the same damn time.

We're flanked by the other guards all the way into the house. They walk with us down the hall into the guest wing and only leave when the main guy gives them a nod. He moves to take Willow into her room, but I stop him.

"I want her in mine… if—"

"Of course."

The way he gently sets her down on my bed, flicks the tip of her nose with his finger… I wish so much this was all under different circumstances. Any other time, any other place, this could be our home. Our people.

But it's not.

He meets me at the door. "You need to stay here," he says, keeping his voice low. "It's nothing personal." He glances over his shoulder at Willow, offering her a quick little smile. "She's a good kid. And it's a large desert. Understood?"

I shiver. He's not saying it to threaten me; I can tell by the way his words are laced with a friendly type of warmth even as he's warning me. But he's pointed out a major flaw in my plan that I completely forgot: we're outside the city limits. I don't know exactly how far, or in which direction, or where I'd even planned to go.

"There will be men outside." He nods at the door. "I'm telling you for your privacy. And your daughter's."

I nod again. I want to thank him, but I can't find the words. He seems to understand, because he squeezes my shoulder again and walks out, closing the door behind him.

The first thing I do is check the windows. They're not barred, which looks promising. But right when I'm about to test the latch, I stop. A tiny red light blinks from a small white box in the corner.

I should have known. Demyen's house has convertible freaking roofs—of course it's going to have an elaborate alarm system.

I pace around the room. Partly because I need to figure out a new plan, but mostly because I'm trying to feel for any signs of sag under the wooden planks. But there's nothing other than solid ground. It occurs to me that it's very likely this isn't even real wood flooring—it could be that click-board stuff that lays on top of concrete.

Willow is now fast asleep on my bed. Her arm is tucked around the stuffed rabbit, holding it close like a second pillow.

The guilt I feel weighs me down onto the bed as I pull the blankets over her and tuck her in. I'm glad she's asleep. That way, she won't see me cry.

And crying is exactly what I do—because there's no way out for us. This moment has been fifteen years in the making. Now that it's here, I don't know what Demyen plans to do with me.

All I know is that I'll do whatever he wants…

As long as he doesn't hurt my daughter.

17

DEMYEN

I hate these fucking pillows.

But good manners require dealing with the lack of lumbar support. As well as the fact that I'm on the floor, without my shoes on.

A waitress dressed like a traditional geisha smiles demurely as she refills the tiny cup I've been sipping from with green tea.

"This shit tastes like gasoline," I mutter. "Needs sugar."

"And insult five generations of my ancestors with that American poison?" Raizo Watanabe smirks and shakes his head. "No. Drink your tea and like it."

I glance around the Yakuza boss's gaudy restaurant. "Isn't this whole place basically an insult to your ancestors?"

Raizo's face grows serious for a moment. Then he shrugs. "What can I say? Tourism pays the bills. And this city is full of tourists who don't know any better."

"So then buy some fucking sugar."

He chuckles, but I know better than to trust the laugh of Raizo Watanabe. Like me, he wears the charming mask of a generous host and benevolent benefactor to comfort her guests... and, like me, he operates a powerful crime organization that oversees a significant chunk of Las Vegas' underworld dealings.

The Yakuza is no joke.

"Now, Demyen..." Raizo nods his thanks to another waitress who sets small plates of sushi in front of us, then turns his sharp gaze back to me. "I know you did not come all this way to criticize my condiments."

Now, it's my turn to play it cool with a shrug. "For all you know, I was just in the mood for a California roll, my friend."

"Remind me to play a few hands at your poker table soon. Your game face is terrible."

This feels like the perfect segue, so I decide to cut straight to the chase. "If you're looking to make good money off me, I believe I have something better and more guaranteed than a card game."

Raizo arches a brow, a bite of nigiri poised at his mouth. "Oh?"

I ignore the annoying churn in my stomach and nod. "Word on the street says you're hosting an estate auction in a few weeks. I'd like to contribute."

That makes him slow his chewing. He eyes me carefully. I don't blame him; I don't typically involve my business with his, and I definitely don't make it a habit to "contribute" to his "estate auctions." Despite our peace treaty, the Zakrevsky

Bratva steers clear of the Yakuza and vice versa, out of a combination of mutual respect and mutual dislike.

Raizo wipes his mouth with a cloth napkin, his gaze never leaving mine. "It's not like you to part with your antiquities. You're quite the collector of the rare and beautiful."

He's not wrong there. The women in my employ who see to the needs of The Meridian's elite clientele are singular in their beauty and grace. Call it prostitution, call it an escort service, call it temporary matchmaking... whatever anyone wants to call it, we've turned some rough and desperate people into exceptional fantasy-fulfillers.

But that's the difference between him and I. My employees are there of their own free will. The women who "work" for him do so without a say in the matter.

"I know when to diversify my assets." I also know what Raizo is trying to pull from me. "Don't tell me you doubt the quality of my products."

Raizo offers another indifferent shrug. "If it's something you're willing to part with, I need to know why."

Fair enough. "You caught me." I flash him an impish grin. "I want to renovate my kitchen. The extra funds will bankroll these lovely imported tiles I've had my eye on."

Raizo genuinely laughs. "And you mock *me* for being ostentatious!" He nods and pulls out his phone from his coat pocket. "Fine, fine. Bring your artifact to the warehouse by Friday for inspection, and then—"

"I was thinking." I cut him off before he can finish telling me what to do. "You should host the auction at The Meridian."

Raizo's eyebrows almost touch his hairline. "Really?"

"Really. It's about time we start working together like the friends we are, don't you think?" We both know that word is very loosely applied to this tense alliance we're in, but bystanders are listening. "I'll throw in an open bar just to make your guests more comfortable. Drive the bidding high with some liquid help."

He leans forward, officially interested. "Exactly what is this… *antique*… to you?"

I feign confusion. "Nothing. I told you: I just want money."

"You're one of the wealthiest men in Las Vegas."

"When has enough ever been enough for men like us, Raizo? So I want more money. Is that a crime?"

Raizo considers me for a long, tense moment. I know he's trying to find fault in my reasoning—or, better yet, fault in the woman I'm so casually pawning off to be sold like cattle at one of his skin auctions. His eyes follow my careful movements as I toss back a shot of sake and hiss at the burn.

But he doesn't find anything, so he nods. "Fair point. Let's call it a sixty-forty split—"

"Eighty-twenty."

He frowns. "Seventy-thirty."

I pretend to think it over. In reality, I couldn't care less if he wanted ninety-nine percent of the profits from Clara's sale. I just want her punished, and I want her off my hands.

The money doesn't hurt, though. She can't pay him back the lost time her lies stole from him.

She might as well pay him back lost wages.

"Who's on the guest list?" I dab a bit of wasabi on my sushi, then add a bit more. I see Raizo watch me with amused interest. I may like my tea sweet, but I'm no weakass when it comes to spicy food. The burn reminds me I'm alive. "Anyone I know?"

"Nice try." He smirks. If I didn't know him to be an underhanded overlord of a dangerous criminal syndicate, he'd give the impression of a classic businessman with what women call a "silver fox" appeal. A few streaks of silver glisten in his perfectly styled hair, and the way it keeps falling into his eyes adds to the boyish charm of that knowing smirk. "You know I don't divulge our guest list."

I lift a hand in mock surrender. "Of course. I was thinking of inviting Detective Everett, but if he's already coming…"

Raizo freezes on the spot. It's almost impossible to see in this dim lighting, but the blood drains from his face.

Interesting.

"Why? He's no antiquities dealer. And his salary barely affords…"

I catch his drift. *Why invite a police detective to a slave auction?* Good question.

"Added security." I take another shot of sake to wash down the wasabi. And to plaster on a far more convincing poker face than his. "It will put your guests at ease knowing there's enhanced protection in all areas."

Translation: plainclothes cops at a slave auction are obviously dirty, so there's no risk of a raid.

Raizo considers this through a narrowed stare. For a moment, I think he's going to call my bluff. But then he sighs and tilts his head. "Done. Adding Detective Everett to the guest list as we speak." He taps something on his phone, then sets it down with an air of finality.

"Do me one more favor."

"I suppose I must, since you're hosting."

"See if his partner will join him." It's a low fucking blow, but the thought of flaunting Clara's worth in front of her deadbeat ex-boyfriend is too tempting to pass up. I want him to see just how goddamned valuable she is, and I want him to realize just how fucking powerless he is and will always be.

Wait—*focus, Demyen.*

This is about revenge. On Clara.

"Why not invite the whole family?" Raizo chuckles and throws back his own shot of sake with a loud smack of his lips. "I hear Everett's daughter is a fine piece of ass. Dumb as rocks, but she doesn't need a brain when she's on her back."

He laughs like it's the most deliciously funny idea he's had all night. I know he expects me to join in. Hell, *I* expect myself to join in with at least a chuckle.

But that churning feeling in my stomach won't go away no matter how much I try to drown it in rice wine and green tea. It roils when he talks about Clara, and my fist clenches around the shot glass.

I have more than half a mind to stab this glass through his fucking eye socket.

I should stab my *own* eye socket. The hell is wrong with me? Clara Everett isn't my problem. She sure as hell isn't mine to protect.

Yeah. Keep telling yourself that.

"We have a deal." Raizo signals to the servers that we're finished, and he gives me one final nod. "Bring your artifact to the auction. I will trust you'll have it inspected and verified beforehand." At my nod, he continues. "I'll cut you the check for seventy percent of the highest bid—"

"Cash." It's not that I don't trust his paper; I just don't trust him at all.

Raizo grins. "Cash, Mr. Zakrevsky. As you wish."

With the deal struck, I take my leave. I'm not inclined to shake hands with him, and he knows what will happen should he double-cross me. He's playing on my turf, by my rules, surrounded by my people.

It's the allure of the unknown—the temptation to find out the secret of my "antique"—that has Raizo Watanabe in the palm of my hand.

He knows what will happen if I close my fist.

18

CLARA

The door slowly opens. I want to jump at the sight of him darkening the doorway, but I don't want to startle Willow from her sleep. So instead, I tuck the blankets around her once more, then slide off the bed to meet him halfway.

I press a finger to my lips. I expect him to tell me to go to hell, that he'll do whatever he wants, but he sees Willow in my bed and nods.

And then he ushers me into the next room over. The firm hand pressed at the small of my back doesn't allow me any room to run. The look on his face dares me to try.

Once the door is closed, Demyen turns on me. But instead of backhanding me or pinning me to the wall, he only smiles. It doesn't reach his eyes.

I almost wish he'd just hit me instead.

"So," he says quietly. "You remember me."

"W-what do you mean?" My tongue feels thick and dry. Even though he's not caging me in, his presence is suffocating.

He scoffs and shakes his head. "Don't play stupid, Clara. You—"

"Don't." The word flies out before I can stop myself. My arms wrap tight around my waist without me thinking about it. I'm cowering. And I hate myself for it. "Don't call me that. I'm not… I'm not stupid."

Demyen's fingers twitch, but he doesn't move. "I know. I know you're not. And that's the problem."

I peer at him through the haze that's clearing as quickly as it came. "What are you talking about?"

"Why did you run?"

Oh. That. I quickly glance at the door separating us from Willow. "It's not safe here," I whisper. Something protective coils inside my chest, and I meet his hard stare with my own. "You… you trapped me. You trapped us."

"You did that yourself, Clara." He folds his arms across his chest as he glares at me. I'm trying my damned hardest to ignore the way his muscles ripple and bulge. "What did you think would fucking happen? You threw my brother in prison. I'm just disappointed I missed seeing the look on your face when you figured it out."

The kind man I knew last night is gone. There's a monster using his voice and working his face like a marionette. That's the only possible explanation here.

And—*Oh, God…*

I *slept* with him.

I slept with him, and I put my daughter's life in his hands.

"Are…" I swallow hard. "Are you going to kill me?"

He doesn't answer.

He is. He's going to kill me.

Demyen suddenly sighs. The sound almost makes me jump. "I'm not going to kill you. I'm not in the business of destroying families and ripping them apart. That's your thing."

I take a step back. "If you're not going to kill me, then... then why am I here? Why bring my daughter into this?"

His jaw clenches. There's a vein in one side that pulses as he continues to glare at me. Actually, the hardness has softened in his eyes just a bit, but it's all the same to me.

It won't change what comes next.

I feel the tremor start in my bones. I close my eyes tight and hug myself tighter, willing it to go away before he sees me visibly shake. It's bad enough he can see how easy it is to keep me hostage—worse yet, how easy it is to use Willow as a bargaining chip against me.

The tremor settles into my limbs. I'm shaking, and I know he can see it.

So I close my eyes so I don't have to see him seeing me shake like a rattlesnake tail.

The shaking is something that started years ago, back when I was a little girl and my father took out his anger and frustrations on me. Sometimes, all it took was for him to walk into the room after a shift and I'd start quivering.

On good nights, just seeing me tremble was enough to make him laugh and walk away. But most of the time, it only irritated him. And then he'd slap me. Pull my hair. Throw me across the room until I stopped shaking because I was too busy sobbing.

The only time I really remember my father being kind to me was when he found me in that warehouse. I'd been kidnapped, stuffed inside the trunk of a car, and thrown inside a crate while men fought with each other and I was forced to listen.

When the police finally showed up, my father pulled me out of that horrible crate and cradled me close. I was shaking harder than I ever had before, but he simply shushed me and promised that everything would be okay. All I had to do was be a good girl and tell the truth.

So I did. I told them the truth.

I told them about how a man had grabbed me from behind, hurt my face when he clamped his hand over my mouth. He stuffed me into that musty trunk, then drove me to the warehouse where he threw me inside the crate. My body was riddled with splinters, and I couldn't stop shaking or crying.

I told them about how someone opened the crate. A different man—except he wasn't old like the first one. Not like my dad. He reached for me, told me I was going to be okay…

And then slammed the crate shut again.

My father interrupted my story to ask if it was the same man I saw holding the gun over Uncle Mike's dead body.

I didn't remember seeing Uncle Mike there. I might have heard him? Maybe he came to save me?

Yes, that was it. Daddy said so. Uncle Mike was there to save me from the kidnapper. And the kidnapper was the one who checked on me in that crate. The kidnapper was the one who shot and killed Uncle Mike and tried to do bad things to me.

When they showed me pictures, I recognized the face that had peeked in on me and asked if I was okay.

When I had to go to court and tell my story in the stands, Daddy reminded me to tell the truth. His hands on my shoulders hurt when he squeezed. The bruise on my face still throbbed. He told the bailiff that I was still healing from my ordeal. He forgot to tell the bailiff about how I'd messed up my story and forgot what the kidnapper was trying to do to me. I forgot, so Daddy knocked my memories back into place so I'd get it right.

I got it right. I told the truth, just like Daddy said.

I told the truth.

I watched them take away the bad guy. He kept looking at me. But I was shaking so hard, I couldn't meet his eyes with my own.

They took him away forever because I told the truth.

I told the truth.

… Didn't I?

～

"Clara."

It's the warm hand on my arm that pulls me back. His voice is gentle, but his fingers wrapped around my bicep make me jolt to the present and immediately yank myself away from him.

Demyen takes a step back, his hands up by his shoulders as if to show me he's respecting my boundaries. It's strange—he's pissed, and he has every right to be. He should be hitting me, pulling my hair, maybe even kicking me in my stomach while I'm curled up on the floor.

That's what everyone else does when they're mad at me.

Why isn't he?

"Clara." He repeats my name. Slowly. Firmly. "I'm not going to kill you. And I'm not going to hurt you or your daughter. You have my word."

"Why?" I press my back to the wall just to calm my shaking. I expect him to corner me there, but still, he doesn't move toward me. "Why not just let her go? I'll do anything you want. Please. Anything you want—just let Willow go."

"Go where?"

It's a challenge as much as a legitimate question.

I'm ashamed to not have an answer.

Now, he does take a step forward, but stops the moment I flinch. He raises a fist, but instead of swinging it at me, he just points an angry finger at my face. "What I want is for you to march your ass into the courtroom, tell the judge you lied, and get my brother out of prison. But you and I both know you're not going to do that. Are you?"

My bottom lip trembles. I don't know how to answer. I'm starting to feel warm, almost overheated. My breaths are raspier than they were a few minutes ago.

"That's what I thought." Demyen lowers his hand. "So you're just going to have to stay here, under my roof, while I figure out what the fuck to do with you."

"But Willow—"

"Has nothing to do with this." His glare softens whenever he talks about her. I wish I could read into that, but I'm struggling to control my own heart rate while my lungs constrict. "She's safe here. And probably safer here than anywhere else."

I nod. At least, I try to.

But the room is spinning now. The floor is rising, fast.

I think I hear him shout my name, but I can't tell. It's all fuzzy and blurred.

And then... black.

19

DEMYEN

I lay Clara's unconscious body in the new—for her—guest bedroom in my wing of the main house. I tell myself it's so I can keep a close eye on her and make sure she doesn't try to run off again. I tell myself it's so the in-house doctor can attend to her quickly without bothering anyone else in the house.

In other words, I tell myself *lies*.

I have to ignore the way panic lanced through my veins when Clara dropped to the floor right in front of me.

She's burning up. Probably got sick long before we met and has just been ignoring the symptoms. I make sure the doctor confirms he's on his way across the compound before I leave her on the bed and close the door behind me.

The guard stationed nearby doesn't need me to say the orders. He knows, with a single nod of my head, that he is to let no one but the physician in or out of that room.

I don't know where I'm going as I storm through the main house. What would be a beautiful starlit night perfect for relaxing by the pool is only irritating me with all that glitter in the sky. I want to close all the open roofs but don't have the patience to wait for each one to slide into place.

I want to scream into a canyon, but the nearest one is half an hour away.

I want to bury myself in the soft warmth of Clara's body and listen to her breathless moans…

…but she's sick.

And my prisoner.

And the woman who put my brother in jail.

Fucking focus, *Demyen*.

I was ready to rip into her when I came home after meeting with Raizo. I'd thought of all the best and scariest things I could snarl to make her cower and beg for mercy as I swung her fate over her head like some proverbial sword. She would be on her knees, and I'd make her earn my mercy… if there were any to give.

But the way she crumpled… that look in her eyes… It didn't just slam the brakes on my plans; it threw them out the fucking window.

And then she started shaking.

Fuck, it took every ounce of self-control I have left to just stand there and watch when all I wanted to do was wrap my arms around her and squeeze until she could breathe again.

It's taking every ounce of self-control I have right now not to drive into town and plant a bullet deep inside her ex's skull.

If this is what he's done to her, I don't want to imagine what he's tried to do to his own daughter.

And that's when I realize where I am: right outside Willow's room.

I'm not going to read too much into it. Probably just walking on autopilot, coming back to grab a change of clothes for when Clara wakes… something like that.

Yeah. Clothes. That's all.

I can hear the kid stirring in her sleep as I brace a hand on the doorknob. No way am I going to risk waking her up—I'm not father material, and I don't do the whole "kid thing." Hell, I don't even have nieces or nephews. So it's just best for everyone involved if I slip in, grab Clara's things, and slip back out without being noticed.

"Mom… Mommy…"

Shit. She may be too alert for me to go in just yet.

I hold my breath and wait. Maybe she'll calm down. Maybe this was just a fluke.

But then she screams.

"Mooommyyy!"

Each scream is loud and shrill and filled with terror. Immediately, I draw my gun and burst into the room, the guard close behind me. The way she's sobbing and panicking and scrambling up the headboard, I'm convinced there's a rattlesnake or worse inside the room.

The guard flicks on the light while I quickly scan the room for any signs of snakes, spiders, boogeymen… I shake off that last thought and quickly gesture for guns to be put away.

"You okay?" I ask the kid.

She nods for a moment, then shakes her head. "Where—where's my mommy?"

Well, this is uncomfortable.

I nod for the guard to resume his post. I've got this.

Well, I'm pretty sure I've got this.

"Hey, Willow," I coo. "Remember me?"

Willow slumps down the headboard onto the pillows, clutching the woven blanket like it's a lifeline. She stares at me for a long, teary-eyed moment, then nods.

"Good." I smile. I'm surprised at how natural it feels to smile at her. "I had to take your mommy to the doctor's. She's sick." Which, technically, is accurate.

More or less.

"Sick?" Willow frowns and hides half her face behind the blanket. "But she was just here."

"I know. I think she's been sick for a while, and just didn't want you to worry. Does she…" *Fuck,* how do I ask this kid without traumatizing or confusing her? "Does she do that a lot?"

Willow looks away. Then slowly nods. "Mommy doesn't want me to worry," she mutters so quietly, I almost can't hear her. "And Martin doesn't like it when we go to the doctor. He gets real mad."

I grab one of the stuffed lounge chairs from a corner of the room and carefully set it down near the bed. The movement gives me an excuse to grab something hard in lieu of punching my fist through the wall like I'd rather be doing. I almost slam the chair on the ground just to be cathartic for myself, but I rethink it when I see the little girl eye me warily.

So instead, I set it down so slowly and quietly, the legs never make so much as a squeak when I settle my large frame down onto the chair. This seems to have the effect on Willow that I wanted: she's stopped sniffling, and she's not cowering away from me. She actually seems curious, eyeing me from behind the blanket.

"Martin?" Again, I don't know the right questions to ask a traumatized five-year-old. I find it interesting that she doesn't call him "Daddy" or "Dad" or whatever.

"Yeah." She lowers the blanket just enough to grab her stuffed animal and hug it to her chest. "He's my dad. I guess."

I do my best to suppress my smirk. "You guess?"

Willow shrugs and starts picking lint off the toy's fur. "He's mean. He's really mean to Mommy."

"Is he mean to you?"

Translation: *Do I need to go load up my men and pay this* mudak *a visit?*

Because, as much as I might not do the whole "kid thing," I sure as shit don't tolerate abuse. Especially not when it's a grown man hitting a little girl.

Even the king of hell has standards.

Willow scrunches up her face. "He yells a lot. He—he—he calls me names sometimes, but Mommy doesn't like that." She hugs the stuffed rabbit closer. "He hits Mommy," she mumbles into the fur.

I have so many questions. So many questions, and not a clue how to get the right answers. I want to know more about this Martin asshole, where he lives, how he got his hands on Clara, who the *fuck* he thinks he is terrorizing such a sweet little girl…

But I don't want to make the kid cry by launching an interrogation. And, frankly, it's none of my business. It's not my problem.

And I'm going to keep chanting that to myself like a fucking mantra so my instincts follow suit.

"Are you gonna send us back?"

Her question yanks me out of my brooding. "What?"

Willow swings her feet around so they dangle over the side of the bed. She's still holding fast to the rabbit, but not as white-knuckled as before. "When Mommy feels better. Are you gonna send us back to Martin?"

Fuck no.

I study her carefully and choose my words with as much caution as possible. "Do you want to go back?"

She immediately shakes her head. Fear fills her eyes. "No!"

"Then no." I slowly rise from the chair and take her moment of visible relief to gently nudge her back down. "It's bedtime. You need to sleep."

"I can't."

Here we go. I fucking swear, if this kid starts asking for glasses of water—

"It's too dark."

Oh.

I guess I hadn't thought of that when I carried her mother away to what is now a makeshift medical wing. This place wasn't built with kids in mind—no matter how many times Pavel and Bambi nudged me to "think of the future"—so there's no night lights or glowing orbs for the bathroom or anything of the sort.

Nothing but pitch darkness. And without her mother to hold her and comfort her and reassure her with her presence, it's probably a hundred times scarier to a tiny thing like Willow.

I think fast. "Wanna see something cool?"

Willow nods and sits back up, holding her arms up to me.

It doesn't occur to me that she probably just needed help sliding off the tall bed. Not until we're already halfway down the large hallway, her head tucked under my chin as I carry her in my arms. I'd swept her up, blanket and rabbit and all, without a second thought and now I'm carrying her around like... like...

Like she's something to me I can't afford her to be.

We reach the solarium and I quickly set her down on one of the plush loungers before she gets too comfortable. She's already started to snuggle me—because she doesn't know what I am.

I'm a mob boss. The leader of an organized crime syndicate.

Mob bosses don't "snuggle."

But Willow neither knows nor cares.

She's a little preoccupied, to be fair. Her eyes grow wide when she sees the open ceiling and the brilliant stretch of the

Milky Way illuminating the room. The starlight makes the palm trees and cacti reflect dark greens and blues, and through the floor-to-ceiling glass wall, we can see the moonlight sparkle on the pool water.

"Is this better?" I ask her. I already know the answer—her face is almost as lit up as the sky.

"Yeah," she breathes.

"How about…" I discreetly pull out my phone and tap a quick text to Bambi. "How about we make this your new room?"

Willow whips her wide eyes to me. "Really?"

I nod. "We'll get some tint for the windows when you need it, add some more furniture and toys, maybe a fluffy rug over there…"

I stop myself before I start sounding like I'm invested in her comfort. I'm not. I just need her to be happy so she stops asking questions and stays out of the way.

That's it.

Bambi quickly sashays around the corner, a bright smile plastered on her face. *Thank God.* I know I woke her from a dead sleep when I texted her to come over and handle whatever this is, but the way she croons her hello to Willow and practically glides across the room in her silk kaftan doesn't give away any irritation she may feel toward me.

Which, great. Whatever. Be irritated, or don't. I have better things to do than to play Daddy Warbucks to little semi-orphan Annie here.

"Miss Bambi is going to help you settle into your new room," I tell Willow as I begin to make my subtle exit from the situation. "Anything you want, just tell Miss Bambi, okay?"

"I want Mommy."

Bambi dives in before I say anything stupid. "Do you want a midnight cookie? Maybe with some ice cream on top?"

Something inside me wants to caution against too much sugar so late at night. It's bedtime. The kid needs to be asleep, not rotting her teeth out.

But I shake that off just like every other remotely parental thought I get around her. Not my kid, not my problem. I give Bambi a quick nod, then wave at Willow when she spots me leaving.

"Goodnight, *solnishka*."

Solnishka. Little sun. A bright spot in a dark desert.

I don't know who or what has possessed me. Phrases like that keep flying out of my mouth—things that only a man who genuinely cares would say.

That same stranger sitting under my skin makes me pause just outside the solarium door so I can listen in on their conversation. Bambi keeps asking questions to figure out what Willow wants, but the kid is too shy to actually answer. I hear a softly muttered, "Mommy doesn't have a lot of money," and Bambi's richer tone assures her there's nothing to worry about.

The mysterious squeeze in my heart strongly disagrees.

20

CLARA

Am I swimming?

Everything is floating around me like I am.

I try to look up from where I'm lying, but even that little effort makes me feel like I'm rolling head over heels with the dizzying vertigo that slams into me.

I groan and give up. My limbs sink deeper into the softness surrounding me... and that's when I realize I'm not swimming at all. I'm sprawled in a bed, tucked under a comforter, cushioned by who knows how many overstuffed pillows.

And I'm alone.

Where's Willow?

Oh, God. I don't know where my daughter is.

I try to jump out of bed, but my legs are weaker than I expected. I crumple to the floor almost immediately. A chair set up next to the bed, for whatever reason, is heavy enough for me to grab and pull myself up with.

The room keeps spinning.

My face feels so hot.

My head hurts, too. Not like a migraine, but more of this dull, throbbing discomfort that twists my insides every step I take. The ground keeps lunging at me, but I'm too determined to find my baby girl to let it win.

I manage to claw my way over furniture to the door. My fingers fumble weakly with the knob, but eventually, it squeaks open. My bodyweight swings me forward through the crack. I nearly trip over my own toes, but muster enough strength to hold myself up where I'm gripping the knob and frame.

No one is in the hall. I don't think so, at least.

Pretty sure this is a trap.

It has to be. There's no way Demyen would allow it to be so easy for me to just… walk… out of…

I need to stop.

The wall feels nice. It's cool adobe, so smooth and soothing where my cheek presses to it. I could stay right here forever; it actually feels even better than the bed.

No, no… I need to find Willow. I need to find my baby and we need to get out of here. Back to walking. One foot in front of the other.

It's harder to walk in this hall. There's not enough furniture to grab and lean against, so I'm mostly just sliding along the wall. I have to move slowly so I don't scrape myself, and because my legs keep wobbling and threatening to give out under me.

God, I hope I'm going in the right direction.

I hear a door open somewhere nearby. I freeze. Voices mutter and muddle, but I can't make out the words. They vanish behind what might be another door. Once I'm sure the silence is permanent, I take another few shaky steps forward.

This time, the door that opens is right in front of me.

"The hell...?"

No. No... no no no no no...

I close my eyes and this time, I allow my legs to fold under me. I crumple to the floor with a soft whimper. I want to cry, but my head hurts too much. I want to scream, but it's a miracle I have the strength to even groan.

Demyen scoops me up like I weigh nothing. His face is etched with deep lines of anger and hatred for me.

I think.

I mean, what else could it be? He's pissed and he hates me. There's no way that's worry or concern weighing down his brows. Impossible.

"The fuck do you think you're doing?" he demands, giving me a little shake.

"Getting... my baby... outta here..." Even in my weakened state, I manage to glare at him. He can torture me all he wants—I won't let him lay a finger on my Willow.

The asshole has the balls to laugh at me. "Is that so?" He grins like it's the funniest thing he's heard all day. "And how exactly do you plan to do that?"

I want to give him my master plan just out of spite, but my head hurts too much to remember the details. Or if I even had a plan. "Fuck… you."

"Let's put a pin in that for now. You're sick."

"*You're* sick."

He smirks and starts carrying me to God-knows-where. I try to wrestle away from him, but for some reason, I'm too weak to do more than wiggle my feet.

Shit. This is going to be harder than I thought.

"Where's Willow?" Aha, there it is. My Mom Voice comes through just fine. It hurts my throat, but I don't care.

"She's fine."

"Where is she?"

Demyen rolls his eyes as we turn a corner. I'm vaguely aware we should have been back to the bedroom by now, but he's turned us in a whole other direction.

I'd be scared, but right now, I'm too worried about my daughter.

He shifts me in his arms, and the movement tucks my head on his shoulder and my face against his neck.

He pretends like this is completely normal.

I pretend like I'm not breathing in his sandalwood scent and drifting off to heaven.

"I want my baby."

"And I want you to not get your baby sick. Think you can manage that?"

Fuck him and his... his... fucking logic.

My nose is suddenly accosted by an array of scents overpowering the warm sandalwood of his skin. I roll my head on his shoulder enough to catch a glimpse of glistening silver metals, sharp objects, strange tools…

Oh, God. This is it. He really is going to kill me. This is his torture room—

He shifts me in his arms again, then grunts as he pulls open what must be an incredibly heavy door.

And then I'm freaking *freezing*.

Until I'm not, because… well… it feels kind of amazing.

Demyen mutters something about a delayed meat shipment and dumb luck. I don't know. It's hard to hear him over whatever the hell keeps rumbling in a wall over our heads.

He kicks aside what sound like boxes on the floor, then carefully lowers me down. I don't know why he's being so gentle with me—unless, of course, he doesn't want to kill me *here*.

I don't even know where "here" is.

My breath comes out in small, cloudy puffs. It's so cold in here, there's frost coating the edges of what appear to be shelves.

Fuck. He's thrown me into a freezer.

I've seen the movies. I know what this is. My heart starts pounding and I'm scrambling to get up, but he simply presses me back down with one hand to my chest. The floor is too slippery and cold for my bare feet; otherwise, I'd keep trying. I'd keep fighting him.

"Stay," Demyen orders me like a dog. He holds his hand out over me like I'm about to pounce back up. "Just... stay here. Don't do anything stupid."

Sheer spite and determination to protect my daughter has me pulling myself up to my feet—but not fast enough.

Demyen walks out of the freezer and slams the door shut behind him.

Leaving me in the frozen dark.

I slump back against a pile of cardboard boxes, feeling weaker than before. Utterly defeated. Tears drip down my face. They're hot at first, but I wonder how long it will be before they freeze to my skin.

I don't know how long it takes for someone to die inside a locked freezer, either.

But I know he's going to leave me here long enough to get the job done.

21

CLARA

Light spills through a thin crack that forms in the frost.

The freezer door opens.

I can barely move. My lips are numb. I tried keeping my fingers warm inside my armpits, and now, I'm permanently frozen in this cross-armed fetal position. Frost has formed on my lashes, from what I can tell in the dim light.

A brighter light clicks on, blinding me.

Demyen is here to collect my body. He's about to be sorely disappointed when he finds out I'm still alive.

He crouches down and scoops me back up in his arms like he did earlier.

"Still… alive… asshole…" I manage to mumble through my frozen lips. It's about as close to a middle finger as I'm able to flip.

He furrows his brow as he looks at me. "What? Of course you are. It's only been ten minutes."

... What?

No. It's been way, way, way longer than ten minutes. I counted every icicle that formed on my breath, flipped through every happy memory of my sweet baby girl while I felt the setting and the rising of the sun... minutes turning to hours... hours into days...

My body shivers for a violent moment. I pretend to completely ignore the way he holds me closer, his solid chest and thick arms warming me up. As he carries me out of the freezer and into what is apparently his kitchen, I feel the frost melt from my lashes and mingle with my earlier tears.

"For the hundredth time," he grumbles, "I'm not going to kill you. And even if I were, why would I put you in my freezer? So fucking dramatic."

"B-but... mafia..." Stupid lips still won't move.

He snorts. He actually *snorts*. The asshole. "Right. I forgot. My apologies. I'll be careful to meet your expectations next time."

Again, I have no idea where we're going. I'm too weak, too cold, too out of it to fight him or even ask him what his plans are with me. For all I know, he could pour me into some cement shoes and toss me into an ocean.

"Clara." He gives me a slight shake and frowns again. "Stay with me."

What is he talking about?

The next place he lays me down is low in the ground and covered in ceramic. Or maybe it's not on the ground, it's just... deep? Deep and white and... filling with warm water.

Oh, God, thank you... That feels so good...

I let out a moan of appreciation and lay my head against the basin. Somewhere nearby, Demyen clears his throat. I don't care. He can leave me to drown in this torture pool of his as long as it stays warm…

Oh. It's a bathtub.

It's the golden faucet that lets me know where I am. My head still kind of hurts, but not as much as it did earlier. I'm able to make out stone tiles, golden lights, thick white towels on a shelf, and eucalyptus wreaths decorating the walls.

I'm in a bathroom. I glance over to where Demyen is—*fuck*, he's taking off his shirt—and realize this is probably his bathroom.

He tosses his shirt aside and turns to me. I swear he's going to take off his jeans, but instead, he keeps them on and calmly saunters over to the side of the tub where he kneels.

"Lift your arms." His voice is soft but firm. It's an order he doesn't feel the need to shout.

And I don't feel the need to make him. I carefully lift my arms as much as I can, which isn't that much, but he doesn't scold me or yell at me. Instead, he calmly dips his hands into the rising water, grabs the bottom of my nightie, and pulls it up over my head.

"Hips."

I stare at him. He stares back. There's no arguing with him, as much as I want to. But the lace is also feeling increasingly uncomfortable as it rubs against my skin under the water, so I sigh and do my best to lift my hips so he can slide those off me, too.

I hate how good this bath feels. I want to glare at him, but I can't. My limbs feel far too relaxed, especially after he pours what look like bath salts into the water and swirls them around with his hand.

Neither of us says a word to each other. I try not to look at him. Or at least, I try not to let him see me look at him. Hate him, fear him, whatever I feel about him... that is one chiseled torso. The memory of my legs wrapped around his waist enters my mind unbidden.

If he notices the way my thighs suddenly press together, he doesn't say anything. His face is a mask of stoic resolve. After a few silent minutes of me soaking in the tub, Demyen just watching me, he grabs a sea sponge and lathers it with some sort of sudsy bath oil.

"Sit up."

I don't know why I obey him. Maybe it's that fucked-up part of me that's been trained my entire life to do whatever a man says. But I do as he says, tucking my knees to my chest while he pushes my hair over one shoulder.

He's *bathing* me.

Demyen Zakrevsky is bathing me.

I want to laugh at the absurdity of this moment, but the rub of the sponge along my aching back feels too good. He presses just hard enough for it to feel almost like a massage, and his movements are slow and purposeful. One shoulder blade, then the other... and then down one side of my spine, up the other side... over and over.

He doesn't say anything when he moves to my arms; he simply takes the one closest to him and lifts it up. He's careful to wash every inch, from my shoulder to my armpit and all the way to my fingertips, where he massages each one with the sponge. When he needs to reach the other side, he moves behind the tub and crouches behind my head.

Demyen lowers my arms back into the water, rinsing the oily soap off my limbs. I think he's done when he drops the sponge into the water, and I try not to feel as disappointed as I am.

But then I hear the sound of the soap pump, the slickness of his hands rubbing together… and he massages my shoulders. He uses the movements to guide me up along the side of the tub more, working the soap into my collarbone and kneading away knots of tension I've probably been carrying for years.

I can't hold back the whimpers of relief that catch in my throat. If they bother him, I don't know, because he still doesn't say a word.

My lips part in a half-gasp, half-moan when his slick hands reach down and cup my breasts. He takes slow, steady strokes, wrapping his huge hands around the base of each one, rotating his fingertips to knead out painful knots I didn't even know could exist there… then slowly, deeply squeezes and slides his hands around until my nipples are captured between his fingertips.

"Demyen…" I gasp his name. I don't know why. I can't see his face at this angle, and everything from his waist down is hidden by the tub.

Instead of responding with words, he does it with his hands, repeating the motion again… and again… until I'm unable to hide the writhing in my hips. Every time his fingers slide to my nipples, he teases them, tweaks them, caresses them, sending wave after wave of pleasure straight to my core.

Only when I'm a panting mess does he release my sensitive breasts and smooth his soapy hands down over my waist. But then he grabs the sponge again, and I have to force myself not to pout.

Demyen shifts his position around the tub to reach my legs, and finally, I can see the stormy look on his face. I'd easily mistake it for rage if I hadn't already seen it on him that night at the hotel.

So I know what it really is.

Lust.

He takes hold of my calf and eases my leg up and close to him. The sponge starts rubbing at my ankle, and I let out another long, low moan of appreciation when he moves it along the arch of my foot.

When he's finished with this leg, he lowers it so it drapes over the side of the tub. He doesn't seem to mind that my toes are dripping suds onto the tiled floor. Demyen simply gets up to move back to his original post and resumes bathing me, taking the same sweet time with this leg.

This time, he doesn't move away when he drapes my leg over the side. He dips the sponge into the water for a brief moment, then smooths it over my waist.

And then dips between my legs.

I bite my lip. Turn my head to the side.

"Look at me."

I quickly do exactly as he says. The order and my submission resonate in a wave of warmth deep inside me. Demyen seems to notice, because a fire lights up in the backs of his eyes and he presses the sponge firmer against my slit. When he rubs over my sensitive, swollen clit, I let out a pitiful mewl and arch my back in the water.

The devil smiles at me. Wicked. Hungry.

He won't stop until I break.

I reach down to grab his wrist, but he moves faster and grabs both of mine with his one free hand. He holds them above my head, and this new angle only manages to press me down harder on his wicked sponge.

"I said, *Look at me.*"

My lashes flutter, but I make the effort to obey. Just the thought of that word—*obey*—makes me shudder with a surge of pleasure. He smirks as I try to ride it out. I look him in the eyes, chewing my bottom lip so I don't do something stupid like cry out his name.

Demyen leans in close, so close I can smell that sandalwood again.

"You're mine." He flicks the sponge away to cup my whole mound in his hand, squeezing just firm enough to make his point.

Fuck, I want more.

"You'll do exactly as I say, when I say it. Do you understand?"

When I don't immediately respond, he kneads the heel of his palm against my clit until my bottom lip pops from between my teeth in another moan. The way he's holding my wrists together above my head has my torso lifted out of the water, and now, my nipples are tightened almost painfully in the cool air.

"If I tell you to drop to your knees and open your pretty mouth, you do it." His thumb brushes over that bundle of nerves and pinches just enough to make me whimper and nod. "If I tell you to bend over my fucking desk and spread your legs, you do it." He pushes one, then two, thick fingers inside me, holding there. "Anytime, anywhere, you will do exactly as I say and you will take whatever I fucking give you until I'm done. Until *I* say I'm done."

I whimper again. I nod, and nod, and nod some more.

His gaze burns into mine; his mouth is so close, I can almost taste him. I *want* to taste him. I want to feel him surround me, fill me, own me.

"And when I give you my word, you'll fucking believe it. Understood?"

I nod again. "Yes, sir," rushes from me in a surprising gasp, punctuated by my own inner squeeze around his fingers.

A flicker of surprise, then dark delight, pools in his eyes. I watch them drop to my lips; I wait for him to devour me.

But then he pulls away.

His hand abruptly slides out, leaving me on the very edge of the release I need—and I suddenly realize, to my horror, he's not going to give it to me at all.

Demyen stalks over to his shirt and yanks it back on.

"Oh, and Clara…"

He turns only enough to glare at me over his shoulder.

"Don't even dare think about touching yourself. I'll know if you do. And then I won't be nearly as kind."

The bathroom door slams shut behind him, leaving me in the cooling bath water to stare up at the ceiling and wonder what the hell just happened.

This time, my limbs are shaking for a whole other reason.

22

DEMYEN

That was too close.

Way too fucking close.

I've been successful in avoiding both Clara and Willow for over a day, with the exception of checking in on Bambi and her new favorite little friend. They ended up going shopping together all day yesterday as a sort of therapy to help Willow break out of her shell and learn how to ask for things she genuinely needs.

Based on the number of bags they brought home, it seems she also learned that what she simply *wants* is also on the "yes" list.

Clara was bedridden the entire time they were gone. Doc said that it was nothing serious, just compounded neglect for her own health. She had a high fever and would be a bit delirious until that breaks. But other than that, and aside from the healing ankle and various bruises Doc found on her body, she was healthy.

I asked him where those bruises were.

I really wish I hadn't.

It's what kept me in the gym for most of the night, pumping weights and slamming bags around until I passed out on one of the benches. I'm not supposed to care, and I have to keep telling myself I don't. I fucking *don't*. But every time I think about that motherfucker's hands holding her thighs apart so hard that his fingers bruised her skin… the cigarette burn on the side of her breast I don't even know how I missed… and countless other marks that are faint now, but still obvious to the medical eye…

Fuck.

I can't afford to care about Clara Everett.

So why do I care so fucking much about how she's treated?

And that's where it all went too far overboard this morning. All I meant to do was speed up her recovery process by breaking her fever. It's something Tolya and I used to do for each other whenever we got sick—we'd go inside the freezer, whoever had the fever, and the other would stand guard outside for around ten minutes. I don't know the medical science behind it; all I know is it shocked our bodies enough to break into that vile sweat and bounce back within a day or so.

That was all well and good.

It's the bath that did me in.

All I wanted to do was help her not stink of sick-sweat and warm up a bit from the freezer. That's it. But the moment I saw her in that tub… the moment she started responding so sweetly to every touch…

I had to rip myself away before I took advantage of her delirium and fucked her fever out.

She's my prisoner, not my woman.

My prisoner. Not my woman.

I'm chanting this to myself as I storm through the halls and across the courtyard. I need a distraction that's as far away from Clara as possible. I can't go back to my office because now, after our little "agreement," all I can think about is bending her over that desk and pounding her open. I can't go back to the gym because all I want is to pin her to the mats and fuck her in front of the mirrors so I can see her fall apart from every angle.

No way am I going to even *try* going to my bedroom.

So, I beeline to the least provocative, most effective boner-crushing section of the compound in existence.

"Hey, Demyen!"

Willow beams as she waves at me from her new hammock suspended between two large palm trees in her solarium bedroom. What used to be an open, airy general space is now officially a homage to all things little girls could ever possibly want.

And it's so goddamn *pink*.

Bambi is reclining on a lounger, scribbling away on her tablet while keeping an eye on the kid. "'Sup, boss?" She squints up at me through her sunglasses, a smile brightening her caramel skin. I've noticed more and more of that lately, with Willow around. Bambi seems to genuinely love the little girl.

"Just checking in on you ladies." I wink at Willow, who giggles and rolls out of the hammock to give me a hug.

Unexpected.

But it's not… unwelcome.

I don't exactly know what to do, so I pat her on the head. That seems to be the correct response. She pulls away and peers around me. "Where's Mommy?"

"She's still resting." I catch Bambi's skeptical stare, but for a change, I'm actually telling the truth. "She's still got a fever, so she's sleeping as much as she can."

Okay. Maybe that part's less accurate.

Bambi's arched brow nearly reaches her hairline. That's how I know she knows, and I keep my happy face plastered on for the sake of the kid while silently shooting mental messages for Bambi to keep her mouth shut. Telepathic or not, she seems to receive those messages and relaxes back into whatever she was doing before I sauntered in.

"Yeah." Willow brushes the hair of one of her new dolls as she scrunches her face thoughtfully. "Mommy works really hard. She's always tired. She needs sleep."

Kids. Gotta love them. Not me, necessarily, although this one is pretty great.

I settle onto one of the overstuffed bean bags. This will be the easiest interrogation I've ever conducted in my life. "Do you know where Mommy works?"

Willow frowns. "Why?"

Sharp kid. She's catching onto something, and I'm impressed. "Well, if Mommy's sick, they'll need to know, right? So they know she won't be coming in until she's better."

"I don't know." Willow shrugs, still focused on meticulously brushing the doll's hair. "She gets all pretty and says she has to go serve drinks to people. She never lets me go with her."

Bambi catches my eye and blinks a few times. That's the signal to check my phone.

BAMBI: *Canyon Sun Cocktail Lounge. They haven't heard from her. Assumed she quit, so no one's looking.*

Fair enough.

"That's okay." I offer Willow a friendly smile. "It's probably for the best. Some places are too boring for kids. And I'm sure your dad wouldn't want you to go, anyway."

Yes, I'm fishing for information. I figure any bits and pieces I can casually glean here and there are better than nothing.

A shadow passes over Willow's face. I suddenly feel an immense hatred for the man who makes his own child respond like that at the mere mention of him.

"He doesn't care." She shrugs and sets aside the doll, then picks up another one. I focus on her words and not the fact that I'm pretty sure Bambi bought an entire zip code's worth of dolls.

"Your dad doesn't care?"

She shakes her head slowly. "He doesn't play with me. Or talk to me. He just tells me what to do. But one time—" Her face suddenly lights up and she looks at me with a smile. "—he took me to the Ice Cream Palace and let me have the biggest sundae I've ever seen! And then we went and got fairy wings and I got to meet a princess."

Both Bambi and I feign awe. "That sounds so cool!" she chirps.

"Did you have fun?" I ask.

Willow nods. But then her smile fades and she picks at the Velcro back of the new doll. "He said he was sorry. He didn't mean to, so he took me out for ice cream and wanted me to be his pretty princess."

I really, really don't want to ask. But I need to know. *Why* I need to know is up for debate. "What was he sorry for?"

She steals a quick little glance at me. Her words come out mumbled. "He hit me."

And just like that, Martin has a death warrant.

I catch Bambi freezing in the corner of my eye. She's never had a taste for the kind of violence I dole out to traitors and assholes, but the fire in her eyes at those three tiny words tells me she may be rethinking her policy.

"He hit you?" she asks the kid as gently as possible. I can still hear it in her voice, though. The shock. The fury.

Willow shrinks back. "Yeah. I spilled his beer."

Thank God I'm sitting too awkwardly to pull my gun out. I have a sudden urge to clean it and, I don't know... play target practice with the bastard's head.

"Hey, Willow." I say her name just firmly enough to get her to look up at me. For a moment, I see fear in her eyes—and that strikes a sharp chord in me that I never want to feel again. "You know that you're safe here, right?"

She blinks at me, then slowly nods.

"No one is ever going to hit you, or hurt you. And if anyone does something you don't like, you run and tell Miss Bambi or me, alright?"

Again, she nods, a little faster this time.

"Bambi." I turn and wink at my assistant. "Did you remember to grab some monster spray while you were shopping?"

Bambi takes only a second to catch on, then quickly sits up and nods. "I even made sure to grab the Anti-Monster Magic Light. Strongest one they have."

"Perfect." I turn back to Willow. "We'll keep the monsters away, okay?" *Including the asshole who claims to be your father.*

I expect her to nod some more and maybe say "okay" or "thank you."

I don't expect her to suddenly jump to her feet and run across the room...

And I *definitely* don't expect her to throw herself into my arms.

Again, I'm not sure what to do. But hugging her back is apparently exactly what she wanted, maybe even needed, because the bright grin on her face when she pulls away is a light in my dark life I didn't know I was missing.

"Thanks, Demyen."

And then she skips back across the room, carrying a piece of my heart with her.

Fuck.

I'm in trouble.

23

DEMYEN

Now that we've settled the workplace issue, I need to make sure the rest of Clara's personal life won't be coming looking for her. Or for Willow.

Fucking hell. I'm growing too attached to that kid.

I steer my focus away from the bright beam of sunshine currently jumping rope on the far side of the courtyard and home in on the door to my office.

The same office I really want to make Clara fill with her moans and pleasure-screams. With the heat of her exhales and the smell of her—

Focus, goddammit!

I swear this family is going to be the end of me.

When we first met—or rather, when we second-met, at the casino—I was under the impression Clara didn't own a phone. Given all that I've been learning about her ex, it wouldn't be surprising if the bastard cut off her communications with the world so she'd have to go through him and him alone.

But it occurred to me, while sitting in Willow's room, that no loving parent who actually cares about their kid would go about their day with no way for schools or other officials to contact them in case of emergencies.

I sure as hell won't let Willow leave this compound without at least ten different ways for people to get in touch if necessary. Or without twice as many guards watching her every move.

Because she's collateral. Valuable collateral.

Not at all because I actually *care* about the kid. Not like a parent or anything.

I glance up to peer across the courtyard before I duck into the hall that leads to my office. *Is she too close to the pool's edge? Is anyone watching her? Where is Bambi?*

But then Bambi materializes from behind a decorative cactus and leads the girl away from the pool and toward a safer area where she can continue counting her jumps.

Satisfied, I finally make it to my office and lock the door behind me. I don't need any more interruptions or distractions for the day. Clara's bag is in one of my locked safes. I quickly turn the dial to pull it out and search for her phone.

I don't know why I haven't cleared out the stacks of money from the bag. I could, and I should; it's my money from my casino and she won't be needing it anytime soon. If ever.

But something keeps stopping me from taking it. I'm blaming my sense of honor for Lady Luck; I have to respect that it was pure chance, a strange stroke of good fortune—for her—and it would be no different if someone else had sat at that machine.

Fuck. What a stupid thought.

Everything would be different if someone else had sat at that stupid machine.

I find her cheap cell phone tucked inside a zippered pocket I almost missed. At first, it seems strange for anyone to put their phone somewhere unreachable... but then, maybe that was the point. Clara didn't have the budget, or the time, to buy a new phone before running from her ex.

My theory is dead on. The passcode to the phone was easy—Willow's birthday, which I had Bambi grab for me along with other paperwork in case this "visit" extends into the school year. No sense in depriving the kid of an education just because her parents are shitty.

I'm quick to switch the settings to Airplane Mode, just in case anyone decides to try using the GPS to locate Clara. I'll have Pavel do a full sweep through just to make doubly sure no one can follow the tech trail here; we can't forget who her father is and who he works for. As much as I'd love the chance to take him out in a firefight, I don't want that shit blowing up my house.

Most of the phone's storage is taken up by pictures of Clara and Willow. Every picture, no matter how happy she seems with her daughter, is tinted with a shadow of sadness in her eyes, a melancholy tightness in her smile.

I'm bothered by how much that bothers me.

Time to close the photo album and look for some real information.

Her friend from that tiny apartment, Roxy, has been blowing up her phone with texts and calls demanding updates. No voicemail, but that's typical, I guess. Mostly just messages in the text inbox saying things like, *Are you okay?* and *Are you still alive?* and *Did he fuck your brains out?*

I snort at that one. There are a few others of this woman referring to me in rather flattering ways. One text asks if I have a brother, and if that brother is single.

Right. That's exactly what Tolya needs—conjugal visits from his accuser's best friend.

Come to think of it, Roxy may be a problem. A serious problem. From the five minutes I spent in her microscopic living room, I got the impression that she's not the kind of woman to just let things slide when it comes to Clara and the girl. She watched me like a hawk from the second I darkened her doorway; I have no doubt she'd comb the desert to find her best friend and pseudo-niece.

What I *am* doubting is my sudden distaste at the idea of getting rid of Roxy. It's nothing different from what I've ordered before; we can't have witnesses or nosy neighbors complicating things. So why does the idea of eliminating Clara's best friend put a bad taste in my mouth?

I shake it off and scroll through more of the texts. The ones that grab my attention are the ones that make my blood instantly boil.

MARTIN: *Where the fuck are you??*

MARTIN: *Pick up the phone, you dumb bitch!*

MARTIN: *Clara, I swear to fucking God, you better bring my daughter back or so help me*

MARTIN: *Want me to call your father? Is that what you want?*

MARTIN: *Your ass better be back home with the brat*

MARTIN: *Baby, I'm sorry. I'm just worried. I'm so fucking worried about you*

MARTIN: *I love you so much*

MARTIN: *Please, Baby, pick up the phone*

MARTIN: *I promise I'll treat you so good when I get home Baby*

MARTIN: *Unless that's it? You found some other dick?*

MARTIN: *Out spreading your legs like the fucking slut you are?*

MARTIN: *I bet that kid isn't even mine.*

MARTIN: *Whore*

MARTIN: *You'll fucking regret this, Clara. I swear to God, you'll regret ever leaving me and you'll be lucky if I take your stupid whore pussy back once you're on your knees begging*

MARTIN: *You're so pretty on your knees, Baby*

No, Martin, I think through oceans of red clouding my eyes. *You'll be the one regretting this.*

It's a miracle I haven't crushed the flimsy phone in my hand. I'm clenching it so tight as I read every text. The other messages he sent are no better and not worth my time.

I do venture a quick scroll into her message history because I've noticed a lack of texts from Greg Everett. Does he ever check in on his own daughter?

It seems not. Not even one call for the last several weeks, according to the phone log when I check.

I'm not sure what I expected, or worse—what I wanted. Do I *want* Greg Everett to be a doting father who tears apart Las Vegas in search of his daughter?

Obviously not.

So why does his absence itch the back of my mind like a bad rash?

I can't afford to feel sympathy. This is purely circumstantial, and I need to know that all the cards in my hand won't lose.

I toss the phone into my desk drawer with half a mind to lock the damned thing up. Not that I want Clara calling in the calvary, but I have a fleeting thought of buying her a new phone—a far better one—and giving her a new number so her dickhead baby daddy and his cohorts in blue can't find her.

Fuck. There I go again. Forgetting she's my prisoner with a debt to repay.

Prisoner. My fucking prisoner. NOT my woman.

24

DEMYEN

I'm relaxing on one of the lounge chairs by the pool, sipping a cocktail I don't know the name of. My chef thought the umbrella and sugar rim would cheer me up.

"Relaxing" isn't the most accurate word, though. I'm more glaring into the depths of the pool, wondering if it's deep enough for the old-fashioned "cement shoes" bit. The one mental image that manages to make me remotely smile is of Martin McFuck drowning down there, his eyes wide and terrified as I fuck his woman on the chair in front of him.

I take a sip of the cocktail to calm the nausea that surfaces at the association of Clara being "his woman."

But she's not mine, either.

I'm about to throw the stupid blended drink into the water when Bambi sashays over, tablet tucked under one arm and the legs of her linen romper billowing with every step.

Clara would look good in that.

"What." I bite the word and close my eyes behind my sunglasses.

"Need another one or three of those?" Bambi arches a brow at my drink as she drapes herself across the coordinating lounge chair. "You're testy."

"Shouldn't I be?"

"You've literally pulled the luckiest hand in all of Vegas, so... no. You should be overjoyed, not glaring at the pool like it just called your mother a whore."

I shift my glare to her, but it doesn't have the effect I want it to. She just snorts a laugh and nods in feigned defeat.

"Alright, alright." Bambi sets her tablet on the table between us and gestures for one of the waiting staff to bring her a duplicate of my drink. "What crawled up your ass and died?"

"I went through Clara's phone."

"Ah. Anything juicy?"

I'm not sure how to answer that, so I just shrug. "Pictures of her and the kid. Basic shit. Her best friend is looking for her, but I don't think she'll be a problem." A boldfaced lie, but that nagging feeling inside my chest doesn't want to risk Roxy's safety. Fucking *irritating*. "Her ex, Martin whateverthefuck—"

"Patterson."

"Patterson? That was it?"

Bambi nods. "He's a police detective. Easy to find. Actually, you'll find this interesting: he's Greg Everett's partner."

"No shit." I make a mental note to order two sets of molds for those cement shoes I really want to try out now. "That explains a lot."

"Does it?"

"No, not really." I sigh and lean back in the chair. "I mean… fuck, I don't know. The guy's a fucking asshole."

Bambi's mouth twists into an amused smirk I know she's trying her damned hardest to suppress. "What makes you say that?"

"You should have seen the way he texts her. The bruises he left on her. And the kid—you heard what she said."

This makes Bambi sober up a bit. "Yeah," she murmurs. "I heard it."

That annoying mental itching resurfaces. "Speaking of the kid: who's watching her?"

"She's asleep. It's naptime."

"Ah." I'm about to leave it alone, but then… "Same time? Every day?"

Bambi nods. "It's important to keep kids on a schedule."

"Fine." Something else occurs to me. "Ease up on the sugar, too. Don't want her rotting her teeth out."

I don't have to turn my head to see the brow creep up her forehead.

"Anything else, *Dad*?"

"Shut the fuck up, Bam."

She snorts a laugh and thanks the server for her drink, takes a very long sip, then lies back in her chair. "You know what I don't get?"

"The concept of leaving a man alone to his thoughts?"

"Aside from that." Her smirk shifts into a slight frown. "Why are you keeping her around?"

I roll my eyes. "We've been over this. Clara lied about what she saw and put my brother in prison on a life sentence, and even though I could just have her recant her testimony, she won't because her asshole father is the same detective who made the arrest and there's no way in hell he'll change *his* statement—"

"The kid, Demyen. I was talking about the kid."

Oh.

Right.

"The kid's collateral."

"With a custom bedroom under the stars and an unlimited menu paired with Daddy Warbuck's black AmEx, no less." The blinking she does is every bit as sarcastic as her words. "You do realize she has a grandfather? An aunt of sorts? Why not send her to them?"

"And explain what when they ask about her mother?"

"She left town."

I shake my head. "That won't pan out. Clara's a devoted mother who sacrificed everything for her child. They're broke as fuck but she's always put Willow first. Even I wouldn't believe she just up and left town without her daughter."

"Fair point."

"Plus…" Again, the absence of Greg Everett in Clara's missed calls, unread messages, her photo library—it all presses an unsettling feeling in my gut that I don't like for a multitude of reasons. "I don't trust the Chief Detective."

"No shit."

"I mean, with Willow. Or Clara, for that matter."

Now, Bambi does a full turn to look at me. "Oh?"

I try to shrug it off. The last thing I need is a therapist prying into the feelings I'm definitely not catching. "Just a hunch. I can't put my finger on what father doesn't check in on his daughter, or notice when she's missing. Is that the kind of grandfather we can trust with his granddaughter?"

"Right. But can she be trusted with *you*?"

"Of course she can." The words fly out of my mouth without hesitation. "I've got a bone to pick and a score to settle with her mother, but I'm not a fucking monster. I'm probably—"

I stop myself before I finish that sentence. The thought accompanying it is far too dangerous for me to say out loud, let alone let it float around in my head.

Bambi doesn't press for me to say it. She knows better. "So, whatever happens to Clara…"

"The kid stays."

That's all I'm going to say on that matter. I don't exactly know what that means, or just how far things will go, but I'll be damned if I throw a helpless child to the wolves.

"Run a full background check on Clara." I'm switching subjects and, if I'm being honest with myself, changing tactics only slightly. Things keep itching in my brain and I need them scratched before I roll the dice on things I can't undo. "Dig everything up."

Bambi furrows her brow, clearly confused. "I thought we already did."

"There's more." I polish off the cocktail and debate getting another one, but I decide against it. Work needs to be done. "Run full specs on Greg Everett, too."

"Again, I—"

"If we had everything, I wouldn't be telling you to get more, would I?" I snap.

She closes her mouth and stares at me. Bambi's a proud bird, and I know I've ruffled her feathers, but she's not about to question my authority.

And I'm not about to apologize, even if I suddenly feel like I should.

A half-assed wave of my hand that might be construed as a silent mea culpa is about the best I can do. "There's more to the story. Things aren't adding up. And if I'm going to be striking deals and getting Tolya out, we can't afford to miss a single detail. We pulled her current information but we didn't look into her childhood."

The tablet is out and on. Bambi scribbles notes with her stylus without looking up at me. "Medical records?"

I nod. "All of it. Dig deep. Dig where we wouldn't normally go. Her father had—and has—the power to erase anything he wants. We need to find whatever traces he missed."

Bambi chews on her lip for a moment. "We did confirm they've lived here their whole lives. At least, Clara has. Never moved, never even changed houses until she graduated from high school."

"Makes it easy, then."

"Easy to pull up school records. And reports."

That makes me pause. "The kind that Everett wouldn't be able to erase."

"Not without raising alarms."

I don't want to find anything. Finding things like child abuse reports from grade school teachers who paid attention to Clara would mean there's far more to her history—and to her relationship with her father. Finding shit like evidence that Detective Everett was a dirty cop on and off the clock means I can't take anything at face value.

But if we don't find anything, and my hunch about Everett is still correct, it would mean that Clara slipped through the cracks, unnoticed by everyone who should have been paying fucking attention… and has been living in a hell she never escaped from.

Not until she ran into me.

And now, I'm a whole new demon determined to make her suffer.

I dismiss Bambi with a final nod and a flick of my hand, which only irritates her more. She flips her tablet closed and huffs away to go do what I ordered. To be fair, I don't make it a habit of treating her, or Pavel, like obedient dogs. I do genuinely appreciate their loyalty and intel.

But right now, I've got a lot of shit piling up in my head and no shovel to dig any of it out. Which makes me moody.

I storm back to my office, needing something to do. Something productive. Something to clear my mind.

Why I think that means opening my laptop to watch the camera feed from Clara's new room is beyond me.

She's still sound asleep, lying on top of the sheets as her body continues to fight the fever. She moans softly and the sound makes me swallow. Hard.

Her legs slide against each other, then spread. It's a natural fall of her knees, just a result of her feverish dreaming, but it's enough to make other things about me very hard, too.

At ease, asshole. She's sick.

The tent in my pants demands to know what we'll do when she's better. I'm not even going to entertain those fantasies. The only thing I need to focus on in regards to Clara Everett is whatever the hell we pull up about her past.

25

CLARA

Everything's burning.

Arms, legs, head, all of it.

Maybe it's because Mama forgot to turn the stove off when she made me grilled cheese. I love grilled cheese. Mama makes it special for me when Daddy's at work. He hates grilled cheese, so it's just our thing.

No. That's not right. Mama's gone. And I'm not a little kid anymore.

It's gotta be the courthouse. The courthouse is always so hot in the summer; why don't they ever put in air conditioning? The fans hanging from the ceiling don't do much and the sweat in my hair is stinging the cuts on my face.

But Daddy says I gotta do it. I gotta go up there and tell the truth.

I don't know what to say. I didn't see much. It was scary inside the trunk of that dusty old car.

It was even scarier inside the box.

And it hurt. I got splinters.

I remember the man... the man who opened the box and asked me if I was okay. He told me I'd be okay—I just needed to stay there and be a good girl.

I'm a good girl. I'm always a good girl.

He's here at the courthouse, too. He remembers me. He looks like it's too hot in here, too. I don't blame him. I try to smile at him, but Daddy squeezes my shoulder too hard and tells me not to look at him and now, I want to cry.

It hurts. Daddy always makes me hurt.

There's too many questions. I don't know how to answer them. They ask me if I saw the nice man at the warehouse... but what's a warehouse? I was in a box. I saw him in the box.

They ask me what else I saw.

I don't know, though. I don't remember. I just remember what Daddy helped me remember... and I can't forget, or he's going to make me hurt again. I forgot things last night when we were practicing and now, I hurt all over... but I have to be a good girl and tell the truth.

I'm always a good girl.

So I tell them what Daddy helped me remember.

The nice man looks so sad. I thought he was angry at me, but when he looks at me, he just looks sad. I don't know why he's sitting there, where the bad guys usually sit. He's not a bad guy. Where is the man who tried to kidnap me? He should be sitting there.

Wait.

This... this isn't right.

I'm not a little kid. Not anymore.

I'm not in that courthouse anymore. I haven't set foot inside there for years.

It's hot because Martin won't fix the air conditioner. It broke yesterday. Willow keeps crying and I'm keeping her in just her diapers so she doesn't overheat. He's acting like he doesn't hear our baby girl screaming from the heat.

"It's too fucking expensive" is his only answer when I ask him about it.

But so are the new shoes he's wearing around the house. So are the season tickets he bought last week. And his new phone, and his new laptop, and everything else he buys for himself while we fend on scraps.

Thank God Willow is still breastfeeding. I'm not sure how I could afford food for her right now; it's a miracle he even lets me eat.

"Gotta watch your weight. Shed those baby pounds." He smacked my ass when he said it, right before he took away my plate of cheap pizza. He didn't offer me anything else.

It's so hot in here. Willow keeps crying and it's too hot to swaddle her. If he won't fix the air conditioner soon, I might have to go stay at Roxy's for a while.

I tell him that as I lay Willow down on a blanket where it's cooler under the ceiling fan. I don't mean it as a threat, or that I'm leaving him—we just need to keep Willow out of the heat.

But Martin doesn't like that. He hears me threatening him to leave. He thinks I'm going to abandon him, abandon our baby—and I would never!

But that doesn't stop him from grabbing my hair. Or from pulling me across the house and into our bedroom by my hair. It hurts so much, I scream and try to kick and pull away.

"Please...please, don't..." I'm sobbing, begging. I don't want him to hurt me.

The back of his hand cracks against the side of my face.

"Please! Martin, please!"

"Clara!"

I sob harder. And even though my chest is shaking with my sobs, I'm determined to get my baby and get the hell out of there. So I scramble for anything, the bed, a chair, a table... anything I can grab to pull myself up even as he's trying to pin me down.

"Clara!"

He grabs me hard by my shoulders. Shakes me. And—

My eyes fly open.

I don't recognize him at first. He kinda looks like the nice guy from the box, but... different.

His hands are on my shoulders, but they don't hurt. He stops shaking me when he sees I'm awake, although I'm not sure if I really am awake. Everything is so blurry, so hard to focus... The room is spinning...

"Fuck." He whispers it under his breath and holds me close. Did I fall? I think he caught me.

The back of his hand feels so nice. It's cool and, against my forehead, it feels so soothing. He presses to my brow, my cheek, and my neck. Is he a doctor? If he is, he's sexy as hell and I am ready for my examination.

"You're burning up."

The room spins again, but this time, it's because he's lifted me into his arms and is carrying me to… I don't know where. I never know. He never tells me where we're going or why; he just scoops me up like ice cream and takes me wherever.

I remember now. I remember his name.

"Demyen…" It comes out way weaker than I intended. Raspy. Good fuck, my tongue is *dry*.

"Stay with me." He shifts me in his arms a bit. My head falls against his chest. He's so warm, but it's nice. Comforting. He's not wearing a shirt, so I can smell the sandalwood on his skin.

I moan.

Demyen looks at me with a frown. He seems more worried than angry. "Hang on," he says, and now, we're moving faster. It's dizzying.

We're back inside the room with sharp things. The kitchen, he said? And then I hear that familiar heavy click, and then—

Oh, sweet God, yes. It's cold. The air is cold.

So much better.

He left me here before. I thought he wanted to kill me. I still think he does, so maybe he'll leave me here again.

But he doesn't leave at all. Demyen sets me down on the cold cement floor, then sits down next to me. This is when I see— he's wearing pajama pants. No shirt, no shoes, just gray pajama pants.

His hair looks ruffled, too.

Did he... did he wake up to check on me?

My head hurts too much to ask these questions. Still too hot, although the cold air helps. Demyen reaches behind us, grabs a bag of frozen peas, and presses it to my forehead. The way he does it pulls me close to him. His arm is wrapped around me to hold the bag in place.

I have nowhere to go except further into him. So I rest my head on his shoulder and close my eyes.

It's freezing in here, but neither of us shiver. He jumps, just for the quickest moment, when I loop my arm around his waist to settle in closer. I'm feeling sleepy, and he's so, so *comfortable*.

The still-functioning part of my brain tells me that I'm sick. I have a fever and it's bad. I've been hallucinating fever dreams and dripping sweat into the bedsheets, desperate for relief.

The rest of my brain is still hallucinating. There's no way Demyen actually cares enough to...

I don't know what he's doing. Or if he's actually here. For all I know, this is all just part of some fucked-up fever dream and I'm in some dirty basement cell where he's keeping me prisoner.

I won't blame him. I deserve it.

Might as well make the most of this dream.

"Dem..."

"Hm?"

I'm able to pry my eyes open enough to see he's texting someone on his phone. Attempting to read the tiny words on the bright screen only hurts my eyes, so I look away and just focus on the frosty shelf next to him. "I'm sorry."

"For what?" He sounds like he's only paying half-attention to me, if that. His phone buzzes in his hand. After a pause, he taps something else in response.

I sigh. It's shaky and makes me wonder if my lungs are on fire, too. But the cold air feels good when I do it, so I won't complain. "Everything."

He pauses. Then lowers his phone. "Everything?"

I start to nod, but that makes me instantly dizzy. "Yeah." The dreams from earlier come crashing back into my mind's eye, making my head hurt more. And my chest. "I messed up. I messed up bad."

Fuck. I don't want to cry. My head hurts too much to cry, and I don't want him to see my tears and think I'm weak or helpless or whatever loser-level names he's probably made up for me.

Demyen doesn't say anything. He just tosses the frozen peas aside and presses the backs of his fingers to my face. For the briefest of moments, it almost feels like he's caressing my cheek.

I'm *definitely* hallucinating.

He shifts me until I'm sitting against the shelves behind us, then stands and walks out of the freezer.

I knew it.

But then he's back, clutching something in his hand, and he rummages through another section where there's piles of boxes stacked neatly on top of each other. When he finds the one he's looking for, he walks back over to me and sits back down.

I have no idea what he's doing. I don't even know if I care. My eyes drift close and I let my head rest against the icy shelf. It feels better than the hot pillow in my room. It's nice and quiet in here, except for the rustling Demyen's doing with whatever the hell—

"Open."

Something prods at my lips. I frown, confused, and try to open my eyes to see what the actual fuck he's doing.

"Come on. Open your mouth."

At this point, there's not much he can do to me that's worse than what we've already done. So I figure, why fight? And I slowly open my mouth.

Demyen shoves it inside my mouth. With… a fork.

It's… strawberry cheesecake?

"Good girl." He pulls the fork away and lets me chew this one bite. It's a painstakingly slow process. My tongue is trying to register what's inside my mouth at the same time my fried brain is trying to register what is even happening.

And then there's another bite. A rich, graham cracker crust coated with a thick layer of strawberry preserves and New York-style cheesecake. If I wasn't sick as a dog, I'd devour the whole box. It tastes incredible.

"Almost forgot these were made today." Demyen's voice sounds like he's also enjoying the cheesecake. "I'm kind of a sucker for this stuff."

He feeds me another bite. This time, I'm able to chew a bit faster and open my eyes as I swallow. "What are... Why?"

"You're tasting this, right? It's amazing, that's why." There's a sudden, heavy silence that settles over him when he realizes what I meant to ask. I almost don't expect him to answer, but again, he surprises me by turning to his side more and holds up another loaded fork. "You haven't eaten in over a day. And I was hungry, too."

I take the bite and chew, narrowing my eyes at him as best I can. "Why don't you just let me die?"

Demyen rolls his eyes. "You're not dying. You just have a fever. Mostly because you don't fucking take care of yourself, though Doc's wondering if your ankle's infected."

That doesn't answer my immediate question. It does answer a few others, though. Still, I shake my head, which is more of a gradual rocking along the edge of the shelf. "Why do you *care?*"

He pauses. The fork is poised mid-stab into the cheesecake resting on his lap inside the cardboard box. He finishes that scoop extra slowly as he thinks.

"I *don't* care," he says at last.

I don't believe him. He sounds like he doesn't believe himself, either.

But also, I'm sick and feverish and this is all a hallucination, so my brain is probably just trying to make me feel better. Gourmet desserts and all.

"You're no good to me dead. That's all. Don't read into it."

I snort. It sounds weird inside the freezer, even weirder with how out-of-it I am, but I can't help it. I snort and I peer up at his face, my mouth twisted in some sort of darkly humorous smirk. "Gotta get me healthy so you can torture me properly?"

He frowns. He doesn't find it as funny as I do. "Why the hell would I do that?"

"It's not fun torturing a sick person. Everyone knows that."

"No, I mean, why would I torture you?"

Now, it's my turn to frown. "Why wouldn't you?" The weight of my nightmares slams against my chest. "You have every reason to."

Demyen seems to consider this. Either that, or my brain has just glitched and can't come up with a response to my own arguments. Then he sets the box of cheesecake aside, stabs the fork into it like the sword in the stone, and fully turns to face me. "Have you ever been with a man—*any* man—who hasn't tortured you?"

I'm not loving the answer that comes to mind. "I wouldn't call it 'torture.'"

"Is that how you get by? Renaming shit to make it seem less terrifying?"

My frown deepens. "You keep acting like you actually care."

"You keep acting like you don't." Demyen shakes his head at me. "Fucking ridiculous. Keeping your kid in that environment, too. It's disgusting."

The second he mentions Willow, my hackles raise. Sick or not, I will fight him to protect my baby girl. I sit up and I'm immediately dizzy, but I struggle against his attempt to press me back down. "Where's Willow? Where's my baby?"

"She's fine, Clara. No thanks to you."

I'm practically seething. "The hell does that mean?"

Demyen glares at me, his face inches from mine. "You kept your 'precious baby' in that fucking hellhole with that sorry excuse for a man. You knew what he was doing and you forced her to live in that terror anyway. Honestly, for that, I *should* torture you."

My heart sinks into my stomach. The cheesecake turns rotten and I want to throw up. "He never touched her."

The instant arch of his brow makes me feel sicker. No— there's no way. I'd always been so careful when it came to protecting Willow.

"You really think that?" Demyen scoffs. "Did you ever bother to ask?"

"He swore—"

"*Her,* Clara. Did you ever bother to ask Willow?"

I want to cry. I want to throw up. I want to smack that indignant look off his face and claw his all-seeing eyes out of his head.

I want to burn the whole fucking world down until it's just Willow and me, finally safe and sound from monsters like him.

But instead, all I can do is lean against the frozen shelves and let hot tears spill down my face. Maybe if he leaves me here long enough, they'll freeze and cool my burning cheeks.

I'm too busy crying to see his face soften, but I hear it in his voice. "Why didn't you just leave when you had the chance?"

Oh, cruel irony.

"I did."

I think the deep, hard strength in those words surprises both of us. But I still don't open my eyes. Hopefully, my tears will freeze them shut so I never have to look at him again.

Demyen remains silent for a breath or two. Then: "What stopped you?"

This time, I pry my eyes open. Just so I can glare at him with all the fire and fury I've been bottling up since the moment those security guys stopped me at the front doors of The Meridian.

"*You* did."

His face is unreadable. He just stares at me, blinking. I stare back until I'm once again too tired and too heartbroken to look at him. Flashes of that night we spent together before either of us knew anything about each other stab through my brain and make everything hurt worse. So much worse.

Why couldn't he just let me go?

I don't know how long we stay like that. I don't even remember falling asleep. But I must, because my dreams get less horrible and I'm vaguely aware of being wrapped up in a weighted blanket on something soft. Every time I struggle against a lesser demon in my nightmares, the blanket tucks tighter around me and the demon scurries away. I can't make sense of any of it, but I don't have the energy to even care.

The last dream I remember is of Willow, laughing and happy in the desert sunshine, surrounded by everything she's ever wanted...

And a handsome father who loves her, handing her a plate of strawberry cheesecake.

26

CLARA

What time is it?

What day *is it?*

I sit up in bed, slowly so I don't make myself dizzy—and realize I'm not dizzy at all.

I actually feel better. Somewhat.

I press a hesitant hand to my brow. Surprisingly, it feels way cooler than I expected. Given the way my hair's sticking to the sides of my face and my neck, I'm wondering if my fever finally broke.

Almost on cue, the door opens and Demyen fills the space. His eyes give me a lingering once-over, and for a moment, I start to wonder why he's really here. But then he closes the door behind him and tosses something onto the bed.

A bottle of water.

It's fancy water, because duh, of course it is. The kind of bougie glass bottle that I always roll my eyes at because who the hell would pay eleven dollars for a glass of tap with fancy branding that doesn't fit in any cupholder known to man?

But I won't turn my nose up at it now. I'm parched. My hands are a blur as I snatch it up and unscrew the cap, tossing it back like I'm shotgunning beer at a frat party. But I miscalculated my thirst with the dryness of my throat. Almost instantly, I'm choking and gagging on the water.

Just as swiftly, Demyen materializes at my side and grabs the bottle from my hands. He cups the back of my head, firmly gripping my hair between his fingers, and waits for me to calm down. Then he tugs my hair just enough to make me tilt my head back, raises the bottle to my lips, and eases a slow trickle of water into my mouth.

I watch his face. He doesn't seem to be feeling one way or the other, but his own gaze is fixed on my mouth. I feel his fingers flex a little bit in my hair, almost like…

No. He's not caressing me.

This is just… necessity. Yeah. Necessity. He's keeping me alive for his own brand of torment.

He pulls the bottle away to give me a chance to swallow. A few drops escape my lips but otherwise, it is easier this time. I feel the droplets splash on my chest and dammit, does that feel good.

Demyen's eyes flick down to follow their paths as they slowly trickle over my skin. That same look he had in the doorway returns.

Thirsty.

No… *hungry*.

But instead of doing anything to feed that hunger, he clears his throat and repeats the motions: tilting my head back, easing sips of water into my mouth, letting me swallow.

After a few sips, he lets me go and screws the cap back on. "You look better," he observes quietly.

"I feel better."

"Good." He's avoiding my eyes, instead focusing on setting the bottle down on the nightstand and wiping the condensation from his palms onto his jeans. I realize in this moment that I haven't seen him so casually dressed—a tank top, jeans, bare feet. I've only ever seen him in immaculately tailored suits.

And his pajamas. But that was definitely a fever dream.

"How's your stomach feeling?" This time, he does look at me, that same unreadable mask on his face.

I think about it. The water isn't making me nauseous, but I'm not sure if I'm ready for a full meal. "Pretty good. I think. I don't know, really."

"You've kept food down so far. Must be a good sign."

I furrow my brow at him. "You… fed me?"

"I made sure you were fed. Big difference."

Right. But I'm not about to argue. I have bigger things to deal with, now that I'm able to stay upright. "Where's Willow? I want to see my daughter."

Demyen side-eyes me. "She's fine."

"I don't believe you." I grit my teeth. "Bring me my daughter. Now."

"No."

I lean back. I may not be fully recovered or able to take on a guy his size, but hellfire and brimstone can't keep me from my child. What makes him think he can? "No?"

"No. You're probably still contagious."

"*You're* here."

"I'm also not five years old."

Damn him. He and his logic can kiss my ass. "I want to see her."

He nods. "I know. I heard you the first time."

"Well?"

Now, he's the one leaning back, eyeing me with something akin to amusement. "Are you still hallucinating? At what point did you suddenly gain the ability to tell me what to do?"

I narrow my eyes at him. "When I gave birth to *my child*."

"Alright, fair." He nods and pulls out his phone. "So where was all this authority for the last five years?"

My fever dream comes back to me. We had a similar discussion then. Was it a premonition of this one that's about to happen? "What are you talking about?"

He starts tapping his thumb on his phone, staring at his screen as he talks. "You're acting like giving birth to Willow officially gave you authority over her well-being and safety. Which—yeah, it did. So why the fuck did you force her to stay in a dangerous house with a dangerous man?"

My stomach turns. I hate déjà vu. "For your information, it's not as easy as you make it sound."

"Try me."

I sigh and slump against the headboard. Anything to put some distance between us. "Other women... they can leave. Go to shelters. Change their names. I don't have that luxury."

His brow lifting is the only response I get. He's still staring at his phone, probably texting someone to ready my firing squad.

"My ex *and* my father are both on the police force. And not just some beat cops or desk workers, but lead detectives. Men of power. Men with resources at their fingertips. They know every shelter from Las Vegas to Reno. Change of name forms are readily accessible by their exact department in case murder investigations need it. And worse—they know how to make things look like an accident." I tilt my head to one side. "Kinda like you, actually. Isn't that what you do? Make things look like an accident?"

Demyen snorts out a laugh and glances at me. "Depends on who's receiving the message."

I'm just going to ignore that. The image of him sending one of my severed fingers to my father is not doing any favors for my roiling stomach. "So yeah. That's why I couldn't just get up and leave any time I wanted. Not until..." I look away.

"So your plan was to buy your way out of Vegas and go... where?"

I shrug. "Anywhere. Anywhere they'd never think to look for me. Mexico came to mind. Maybe keep traveling south to Brazil. Hide in the rainforest with the monkeys." It sounds ridiculous, but it was one of the many options I'd dreamed up between the slot machine and the cashier's desk. I smile a little when Willow's awestruck face appears in my mind. "Willow loves monkeys."

Demyen holds my gaze for the longest moment, not saying a word. It's a tragedy that a man so dangerous and deadly can have such beautiful, stormy eyes. Even his lashes are long and dark.

If he wasn't my prison warden, I'd let him see how much "better" he could make me feel.

He glances away, back to his phone. Then holds it up to me.

It's a camera feed from what looks like a lavish outdoor courtyard. A marble fountain pours intricate, sparkling patterns of water in the middle of an Olympic-sized pool…

… and Willow is playing hopscotch by the garden.

I suck in a sharp gasp and grab his phone. Demyen's grip tightens, but he doesn't pull it away from me. I all but climb on his lap just so I can get a better look at my baby girl.

"Willow?" Tears sting my eyes. My throat tightens. "Is she okay?"

Demyen rolls his eyes. "No. We made her walk on a cactus, hence the hopping." He gently eases his phone from my fingers and turns the screen off. "My God, woman. Did you not see the army of dolls lining the courtyard? If anyone needs to be worried about an attack, it's me."

I stare at him like he's grown a horn in the middle of his head. "Wha… *Why?*"

"Why what?"

"Why *that.*" I gesture to his phone.

He shrugs like it's no big deal. "The kid's not my problem. *You're* my problem. And you're my prisoner. She's just my guest."

"Can I—"

"No." He slides off the bed and turns to stare at me. He's all business again. Any trace of kindness gone like it never existed to begin with. "Now, Clara Everett, here's the big question: are you going to do exactly what I say, when I say it, no questions asked?"

The terrifying part is not knowing what he plans on asking me. It could be anything.

No, scratch that. The *really* terrifying part is knowing what he *could* ask of me.

And the fact that I'd want to do it for him.

Especially if he keeps looking at me like that.

"Yes." I nod with the word, just in case it sticks to my tongue. "Anything. I'll do anything—just keep my daughter safe." Out of some deep-seated instinct, I crawl on top of the blankets and kneel in front of him, literally on my knees to beg for Willow's safety. "Anything you want. As long as Willow is safe."

Demyen steps closer to me, so close I can smell his musk through his shirt. *Just like my fever dream...*

He tucks his fingers under my chin and tilts my head up to look him in the eyes. One knee settles on the bed, then the rest of him leans down until I'm surrounded by him.

Nowhere to run.

Nowhere to hide.

Nowhere he can't get me.

"And if I want to start collecting on your debt now?" His mouth hovers over mine. I catch his eyes flickering between mine and my lips, dipping down lower for half a millisecond. At this angle, he can probably see clear down the threadbare top barely covering me as it is. "Right here, right now." His thumb slowly rubs over my bottom lip as he holds my gaze. "You'll be my good girl and do exactly what I say?"

The stubborn mother in me needs to keep demanding for more leverage.

The heat quickly pooling between my legs wants him to start making more demands.

"Show me Willow again." I need to make sure I don't lose focus on why I'm doing this. "Please."

I expect him to get angry, or slap me, or something else for my bold demand. But instead, he regards me for a moment, then pulls out his phone. A few taps later, he holds up the screen so I can see her.

She's in the same stretch of garden, now a few yards away from where I can just make out the chalked hopscotch grid. A beautiful, richly-tanned woman is with her, and they're laughing and pointing at different desert flowers and exotic cacti.

"Okay." I swallow back the lump in my throat and nod. My gaze meets his and I nod again. "I'll be good. I promise."

A smile tugs at one corner of his mouth. He tucks his phone back into his pocket. When his hand lifts, I inwardly brace myself for him to grab my hair and pull me somewhere to do something salacious and dirty.

He cups my face, leans in close. "First thing? Take a shower."

I blink. *What?*

"Bathroom's around the corner, through the double doors." He nods his head toward an archway I hadn't noticed before. This room is a hell of a lot bigger than I thought. "Don't take too long. You need to eat something before the real work begins."

I swallow hard. "Yes, sir."

That flame of hunger lights up in his eyes at my word choice. He hesitates before he pulls away and strides to the door.

When he's a safe distance away, he turns to look at me once more over his shoulder, hand lingering on the doorknob. "You might survive this after all."

And then he's gone.

27

CLARA

I should be righteously offended that anyone, let alone Demyen, told me to "take a shower."

But one sniff of my shirt tells me the man's got a point.

Woof.

I'm pretty sure he's got this place rigged with some sort of alarm system, so it's pointless to try and sneak my way out of the bedroom. But the bathroom? No one with a shred of decency would rig a bathroom...

Right?

The plan: find the weak spots. Take a shower. Convince him to bring Willow in here. Make a run for it.

I make my way—slowly, still a bit wobbly—to the archway and lean heavily against the mosaic-tiled column to hang a left. I am feeling better; it's just been a few days since I last actually walked.

Good Lord. This man lives in a palace.

The bathroom is huge. Everything is white: white tiles, white walls, white fixtures, all accented by gold faucets and light fixtures. Even the toilet handle is gold. It would be ostentatious if it weren't for the exotic plants hanging in beautiful pots, lining the frosted windows, and decorating the vanity.

Exotic plants and flowers have always been my secret passion. If I'd been allowed to go to college, I would have studied botany and found my way to far-off lands with new species to be identified and cataloged. I used to dream about it in high school. Even prepared a persuasive speech for my father when I chose my dream college.

But then he introduced me to Martin. And once I turned eighteen, the only place I was allowed to go was Martin's house, Martin's bed.

I'm distracted by the plants inside this bathroom, so much so that I almost forget why I'm here. My mind is racing with facts. Preferred humidity points and foliage patterns and rooting systems. I can close my eyes and picture the textbook I learned it all from, a thick beast of a book with hand-drawn illustrations and a spine permanently bowed from how many times I cracked it open when I was still young and hopeful.

I could live in this room.

Shower. Focus.

I shuffle over to the huge sliding glass door of the shower and step inside. Of course, it's the kind that has a rainfall showerhead suspended from the ceiling, jets that let out steam for one of those steam bath experiences. I'm pretty sure you can pay extra for a feature that screams, "Look at my riches and weep, peasant!" to anyone with a net worth less than yours.

I'll be lucky if I can even figure out how to use the stupid dials.

It takes a few tries, but I finally manage to get the water flowing and at a decent temperature. I'm used to taking five-minute showers because Martin always goes first and uses up the hot water, leaving only enough for me to do the basics and then finish up in the sink.

But I'm not there anymore. And Martin's not here.

And I bet... I *bet*... this hot water will last for hours.

I stand underneath the rainfall until I realize I haven't even taken off my once-sweaty, now-drenched clothes. I peel those off and toss them into a corner to grab later.

The water on my skin feels so good. I almost want to cry; everything feels so good despite being in such a bad situation. It's confusing the hell out of me and I don't want to lose myself inside this twisted game Demyen's playing.

But I don't want to lose Willow, either—which means I have to play the game regardless.

I look around the shower walls for soap, shampoo, anything to freshen up. A stone alcove layered to look like natural sandstone forms the shelves holding natural sea sponges, a bristle brush, and several bottles labeled with French-sounding brands I've never heard of before. I find one that says "hair wash" and figure that probably means "shampoo," so I slather some onto my palm and work it into my scalp.

Ohh, it smells *amazing*. And familiar, too, weirdly enough. I can't put my finger on why that would be. But it tingles my scalp and feels as incredible as it smells.

I rinse and repeat—I need to experience that bliss again—and then look for what might be conditioner. Another bottle that looks like the first one says "rinse," so maybe? I slather that in, it feels close to what I'm looking for, and I let it soak in while I look for body wash.

And he gave *me* grief for renaming things. Wealthy people are on a whole other level.

At least the body wash is labeled clearly. But it's also clearly a man's bottle, all masculine in how the label is designed. I take a sniff of the liquid—

Oh. This… this is Demyen's body wash.

I recognize that smell.

And suddenly, it clicks with the shampoo, why that smelled so familiar.

It smelled like Demyen.

This… this is Demyen's shower.

This is Demyen's bathroom.

Which means…

I've been sleeping in Demyen's *bed*.

I focus my shaking hands on grabbing a sea sponge so I can at least scrub while I sink into these shower thoughts. The moment his scent rubs against my body, however…

It's one thing to smell the rich spice on his skin. It's something else entirely to be wrapped up in it, surrounded by it, covered by *him*.

None of this makes sense. This whole place is huge. There have to be at least a dozen guest rooms and just as many baths, showers, whatever—so why am I in his? Why did he have me sleep through my fever in *his* bed?

And then something occurs to me.

When I woke up today, there was no weighted blanket on the bed. Or the floor.

Did he…?

No. No way. There's no way.

Despite taking me away from a life that was killing me, despite nursing me through an illness and making sure Willow is safe and comfortable… I know that he's still probably going to kill me himself. He blames me for his brother's life sentence, and in a way, it's a life for a life.

Which is why I have to plan our escape.

Something that does hamper the plan is the one guard's voice echoing in my mind: the desert is a large, lonely, and deadly place. Even though we're probably only twenty minutes by car from the city, that's a lot longer of a walk for an adult, let alone a small child, when nature is actively trying to steal every drop of moisture from your body. I'm going to need to figure that part out before I make the actual attempt.

Until then, I might as well enjoy what I can. Demyen's razor, for example. I'm in desperate need of a shave and he's been so kind as to lend me his bathroom, so, y'know—when in Rome…

One shower and dolphin-smooth shave later, I'm sitting on the marble vanity slathering lotion onto my arms and legs. It's more of his scent, which makes it all the better. He doesn't need to know I'm taking my time to massage it into every inch I can reach.

He doesn't need to know I'm imagining his hands doing this for me.

I'm about to leave the bathroom when I figure I might as well brush my teeth, too. And oh, opportunity of opportunities, there's only one toothbrush in here.

My teeth are squeaky clean when I finally wrap the biggest, fluffiest towel I can find around me and tuck the ends in. I figure it's best to let my hair air dry, especially with how hot it is this time of year, so I make sure I'm not dripping everywhere before I saunter back through that archway into *his* bedroom.

I'm clean. I'm refreshed. I'm ready to take on whatever he throws at me.

Except I'm not ready for the sight of him, shirtless and sitting on the bed, with a platter of fruit and veggies next to him.

Demyen looks up from his phone. The way his face shifts hints that maybe he wasn't expecting me to walk in looking like this, either. His eyes roam from head to toe and never once leave my body as he tucks his phone back into his pocket.

I've stopped. I don't know what he wants or what he wants me to do. And I can't afford to fuck anything up.

"Come here."

The order is clear, but there's a slight gravelly sound in his voice. He leans back on his arms as I slowly walk over to him, and yes, maybe I do add a little bit of sway to my hips.

Might as well work it up to get on his good side.

I swear that's a growl of appreciation I hear in his throat. It's low and Demyen acts like I'm not affecting him in any way. But I hear it.

And then his hands are on my waist, pulling me onto his lap.

"Ready to be my good girl?"

Every time he says those words, something shoots straight from my head to my core. I can't explain it, and I don't think I want to dig into the why. All I know is, his voice, his words, make me nod my head and rest my hands on his shoulders for balance. He's made me straddle him, and I'm pretty sure one wrong move will have this towel dropping to the floor.

I'm also pretty sure he won't mind that at all.

Demyen stares at my neck. Breathes me in. I know he smells it—and his one arm around my waist tightens just a little more. His other arm reaches for the platter, picks up a piece of fruit, and lifts it to my mouth.

"Open."

I do as he says. It's honeydew, cold and juicy, and I can't help myself. I let out a soft moan of delight when the sweetness bursts on my tongue. My lips wrap around his fingertips and I flick my tongue over them to catch any drops of juice still there. I'm not even thinking about what I'm doing—I'm just savoring the moment, the flavor.

When I settle down to chew and swallow that delicious bite, I look at Demyen.

He's transfixed. Staring at my lips, his own slightly parted. The hungry fire in his eyes is blazing and I feel the undeniable evidence of what I'm doing to him press between my spread thighs.

But he doesn't say anything. He just reaches for another piece of fruit and feeds it to me. This time, I gaze into his eyes as I bite into the fresh strawberry and suck on its juices. It takes a few bites. I'm slow and careful with each one.

Demyen growls his approval again. His arm pulls me closer, makes me sit on his lap a bit firmer.

I really can't help myself. I roll my hips, just slightly, as if I'm trying to get comfortable.

He sucks in a breath. The hand that was feeding me grips my bare thigh. It feels like he means to stop me, at first, but when I do it again, his hand only rubs, slowly, from my knee to my hip.

Now, he truly pulls me onto him. There's no mistaking what we both want.

"Clara..."

"Yes?" My lips are barely inches from his. I won't close the distance; I know better to wait for him to give me permission. "... Sir?"

Demyen sucks in another deep breath, and when he lets it back out, it's with a string of curses I can't quite decipher.

The spell is broken. I figure as much when he reaches to another spot on the bed and holds up a scrap of shimmering gold fabric. "Put this on. After you eat," he quickly adds.

I squint at what can't be more than two square feet of fabric. Total. "*That's* clothing?"

"It's your uniform for tonight. I'm hosting a dinner party for a few business associates, and you're going to be my waitress." He holds the...dress, I guess you'd call it?...between us. "You do your job well and I'll let you spend a day with your daughter."

He's playing dirty. And he knows it.

I can, too.

"Yes, sir."

Demyen looks like it's taking every ounce of self-control to ease me off his lap and head toward the door. To be fair, it's taking a good amount of my own not to cling to his waist just to hump out the ache where his erection had been rubbing so nicely.

"You've got an hour. Eat, get dressed, then meet the guards at the door. They'll escort you to the event."

"Wait." A sudden panic hits me. "What about Willow? She's just a little girl, and—"

"Oh, don't worry. We sized her uniform down to fit."

The look on my face must match the horror I feel, because Demyen genuinely laughs. He calms down when he sees the tears brim my lashes and shakes his head with a sigh.

"Listen, Clara. Every time you ask me some terrible fucking question about how I'm treating your daughter, I'm going to give you an equally terrible answer." He takes a few steps back toward me and wraps his large hands around my arms. The gesture actually feels comforting. I hate that. "I'm an asshole. I'm a murderer, a thief, and I won't think twice before putting a bullet between a man's eyes just for blinking at me wrong. But I'm not a monster. I wouldn't do that to her."

"You're a contradiction." I don't know why I mutter it; the thought just slips out of my mouth. I brace myself for the consequences.

Demyen chuckles and nods. "That's exactly I am. It's in your best interest to remember."

And that's how he leaves me. Hot, flustered, and frustrated as all hell. Even watching the door close behind him is torment because it gives me a view of his bare back, all rippling muscle and golden skin.

He wants to play this game? Fine.

Let's play.

28

CLARA

I might as well go out there naked.

This dress—if you can even call it that—is going to fall off me if I sneeze. It's a slinky gold fabric that ripples with every movement, cut into two panels with one in the front and the other in the back to just barely cover my assets. They're held together by delicate, thin straps at my shoulders and even more delicate gold chains crisscrossed on either hip.

There's no way a bra or panties works under this "outfit," which means I'm going commando.

I'm thanking my lucky stars that breastfeeding Willow didn't make my boobs sag like I'd feared. I grew a cup size and a half, hooray, but otherwise, they're staying where they need to.

Not that I want Demyen to *like* what he sees, or anything...

Anyways.

One small act of mercy he granted me was a choice in shoes. I received two pairs when the guards arrived at the bedroom door: one pair is at least four or five inches tall, poised on lethal stilettos and glistening with gold straps to match the dress. The other pair is identical in design, but only about two inches high.

He remembered my ankle.

My stupid, stupid ankle that no longer hurts, is no longer bruised, and can probably withstand the skyscraper heels.

I bet he's expecting me to choose the shorter pair. I bet he's ready to see that I wussed out and went for the safe route in the two-inch heels.

So I slip on the femme fatale heels, do a little practice stroll around the room to check my balance, and smile to myself when I stop in front of the floor-length mirror.

Eat your fucking heart out, Dem.

My hair tumbles in waves over my shoulders, air-dried and au naturale. I hold my head up high as I walk between two guards who are doing their absolute best not to look at me, enjoying the cool desert breeze as it tousles my hair. The moon is a perfect crescent illuminating the grounds. A part of me wants to simply lie by the pool and marvel at the expanse of stars overhead.

But I'm led to another end of the compound—pretty far removed from the main house, actually, or at least from where Willow and I have been staying. The main courtyard is quiet and softly lit by solar lights enough to see one's way around the pool. Several guards are sitting on deck chairs, casually strolling around, or standing at attention around one particular room that must be a VIP guest situation.

We walk past all that and down through a series of open archways toward the faint sound of laughter and music. As we get closer to the sounds, I'm able to see that it's a secondary courtyard of sorts, with another pool and a larger area set up for formal dining. Strings of lights drape across the courtyard, casting a warm golden glow over Demyen's guests.

And there are so. Many. Guests.

I don't know what I expected. Ten? Maybe twenty? But no, there's gotta be at least fifty or more people here, eating, drinking, and schmoozing with each other over fancy little cocktail platters and what must be an endless round of expensive champagne.

And of course, the actual serving staff is all appropriately dressed for such an event.

I'm the only one who looks like a prostitute.

The guards stop at the main archway that opens into the courtyard. They must be expecting me to just sashay my almost-naked ass in there as if I know what I'm doing.

Riiight. Joke's on them.

I haven't known what I'm doing since the day I was born.

But then I see him, several tables away and laughing at something the man next to him muttered in his ear. The whole table is full of men, young and old, all obviously wealthy and important enough to sit with the host.

There are women here, too, but most of them are draped on the arms of men that Demyen is either trying to impress or intimidate with this display of casual extravagance. Like me, they're here for show. Living ornaments meant to make the night pretty.

*Un*like me, they don't have to deal with the asshole in the tailored linen suit.

He hasn't called me over, but I don't fucking care. I know what he wants—to humiliate me in front of everyone, dressed like this and serving him—and while I'll be at his beck and call, I won't be groveling for his attention.

So I put my cocktail serving skills to good use and weave my way through the tables. No pause, no hesitation, just inner determination to prove a point and the familiar mask of happy servitude on my face.

When Demyen looks up and sees me, the champagne flute he was about to toss back pauses at his lips.

He's frozen.

Staring.

I know that between the heels and my need to not trip over chairs, the sway in my hips is more pronounced than usual. And with the way this fabric keeps shimmering and rippling over my curves, well…

Let him choke on that bubbly.

He sets the flute down and clears his throat. His own mask settles on his face—the boss who gives orders and expects to be instantly obeyed. He gives me a once-over when I approach his side and simply grunts his disinterested approval.

"What can I get for you?" I smile benevolently at him. Not too sweet, but enough to show I'm willing and happy to play his game. And just for added fun… "Sir?"

Demyen leans back slightly in his chair, his eyes narrowing as he regards me. "Get me a Rum Martinez. Cuban."

Oh... Fuck. You.

I smile and bat my lashes like the slutty bimbo he wants me to play. "Right away, sir. Anything else for the table?"

The hungry looks in their eyes have me feeling like *I'm* on the menu. A few of them chuckle and mumble how they have "something they can give me."

But Demyen shoots them a glare and the table instantly quiets. "No. You're to serve me exclusively. Just the Rum Martinez and a Cuban. For now."

"Understood, sir."

I turn and make my way to the bar, making sure the sway in my hips is as sensual as I can manage in these heels without toppling over. Demyen's pretending to not be interested, but I'm pretty sure one shift in the tablecloth would blow his bluff.

The bar is as lavish as the rest of the party, and as much as I've been doubting if such a cocktail would be possible, it occurs to me that Demyen isn't the kind of man to shortchange his guests or himself. If he orders a stupidly complicated drink, he'll get the stupidly complicated drink.

"One Rum Martinez and a Cuban, for Mr. Zakrevsky." The bartender was only half-paying attention until I mentioned Demyen. As soon as I drop that, he goes double-time.

Just as I guessed—they're fully equipped to create the smoky infusion of rum and bark. The bartender even plates it on a thin round of mesquite wood, with a small but decorative prop to hold up the lit cigar. The whole process can't be rushed and it takes a good five minutes at least for the bartender to go through the whole smoke infusion process.

When he's done, he slides the plank to me and quickly moves on to the next drink.

I carry the wood on one hand, weave through the maze of tables, and smoothly place the drink and cigar tray in front of Demyen. "Your cocktail, sir."

Demyen's brow tics, but otherwise, there's no other sign of approval at my swift and confident service. Not that I would expect any. He takes a long draw on the cigar, blows the smoke out, then lifts the glass for a sip.

He sips a good amount, lets it sit on his tongue, then swallows.

"It's terrible. Take it back and get me a new one."

"Excuse me?"

He quickly looks up at me as if I've just insulted his mother. "Is there a problem?"

"No, sir. I just need clarification for the bartender—"

"It tastes like shit. Get a new one."

He even has the audacity to shoo me away with a flippant wave of his fingers before returning to his riveting conversation about racehorses.

I've dealt with customers like him before. This is nothing new.

I just never *fucked* any of those customers before they treated me like this. And they never nursed me back to health, or put a roof over my head, or—

Or made me work practically in the nude.

So as much as his attitude stings—and I *hate* that it does—I'm determined not to let him and his ego get to me. I scoop up the mesquite tray, resist the urge to pluck the cigar from his mouth, and weave my way back to the bartender.

"You're kidding me, right?" he asks when he sees me coming.

I don't know what to tell the guy. "He says it tastes like shit. He wants a new one."

The bartender gestures at the counter full of elegant supplies. "What does he want? What's wrong with it?"

"I wish I knew what to tell you." I sigh and flip my hair over one shoulder, leaning against the counter for a quick break. "I'd just make it the same exact way and see what happens. His taste is probably shit."

He smirks and gets to it, taking my advice.

Three years in the food service industry, and I can promise anyone—half the time, it's the customer who can't taste worth a damn.

"I'd be careful if I were you."

I slide my gaze to the side where the gentle voice full of warning came from. The woman from earlier, the one who played with Willow in the garden, is leaning against the bar with a martini in her flawlessly manicured hand. She's eyeing me with something like interest mixed with disdain.

If I remember correctly, I think she's Demyen's assistant.

"Oh?" is all I can think to ask. I need to be careful, like she said.

"He has eyes and ears everywhere. And he won't hesitate to make you pay for the slightest insult."

"Oh." I need her to like me, or at least like me enough to keep being good to Willow, so I play the demure, obedient waitress and lower my eyes. "Well, I hope Mr. Zakrevsky's ears won't mind a little frustrated joke."

She stares at me for one heavy, silent moment. Then smirks. "His ears heard nothing. And his taste buds haven't clocked a good cocktail in years."

Someone beckons her to their table, so she glides away without a second glance at me. It's just in time for the bartender to slide a new Rum Martinez across the counter, and then I'm back to pretending I actually enjoy serving Demyen hand and foot.

Just as I expected, he takes one sip and nods his approval.

"Much better."

The threads on my self-control are working overtime. It's a literal miracle my eyes don't roll back in my head.

"Give this to Tarken." Demyen holds up a folded slip of paper between his fingers. He's too focused on flicking his Cuban cigar to look at me or bother to explain who the fuck Tarken is.

I know better than to ask. "Yes, sir." I take the paper from his fingers, making sure to glide mine over his in a subtle move to get some sort of rise out of him.

The way he stills, just for a moment, tells me that it worked.

I walk away to deliver whatever this message is, or receipt, or death threat—I don't even know, and I don't care at this point. I just need to know who Tarken is and where he's sitting or standing or—

Someone squeals with laughter and playfully smacks her companion's arm. She tells him he's "so bad" and says his name.

Bingo.

I walk over to the couple and hold the note out for Tarken. He's gotta be a decade or two older than Demyen and ten times as sleazy. He looks me up and down and the smile on his face grows into something larger and lecherous.

I ignore it and maintain my own customer service smile. "This is from Mr. Zakrevsky."

Tarken takes the note, but not before enveloping my hand in his. Clearly, his lady companion either doesn't care or isn't paid enough to pretend to.

He reads the note, nods, and tucks it into his jacket pocket. "Tell Mr. Zakrevsky I'd love to. I'll be in touch. And while you're at it…" He steps closer and smooths a hand along my ribs, tracing my exposed skin lightly with his fingertips. "Ask him how much he wants for your lovely company."

I keep that damned service smile on and tilt my head to one side. It's about as flirtatious as I'm gonna get with this creep. "I'm afraid I'm exclusive to Mr. Zakrevsky. Shall I have him send you someone else?"

"If you have a twin, then hell yes." He laughs, and his companion laughs with him. I don't think she even knows what the joke is; she's been staring off at the pool fountain with boredom. Tarken pulls me closer to him and leans in to breathe in my hair. "Please assure my good host that no amount is too high. You are worth every penny, I'm sure."

I carefully slip away before his fingers have a chance to slip beneath the dress. "I'll see what Mr. Zakrevsky can do."

That seems to satisfy the creep. He returns to entertaining his lady with more bad jokes.

When I return to Demyen's side, he's got a stack of playing cards fanned in one hand and the cigar poised between his other fingers. "What did he say?"

"He says he'd love to and he'll be in touch."

Demyen nods. I'm this close to adding Tarken's second request, but I hesitate. Better not.

"And?"

Damn. Caught.

"And…he wants to know how much you want. For me. For tonight."

Demyen folds the cards into a neat stack as he leans back in his chair. Still, he doesn't look at me. But I see the vein in his jaw tic once, twice. A dead giveaway.

He's not as unaffected as he's pretending to be.

"What did you tell him?"

The hell kind of question is that? "I told Mr. Tarken that I'm exclusive to you."

"And?"

"And he assures you that no price is too high."

Demyen snorts a laugh and finally looks up at me. "As if anyone could put a price on you."

I… I'm not sure how to take that. If it's a compliment, it's the weirdest one I've ever gotten.

Even weirder is how it makes me feel.

Before I can puzzle it out, he snaps his fingers and a different server appears out of nowhere. "Invite Tarken to our table. Make some room for our honored guest and his companion. And *you*." His gaze slides back to mine. "Bring me a charcuterie board."

Right. Because I know where to find a fucking charcuterie board.

I give him my best "right away, sir" smile and turn to go hunt down yet another impossibly difficult whim.

And as I go, he slaps my ass.

The table erupts in chuckles and good-natured ribbing. I quickly walk away just so I don't have to hear them talk about me like I'm a piece of meat. I also need to get away from Demyen as quickly as possible because… because…

Well, because that slap landed in a very unexpected way.

And we're in public.

Sort of.

I watch the servers carrying food around and figure out where they're streaming from—and thank the stars, there's a buffet-looking table with charcuterie trays all over the place.

I have no idea which one he wants, but I also don't know if he cares. So I grab the fullest, most varied one I can find, and carry it all the way back to the table. I should have picked a lighter one, but oh well. Here we are.

And there Tarken is, making himself comfortable at Demyen's table. The woman with him is now sitting on his lap, draping herself around him like a human scarf, but he hardly notices. His gaze follows me the second he notices me approaching, and his grin widens.

"There she is. Goddamn, Zakrevsky. What a beauty you caught."

I place the heavy board on the table in front of Demyen. But before I can straighten, he reaches up and caresses a strand of my hair between his fingers.

"That she is." Demyen's voice is gentle. Not at all the demanding asshole of five minutes ago.

I think I missed something.

His arm slips around me, and the next thing I know, I'm sitting on his thigh. The way he tucks me close to him forces me to lean against his chest, my head nestled in the crook of his neck.

His hand smooths down my side to rest possessively on my thigh, right where it flares into my hip. His fingertips flex for a moment, almost like a subtle caress, then still.

I *definitely* missed something.

"Grape."

I blink at him. He still doesn't look at me, and I'm not sure if I heard him correctly at first. But then his fingers dig into my thigh and I realize yes, I heard him.

Of all the...

I keep that smile plastered on my face and pray that he chokes on the fucking grape that I pluck from the board and gently pop into his mouth. As he slowly chews, he looks around the table at his guests until his eyes land on one in particular.

"Tarken, old friend." His voice is calm, but I'm starting to pick up on his little tells more and more: he's not as happy as he seems. "I have some concerns about our new contract."

Tarken frowns just a little, but laughs it off. "Oh? What about? Everything looks good on my end."

"You seem to misunderstand a few very important terms and conditions."

Now, the man is more confused. "I don't understand."

"No, you don't. When I say 'exclusive,' I fucking mean 'exclusive.' Non-negotiable."

The men playing the card game slowly lower their hands and look uncomfortably at the tablecloth. Tarken turns an interesting shade of red and sputters. "But, Dem, I—"

"Thought you could buy me off? Disregard my terms with money?" Demyen laughs, but the smile doesn't reach his eyes. Those are cold, calculating, and deciding this poor man's fate. "What could I possibly want with *your* money?"

"But the contract—"

"Will need another review by my lawyer. We'll be making a few adjustments as well. Your cut is now dropped to thirty percent."

"You can't—"

"Fifteen percent."

Tarken slumps in his chair, beet red and practically foaming at the mouth. But he knows he's defeated. He looks at me, but instantly looks away again when Demyen clears his throat in warning.

Demyen's hand travels from my thigh to my side in a long, slow caress of his fingers. "You're lucky I'm feeling so generous and we're at a party. I'm not in the mood to make my staff clean your brains off the linens. Am I understood?"

The man nods. Some of the other men nod, too, just to be safe.

I pick a cube of gouda and feed it to him. I figure he's probably expecting me to keep going regardless of what's going on. His glare is fixed on his "business associate," but he accepts the cheese with a small grunt of what might be gratitude. Maybe.

But when I feed him another grape and the juice accidentally bursts between his lips, he looks at me as I grab a napkin and gently dab his chin clean.

Our eyes meet. For a breathless millisecond, I could swear I see something glimmer in his eyes that isn't anger, or calculation, or desire.

It's new.

It's raw.

It's *dangerous.*

And it's quickly shuttered behind his boss mask the moment I spot it.

"If you weren't our generous host, I'd call you selfish," chuckles one of the other men at the table. He seems decent enough, but I'm quickly learning to never trust appearances when it comes to Demyen's friends. "Keeping such a beautiful woman all to yourself. And obedient, too."

That last comment lands right when I'm feeding Demyen a chocolate-covered almond. My fingers still. Suddenly, I'm not enjoying this as much as I was two minutes ago—if that could be called "enjoying"—and I want the ground to swallow me whole.

It's one thing for Demyen to do whatever this is.

It's a whole other thing for someone else to see me as a literal obedient lapdog.

He must sense the shift in me because, instead of absentmindedly taking the almond from my fingers, he looks into my eyes as he wraps his lips around it—and my fingertips. His tongue flicks lightly against them, then stops.

That's when I know he sees the tears brimming my lashes.

I'm not going to cry. I'm not going to humiliate myself any more than he's already managed. But my stomach is in knots and I really wish I could just disappear from this dinner party, from this compound.

From this *life*.

Regret flashes in his eyes. It's a fraction of a millisecond, but it's there. Were we in any other situation, I might dare to dream that he'd actually apologize for the way he's treating me and defend my honor against his horrible guests.

But this is reality.

Demyen smirks and takes a long pull from his cigar. "You know me. I'm a selfish son of a bitch when it comes to a beautiful face and a tight ass. I just can't help myself."

And just like that, my self-pity snaps into anger.

"It's too bad you have to pay for it," I casually muse, plucking another chocolate almond from the board. "But hey, the more you pay, the bigger and better you are, right?"

No one finds my little joke funny.

Least of all Demyen.

He taps the ash off his cigar into the ashtray, then slowly presses it out. After a long silence, he smiles at his guests.

I don't like that smile. It's full of promises I don't want him to fulfill.

"If you'll excuse me, gentlemen. I have some business to attend to."

His hands are on my waist. I'm suddenly on my feet.

And he whisks me away from the table, confirming my blooming fear: *I'm* the business in question.

29

CLARA

How many walkways-slash-hallways-slash-paths does this place have? I've lost count and Demyen shows no signs of slowing down as he hauls me away from the party. It's another open archway path he steers me to, abandoned by guests and staff and dimly lit by solar lamps perched on each column. One of those columns is now pressed to my back—and he's caging me in.

"Remind me, Clara: didn't we have an agreement?"

I look anywhere but at his face. I'll stare at his chest if I have to. It's not a bad sight, either. The top buttons of his linen shirt are undone and the low lamplight makes his golden tan glow.

"Yes."

"Yes, what?"

I swallow. My mouth is suddenly dry. "Yes, sir."

"You promised to play nice. You promised to be a good girl." He braces a palm against the smooth column above my head as his other hand lifts to play with the ends of my hair. "You gave me your word."

"I… I know."

"You've got a lot riding on this, Clara. A whole hell of a lot. You owe me."

I suck in a deep breath. *Bad mistake.* All I can smell is him and it's so distracting. "I don't deserve to be treated like a slave. I'll do whatever you want, but I won't give you my dignity."

The fingers playing with my hair slide up and tangle at the nape of my neck—and with one sudden, firm pull, he forces my head back to look up into his stormy glare.

"You'll give me whatever the fuck I want."

I try to shake my head, but I can't. He's holding me in place.

What's worse—it doesn't hurt at all. It actually, kinda… feels *good.*

The hell is wrong with me?

"Let's get one thing straight, Clara Everett." Demyen over-enunciates every consonant in my name as he leans in closer. "You. Belong. To. Me."

My heart slams inside my chest. But my God, am I feeling stubborn. "I'm not your fucking plaything."

Those fingers tug just a fraction harder. And instead of wincing or whimpering or squinting in pain, I *moan.*

I fucking *moan.*

Demyen's face breaks into a wicked smirk. "Oh, I beg to differ."

"Please." I sputter to regain some traction, some shred of dignity before it completely vanishes. "I'm sorry. I forgot—I'll be good, I promise."

He clicks his tongue at me. "Tsk tsk. You said that before. You promised me you'd be good so you could see your sweet daughter. What will Willow think when Mommy isn't there for her playdate?"

My eyes widen in horror. "No! Please, I'll do anything!"

"That's my fucking point, Clara." He gives another slight tug just for emphasis. "You'll do anything and everything I say because you don't have a fucking choice."

This time, I try to nod even with his fist in my hair.

Demyen's gaze lowers to my trembling lips. "I wanted to go easy on you. Let you prove yourself. Let you show you mean it. While I show the world who you belong to."

"I'm sorry. I'm sorry." I bite my bottom lip to stop it from trembling so much.

His other hand leaves the column and cups my face. With an odd gentleness, his thumb eases my lip from my teeth and remains there, massaging the swollen flesh.

"You owe me." Demyen leans in closer. "Which means I own you. If I tell you to get me a drink, you bring me a drink. If I tell you to go out there and bend over the table, you'll spread those beautiful legs and bend over the fucking table. If I tell you to scream my name while I fuck you open in front of the whole party, you'll do it and beg for more. Am I understood?"

Fuck.

I'm squirming. And it's not because I'm scared.

His hands ease from my hair and slide down my neck to caress my sides. I feel him pluck at the delicate chains before he presses and caresses under the slinky fabric.

"Is that what you want?" A darkly amused smile tugs at his lips. "Is that what my good girl wants? You want me to fuck you hard in front of everyone? Show the world who owns you?"

God help me.

I do. I kinda, really do.

I won't say it, though. Never in *this* lifetime. No matter how hot the inferno now dripping between my thighs burns, no matter how much his silky smooth voice rumbles such dark promises against my skin as he presses his lips to the rapid pulse below my ear…

"You'd enjoy it. I promise."

His teeth capture my lobe and softly tug.

I let out a whimper. My hips writhe against the column. "Please…"

"Please, what?" Demyen moves a hand even lower and presses between my thighs. The moment his palm cups my mound, his fingers teasing my slit, I shudder. He feels how wet I am for him and the look on his face is pure pride.

The heel of his palm kneads into my mound, teasing but not quite rubbing my clit. His fingers stroke back and forth over my lips, coaxing more delicious tremors from me and another pitiful moan.

"I should fuck you right here." The words are breathed along my neck, his mouth skimming my flesh without fully pressing in. "You want it. You *need* it, don't you?"

I want to protest, but I can't. Without even realizing it, I've grabbed his waist and started grinding myself against his hand. When I roll my hips a bit harder in response, he uses that moment to cup my whole pussy in his hand and squeeze.

"Who owns you?"

My head is foggy. I can't think straight. Something echoes in the back of my mind that I need to fight, need to protest, need to hold my ground.

The rest of my entire body screams the answer he wants, though my voice can barely whisper it. "You."

"I can't hear you."

I moan again. He's moving his hand, kneading my clit with the heel of his palm now. "You, s-sir! I belong to you."

"That's fucking right." Demyen breathes me in, burying his face against the curve of my neck. "But you knew that already, didn't you? That's why you smell like me. You're covered in me. It's been driving me fucking wild all night."

Hold on... what?

But any cohesive thought in my head vanishes when he presses one finger, then two, inside me. And when I groan, he sucks on the skin where it vibrates through my throat.

"I want to fill you with me. Over... and over... and over again."

Each word is emphasized by a deeper thrust of his fingers combined with a coaxing rub against something wholly unfamiliar inside me. I don't know what he's doing, or what he's pressing, but he keeps working his fingers inside me over the same spot.

I'm clinging to him for dear life. My toes are curling to the point of almost hurting from the strain.

And I don't want him to stop.

Demyen's eyes are boring into mine, his mouth barely an inch away. His breath is ragged, like he's trying to maintain control of himself as much as he's controlling me.

"There's my good girl." It comes out in a whisper, almost like a prayer. "But you were naughty, weren't you?"

I bite my lip and nod.

"Do you know what naughty girls get?"

My head barely shakes, but it's enough of an answer to him.

I don't know what registers first—the sudden emptiness inside me, the wet slap, or the heat suddenly spreading through every inch of my pussy.

And when it does register, all at the same time, the only thing keeping me upright is his hand massaging the sting.

I'm so close. I'm so fucking close.

He does it again. He spanks my pussy and I don't feel a sting at all—only heat, tingling heat, that spreads from my clit to my ass and makes me practically gush all over his hand.

This time, I almost cry out, but he cuts me off with a kiss. It's hard and hungry, demanding, his tongue invading my mouth the same time his fingers plunge inside me again and work themselves against that same spot.

"Don't come—" He kisses me again. "Until I say so. Show me you're my good girl."

I can only nod. The pressure is building beyond my limits. The only way I can think of holding back is to squeeze my thighs tight around his hand to slow his movements... but that only helps him massage my clit even better.

I don't know if I can hold back much longer.

"Look at me, Clara."

I do. I look up at him, deep into his eyes, and see that same raw *something* from earlier. He wants me as badly as I want him, and I'm so fucking tempted to beg him for more than just his fingers. I want him to look at me just like this while he impales me on his thick cock, and—

"Ahem."

Demyen freezes.

So do I.

His assistant stands a few feet behind him, clearly resisting the urge to arch a brow. "You're needed at the main house."

The growl in Demyen's throat rumbles enough to scatter stones. "Are you fucking serious—"

"We've got company."

The way she says it has him easing his hand from me and discreetly wiping his fingers against his pants. "Who?"

"Detective Patterson."

No.

No. No, no, no, no, *no.*

Anyone but Martin.

30

DEMYEN

Motherfucker.

I despise being interrupted under normal circumstances. When I'm eating, when I'm drinking, when I'm speaking, don't fucking interrupt me.

But when I'm intoxicated on the way Clara's scent is wholly mine? When I'm working her deliciously sweet pussy to the brink of release so I can hear her moans and taste her sighs?

I don't care if he's a cop—I'm going to fucking murder him.

I can't immediately place why that name rings a bell; I'm too distracted by the way Clara's breasts strain against the flimsy excuse of a dress as she gasps to catch her breath. Those hard nipples are begging to be sucked, and I'm—

Focus. Fucking focus, dumbass. The cops are here.

"Demyen." Bambi's voice is as effective as a snap of her fingers. "What do you want to do?"

Shoot him in the head.

"What the fuck does he want?"

Bambi cocks a brow. "Do you really have to ask?" But when she sees my glare, she erases the attitude. "Patterson, Dem. *Martin* Patterson."

And the name clicks into place.

Fuck.

I glance at Clara and immediately realize those tremors aren't from the tension of an interrupted orgasm. She's terrified. Not even looking at me with her soft green eyes, which are widened in horror and staring off into some dark abyss only she can see. She's slumped against the column, shaking and sinking into some mental zone that honestly kind of scares me.

I've been intentionally cruel to her all night, but I enjoyed her fire. I'll never say it out loud for as long as I live, but I actually *want* her rebellion.

Seeing that fire snuffed out, watching the dark shadows that haunt her suddenly overwhelm her entire being—and at the mention of *another man's name*—has me forgetting all about how I'm supposed to be punishing her.

"Clara."

It takes a moment, but she looks at me.

"Come with me."

She meekly nods and trails along. I almost take her hand, but I stop myself before I do anything quite that stupid. She manages to keep up with my furious pace across the compound to the main house, with Bambi close behind and on her earpiece muttering orders to various staff.

"Check for drugs," I remind her.

"On it."

"Weapons stash?"

"Already sealed."

"And our guests?"

"Distracted and entertained. Pavel made sure to keep Patterson on the other side and well out of view."

"Good."

"What about Willow?" Clara suddenly grabs my arm. "He can't get Willow!"

I only nod and shake off her hand.

We're just entering the main courtyard, so I don't see a need to explain it all to her. The guards I have stationed around Willow's bedroom are on full alert, hands near their weapons just in case. The one standing in front of the kid's door nods to me, ready for orders. "Sir."

"How is she?"

"Sound asleep." He cocks his head toward the darkened room. I can just make out the small sleeping form nestled under blankets in her hammock. "Went down around three hours ago."

Clara rushes forward to check on her, but I grab her arm and hold her back. "I need to check on my daughter!" she hisses at me.

"You need to shut the hell up and pray she stays asleep." I yank her back behind me and return to the guard. "Double the watch here and make sure no one gets within fifty feet of the girl. If anyone, and I mean *anyone*, pushes that—shoot on sight and get her out of here. Arrange a getaway vehicle out back just in case."

"*Da, pakhan.*"

I turn around to storm off to confront the asshole, but Clara is standing in my way. This time, her wide eyes are staring at me in what can only be awe.

"Thank you," she whispers with tears brimming in her eyes. "Thank you."

I shrug it off and glower at Bambi. "Get rid of her."

Clara gasps in horrified shock as Bambi grabs her by her arms and quickly leads her away. I pretend those sounds don't make my chest seize up as I turn and prepare for whatever mess this woman-beating *mudak* is bringing to my doorstep.

From the sound of it, Patterson came alone, so there shouldn't be a "worst-case scenario" that tears holes into my walls. But then again, I can't afford to underestimate the stubborn resolve of a man hellbound to get his woman and child back. I know if I were in his shoes, I'd—

No. Not going to think like that. Clara is not my woman; Willow is not my daughter. If they go missing, it's none of my concern.

Which means the very loud protective instinct in my body can shut the hell up.

I'm flanked by two of my men as I storm through the house to the main entrance. I slow my pace once I hit the hallway leading to the columned archway and take a moment to smooth out my hair and suit.

That's the key to a poker face: Be calm. Be bored. Be aloof. But always be watching your enemies for their tells.

Pavel is the first to greet me with a nod and a grunt. "Over there."

I flick my gaze to the corner of the room behind him…

And almost burst into laughter.

Him?

31

CLARA

"What are you doing?!" I half-hiss, half-shriek at Demyen's assistant when she grabs a zip-tie from a guard and binds my wrists together in front of me. My heart is pounding in my ears so loud, I'm not sure I can hear her answer.

Bambi's face is a mask of grim determination as she tightens the zip-tie and then moves to my legs. "I'm following orders."

"Oh, God... you're gonna kill me."

That's what this is. It's an execution. She's trussing me up like a turkey right before the men slaughter me. What about Willow? I can't—I don't—

"Will you calm down?" Her voice is soft but there's no mistaking the authority in it.

I shut up instantly.

"Good. Listen." Bambi straightens and holds her hand out to no one in particular, waiting until a guard hands her a clean handkerchief. "You panicking? That's too risky. You're going to get us all shot, or worse. That's why the boss said to shut you up."

"But he said to get rid of me—"

"Out of sight. Away from the prying eyes of your asshole ex." She twists the fabric in her fingers, then wraps it around my head. "Bite down. It's clean, promise. Won't taste great, but the plan is to not need it for long."

My "why" is more of a muffled grunt as I do what she says. She's right—it tastes terrible. I'm not loving the dry cotton in my mouth.

Bambi sighs as she tightens the knot behind my head. "Because if things *do* go south, it will be better for you if you look like an unwilling participant. A *captive*, Clara," she adds a little impatiently when she sees the questions in my eyes. "Think about it: if Martin does find you, would he beat you up for being a kidnapping victim? No? What about if you were the woman warming my boss's bed?"

Shit. She has a point.

"That's what I thought. Willow will be safe. Extremely safe. To be brutally honest, between the two of you, you'll probably go down first as live bait before we let anyone get their hands on her."

It's a horrible vision in my mind, but one that I'm honestly okay with. I'd rather Martin kill me slowly if it meant buying time for my baby's escape.

Bambi offers me a small smile, but it's genuine. "She's a great kid. You've done a great job, despite everything you've had to deal with. She's polite, she's sweet, she's *insanely* intelligent…" She sighs again and rests a hand on my arm.

"So I can promise you right now, cop or not: if he lays one finger on her, I'll shoot him myself."

And then I'm shoved backward into some sort of utility closet.

Into the dark.

Into the silence.

Into the depths of my own hyperventilating mind.

It's just like the box.

I'm back in that damned box.

No—the box was warmer. This is… not cold, but also not wood. I'm in a closet, not a box. But it still *feels* like that damned box.

At least the box was better than being in the trunk. The trunk was too cramped, too scary. Everything rumbled beneath me; every turn made me roll around and slam into things. I felt like I was suffocating in the trunk of that godforsaken car.

I don't even remember how I got in there. How I got so close to someone who wanted to hurt me bad enough…

Sometimes, it feels silly, being a grown woman drowning in her own memories over something that happened years and years ago. I was rescued, I was healthy and unharmed, and I was home in Mama's arms by morning. I fared far better than the dozens of missing children my father tried to find in all his years as detective.

But other times, like right now, it's easy—*too* easy—to wallow in the sea of memories that horrible night seared into my mind.

Especially when the clearest memory is the one that put a man in prison for life.

I can't blame Demyen for his anger. I don't know what I'd do in his position, if someone I loved was suddenly locked away and I believed they were innocent.

All I can do is pray he keeps Martin away from Willow. My baby. My sweet baby who doesn't deserve any of this, who deserves far better than what I've ever been able to give her.

Demyen does his best to hide it, but I see it: he's got a soft spot for Willow. I wasn't sure if that's what I was seeing at first, but it's been little things over and over again. The way he ordered his men to protect her at all costs. The way his voice shifts into something softer when he talks about her. The way he's so defensive over her, even against me.

I know I'm his prisoner here. I know my survival chances are extremely low.

But maybe, just maybe...

Willow actually stands a chance.

32

DEMYEN

I cannot for the life of me figure out how the hell *she* ended up with *him*.

Martin Patterson—*Detective* Martin Patterson—is a short, pasty, chameleon-eyed excuse for a man currently sniveling in the corner of my entryway. His hair, what little he has left, clings to his scalp in a sad combover with too much oil. What looks like a failed attempt for a handlebar mustache glistens above his lip with a mixture of sweat and snot.

And the rest of him? I doubt he engages in any hot pursuits on foot. Between the softness around his middle and the limpness in his limbs, I'm guessing I could take him out just by challenging him to a light jog.

The fact that he ever reproduced is a miracle in itself. The fact that he made Willow is proof that either God or the Devil definitely exist, because there's no way *she* came from *this* motherfucker without divine intervention.

Almost instantly, the thought turns sour.

This son of a bitch? Between *Clara's* legs?

Absolutely not.

I pray he gives me a reason to kill him.

"What can I do for you, Detective?" I'm all Casino Host and Esteemed Pillar Of The Community, making sure my charm oozes more than his mucus.

"Ah, Mr. Zakrevsky." Patterson straightens up and holds his hand out to me. "Detective Patterson, although I'm pretty sure your men filled you in."

"They did." I shake his clammy hand and make a mental note to bathe in antibacterial gel later. Either that or burn the skin off. "Has anyone offered you a drink?"

Not that I want him to get comfortable and stay. But if he chokes on a maraschino cherry, I'm not going to be heartbroken.

"Yes, thank you, but unfortunately, I'm on the job. Speaking of..." He opens his jacket and pulls out a stack of photos from the inside pocket. "I was wondering if you could take a look at these and answer a few questions."

I frown. "Are you questioning me, Detective?"

Patterson chuckles. "Not at all, Mr. Zakrevsky. But as the owner of The Meridian Hotel and Casino, I was hoping you'd be able to shed some light on a missing persons case."

The first image he shows me is a still from one of my cameras inside the main floor of The Meridian Casino. In it, I'm standing next to a woman at the bar, talking to her while my guards hold a man by twisting his arms behind his back.

"Is he missing?" I ask, pointing to the terrified man in the photo.

"No, no. He is, however, the one who filed a report with LVPD regarding the assault."

"Assault?" I laugh pleasantly. "We have a strict policy against sexual assault and offenders in our establishment. He was harassing one of our VIP guests and we took care of it."

Patterson shrugs with a nod. "I can understand that. It's not my department, anyway. But what brings me here is something we caught in the corners of these images… and then here. And here."

The next several photos are more stills from different cameras, first focusing on the march of doom we gave the man into that interrogation room to make him sweat it out… but then I stop.

Fuck.

That's the same night Clara showed up and won the jackpot.

Sure enough, she's the star of each subsequent photo, seemingly wandering around the main floor in awe and uncertainty. *How did I miss her?* A few of the images even show us walking right by each other, but I didn't even so much as glance in her direction.

"Missing woman?" I force myself to keep my voice calm and unbothered.

"Yeah." Patterson sighs, taking the photos back and tucking them into his jacket. "She's been missing for a few days now and this is the first major lead we've had."

"I wish I could help you, but as you can see, we get hundreds —thousands, on a good weekend—coming and going in that place."

"Seems like you bumped into her more than a few times, wouldn't you say?"

I hide my irritation with a good-natured chuckle and shrug. "Her and dozens of other women that night alone. I'm sorry, Detective, but I don't keep a ledger of names of every single person I brush elbows with."

Patterson eyes me for a silent moment. "I'll be honest, Mr. Zakrevsky: she's my woman. My woman and the mother of my child, who she kidnapped in the middle of the night. I'm very concerned for both their safety."

Of fucking course you are. "I thought you said this was a missing persons case? Not a kidnapping?"

"He better make it exceptionally clear which one we're talking about." Bambi's voice carries across the foyer as she sashays into the room, every bit the lethal lawyer I pay her to be. "And I *know* he's not questioning you without me present."

Patterson almost shoots her a glare, but I watch him catch himself and cough. "Of course not. As I said before, we're just pursuing leads at the moment." He glances at her, then turns his focus back on me. "My daughter, Willow, is the true missing person. She's only five and I'm just worried sick about her. Her mother, Clara... she's not stable. Never really has been, but what can I say? I fell head over heels. But she got hooked on the meds after giving birth and... well, I just can't sleep knowing my baby girl is somewhere out there with a crazy drug addict."

If there's one type of man I can't stand in this world, it's liars.

If there's two types, it's liars and abusers.

Detective Patterson is both.

I know he can see my smile harden. "Sounds like you need the Narcotics division. I can't help you." I give him one final nod and turn to leave.

This interview is over.

And I need to walk away before I beat a police officer to death.

"She's only five, Mr. Zakrevsky. She's my whole world. I'll do anything to get her back."

What strikes me as interesting is how, now that I'm not looking right at him, the bullshit smells even stronger. He says all the right things, but there's something about the way he says them that just doesn't convince me he's in this for Willow.

I'd place a good wager that he's planning to use Willow as leverage. The fucking snake.

Like what you're doing now, hm? pipes up the little devil's advocate in my head.

I squash that thought back down the second it pops up. This is about Patterson, not me.

"You know what?" I snap my fingers and spin back around on my heel. "I just remembered. You're right, we did bump into each other at the casino."

Oh, I bumped into her, all right. Repeatedly. Until she screamed my name and came on my cock, you worthless piece of shit.

Patterson perks up. "Oh?"

I nod and glance at Bambi. "You remember, right? The one our concierge flagged us down for. He had some concerns for her safety."

Bambi stares hard at me for only a second before she catches on. "Yes. I believe I recall something about injuries…?"

This makes Patterson pale just a smidge. "Injuries? She was injured?"

"Well, that's what our concierge was concerned about. And, of course, we take safety and security at The Meridian very seriously." I hold my hand out for one of the photos of Clara, but Patterson takes a step back.

"That's okay, Mr. Zakrevsky, I—"

"Got it." Bambi smiles her professional smile, but I know that gleam in her eyes as she turns the tablet in her hands to show us actual footage of Clara speaking with one of our concierges, then Bambi herself. "Is this who you're speaking about, Detective?"

Patterson clears his throat, wipes his nose, and nods. "Yeah. Yeah, that's my Clara."

"Oh, well, that's a relief." Bambi turns off the screen and tucks the tablet under her arm. "We were so concerned about the bruises on her arms and especially her ankle. We almost felt the need to send her to the hospital. But it's reassuring to know she's in the safe hands of Las Vegas' finest."

Bambi Watkins's most powerful weapon is her tongue. I've seen her make ADAs burst into tears in the courtroom hall after she flayed their cases apart.

And by the look on Patterson's face, she's stabbed him through his lies and twisted the knife.

"Where did she go after you spoke with her?" He takes out a small notepad and pen as if he's actually going to take notes.

I laugh. "How should I know? We offered to call her a cab, even offered to escort her to the hospital for the ankle injury. But she stubbornly refused and went on her way."

"And how much did she cash out before she... 'went on her way'?"

The fuck is it to you? "I'd need to pull records for that—"

"With a warrant." Bambi cuts me off. "Which you'll need probable cause for, Detective. And it's becoming abundantly clear that you have none."

Patterson turns his focus to her fully now and it's like something switches off in his mind. His smile fades, his gaze hardens, and every word that comes from his mouth is dripping with disdain. "I know all about your 'business,' Mr. Zakrevsky. Business that not even this lap dog bitch of yours can protect you from serving time for. Business that can get her a prison sentence, too."

Bingo. We've found his weak spot.

He *hates* women.

So I am more than happy to let Bambi take care of him on my behalf. I signal to her with a subtle nod.

"We're done here, Detective." She strides into his space, which makes him take several steps back. "Demean me or threaten my client again and you'll be slapped with defamation charges that will make your head spin. As for Miss Clara, we wish her all the best. If she *is* a drug addict, it's easy to see why." The way her eyes scan him from head to toe lands that message loud and clear.

"But you—"

"Will not be insulted and blackmailed by a corrupt cop over baseless accusations and a misplaced hunch. Now, unless you have that warrant, kindly allow us to escort you the fuck off the premises."

I signal for Pavel to lead a few men out with Patterson, who is desperately struggling to think of a comeback, any excuse to stay, *something*. But he comes up empty.

He does stop at the doorway to glare at me. "This isn't over, Zakrevsky. I've got eyes on you."

"I sure hope they're better eyes than the ones you had on Clara."

I grin. Then, because I can't resist the urge, I wink at him.

And that's when he knows. I *know* he knows, because he goes beet red in the face and tries to shove through my men.

But Pavel is a brick wall between us. All Patterson manages to do is get himself firmly escorted outside to his car, with Bambi's reminders to bring warrants next time echoing across the driveway like the law itself kissing him goodbye.

33

CLARA

Their voices are muffled as they approach, but what matters to me is that they're approaching. Will I finally be let out? It feels like an eternity has passed—but, knowing me, it's probably only been ten minutes. Keeping track of time in solitary confinement is not my strong suit.

"… and if he comes back with an actual warrant?"

"We'll burn that bridge when we get to it."

"That's not how—"

"Meaning we'll obliterate him anyways, Dem. There's nothing he can do, short of a SWAT team raiding this place. And should that day come, we'll already have a plan."

"That plan better involve keeping the kid far as fuck away from him."

"And Clara?"

I hold my breath, wanting to hear the answer. *Yes, and what about me?*

But instead of Demyen's deep voice answering, he opens the door to the closet. I'm immediately met with his glare and I flinch.

He looks *furious.*

"The fuck, Bam?" Demyen lunges forward and grabs the zip-tie around my wrists. "The hell did you do this for?"

"You said—"

"I know what I said." He mutters something under his breath about words being open to interpretation and takes out a switchblade from his suit pocket. In the blink of an eye, the tie snaps apart and I'm free to rub my sore wrists. Even though Bambi had been careful, the plastic still bit into my skin. He's quick to cut my ankle tie as well, then he closes the knife before reaching up to undo my gag.

When our eyes meet, he pauses. I would give anything to know what thoughts are flowing through his mind as he stares at my face, his fingers slowly untying the handkerchief knot at the back of my head.

"She wasn't going to shout for Martin." When he pulls the gag away, his hand reaches up to cup my face. "Right?"

All I can do is nod.

I don't begrudge Bambi for her idea. She had a solid point—it's better for Martin to think me a victim than a traitor.

But I have to confess, even if just to myself, there's a warm spark of reassurance in the way Demyen is caring for me right now. He lowers his hand, but only to take mine and help me to my feet.

"Shut the dinner down." He turns to Bambi as we leave the closet. "I want everyone gone in fifteen minutes. Make up whatever excuse you need to."

She nods and quickly leaves to go carry out his orders, leaving us alone, save for the guards still sprinkled through the halls and walkways.

Demyen stares at me for a moment. Then he takes my hand and leads me through the hall. I don't know what to say, so I don't say anything at all, but it's just as well. The heat that spreads from our hands through my body is far too distracting to focus on anything else.

When we reach one of the marble fountains that has a wide bench wrapped around it, he sits me down and then settles onto the cool marble next to me.

"So…" He looks up at the stars. "I met your ex."

"Yeah."

"Interesting guy."

I snort. I can't help it. "You're not going to insult me by being honest."

"Then let me correct myself: he's a fucking asshole." Demyen lowers his gaze to stare at me again. "How did a woman like you end up with garbage like him?"

I'm way too nervous to ask him for clarification. *A woman like me?* "He wasn't always that bad." Which is true. There's no way I would have ever gone on a date, or several, with an *obvious* asshole.

"Was that back when he had hair?"

Now, we both snort with laughter, trying our best to keep our faces straight. Demyen puts on a good front as this Big Bad Bratva Boss with all his men and guns and demanding, commanding presence... but moments like this are what make me wonder just how bad he really is. His dry sense of humor, his soft spot for damsels in distress...

"Do you ever think of going back to him?"

"Absolutely the fuck not." I snap the words before I can remind myself to watch it with this man. But he doesn't yell at me or scold me for having an attitude. He simply nods, so I sigh and tack on a better explanation. "I've thought about it, yeah. It always involves a lot of blood, a few knives, and one of us dead on the floor."

Demyen's brow arches a tick. "You lose fights in your own daydreams?"

"Only sometimes. But either way, it's obvious I can't go back. I never will. I refuse to put Willow through that hell again."

"Where would you go? If you could leave here."

If you could leave here... Like I need another reminder of how I'm basically his prisoner. I shrug and sigh. "Depends on how far I could get. Pay our way to disappear. Maybe Alaska. Willow loves the snow."

His mouth twitches at the mention of Willow. "How would you get there? In this daydream plan of yours."

"I don't know. How much do you want for one of your cars?"

Demyen shoots me a look before he softens and actually, genuinely, chuckles. "Even with your newly padded bank account, my car collection is out of your budget."

I'm about to ask him what *his* plans for Willow are when he surprises me with a heavy sigh.

"Look, Clara." He leans his arms on his thighs and runs a hand through his hair. "Your ex's meddling changes things. A lot of things, actually. But mainly, we need to figure out what to do with you."

"I can't—"

"I'm hiring you as one of my maids." He looks at me. In the moonlight, it's a little hard to read his expression as thoroughly as I want. But what I can see is... promising? I think? "You'll get a uniform and a stack of paperwork to file for taxes—"

"You're hiring me?" I frown. *What's the catch?* "Why?"

"Because the detective is one of many in Las Vegas itching to dig into my operations and find a reason, *any* reason, to get a warrant signed and do a full search just to prove their suspicions. I can't have you here without a justifiable reason."

I think I understand. "So hiring me..."

"Provides all the necessary paperwork to verify that's why you're here. And it will also make it difficult for anyone to remove you, since your employment contract will include room and board."

I try to force my heart to stop slamming against my ribcage. The last thing I need is for him to hear the excitement thrumming through my veins and suddenly change his mind. "Does this... does this mean I can see my daughter?"

He nods.

The fact that he doesn't hesitate makes me feel even more hopeful.

Demyen sits up and turns his body to face me. "I'm going to be honest, and I'll deny it ever happened if you bring it up. But I'm not sure what to do with you. I'm still fucking pissed, and you still fucking owe me."

I suck in a breath. "But?"

He rolls a shoulder in a half-shrug. "But I'm not sure what kind of punishment could ever be worse than sharing a bed with *him*. So, for the time being, you're safe here. You and your kid. Until I figure out what to do with you."

I'll take it. I'll fucking take it. His promise, his security... even the way he's looking at me with a softness I'm not used to seeing on his face.

"Thank you," is all I manage to mutter.

Demyen nods. He looks like he's about to say something more, but he stops in his tracks when he sees Bambi approaching. And just like that, his boss mask slams back into place.

"They've all left," Bambi informs him. "No one asked any questions; no one straggled behind. Staff is cleaning up now."

"Good." He nods once and stands. "Show Clara to one of the guest rooms next to Willow's new room. Tomorrow, have someone grab her the basics, a few maid uniforms, and whatever else you can think of."

Bambi glances at me, her brow stitching together. "Sir?"

"Clara is joining the household staff as a maid. See to it her paperwork is filled and filed."

Realization dawns on Bambi's face. "Done." She nods for me to follow her, so I stand and cast one last quick glance at Demyen for permission to leave.

But he's already walking away.

With a weird squiggly feeling in my stomach, I follow Bambi toward the main courtyard, my heart soaring with the mercy he's showing by allowing me to stay near my sweet baby.

"You can stay here tonight," Bambi informs me.

"Great." I don't stick around to ask follow-up questions.

I tiptoe over to Willow and carefully roll myself into the hammock with her. It's just big enough to hold both of us, and after I tuck a warmer blanket around us, I use my good foot to nudge us into a rocking motion.

I don't want to cry. But as we rock to sleep in each other's arms, as tears sting my eyes, as I catch glimpses of Willow's new toys and the life our captor has given her...

I thank the stars above for guiding us here.

34

DEMYEN

It's almost two in the morning, and I can't fucking sleep.

I thought running a lap on the elliptical would help. Nope. Maybe throwing some weights around until my body burns would do it. Negative.

Neither did taking the coldest shower possible and climbing into bed. That turned out to be a monumental mistake, because all I could think about was how Clara's soft curves feel tucked next to me when she's sleeping... how she tastes when I explore her body... how she sounds when she's awake and losing herself to her passions while I'm impaling her on my—

I drop the barbell onto the hooks above me and sit up. I can't even fucking bench press without tenting my shorts. *Fuck*.

As much as I hate liars, I also hate being honest with myself. Because that requires admitting things, confessing things, and those things usually involve some part of me losing control over the situation.

Like Clara.

I'm supposed to hate her very existence. I'm supposed to have her locked up in some dirty dungeon cell, sobbing and pleading with me for mercy that I have zero plans on giving. I'm supposed to be exacting vengeance on her for what she did to Tolya. Her life for his life.

What am I *not* supposed to be doing?

Protecting her from abusive scumbags like Martin fucking Patterson. Nursing her back to health through a serious fever and possible infection. Showing her off like my prized possession. Growing attached to her offspring.

In other words… literally everything I've been doing.

I don't understand it. She's not the first damsel in distress I've ever come across. Bambi's a testament to that—I stumbled upon her when she tried to shop for johns in my establishment and I nearly had her arrested. But she was so young and so terrified. I felt more compelled to help her than hurt her. I paid for her apartment, her education, supported her through her bar exam, and then hired her as my jack-of-all-trades.

But I never obsessed over her. Not that she isn't a walking sculpture who could have any man or woman she chose—I just never felt the compulsion. I respected her too much. Still do.

So why the ever-living *fuck* is Clara so deeply embedded under my skin?

My deep thoughts are interrupted by a water bottle flying at my head. I catch it and glare up at Pavel, who sports a sheepish grin.

"Sorry, dude. Thought you were paying attention."

I should be, that's for damn sure. But instead of admitting it, I just grunt. "Yeah, well." I chug down the icy water and drop the bottle to the floor with a plastic *crunch.*

Pavel sits down on a bench next to me and sighs. "Want the updates?"

"Shoot."

"We located the guy from the bar. He has officially retracted his complaint filed against you with LVPD and admitted to his own crimes. They're taking him in for arraignment once he's discharged from the hospital."

I smirk. "What happened to him?"

Pavel casually shrugs, but the mischievous smile tugs at his mouth. "He tripped and fell through a window."

"How many times did he fall through that window?"

"Oh, there were a lot of windows. Terrible stroke of luck. Or *strokes,* rather. But the police are betting each window has a name attached to one of his victims, if you know what I mean."

I raise a brow. "Victims?"

Pavel nods. "Serial rapist. We only figured it out because he kept getting the names wrong when we questioned him. Seemed interesting, so I had one of our guys hack in and run those same names through the system. Rapes and assaults, all unsolved."

"I hope you tied him up with a big red bow for LVPD."

He snaps his fingers in exaggerated disappointment. "Dammit, I went with blue."

We share a chuckle. Pavel makes a perfect second-in-command for me not only because he gets every job done three times over, but also because he's got a wry sense of humor that comes in handy when I'd least expect it. For instance, when I'm about to go and do something stupid, like wake up Clara Everett and carry her into my bed.

Fuck. She's back. *Dammit.*

"And while our guy was in, I had him dig up dirt on that cop. Patterson."

That catches my attention. "Anything good?"

Pavel's eyebrows nearly reach his hairline. "Dude definitely has friends in high places; otherwise, he would have been fired years ago. Every case he's ever caught has a perfect arrest record, but over half of them have formal complaints filed against him."

"Evidence tampering?"

"That. And assault. Mostly assault. Victims claiming he beat them into confession, threw them around a bit before slapping the cuffs on, stuff like that. One was a woman who said he forced her to suck him off in exchange for leniency and then he arrested her anyway. But he didn't take her to the precinct until after he was done with her."

Bile creeps up my throat. "And he's *still* on the force?"

"A police detective's word against a strung-out prostitute from the wrong side of the Strip?" Pavel looks as disgusted as I feel. "You know how this goes, man. Who would believe her?"

Something strikes a solid chord in my chest. It's familiar and yet I can't quite put my finger on it.

Who would believe me?

Did Clara say that? Or did I imagine it? Either way, it's something that's been bothering me for a while now—how could anyone mistreat a woman like that, let alone her kid, and get away with it?

I give myself a little shake and force myself to focus back on Pavel's investigation. "So the big question is, who's paying him off? Who's pulling the strings? Is there a rival organization we need to watch out for?"

Pavel scrunches his nose. "It's unclear right now as to why he's doing what he's doing. Or how he keeps doing it. We couldn't find any connections to another Bratva or mafia or motorcycle club or even the damn IRA, and believe me, we looked everywhere."

I do believe him. He never cuts corners and he's not about to start now. Not when everything and everyone we've been hunting for over a decade is finally in our hands.

Which is the other thing that bothers me enough to keep me awake at night. Everything is finally falling into place, but I'm left with more questions and unsolved riddles than actual answers and closure.

At this rate, I'll get closure when I'm dead.

"Detective Everett." I pick up the water bottle and turn it in my hand, half-tempted to throw it across the room just to watch something explode. "He's been quiet lately. Too fucking quiet. Should we be worried?"

Pavel's scrunched face instantly shifts. I know that look. It's the set jaw, tongue-over-teeth that he always does right when someone says something to piss him off. And I know I'm not the one pissing him off right now, so I lean forward.

"Pav?"

"There's no record of him ever visiting Clara in the hospital."

I shrug. "So?"

"Ever." He focuses his gaze on me. "And I mean, *ever.*"

I still. The first thing that comes to my mind isn't of Clara the other day, sick as a dog and struggling to maintain her sanity. It isn't of her injured ankle, or the look of pure terror in her eyes when Bambi told us Martin was here.

It's the image of a little girl, trembling with fear in the witness stand. Quiet, sniffling, covered in cuts and bruises.

Everyone automatically assumed those injuries were from my brother when he tried to kidnap her and murdered the other cop who came to rescue her. No one could prove any motive for the kidnapping, so those charges were dropped. But it didn't stop people from coming to their own conclusions about Tolya—or Clara.

"He was there when they took her to the hospital. After they found her."

Pavel slowly shakes his head. "He filed a report. But there's no record of him signing in and we can't find anyone who remembers seeing him visit her."

I frown. Something sick and heavy forms inside my gut. "What about when she had a baby?"

Again, Pavel shakes his head.

None of this makes sense. Greg Everett was a loving father who couldn't be more relieved to have his only child, his little girl, found safe and sound inside that warehouse. He said so right there in court; I've reviewed the transcripts so often I've practically memorized every word. He and his wife thanked the whole of Las Vegas for their love and support—according to him, anyway. His wife never spoke a word during those press conferences.

Come to think of it, Clara hasn't mentioned her mother once. "What about Mrs. Everett?"

"Those who were there do remember seeing Clara's mother sit by her side after they found her. But they also remember she was a very quiet woman. Didn't say much to anyone, except to get water or ask for the bathroom."

"And now?"

"Dead. A few years after the trial. Suicide."

Something very close to empathy washes over me. *Too* close. I rub a hand over my jaw as I try to process all this information—and as I try to ignore the nagging feeling that we've only scratched the surface.

This was all supposed to be easy.

It's been anything but that.

Pavel sighs and runs a frustrated hand through his hair. "Look, I'm nowhere near being a prime example of father material. God help the poor bastard who comes from me. But I gotta say… if *my* kid was lying in some hospital bed? Cold, flu, broken arm, beat all to shit, I don't care—I'd be there. No matter how old they are." He tilts his head to one side and gives me a knowing smirk. "And you can't tell me you wouldn't set up camp in that little girl's room, either."

I should punch him right in that smug smile, just to make me feel better. But damn it all, he's right. I'm the exact opposite of Father of the Year—hell, I'm not even in "Fun Uncle" range

—but the moment I imagine Willow wearing a black eye and cradling a broken arm, I feel myself simultaneously wanting to run to her side and go to war.

So what the fuck is wrong with Everett?

"Get eyes on Greg Everett. Twenty-four-seven, every fucking day until we figure this shit out or he falls through a window himself." I stand and stretch the tension out of my shoulders. Pavel stands with me, already tapping the orders in a group text to the Bratva's rank-and-file. "I want to know when he so much as sneezes in our direction. Send a plant into LVPD and make sure his relationship with Martin is strictly professional. I'm not going to lose everything just because we read lips wrong."

Pavel nods. "Done."

Oh, how I fucking wish it was.

35

DEMYEN

I'm only halfway down the hall from the gym when Bambi turns a corner and almost runs into me. She jumps, then quickly straightens and gives me a respectful nod.

"Does no one sleep in this place?" I growl.

"I heard you were up," she replies, smoothing a hand over her tunic. "Reports came in from the schools and I thought you'd want to know right away."

The fact that reports only *just* came in tells me that, as usual, Bambi went above and beyond to get what I need. When she hunts down records, she hunts down people as much as paperwork, until even the janitor has given a witness testimony.

Pavel does, too, but his methods are a bit... messier. More windows get broken. Usually by someone's face.

I sigh and nod. "You thought correctly. But before you tell me—do I need a drink for this?"

Bambi's expression darkens. "We'll both need a drink."

That's how we end up in the now-empty party courtyard, perched on stools at the abandoned bar with an open bottle of liquor for each of us and only the crescent moon lighting the glasses enough to see how much we pour.

I'm tempted to chug straight from the bottle. It's a smuggled import from Russia, one of my father's personal favorites. Strong as fuck. With any luck, I'll be facedown at the edge of the pool and blissfully incoherent to the shitty mess around me in about three solid chugs.

Unfortunately, that stupid thing called "responsibility" whispers in the back of my brain to pace myself while Bambi turns on her tablet and dives into her report.

"I had a few of my colleagues interview retired teachers, school nurses, whoever we could track down within the city limits." She scrolls through her notes app and I catch glimpses of photos and personnel files that I'm pretty sure she is not legally supposed to have possession of. "It took some squeezing, but I was able to get files unsealed long enough for a quick peek."

"And?"

Bambi purses her lips. It's too dark to see her clearly, but I can see enough between the moonlight and her tablet to know she's deeply troubled.

"Can you promise me something?" she suddenly asks.

I sit up. She'll come to me for supplies, necessities, clarification, the essentials... but it's rare that she'll ask me for a personal favor. "Shoot."

"Exactly that." Her eyes meet mine, even in the dark. "*Shoot.* When you find Greg Everett, when you bring him in to clean up this whole mess… shoot that motherfucker right between the eyes."

I was already planning on it, but I bite anyway. "Tell me."

"They knew." She pours herself a shot to the brim and tosses it back. "Her teachers, the school nurse… they all knew. Several tried to file a report, but they were dismissed because the case files went straight to LVPD at the same time Child Protective Services received them. Her fourth grade teacher nearly lost her job because Everett tried swinging the accusations back against her, but there was no evidence."

I don't want to ask. The vodka is already starting to churn in my stomach. "How far back does it go?"

Bambi opens her mouth to tell me. But she doesn't. She can't. Tears brim on her lashes. It's the first time I've ever seen her come close to crying since the day I met her.

Instead, she taps the screen of her tablet and slides it across the counter to me.

I shouldn't have looked while downing another shot. The liquor almost goes up my nose; I'm that shocked at what I see.

They're the standard pictures the Emergency Room takes for CPS whenever there's a suspicious case in their midst. Pictures of fingerprint-shaped bruises, swollen eyes, cut lips, patches where hair was torn at the scalp. Broken skin in stripes across her back, like someone lashed her with a leather belt. In one photo, the clear imprint of a belt buckle can be seen on her ribs.

What makes me want to vomit and eviscerate Greg Everett at the exact same time is the oldest photo of the bunch.

Clara can't be more than three years old.

She's not looking at the camera, but it's easy to see the tears streaking her tiny face. Picture after picture, she grows older. The tears lessen. Her face, what can be discerned, becomes more and more haunted.

By the time I flip to the pictures taken the night she was found at the warehouse, she's a shell of a person.

"How." I force myself to grind out the words through my fury and nausea. "How the *fuck* did he get away with this?"

"You've seen him." Bambi does what I've been aching to do and pulls a swig straight from her bottle. "He's a charmer. Handsome, charismatic. A *hero*."

I hate so fucking much that she's right. I don't make a habit to play cards with Everett, but he's on the news often enough regarding one case or another—and I remember him well from Tolya's trial. He oozes charm and congeniality; as far as the local news is concerned, he's a badged crusader who loves his city and cares for his people. The high school quarterback who grew up to become a beloved lawman with a beautiful wife and little girl. I can just imagine the way he'd act horrified at the news that someone laid their hands on his sweet angel, and then probably even more horrified that anyone would ever consider *him* to be a suspect.

My hunch is right when Bambi takes her tablet back and reviews the rest of the files for me.

"No one wanted to believe Everett was beating his own daughter," she explains. "He responded to so many domestic calls, carried children out of dangerous situations, advocated for protective orders… Did you know he even gave a talk at a national convention for domestic abuse survivors? Telling them how to 'notice the signs' that their partner could be dangerous. Gave out hotlines to call if they're in need. And that's not even including the Career Days he attended at Clara's schools to teach kids about personal safety."

There's a special place in hell for people like Greg Everett.

I intend to escort him there myself.

I take my own swig from the bottle now. I'm going to need to knock myself out just to sleep through the horrible images now seared in my brain. "How the fuck did he get mixed up with Martin Patterson?"

At this, Bambi shrugs. She turns her tablet off and sets it aside to nurse the tequila. From the way she was gripping that thing, I'd guess she was close to breaking it in half and throwing the pieces into the pool.

Which would have been fine by me. I'll happily buy her a new one—one that's devoid of those sickening photos.

"Just going off the staff reports and intel," Bambi clarifies, holding a finger up, "I'm guessing he threw Clara out of the frying pan and into the fire. Made sure she went with someone who would keep her under control once she was out from under his own thumb."

Someone like me.

I hate that thought even more. To be compared to either of those assholes is a whole new version of disgusting. But "control" is exactly what I'm doing to Clara, even if my motives are actually valid.

"This doesn't change anything." The burn in my throat makes my voice gravelly.

I actually sound like I mean it. Because I have to. This can't change anything.

"Doesn't it, though?"

I look at Bambi in surprise. And, to more of my surprise, she stares right back at me with the kind of fierceness that would usually get her reprimanded.

I'll chalk it up to the alcohol.

Not the feeling in my gut that I deserve it.

"No. It doesn't." I set the bottle down hard on the counter. "Clara fucking lied on the stand. She stole Tolya's life. She has to pay for what she did."

"Really?" Bambi flicks the screen back on and slides the tablet under my nose once more. "As if *that*—" She points at the pictures. "—wasn't payment enough?"

I shove the tablet away before I'm the one hurling it into the pool. "Nothing changes."

"*She* did." I look at Bambi again. She leans toward me. "She grew up, Demyen. She was a little girl on that stand. Scared, alone, with no one who would believe her even if she did tell the truth. She was a little girl, and then she grew up."

"Still—"

"You were a kid, too."

That stops me.

"You were a teenager, whatever, but you were still a kid. And you were just as scared as she was. Scared of losing your brother, and scared of losing your last line of defense against a world you never wanted to be a part of in the first place."

It's the liquor talking. I tell myself that so her words don't land as hard as they feel.

"The difference between you and her? She grew up. She left that courtroom and she grew up. Did you?"

36

DEMYEN

I don't know what time it is. I don't even know if the moon is still up. All I know is that the bottle of vodka is empty and the sound of it shattering against the adobe column makes me feel a little better.

Sort of.

Bambi left a while ago. I've been nursing my pride with my father's favorite vodka alone in the darkened outdoor bar, debating on whether I should jump in the pool or just throw up in the cacti and call it a night.

Instead, I slide off the barstool and stumble down the pathway toward the main courtyard. It takes some effort— my vision is blurry as fuck—but I manage to navigate my way to my room.

Except… it's not my room, I realize when I walk in.

I trip over a stuffed hippo in a tutu and almost immediately fall on top of a dresser low enough to damage my chances of ever having my own children—which I narrowly avoid by grabbing for the overhanging net holding even more stuffed animals, all of which promptly fall on top of me.

Fucking hell. Why am I wasting capable men guarding this place? The kid's got it booby-trapped.

By the time I manage to drop onto the beanbag chair next to the hammock, I'm sobering up just from the adrenaline of almost dying. I have to check my feet just to make sure those landmines they call "building blocks" aren't deeply embedded into my soles.

I'm not sure if I want to teach Willow how to clean up her room, or have her teach my men how to string up tripwire.

I settle into the fluffy beanbag chair and watch the way Willow nestles into Clara's arms between soft little snores. Mother and daughter bear such a strong resemblance to each other. I'm struck by how much Willow reminds me of the little girl in the photos on Bambi's tablet.

So much that I'm almost terrified the same injuries are on her skin, too.

What's left of my sober brain reminds me that Willow is safe and sound. Uninjured, no bruises, and far away from the monster who dared to threaten her.

Thanks to you.

I bat that thought away. I'm not the good guy. I'm nowhere remotely close to being anyone's hero.

Still… the more I watch them sleep, the more I feel a sense of pride welling up in my chest.

Yes. Pride. Only pride. Nothing else.

I'm no one's hero, but I can be their protector. I can keep them safe from the sick bastards who thought they'd get away with beating helpless women and children because no one wanted to admit what was really going on.

I try to stand back up, but that's a bigger challenge than I anticipated. So instead, I scoot the beanbag closer to the hammock until Clara's face is inches away from mine.

It's the vodka in my veins that makes me tuck a strand of hair from her brow, that makes my fingers linger in her silky waves. It's the liquor blurring my focus that makes me lean in and press a warm kiss to her full lips.

And it's nothing but my drunken imagination that makes me feel like she's kissing me back.

37

CLARA

I haven't seen Demyen for a few days, but that's just as well. I'm too busy holding up my end of the bargain as his newest maid to play his confusing mind games.

I also don't have the courage to ask him what he was doing in Willow's room the morning after that dinner party. Both Willow and I woke up with the first few rays of dawn and, to our surprise, Demyen was right there. Fast asleep on an overstuffed, outrageously pink beanbag chair, face smoothed clear of all its usual pent-up rage.

Willow had to clamp a hand over her mouth just so her giggles wouldn't wake him. We took extra care to tiptoe over him, grab some clothes, and left to change in my new room.

Ever since then, I've been doing my damned best to forget how good it felt to have him watching over us.

Gloria, the head housekeeper, was the one who found me eating cereal in the kitchen and set a stack of clean, folded uniforms on the table next to my bowl. "The workday starts at seven," was all she said before she quickly turned on her heel and left the room.

She's a stern but kind woman, and always ready to help me figure out where everything is. One thing she didn't have to teach me was *how* to do all the cleaning—I've been scrubbing Martin's mud off the floors for years. And even before him, my father made me do all the household chores after Mama died.

The only thing Gloria has needed to teach me is how to not flinch over every little mistake.

I got the ratio of cleaning solution to water wrong and it started rubbing off the paint in one of the sunrooms. I panicked so hard, I started shaking and couldn't breathe.

"*¡Dios mio!*" Gloria muttered when she found me kneeling and bawling over the sudsy bucket. "Pull yourself together, *mija.*"

"B-but Dem—I mean, Mr. Zakrevsky—"

"Won't know and won't care." Gloria pried the sponge from my clenched fingers and tossed it into the bucket. "Breathe. In through your nose... Good, *sí...* Now, out through your mouth. And now, we start again."

"But the wall—"

"Will be fixed by Maintenance. Come." She pulled me to my feet without waiting for me to respond and wiped away the tears I didn't even know had fallen. "Look at me, *mija.*"

I did as she said. She's older, probably old enough to have grandchildren, and despite her brusque way of going about her business, she exudes a warmth I've been missing since Mama.

"Wherever you were? You are not there now."

I sniffed. At first, I didn't know what she meant. She must have seen the confusion in my eyes, because she gently took my chin in her grasp and gave me a soft little shake.

"Mistakes happen. And anyone who can't forgive them doesn't deserve your time or your effort. Especially you, *mija*. You are far too lovely and far too strong to waste time on men who don't respect you."

"*'Strong'?*" I snorted. "Hardly."

Gloria clicked her tongue at me and shook her head. "Look at where you are. And look at where you've been. No, Mr. Zakrevsky did not tell me anything. He doesn't have to. It's all over your face, in your eyes, in that forced smile of yours. You have seen hell." She grabbed my chin again, gently, just to make sure I was still looking her in the eyes. "But you are not there anymore."

That was the only time we ever discussed my past. And, if I'm being honest with myself, it was a moment that made me reconsider my situation and zone out through most of my chores for the rest of the day.

She was right: I'm not in hell anymore. As much as Demyen lords himself over me, it's completely different from Martin. With Martin, the slightest mistake could set him off. I never knew when, either. One day, he'd laugh off a glass of spilled milk, but a week later, he'd backhand me for being so clumsy and careless with his food.

Gloria forced me to pull out of those shadows and realize I keep waiting for Martin to appear and throw me against the wall. But he's *not* here. He doesn't live here, he doesn't have

access to me or my personal space, and, more importantly—
he doesn't have access to Willow.

If there's one thing that constantly reminds me of how much
better life finally is, it's my sweet little girl. She's flourishing
here. I've always loved her smile, but I never realized how
much her father dimmed her joy until we started living here.
I never knew how brightly she could grin and laugh and
squeal with joy over the simplest things, like a butterfly
landing on a cactus blossom, or a few extra sprinkles on
Bambi's signature ice cream sundae.

Finally, last night, I laid in bed and cried. It felt like a "finally"
because some sort of deeply-buried pressure was released.
Emotions I never allowed myself to feel came to the surface
and I was finally, finally, *finally* able to let them out.

As much as I wondered where Demyen was, I needed the
time and space apart. I needed the distance from all men, any
men, and I think even Bambi and Gloria understood that.
The usual guards were still around but watching from a
broader distance. Groundskeepers and maintenance men
only came around after I left the room.

For the first time in my life, I'm surrounded only by women.
And somehow, they *know*. They know and they understand. I
am never pressured, never criticized, never ridiculed. I am
respected as Willow's mother and encouraged as a new
employee.

Willow is my little shadow, following me around while I try
to get work done. It's a challenge to do a thorough job when
my curious little one is constantly asking questions or trying
to make me watch her try a new trick—usually involving
jumping on the bed I just made—but the fact that she's even

allowed to be near me is a gift I don't take for granted. She's allowed to play by my side while I work, free to be herself without Martin glaring at her or scolding her for being a nuisance.

That's the part that really tugs at my heartstrings in ways I'm terrified to allow: not once has Demyen ever called Willow a nuisance or acted like he doesn't want her around. In fact, I'm strongly suspicious that he's been avoiding me but sneaking in time with Willow, because every day for a week —the same week I haven't caught a single glimpse of him— she's found me in whatever room I'm cleaning, squealing excitedly over a new toy he gave her.

They're *good* toys, too. The kind that never in a million years would I be able to afford "just because," and Martin sure as hell would never bother to remotely consider.

The consideration goes beyond just toys and baubles. The new doll he gave Willow the first day after the dinner party was designed to look just like her, paired with matching sets of clothes for her so she could coordinate outfits.

On the second day, he gave her a set of fairytale books that she was then instructed to practice reading with me.

Now, it's the end of the week and Willow is the proud owner of a butterfly growing kit to nurture her interest in biology, a small piano to explore music, a kids-level pottery wheel "for functional artistic expression," and a sparkly pink tablet.

The tablet in particular gave me panic. The internet is a terrifying place for a parent to send their child, especially one as young as Willow, and at first, I felt the urge to march into Demyen's office and demand to know what the actual hell he was thinking.

But when Willow handed it over so I could at least activate the parental controls, I froze.

They were already on.

Demyen had her tablet locked tighter than Fort Knox, even though she unwrapped it straight from the box right in front of me. Screen time limits are set at half-hour intervals, educational apps downloaded and activated (and paid for), and the lock screen is a collage of selfies Willow took with me... and Demyen.

I think that's what made me finally cry. What made me sob myself to sleep, unleashing all the emotions I couldn't begin to name if I even had the energy to try.

Whatever is going on between Demyen and me, it's complicated and messy and I don't know where it's headed. I can't wrap my head around how he feels about me or thinks of me, and I sure as shit can't figure out my own thoughts or feelings about him.

It's the selfie of Willow and Demyen making silly faces for the camera that has me wishing I could undo the past.

It's the selfie of them giggling together, her face glowing with joy and his usual mask shattered apart by the unadulterated grin that actually flows into his eyes.

And it's the selfie I know he didn't plan to take, the one that caught him completely by surprise when Willow must have suddenly turned and kissed his cheek right as she hit the button.

That's the realest smile of all of them.

I'm used to being scared. I'm used to being terrified.

I'm *not* used to being safe.

Or loved.

And I'm even more terrified that neither is Willow.

38

CLARA

One thing I'm very grateful for: I'm not expected to clean the entire place in one day.

It would be literally impossible—and something I completely expect Demyen to suddenly pop out of nowhere and demand I start doing immediately.

For all I know, that might have been his plan if it weren't for Gloria's strict cleaning schedule. She has the whole compound broken down into monthly, weekly, and daily schedules, with tasks delegated to the cleaning staff by name and the requirement that we only do what we are assigned.

No trading, no laziness, full accountability.

The image of Gloria shooing Demyen away from her carefully-guarded calendar like some naughty child makes me snort with laughter as I carry the bucket of cleaning supplies into the study. Willow glances at me curiously, but doesn't ask what's so funny because she's trying to balance her new storybook in one arm while the other carries her newest doll.

It felt appropriate to encourage her to read while I clean the study. There's plenty of comfortable chairs she can curl up in —and hopefully, also nap in—until I'm done.

And given how large the library part of this room is, it's going to take the whole day.

Gloria had a ladder sent in ahead of me. I stare up at it as I swallow back my fear of heights. It's a job, it's keeping me busy, and it's ensuring our safety as well as housing. I can stomach a measly little climb so my baby gets to have good food in her stomach.

"Whoa!" Willow gasps when we settle into the study. Her eyes are wide as she scans the tall bookcases, taking in the dozens of books stored on the shelves. "Demyen loves stories."

I don't have the heart to tell her that half of these books are on law and real estate. "He sure does."

"Oh! Guess what?" She carefully nestles her doll—Maple, she decided yesterday after asking me to list every tree name I could think of—into the corner of an overstuffed reading chair and straightens out the tiny skirt. "Demyen says if we're really good, he'll take us to Disney World!"

If we're really good. Right. I know his game. And the protective maternal side in me wants to slap his face for playing it with my little girl.

"That sounds fun, baby."

I sigh as I stare up at the top shelf of the first bookcase. It makes sense to dust first, scrub second, but that means I have to climb all the way to the top of the ladder just to reach with the feather duster.

And the part of me that insists on being super thorough in everything I do is whispering the fact that I really should take all the books off the shelf to wipe it down with furniture polish.

Dammit.

With a sigh, I start the journey upward.

The first trip up isn't as bad as I expected. The ladder is new, stable, sturdy, and doesn't creak or groan when I pile books on the top rung so I can spray the polish and do a quick wipe-down. My left hand is white-knuckling the ladder while my right hand sweeps the microfiber cloth around in circles, but I do it as quickly as possible so I can climb down as soon as possible.

"Mommy, I don't know which story this one is."

I literally cannot look and see which one she's talking about, even though I know that's what she wants me to do. "It's okay, baby. We're still working on words. What do the pictures look like? Tell me the story from those."

I hear her hum in concentration and I hide the sigh of relief. *Whatever keeps her busy.*

"She's pretty. But she looks sad. And dirty. Really, really dirty."

"What is she doing in that picture?" I move the next set of books onto the top rung, preparing to tackle the second half of that shelf.

"It looks like she's cleaning the fireplace."

I'm pretty sure I know which story she's opened to. "Are there mice? And birds?"

"Yeah!" Willow giggles. "And they're helping her clean!"

Willow sometimes helps me clean. Sometimes. Her attempts usually cause more mess, but Gloria never says anything and I don't ever want to discourage Willow from volunteering to pitch in. Lord knows she could stand to apply that energy to her own room.

"Her family looks mean." I hear the frown in her little voice. Without looking, I know she's pouting. "They're making her do all the work."

Been there, done that.

I'm finally able to move to the next shelf down, which means the next ten minutes will be spent a foot closer to the ground. *Thank God.*

"Ooooh! A fairy! She's really pretty, Mommy. And she made a new dress!" Willow grins and points at the page. I spare a glance this time, now that I'm not clinging for dear life. "Look! It's white and sparkly, just like that one you wore!"

I pause. It is, actually. "Well, look at that. You're right!"

"Where's she going, Mommy?"

I sigh with a smile and start pulling books from the shelf. "Oh, you know. Girl just needs a night off. Away from all the chores, all the screaming. She just wants to go somewhere where nobody knows her so she can wander around and get lost in all the lights and magic."

For a moment, I'm not sure if I'm describing Cinderella's experience or my own. Because that's exactly what I wanted the night I put on a new sparkly dress and wandered into The Meridian.

Willow gasps. If I didn't have fifty pounds of leatherbound legalese balanced in one arm, I'd whip around to see if she's okay. "What?"

"She met the prince!"

Again, I pause. And then I almost laugh at myself for the thought that follows.

So did I.

Nope. Not even going to begin to go there. I didn't meet The Prince or *any* prince or nobility—I met The Devil in an expensive suit and promptly spilled champagne all over him.

And instead of Happily Ever After, I got... whatever this is.

You got your back blown out. Your toes curled. And your vagina permanently ruined for any other man.

That's *what you got.*

I give myself a little shake to clear my head before the aching heat has time to build deep in my core. I've never been one to actually want sex—and God knows I've never experienced "lovemaking"—so the fact that I'm physically craving Demyen's touch is weird to me.

Weird, and yet... not entirely unpleasant.

I just wish it wouldn't pop up at the worst possible times. Like right now, when I'm on top of a ladder trying to clean and pay attention to my daughter at the same time.

"Mommy? Moooommyyyyy..."

"Huh?" I must have zoned out there for a second. "Sorry, sweetie. What's up?"

"Do you need any help?"

Oh, boy. I want to be honest and say that yes, I do, because help really would be great in balancing these heavy books. But just one of these is almost as big as she is, so the correct answer is, "Thanks baby, but I'm good."

Willow scrunches her little face at me. "Are you sure?"

I flash her a genuine smile. She really is a sweetheart. "I'm sure. Thank you, though."

I return to pulling the books off the shelf, stacking them on the next rung down as well because they're so thick, they won't all fit on just one.

One of the heavy books starts moving in the corner of my eye. When I look to see if it's falling, I realize it's Willow trying to "help" by nudging it closer and closer to the edge.

"Willow! No!"

The book tumbles from the rung, right on top of her head.

But instead of striking her, it lands on the floor—because a man's arm shoots out of nowhere and yanks her out of the way.

She trips over her own foot and stumbles into an end table, knocking a vase to the ground instead. The ceramic shatters, water spills, and Willow starts crying.

I barely have a second to register that I, too, am falling off the ladder before I'm wrapped up in very familiar, strong arms. And breathing in his all-too-familiar scent.

Demyen's eyes meet mine and, again, I see something new in them that isn't anger or irritation or hatred. He actually looks... concerned?

Not possible. Maybe that book fell on *my* head.

He sets me on my feet and quickly turns to Willow. She's trembling, sobbing, and cowering behind the toppled end table. Shards of ceramic float among the spilled water and broken flower stems, staining the expensive wood floor.

Oh, God. No. No, no, no, no, no.

I'm ready to launch myself in front of Willow to take his anger, but before I can, Demyen steps over the broken vase and crouches in front of her.

"Are you okay?" he gently asks.

Willow doesn't want to look at him. She's so scared. But he sees that, and ever-so-lightly tucks a finger under her chin to make her meet his gaze.

Demyen offers her a warm smile. "Hey, *malysh*, it's okay. Are you hurt?"

She shakes her head. And hiccups.

"That's good. You know you can tell me if you're hurt, right?"

She pauses. Then nods. Her teary eyes land on the shards and well up again. "I-I'm s-sorry...!" She starts sobbing again, balling her fists in front of her face.

But instead of yelling at her, or hitting her, or calling her names and scolding her for being so careless, Demyen shocks both of us by gently easing her fists down and pulling her into a hug.

"Shhh. It's okay." He rubs her back until her sobs turn into hiccups and then soft little sighs. When she's calmed, he eases her away just enough to meet her gaze again and cups the side of her face in his hand. "Things can be replaced. You can't. Please be careful next time, okay? And listen to your mom. She's only keeping you safe."

Willow nods and a small, wobbly smile tugs at her lips. "Okay."

Demyen smiles and gives her a wink. "We good?"

"Yeah."

He holds his fist up and she meets it with her own. They ease into a secret handshake that, apparently, they've spent enough time together to create, and Willow's smile widens.

When Demyen rises to his feet and turns to me, I'm ready. I'm grateful for his kindness and warmth to Willow, and my God am I floored, but I'm also very aware he has a limited patience.

One of us is going to pay for the incident, and now, I know for sure it's not her—thank God.

"Demyen, I'm so sorry—"

He stops me with an arched brow. "For what?"

He follows my glance to the broken vase, the mess of damaged plants and dirty water, and his slight frown deepens. But then he looks back up at me, and it's not an *I'm-going-to-hit-you* frown. It's more…

"Relax. It's just a vase." His eyes give me a quick once-over and I suddenly feel very naked. And very achy between the legs. "But do be more careful. Maybe actually watch your child while you work."

And with that, he walks away.

39

DEMYEN

There's something seriously fucking wrong with me.

I should see a therapist, but I won't. I handle my own shit. Some overeducated moron in an expensive office can't even scratch the surface of the bullshit I deal with on a regular basis.

At least, that's what I chant to myself as I watch the live camera feed coming from inside Clara's bedroom while she's sleeping. I'm at the casino, pretending I have an important text that just came through—so important that it's worth interrupting a game of poker in the High Rollers Lounge I'm intent on winning.

I'm just not as interested in reminding these idiots that the house always wins as I am in trying to decipher what Clara's dreaming about.

She mutters something. I'm a terrible lip reader and the sound is muted because, again, this is supposedly a text from one of my men. Texts from the Bratva don't sound like the soft moans and mutters of a beautiful woman asleep in her bed.

She should be asleep in *my* bed. Why did I move her again?

The camera feed leading to Willow's room reminds me why. Because I'm not an asshole who keeps an innocent child away from her mother.

I'm an asshole. Just not *that* kind of asshole.

"Shit, Zakrevsky. Did they send you a novel, or what?"

Shit. I forgot where I am. I was too focused on making sure the windows to Willow's room were securely shut and the guards actually paying attention outside her doors.

"Racetrack figures dropped. Got distracted." I force myself to shove the phone back in my pocket and return to the game. I don't even know if my hand is any good compared to the others, but I'm the master of bluffing. I casually shove my large stack of chips to the center of the table. "All in."

The other men chuckle. But when they see what cards I'm holding, the laughter stops.

Like I said, the house always wins.

I get maybe four hours of sleep before I'm up for the day. I used to get in a solid eight, but ever since a certain someone moved into my home, four of those hours are now spent counting the reasons why I can't just drag her into my bedroom and fuck her brains out until my dick is raw.

One: she sent my brother to prison.

Two: she *lied* to send my brother to prison.

Three: I have more self-control than that.

Four: I need to prove I have more self-control than that.

Five: My dick likes her a little too much. It doesn't care about the pain she's wrought, and that's a problem.

Six: She has a kid. Don't wanna scar the kid.

Seven: The thought of her carrying *my* kid should not make me as hard as it does.

I count those reasons like normal people count sheep jumping a fence to fall asleep. Except, instead of drifting off mid-flock, I find myself believing each one less and less.

Especially that last one.

Fuck.

I'm on my third cup of coffee when I realize what time it is—and I don't even have to glance at the clock to know. It's the camera feeds on my laptop, showing Clara and Willow's sudden absence from their usual spots, that informs me it's probably close to lunchtime. Noon-ish, give or take.

And I've ticked off literally nothing on my To Do list.

Giving them distance was supposed to make this all easier. I pried myself away from Clara after realizing just how much my presence might actually be making things worse for her and for her kid.

I've said it before and I'll say it again: I'm not a good guy, but I'm not a fucking monster. And I'll be damned if I ever remotely resemble either of the sick bastards haunting Clara's past.

But it's impossible to stay away from Willow. The kid's got a magnet embedded somewhere in that toothy grin of hers.

Either that or fucking witchcraft. It's the only logical explanation as to how and why I, Demyen Zakrevsky, *pakhan* of the powerful and deadly Zakrevsky Bratva, found myself asking a toy store clerk which clothing sets go with their *Twinsies Forever* dolls. And did they sell the hair accessories, too, or was that online-only?

I questioned my sanity as I walked out of the store, the boxed doll tucked under one arm and a bag of clothes draped over the other.

I wondered why I couldn't just send Bambi to do this shit while I took care of literally anything else.

And yet I immediately forgot every ounce of doubt the moment Willow squealed with joy and hugged me, asked me to help her open the box, and immediately introduced me to her new as-yet-unnamed friend.

The warm feeling I get in my chest whenever that kid smiles at me is just my pride. Pride in knowing *I'm* the one to make her smile like that. Pride in silently reminding her that I'll always protect her from the demons in the dark.

I give myself a little shake to pull out of yet another daydream. My fucking *Lord*, I've never spaced out this easily. My stomach rumbles, reminding me I didn't eat breakfast, so I force myself to close my laptop—which is easier to do when I remember I can still access the feeds on my phone if I need to.

I might have a major fucking problem.

It's hot as hell the second I step out into the open walkways that connect the different buildings into one large villa. At the time, it seemed like a great idea to have this place designed for desert living, keeping everything open as much as possible to allow breezes to naturally flow through the compound. It's energy-efficient, aesthetically pleasing, and continues the sense of ethereal magic that makes The Meridian so memorable to guests and clients alike.

That's what the architect told me. I didn't really fucking care about the why, just that it got done as quickly as possible.

But I should have added outdoor A/C units to the paths, additional costs be damned. It's less than a minute of a walk from my office to the kitchen, and my shirt is already sticking to my chest.

The second I open the door to the outer foyer, I feel the air cool and I pop the top buttons of my shirt. When I yank the refrigerator door open, cold air washes over me. I stand there and sigh gratefully.

It's the giggling that pulls my head out of the ice box.

Clara is standing over Willow at the kitchen island, her eyes glued to me with surprise while the kid grins and gives me a little wave. She's holding a crayon in that same hand, apparently mid-coloring session while her mother works on cleaning the kitchen.

I give Willow a wink as I take a swig from a water bottle. This seems to be enough to appease the girl, and she returns to her coloring book. "And then what happened, Mommy?"

Clara blushes. It's definitely not from the heat; her eyes are wide as she watches me watch her.

"Oh, well… um… Right." She turns back to Willow and simultaneously moves to the microwave, spraying the inside with a cleaning solution. "Well, a promise was a promise. And even though she lived with him, she still needed to kiss him."

Interesting.

Willow darts a glance up at me and giggles again. "But he's a frog!"

Ah. That one.

Clara laughs as she scrubs. "Yes, he is. But she made a promise and a promise can't be broken. So it doesn't matter if he's a frog, or a toad, or a super warty gremlin with horns —if she promised to give him a kiss for helping her, that's what she needed to do."

"Ew." The kid scrunches her face in playful disgust. "I wouldn't kiss a frog."

"I don't blame you," I rumble. Clara nearly smacks her head against the microwave door when she hears me chime in. "Some frogs are venomous. You wouldn't want to kiss those."

Willow's eyes nearly bug out of her head. "Really?"

I nod and pull out a tub of cookie dough ice cream. "Really. They live deep in the rainforest, and they wear bright colors so you know not to touch them."

"That is *so* cool!"

"It's usually the prettiest frogs who'll do the most damage," Clara murmurs.

I narrow my eyes at her. She notices. Her guard was already up, but now, that wall is sky-high. She's instantly finding nonexistent grime to wipe up on the kitchen island.

I recognize that maneuver for what it is: she's planting herself squarely between her daughter and the big, bad, venomous frog currently digging through the fridge for some goddamned chocolate syrup.

I saunter over to the island and set my armful of junk food down. Willow eyes the tub of ice cream, darting her hungry stare between it and her mother. I don't bother looking at Clara—I feel her stiffen at my close proximity to her.

And, as luck would have it, the bowls and spoons are inside the drawer right in front of where she's standing.

"So, what happened next?" I ask coolly.

"Yeah, Mommy! Tell us!"

Clara continues wiping at the same spot on the counter while she tries to gather her composure. "Well, one day…"

I stop paying attention to the story and crouch down to get into the cupboard in front of her legs. Her beautiful, smooth, silky legs are bare from ankle to mid-thigh thanks to the housekeeping uniform she's wearing.

If it weren't for the kid, I'd make her wear a French maid's costume instead, underwear not included. But I have to settle for the fact that I'm at least able to wrap my hand around her bare thigh as I dig around for the bowls.

I find them almost immediately.

But I also find myself unable to pry my fingers from her skin.

My hand strokes a slow, languid path from the side of her knee to just below the juncture of her thighs and right when I'm about to tease my fingertips over that sweet center—

Clara snaps her legs shut. My hand is trapped between her thighs, and not in the way I'd prefer.

I look up at her. She's doing her damned hardest to pretend like nothing's happening. She hides the sudden waver in her voice with a cough, then another clearing of her throat that actually sounds like a warning.

I grab the bowls with my other hand and stand back up—but not before pulling my hand from those creamy thighs and trailing my fingers over the sweet curve of her ass. *Under* her skirt.

Clara shoots me a look while clearing her throat again. I frown back at her. "Need some water?"

"I got it!" Willow cheerfully hops off her chair and skips over to the fridge to grab a fresh bottle for her mother.

I busy myself with scooping ice cream into a bowl, pointedly ignoring the various expressions flickering across Clara's face. She's flustered, she's protective, she's uncertain.

I know for a fact she's also *aroused*.

And unable to do a damn thing about it.

40

DEMYEN

Willow quickly returns with the water and hands it to Clara before climbing back onto the bar chair and sorting through her crayons. Clara mutters something that vaguely resembles a "thank you."

"Did you eat lunch?" I ask the little girl.

She nods. "Yup! Mommy made sandwiches and carrot sticks."

"Did you eat all of it?"

Willow hesitates and glances at Clara. "Maybe…"

Clara takes this opportunity to nod at a crumb-covered plate that's been shoved aside. "You still have two carrot sticks left."

The girl makes a face, but her eyes are glued to the ice cream scoop in my hand. When she glances up at me, I gesture to the carrots with a quick tilt of my head.

The deal is struck. Willow chows through her carrots and offers her empty plate to Clara, who takes it to the sink.

When she returns, she finds her daughter digging a small spoon into a generous bowl of chocolate syrup-drizzled ice cream.

"Dem—"

I cut her off by sliding another bowl in front of her.

Clara sighs, a small smile playing at her lips, but she nudges the bowl away. "I'm not hungry."

"Bullsh—Liar." I glance at the little tyrant who's taken over my freedom of speech and back at her infuriating mother. "I only see one plate. You didn't eat."

"I finished early."

"Never tell a lie, Mommy," Willow quietly slips in. Her tentative smile grows when I wink at her, my little informant-in-training.

"Yeah, *Mommy*." I cage Clara in against the island, one arm wrapping around her waist while the other slides the bowl back in front of her. "Never tell a lie." I grab the spoon and dip it in, pick up a bite, and hold it to her lips. "Take a bite."

Clara narrows her eyes at me, but the sound of her daughter's laughter seems to do the trick. She wraps her lips around the spoon, her gaze never leaving mine.

I'm suddenly very aware of the way she feels pressed so close to me. The way the soft fullness of her breasts rubs the side of my chest. The way she fits so perfectly tucked inside my arm.

She blinks at me for a moment before quickly turning around to face Willow. But I don't let her get away that easily. I'm too addicted, and she's just given me a taste of what I want.

Both my arms wrap around her waist, slowly but firmly pulling her into me. I bury my face in her hair, breathing her in.

She smells different. Not bad, just... different. Like sweet melons and sunshine, not the rich spice of my own scent.

I have no idea what mother and daughter are talking about as they eat their ice cream. And I've completely forgotten about my own bowl. I'm too busy trailing my mouth down the nape of her neck and inhaling her, trying to catch a whiff of myself on her skin or her clothes or anywhere, really.

"You smell different," I finally whisper against her shoulder.

Clara blushes a beautiful shade of pink and finishes the last bite of her ice cream. "New shampoo. And body wash. Do you... do you like it?"

My arms tighten around her waist. "I like the other one better."

That pink melts into a red as she realizes what I mean. "Oh. Sorry. I don't, um..." She straightens and collects the now-empty bowls for the sink. "I need to get back to work."

One minute, she's warm and pliant in my arms.

The next, she's gone.

Suddenly, I don't like how the cold air feels.

My gaze lands back on Willow, who has been watching raptly this whole time. *Fuck.* I need to be more careful. I can't afford to go and give the kid any grand ideas.

Or break her heart.

I swing a bar chair around the counter to sit across from Willow at the island, finally digging into my own half-melted bowl. "So, kiddo." I take a bite and wait for her to look up at me. "I need to ask you something."

"Sure!"

Except, now that the door is open, I'm not sure how to walk through. "Do you, ah…" I wait for her to stuff her face before I just rip the bandage off, keeping my voice low. "Do you miss your dad?"

Willow slows her chewing. She looks at me, then down at the bowl. My stomach twists as I watch her start to pull into herself.

"Hey," I murmur, reaching for her hand. It's an instinct that comes out of nowhere—my fingers resting on hers, not grabbing or squeezing, simply… *reminding.* "It's okay. I just wanna make sure you're happy, okay? That's all."

I'm not lying. I really do want her to be happy. And as much as I'm chanting to myself that it's all part of The Ultimate Strategy, *that* feels like a lie.

Willow sighs and pokes at a chocolate chip with her spoon. "I feel bad."

Shit. "Why?"

"Because…" She takes what feels like an eternity to finally continue. When she does, she blinks up at me with those long, dark lashes and I'm starting to understand why my best, most battle-scarred soldiers all turn to mush around her. "I don't miss him. And... and he's not... He's not really my dad."

I pause. That's not at all what I expected to hear. "What do you mean?"

The kid's only five, but she starts talking to me more like she's fifty. "I know he's my *father*, because Mommy told me so. But I don't think he acts like my daddy. Not like daddies are supposed to act. He yells too much and he scares me. And he hurts Mommy all the time. That scares me even more."

I swallow down the fury that roils inside me along with the ice cream. "He hurts Mommy?"

Willow nods and glances over to her mother, who is diligently washing the windows on the other side of the adjoining dining room. "She used to cry a lot. Especially after storytime, when I was supposed to be asleep."

I can't ball a fist like I want to. I can't punch a wall like I want to. I need Willow to know she can come to me and tell me anything, everything, without fear of anger, violence, or other repercussions. I need her to know this is a safe space where she can rat on the monsters in her life.

But I also really fucking need to hang Martin fucking Patterson on a hook and use him as my new punching bag.

"That must have been scary."

She nods again. "It was. I don't like it when Mommy cries. And I hate it when she screams."

Now, I do freeze. "She screams at you?"

Willow fervently shakes her head. "No! Never. I mean, when *she* screams. Because of the way Martin hurts her."

Just like that, the kid's on a first-name basis with the man who's supposed to be her dad.

And just like that, she and I have a lot more in common.

"What about now?" I play it cool, aloof. Like I don't care what her answer will be, no matter how hard my heart starts pumping inside my rib cage.

Willow's sad little face suddenly breaks into a bright grin. She even blushes. "I love it here. And Mommy does, too."

"Oh? How do you know?"

"I never hear her cry. Or scream. We're safe here." The kid eyes me with a twinkle of knowing mischief. "And she really likes you."

I damn near choke on a ball of cookie dough. "Is that so?"

Willow nods with that same grin stretched from ear to ear. "She talks about you a lot. And she looks for you all the time." She leans forward and cups a tiny hand around her mouth. "I think she *like* likes you," she whispers fiercely.

"And how would *you* know?"

She shrugs. "Mommy told me."

Hm. Sounds like Mommy's been doing a lot of talking when I'm not paying attention to the CCTV, which is quite a feat, since I'm never *not* paying attention. And despite Clara's hesitation and clear attempts to stay as far away from me as possible, I'm less inclined to believe it's because she despises me.

"Demyen?"

I tear my gaze away from where Clara's bent over a table and give Willow my undivided attention as much as humanly possible. "Yeah?"

"Why don't you have any kids?"

Well, fuck. I'm not ready for this question, nor am I prepared for the way it backhands me with her sweet innocence as she asks it.

I blow out a puff of air. Shit, she should start coming with me to interrogations. I haven't broken into a sweat like this since I was tied to a chair at seventeen. And it's not because I'm afraid of giving her the wrong answer.

It's because I'm afraid of the answer that comes immediately to mind.

"I'd be a terrible father. I don't know the first thing about dealing with kids, and I sure as shit don't know how to be a good husband. And I don't want to have kids with just anyone because if I ever did have children, I'd need to know their mother loves them as much as she loves me. And no one is stupid enough to love me. That's just fucking dangerous."

The kitchen falls silent. I'm painfully aware I've just dropped some juicy word-bombs in front of a five-year-old who is officially staring at me like I've grown three extra heads.

From the sounds still coming from the dining room, Clara didn't hear a word of it.

Thank God.

Willow tilts her head to one side and peers at me. But then she smiles. "You're silly."

I slide the chair back and take the empty bowl to the sink. "Thanks."

I nearly drop it into the soapy water when I suddenly feel a tiny human wrap herself around my leg and squeeze. I don't know what to do. Willow is hugging me like her life depends on it, and when I look down at her, she beams up at me.

So I do the only thing that seems rational and I very lightly pat her on the head.

"See?" she asks like I should know exactly what she's talking about. "You're a great daddy."

And before I have a chance to process *that* bombshell, Willow lets go and skips away to join her mother in the dining room. She leaves me to clean up the ice cream, and worse—she leaves me with my darkening thoughts spiraling into panic.

What the fuck have I gotten myself into?

41

CLARA

"Mommy?"

"Yes, baby?" It's a half-attentive response, since I'm more focused on weaving her braids tight so they won't fall out in the middle of the night. Sometimes, I have the perfect grip and rhythm, and other times...

Well, none of those other times ever involved me being distracted by a strong, chiseled, dangerous man who makes me flush with heat every time I think about him.

"When are we going home?"

My fingers pause mid-weave. I swallow hard, trying to quickly come up with an answer that won't upset her. "I don't know." I also don't think we'll ever actually go back to that place—not if we can help it.

"Oh." She doesn't stop brushing her doll's hair, so I can't tell if she's bothered by what I said or not.

"Do you want to go back home?"

At that, she does hesitate. Then: "Not really."

"Okay. We won't go back if you don't want to." Which is my way of breathing a prayer of thanks that we won't have to wrestle over her limited understanding of the situation.

Willow tries to braid Maple's hair the same way I'm doing hers. It's going to take her a few tries, but it's still heartwarming to watch her. She's always been a gentle and careful child, compassionate and considerate of her surroundings.

I'm just constantly afraid it's because of the hell she was born into, more than it's a natural part of her soul.

"If you could go anywhere in the world," I ask her with a mischievous smile, "where would you go?"

"Anywhere?"

"Anywhere."

"To see the mermaids." Willow states this so factually that I have to stifle a laugh.

"So what you're saying is, you want to see the ocean?"

"Yeah!"

We do actually have enough money to fly to Hawaii. Or I could take us in the opposite direction and confuse every possible trail among the Caribbean islands. As I finish the last of her braids, I hum the Beach Boys song to myself and make a mental note of each island listed. Not a half-bad idea.

"But I wanna see the snow, too."

Alaska is perfect for that. We won't need passports and I've heard stories about how it's almost *too* easy to lose people in the Klondike. Just what we'd need.

If we're going to truly escape, we need to go somewhere I know for a fact we can easily hide, should someone track us.

I know, deep down, the one person who would always find us is Demyen.

"If we go, can Demyen come with us?"

I pull back the covers of her bed to distract her from the way my face falls. "Baby, I need to talk to you about something."

Willow obediently wriggles under the covers and smiles up at me, cradling Maple to her chest. "What's up?"

It's easy to muster a smile hearing Roxy's influence in her tiny voice. "I know you really like Demyen—"

"He's my friend."

"Right." I tuck the covers around her and stroke a stray lock of hair back from her forehead. "And I am so glad you're happy and making new friends. But we need to be careful."

"Why?"

"Well…" I sigh. There's no parenting manual on how to explain to a small child that their new friend is the deadly leader of an organized crime syndicate. "If we get too attached, it will be hard for us to leave."

Willow frowns. "But I don't want to leave. I like it here."

"Sweetheart, I know. I do, too." *In some ways.* I can't overlook how the security measures are just as effective at keeping Martin out as it is keeping us in. "But Demyen… he's a dangerous man, baby. And pretty soon, we're going to have to leave him. To stay safe."

She furiously shakes her head as tears spring to her eyes. "No! I don't wanna leave! Demyen's my friend! He keeps me safe! He fights the monsters!"

He is a monster, babygirl.

But then his own words echo in my mind, reminding me that even he has limits. He basically accused me of accusing him of being the worst of humanity, and to my surprise, he seemed genuinely insulted.

I'm not going to deny it—my first instinct was to think exactly that of him. He's so quick to exact vengeance against me for something I did in my childhood.

What's stopping him from taking it out on my daughter, too?

I press warm kisses to her sweet face and snuggle her deeper under the covers. "Shhh, my sweet Willow-tree. We're not going anywhere right now. You're safe. And I love you."

"I love you, too, Mommy."

We stay like that for a few more minutes, until her eyes drift close and her breath evens. I slowly, carefully pry myself from her bedroom and tiptoe the few yards to my own room, closing the door behind me at molasses speed so the clicking sound doesn't wake her up.

One day, hopefully, she'll be a heavier sleeper. But that day probably won't come until we're able to stay somewhere long enough for me to hire a therapist for her. Until then, her traumatized little ears pick up on every sound that might mean danger is near—the closing of a door, heavy footsteps on wood floorboards… Even hushed whispers can wake her if they sound aggressive enough.

I wonder if Demyen knows a good child therapist…?

I slap that thought away almost literally. Go to Demyen for help? For mental health, and for my child? Am *I* losing my mind?

But then I remember the way he was with her today. So warm, so kind and funny, not an ounce of tension in his body. He took time out of his busy day to sit and talk with her, and even though I have no idea what it was about, I could clearly see the way Willow leaned into him like she felt she could trust him.

And not only did he treat her with kindness and respect, he treated *me* with respect as her mother. None of his overbearing, demanding, overlording assholery made an appearance. He acted like a man teaching a child to respect her mother's wishes by setting the example.

He acted like a father.

Like the father Willow never had.

The father she deserves.

The realization should bring me to tears, but something else happens instead—my mind wanders to another version of that same thought.

Demyen Zakrevsky, powerful and dangerous leader of Vegas' underworld.

Father to my children.

It's a thought that should make me shudder with fear and disgust, but instead, heat blooms deep within my core and flows between my legs.

Demyen, strong and possessive, holding me in his arms as his hands caress the swell of my stomach where he's filled me with his baby.

Demyen, firm and demanding, whispering in my ear for me to give him what he wants as he presses me into the bed and works himself deep inside me.

I'm standing at the foot of my bed, so I imagine him there. Reclining on the mattress, propped up against the soft stack of pillows like some dark king of the underworld beckoning me to service him.

No—beckoning me to *surrender* to him.

I won't do that.

I can't do that.

But for just tonight, for just a little while... I can pretend, can't I?

42

CLARA

I can pretend, can't I?

I close my eyes as I slip my dress off, feeling the cool air of the room caress my skin as the fabric pools around my feet. I don't have a bra to wrestle with. My nipples tighten as they're stroked by the breeze from the vents. I try to pretend it's Demyen standing behind me, teasing them to stiffness.

When my hands smooth up my stomach to cup my breasts, it's Demyen in my mind doing it to me.

When I pinch, then roll, my nipples between my fingers, I can almost feel his calloused fingers instead.

I realize in the back of my mind that this is *mine*—my room, my fantasy. Demyen can be whoever I want him to be. I can make him touch me and speak to me exactly how I want him to.

So I'm surprised—and aroused beyond all reason—when I feel myself slide my panties down my hips and cup myself in my hand.

Because even in my fantasy, in this moment I have full control over...

... Demyen still has full control over me.

We're back at the dinner party—truly back, and not just grinding against each other up against an adobe column under the solar lamplights. Of course, in my fantasy, we weren't interrupted by anyone or anything and his wicked fingers made me come while he whispered such delicious things in my ear.

He pants against my skin. He doesn't want me to know how close he is to losing control, but I can feel it in the way his breath fans over my neck. Hot, heavy, labored.

When he pulls his fingers from me, I whine. I don't know why I do, other than the aching emptiness at their absence. It makes him chuckle, and he nibbles my earlobe as he uses that same hand to grip my ass under my dress.

"Such a needy little thing," he murmurs. "Was that not enough for you?"

It should be. I know it should be. And I know I should be grateful that it's all he's done to me, especially given how furious he was when he first dragged me here.

So why do I feel this ache for more?

"Please," I breathe. When he leans back to gaze into my eyes, I feel myself reaching for him like he's really, truly my lover. Like he doesn't hold my life over my head. "Dem, I want..."

But I don't know how to tell him what I want.

What I really want.

It's too dark. Too extreme.

But he already knows what it is. His mouth curls in a wicked smile and that hand in my hair tightens, pulling me to him as he lets out a low, sexy growl.

"Mmm," he rumbles against my lips. It's the barest of kisses, but it makes me squirm with need. "Are you sure?"

He's asking me for permission. Like he always does, despite the fact that he could just take from me no matter what I say. There's something to unpack there, but I'm too fucking horny to care.

"Yes." It's a sigh and a plea as much as it's consent. "Please."

His eyes harden. "Why?"

It's a fair question. One that I'm probably asking myself. And considering the truth will never leave this moment...

"Because I want them to see. I want them all to see who I belong to." I trail a finger from his jaw to his chest, slow and languid. "I want the whole fucking world to watch you own me like they never can and never will."

Demyen growls again. I feel his hands wander over my body, claiming me right here and now, and I half-expect him to scrap the idea and just fuck me here.

But he pulls back again, this time to take my hand in his and wrap his other arm around my waist.

"After you, my queen."

And then we're back at his table, surrounded by the leering men and bored women—but this time, everyone is watching with rapt attention. Rouged lips part with aroused gasps as Demyen holds me from behind and snaps the thin gold chains on either side of my dress, one by one, until the fabric puddles on the mosaic floor.

His hands are everywhere. Cupping, kneading, squeezing, caressing. He moves my hair to one shoulder so he can mark a path of lovebites from the tip of my shoulder to just below my ear, all the while staring darkly at the men who dare to lay eyes on his woman.

His woman. Me.

His.

A sweep of his arm scatters the cards and chips off the table, and I'm bent over the edge without warning. It feels softer than I expected. The tablecloth rubs over my sensitive nipples and I let out a breathy moan.

Demyen kicks my feet apart. I go the extra mile and spread even more for him, arching my ass up for good measure. His hands knead my cheeks with an appreciative rumble in his chest before he lands one, then two, slaps.

It should hurt, but it doesn't. It only makes me cry out. "Yes, sir! Please!"

"Please what?" He drags a finger through my dripping slit just to torment me. "Be my good girl and use your words."

I can't. I want to but I just can't. Not even here, not even now. "There! Right there. Please."

And again, he knows what I want—what I need—as if he's reading my mind.

And when his palm connects with my pussy, the stinging heat spreads from my clit to my ass and makes me throw my head back. I'm gasping, I'm sobbing, I'm babbling for him to give me more.

His hand threads in my hair again to hold me up. Demyen wants them all to see my face when he shoves himself deep inside me. One thrust—one hard, solid thrust that drives the air from my lungs and makes my eyes roll back in my head. But then, instead of just plowing ahead like I expect him to, he grinds it in just so I can feel him stretch me open in ways no man has ever made me feel before.

"Is that what you need, baby?" His voice is suddenly in my ear. I feel his chest press along my back as he leans over me and continues grinding his huge cock into me. "Does this feel better?"

All I can do is whine and nod and fuck myself on him since he won't do it for me.

"So fucking eager. So fucking beautiful."

He releases my hair and wraps his arm around my chest, returning his fingers to my tangled waves in a half-caress, half-grip on the side of my head. The way he's holding me feels so fucking possessive... and intimate.

It makes me ripple and squeeze around his cock, which finally—finally—makes him thrust inside me.

"Open your eyes, baby." Demyen presses a firm kiss to my brow, then to the outer corner of my eye as he slowly works his cock in and out... in and out... Slowly. Deeply. "Open your eyes."

So I do as he says. I open my eyes and I look straight ahead.

Martin is sitting there, right there at the table. Bound, gagged, and forced to watch Demyen fuck the ever-living shit out of me.

Demyen holds me up more, just enough for everyone to see the way my breasts bounce and sway with every hard thrust inside my body. I grunt whenever he bottoms out—and that's almost every single time. I can hear the loud clap of his thighs against mine, a steady rhythm of a man fucking his woman for the world to see.

No, not fucking.

Claiming.

Marking.

Breeding.

His other hand spans over the soft swell of my empty womb and presses. He kneads me there, firm but loving, and it makes that sweet spot he keeps hitting inside me radiate pleasure with an intensity that makes my toes curl.

"Who does this belong to?"

I stare Martin in the eyes as I answer Demyen. "You."

Demyen rocks into me a bit faster. "That's fucking right. Tell him." He follows my glare to the excuse of a man now writhing pitifully in his ropes. "Tell him who fucks you better than he ever could."

"You do!" I sob with pleasure, feeling that hot pressure quickly build deep inside me. "Demyen! Fuck! You do!"

"I what, baby?"

"You own me." My whole body trembles from head to toe as he holds me in place, not letting me move save for the unavoidable rocking of our bodies together. "You fuck me so good. You fuck me better than him. Better than anyone."

Demyen growls his approval and suddenly stills. The world spins for a dizzyingly swift moment, and I'm suddenly sitting on his lap as he sits on his chair.

It's more throne than chair now. Demyen is the king of the underworld, and I'm his queen impaled on his cock as he shows me off to everyone who ever dares challenge him.

Who ever dares challenge us.

His hand slips around my throat, but not to strangle me. Only to pull me back so his bare chest, damp with perspiration and heaving with his own gasps, is flush with my spine.

His other hand dips between my legs, which are spread wide on either side of his own. He finds my clit and when he rubs, I cry out his name again.

"Show them, baby. You want this. Now, take it."

I do. I fucking take it. I take him, rolling and writhing my hips until I work up a rhythm that has both of us groaning and gasping out of control. I'm so fucking close and I can feel that he is, too.

"Show him. Show him how beautiful you are when you come on my cock. Show him the way you look when I fill you up."

Demyen pulls me down hard as he thrusts up, thickening inside me even more.

"Me. Not him."

Another hard thrust.

I'm almost fucking there.

"You're mine, Clara. Only mine." Demyen uses his fingertips to turn my face to his. "Don't fucking forget it."

I'm bucking. I'm screaming. I'm muffled by his mouth slanted over mine, swallowing his own cries as he fills me with liquid heat I swear spreads all the way to my toes. I can't stop writhing on his cock and he won't stop coaxing every toe-curling spasm from me.

We're falling together and we don't care who watches us. We don't fucking care as long as they get the message loud and clear. One message. Five little words.

I belong to Demyen Zakrevsky.

I don't know how long I've been passed out like this. Facedown, ass up, legs spread like I'm in heat and waiting for my stud to walk in.

And the long end of a hairbrush slowly easing from my soaked slit.

The only reason I know I've been biting down on my pillow is because my teeth are still pressed around a solid chunk of it. Unlike the sopping mess between my legs, my mouth is dry and tastes like cotton.

Cotton, sweat, and shame.

I have nothing to be embarrassed about. Logically, I know that. But I cannot believe that, out of all the fantasies my brain could possibly come up with, *that's* the one it conjured.

Just remembering it suddenly makes my thighs quiver.

Nope. This was a one-time thing. Demyen is not allowed to take advantage of me in my own fantasies; he's already living rent-free in my head.

Once I'm finally able to feel my legs again, I roll off the bed and angrily yank on the first tank top I can find. But then I realize I should probably take a shower, so I yank it right off again and shuffle my way to the bathroom.

The sight of Demyen's body wash in place of my own makes me sigh. Not because I'm irritated.

But because, despite the promise I *just* made myself, I know I won't make it through this shower without imagining him in there with me. Taking care of me tenderly after using me like he did out there on the table.

Rewarding me for being his good girl.

Fuck.

43

CLARA

I can't sleep.

I took a shower—and then I took a *cold* shower—and I even tried making myself a cup of tea in the little kitchenette part of the suite.

But I still. Can't. Fucking. Sleep.

"Earlier" definitely took the edge off something. What that "something" is, I don't know, but I feel a distinct lack of tension in my limbs.

Imagine how it'd feel if he—

Nope. Absolutely not. I'm sure that, on a scientific level, reenacting my little fantasy with the real-life Demyen would melt every knot in my body for the next twenty years.

But he can never know what I did. Or what I thought about while doing it.

Maybe that's what's keeping me awake: anxiety over the remote possibility that he'll *know*. He'll know, somehow, that

I worked myself to a toe-curling orgasm while hallucinating a scenario straight out of his own twisted fantasies.

I need air. I need cold air and cold water and just… whatever works to calm the heat spreading through my veins all over again.

When I slip outside of my room, I glance around and tiptoe past the guards who are more interested in catching a few winks than catching me doing a walk of shame they don't even know about.

I don't bother grabbing shoes or flip-flops; I'm too antsy to waste any more time and just need to go somewhere, anywhere, to clear my head.

I break into a light jog when I decide to follow the darkest walkways to the darkest part of the villa I can spot from the main courtyard. It's not even about dodging the curious gazes of Demyen's men—it's more about how the darkness of the night feels more comforting and less like I'm constantly being watched.

After a few turns down the open walkways, I realize where I'm going. Because I've been here before, both literally and… well, "recently…"

The archway over the entrance to the dinner party courtyard feels more ominous than it did that night. The golden orbs and delicate strings of lights added a kind of ethereal warmth to the architecture that, right now, bathed in shadows and slivers of moonlight, seem cold. Looming.

All the tables and chairs are probably in storage. The courtyard feels even larger now that it's not filled with makeshift furniture and dozens of people from Las Vegas' elite echelons and corrupt underbelly. The pool in the center glows with the safety lights under the water, but it's not enough to luminate the space on its own.

What *is* enough to light the mosaic tiles swirling beneath my feet is the glittering stretch of the Milky Way high overhead in the midnight sky.

Within the city limits, a few stars are able to peek through the light pollution from all the neon signs of casinos and hotels and showtime banners. But it's not the same.

It's nothing compared to the breathtaking beauty of the heavens at midnight, out in the deep, dark desert of Sierra Nevada.

"Planning your escape?"

I about damn near jump into the pool—Demyen's voice right behind me is so unexpected, I do actually jump and clutch a hand to my chest.

When I can finally feel my heart actually beat again, I suck air into my lungs just to let out a sardonic, breathless laugh.

"Ha. No."

He peers at me like he doesn't believe me. Or like he wants to devour me. In the *good* way.

He knows. I don't know how he knows, but he fucking knows.

In reality, he probably knows absolutely nothing and it's all in my head. Demyen could just be looking at me like he's a starving man eyeing a filet mignon because... he wants to? And because he's a guy, and it doesn't take much for the blood to drain from a man's head to his... other head.

Yeah. There's no way he knows. It's just him being him.

"I wondered. You wouldn't get very far." He gestures to my bare feet, a wry smile twisting his full lips that, in my fantasies, branded me everywhere anyone could see and several places they couldn't.

I clear my throat to hide the wheeze. "I just needed some air." I straighten my back, wanting him to see I'm not in the mood to be toyed with. "Don't get me wrong—we *will* be leaving soon. Just not right now."

Demyen just nods. I can't tell if he's pissed or actually taking my words to heart. "I needed a drink." He holds up a bottle of something undoubtedly alcoholic and inclines his head toward a row of sunbathing chairs. "Care to join me?"

A part of me wonders if this is a dream. Some weird way for my fantasies to continue while I'm sleeping.

I'm surprised that he actually wants to spend time with me in any capacity other than to torment me.

I'm even more surprised that he just casually glossed over the fact that I announced, to his face, that I refuse to be his prisoner for much longer.

But it's hard to deny this is real. Especially when I feel him tug on my hand and then pull me on top of him where he's made himself comfortable on the lawn chair. And instead of doing something to seduce me—or chastise me—Demyen simply tucks his arm around me and we lie there just like that, side by side, gazing up at the stars in the midnight sky.

"What's your favorite color?" he asks.

I snort. *Come out of left field, why don't you?* "Um…purple?"

"Bright purple? Or one of those wisty pastel types?"

I have no idea where any of this is coming from, but I'm not going to fight it. Or question it. I don't have the willpower. "You know those cactus blossoms that aren't really pink, but they're not, like, a plum or a grape color, either? That. In general, I mean. But in clothing and stuff, plum."

Demyen nods and takes a swig from the bottle. It's strong stuff; I can smell it from here. "Plum's a good color."

Silence settles between us. Now, I'm pretty sure I'm dreaming, because this is weird as hell.

I turn my face to look at him. "What about you?"

"Silver." He answers without hesitation. I think I know why.

"Ha. Like silver bullets? Knives? Chains?"

"No." Demyen points at the moon. "Like that. That kind of silver. Where it's not really what people say it is, but there's no other word to describe it. I like things like that. Things that defy explanation. Things that can't be captured."

I don't...

I don't know what to say in response to that.

Someone calm and poetic has taken over Demyen's body and it's *weird*. And oddly enough, kinda nice.

"That's beautiful," I murmur to myself.

Because it is. I just never would have expected it to come out of *his* mouth.

Demyen shrugs. That same silence returns, but it's not as heavy. I don't know what else to say, so I just gaze up at the stars and wonder how long it will take for me to count them before I fall asleep.

And it's then that I wonder if Willow's room was placed for this exact reason. So she can count the stars and drift to sleep under their silvery light, her bed canopied by the heavens and her windows curtained with the lush ferns and foliage of the solarium.

The thought makes my heart squeeze.

And then pound with fear.

I can't have these thoughts. I can't afford to assume the best of Demyen. Thoughts like that are how I end up in serious trouble.

"So..." He sighs and takes another swig. "Heard from your dad lately?"

"Nope." The answer flies out too easily. It's an honest answer, but still. I shrug. "He's busy."

"You've been gone for a while."

"He probably hasn't noticed."

"Seems odd for a detective. To not notice his own kid is missing."

I frown. "I'm hardly a kid."

"Doesn't matter to a parent. Not to a *good* parent, anyway."

"Well, there you go. You're assuming he's a good parent. And you know what they say about people who assume."

"I know I'm an ass. I just never thought I'd hear you admit you're one, too."

I snort. It's an ugly laugh that comes out of nowhere, and I'd be embarrassed if Demyen didn't also just snort his own ugly laugh in response. He turns his face to look at me with this half-amused, half-perplexed expression.

"Admit it," I tease him with a nudge of my arm against his. "You like my ass."

"Hm." He narrows his eyes at me, but that smirk doesn't entirely vanish. "It's kept you alive so far."

I know he's returning my tease, but it still makes my mind go places. Reminding me of who—or really, of *what*—he is. I shift onto my side to face him more, unintentionally tucking myself closer to him in the process. And I do my damned hardest to ignore the way his arm around me tightens a bit more, his fingers just barely stroking my skin.

"So, is that what you usually do when you make people disappear? Kill them and, I don't know… bury them in your garden?"

"Cuts costs on fertilizer." Demyen sets the bottle down on the ground next to him. "No, I usually don't make it a habit to 'disappear' people. Brings too many detectives sniffing around and one dead man isn't worth losing an entire empire. If I have to kill someone, I make sure it gets called in. Better they find the body and follow a vague trail somewhere else."

"So that's why you're asking about my father."

He cocks a brow but doesn't look at me, his gaze returning to the stars. "No. I'm asking about your father because he's your father. And a detective. And you're not dead, just 'disappeared.' And he *hasn't* come sniffing around."

"Martin did," I point out.

"*Martin.*" Demyen scoffs. "I still can't believe you and him were ever a thing."

Why does that feel like a punch in the gut? He didn't lob any accusations or insults at me and yet it feels like he might as well have just called me an idiot. I try not to curl up into myself, not to wallow in the sudden self-pity drowning my nerves.

"Everyone makes mistakes."

He stills. Then nods. "Sure. So what was that 'mistake' like? Living with him."

"Why? So you can take notes?"

Demyen turns to frown at me. "Easy there. It was just a question."

Shit. I snapped at him without thinking—but at the same time, I can't deny it feels good to stand my own ground. "Well, it sure wasn't a life inside a desert villa with our own personal chef, I'll tell you that much. Well, maybe for him it was. I was his personal chef, and maid, and accountant— except for when he didn't want to hear the truth."

At Demyen's silent nod for me to continue, I sigh. "The truth was—and probably still is—that he spends outside his means. And never on anyone but himself. He was first in line at the Apple store for their newest laptop, but I was first in line at the food pantry just so Willow would have enough to eat for the week."

Demyen's expression darkens. "He's a detective. That's not a small income. The fuck kind of man doesn't provide for his family?"

I know I'm probably digging my own hole in whatever ditch he'll end up throwing me in, but oh well. I've come this far. What's one more nail in the coffin? "The kind who makes sure to never marry his live-in girlfriend so she can't hold any claims for his finances. It only worked for him during tax season, when he claimed Willow and me as dependents."

"And yet you stayed with him."

"Where else was I going to go?"

I've had this conversation before—with Roxy, who would make sure at least once a week for the past six years to beg me to leave Martin once and for all. Pretty sure she had it as a recurring calendar event.

I just... couldn't bring myself to do it.

I wish I knew why.

Demyen lies there in silence for a while. I don't feel like breaking it with my own questions. Not yet, anyway. I'm feeling too raw and too exposed under his scrutiny and judgment to launch my own interrogation.

Even though I have to admit, this feels less like an interrogation and more like... like he's wanting to *get to know me.*

Which is ridiculous. We don't have that kind of relationship. We never, ever will.

"At least you're out of there now." Demyen picks up the bottle and downs a hard swig before putting it back down on the tile.

"Yup," I sigh. "Out of the frying pan and into the fire."

He stills.

Me and my big mouth...

But instead of chastising me or worse, Demyen simply slides his gaze to mine without turning his head. "If things were so bad with Martin, why not run to the police? To your father?"

I scoff. "Seriously? They *are* the police. And who do you think introduced me to Martin in the first place?"

How thick is his skull that he can't put two and two together? *Run to the police.* Like I hadn't tried that already, multiple times, even *before* I met Martin.

Back when Mama was still alive.

The memory stings my eyes and I shove myself away from him. I don't care that it makes me clumsily roll off the chair —I need to get away from Demyen and his painful, prying questions he has no business asking. He's never cared before, so why start now?

"Clara."

I feel him reach for me, but I dodge his hand. Time to leave.

I'm about three yards away from that looming archway when his arms wrap around me from behind. The gesture feels so warm, so intimate, it almost makes me want to cry.

Cry from frustration, to be clear.

But also because I want so much that which I can*not* let myself have.

"Clara." Demyen's voice is gentle in my ear. I can smell the vodka on his breath. His hold eases when he feels me slow to a stop, enough for him to move his hands to my waist and hold me there.

I try so hard to ignore the way his thumbs trace slow, lazy circles along the small of my back. Or the way his mouth presses something like a kiss to my shoulder, then my neck, before he speaks again.

"Let me know if you need something better than a hairbrush next time. I'll be happy to accommodate."

Shit.

Shiiiiit shit shit shit shit.

He knows. I knew it. I'm actually amazed that he lets me pull away to run back to the main house; I half-expected him to try and seduce me right then and there.

I'm more amazed to feel kind of disappointed he didn't.

44

DEMYEN

Coffee used to be the best fix for a mild hangover.

Used to be.

Until a certain siren moved into my home.

Now, it seems like she's the only fix for anything—and I'm the sailor losing my fucking mind with this obsessive need to be near her. To touch her. To look at her.

Fuck the consequences, as long as I can fuck *her*.

What's left of logic in the back of my mind whispers reminders of why I can't just abandon The Plan just so I can bury my dick inside her whenever I want. Logic is pretty damn convincing, as it turns out.

So I do the next best thing.

This time, I'm still in bed, up before dawn as usual. Everyone else is still asleep, which means I have a rare period of free time before anyone needs me to attend to things.

Right now, I have my own thing that needs "attending to."

The laptop rests on my lap on top of the blankets. The screen is showing me clear footage from yesterday's little adventure inside Clara's bedroom. I promised myself I was just going to check on the current live feed, but…

This is ridiculous. It's not like I haven't seen this before.

She's standing at the foot of her bed, naked. It's slow, but her movements soon reveal she's touching herself. First, her stomach, then her breasts. It makes my mouth water just watching. When she lets out a breathy moan, I have no choice but to shift the laptop enough for me to ease my hard cock out from under the blankets.

I shouldn't.

But I'm going to.

It's impossible not to, with the way Clara slowly peels off her panties and exposes her sweet ass to the camera. I can just make out the details of her pussy framed between her thighs and I wrap my fist around my cock at the sight. I'm practically salivating, needing to taste her again.

"Please," she moans to no one in the room. "Dem… I want…"

Yes, baby. Tell me what you want.

In my mind's eye, I'm there with her in the room, standing behind her and kissing her neck as if it's *my* hands wandering over her body. *My* hands cupping her breasts and rolling her plump nipples between my fingers. *My* hands caressing her silky skin and sliding down to spread her legs so I can give her exactly what she wants. What she *needs*.

The fact that the only words she continues to moan and sigh are "please," "yes," and "sir" makes my dick throb and my hand move a bit faster. I want to take my time and draw this out, but then she bends over the edge of the bed and slides onto the mattress like she's in fucking heat.

Never mind. Forget taking my time.

At this angle, I can see her fingers work in circles between her spread thighs. It's a fucking crime that I'm not there, touching her right there, making her moan for me even more by replacing my fingers with the tip of my cock.

I'd rub her clit with the head until she begged me for more and then I'd keep teasing her until she was sobbing with desperation.

I wish so damn much I knew what was playing out in her mind right now. Where does she imagine us being? What does she envision me doing to her? What sort of things does she want me to tell her while she rolls her hips and fucks herself on my cock?

Whatever it is, it's enough to make her blindly reach for the hairbrush lying next to her on the bed.

And just like the dozen other times when I've watched this footage, the sight of her pushing that handle deep inside her dripping pussy nearly makes me cum.

Goddamn.

Clara fucks herself with the handle and I fuck myself with my hand. I can't tear my eyes away from the sight of her quivering and undulating, working herself with an aggression I definitely did not expect the first time I saw this. I expected her to go easy, gentle, slow… you know, intimate girly shit.

What she does and what her moans beg me specifically for is *hard*. Deep. Fucking *intense*.

Whatever she imagined me doing to her, I know for a fact I'd happily do it right here and now.

All she has to do is ask.

The laptop slides off my lap onto the bed and I don't give a shit. My head leans back against the pillows as my fist works my aching cock harder, slick with the precum that keeps dripping from the tip with every moan and gasp and cry that woman utters. I can't see the screen but I can hear her, and it's almost better because now, I can play out my own fantasy.

Of going to her room and finding her like that on her bed—face down, ass up, legs spread and pussy swollen and dripping for me.

Of rubbing her hips and promising her I'll make it all so much better.

Of grabbing those same hips and plunging my cock inside her, burying myself to the balls with one thrust. Just for the pleasure of hearing her gasp, groan, and sputter my name.

I'd fuck her so much better than that pathetic wooden hairbrush. I'd fill her better, stretch her better, and make her take *my* rhythm. Sure, we could go slow and really massage the walls of her tight pussy, but I can tell she needs more this time.

She needs to be *fucked*—and I'm the man to give it to her.

I have the presence of mind enough to turn the screen toward me again right when she starts coming on that stupid fucking hairbrush. In my mind, I'm holding her as she starts to buck and writhe and sob my name over and over. I'm shoving in as far as it will fucking go and holding her there, making her feel every solid throbbing inch as her pussy ripples and spasms and milks me into her.

In my mind, I'm growling in her ear and sucking on that sweet curve of her neck until I grunt out her name, my own release pouring into her.

In reality, I've just covered my stomach with my cum and made a mess.

And she's not here to lick it up.

That thought—that *image,* Clara on her hands and knees lapping my abs with her soft little tongue—makes my cock twitch again.

FUCK.

Fucking hell. I literally just jacked off and came hard to her security footage, and already I'm wanting to go for round two?

No. Hell no.

I'm going to take an ice-cold shower, get dressed, and actually get some goddamn work done at the casino. Far, far away from the siren song of Clara Everett.

Far, far away from the one sin I cannot commit.

45

DEMYEN

Did I say I was going to get some work done?

I will.

Eventually.

I scroll through the personnel files of each and every escort on Meridian's payroll as if I'm simply checking ranks and evaluating employee performance. In reality, I'm desperately trying to find someone, *anyone*, who looks remotely close to Clara so I can safely and sanely work off the edge of all this tension between us.

It wouldn't be difficult at all to convince any of my escorts to join me inside an executive suite for an hour or two. Bambi has always been an encourager of dipping my pen into company ink, so to speak.

But even though I do find one or two women on the roster who bear a slight resemblance to Clara, it's not the same. I know either one would do their best to make me happy, but I don't want a performance; I want the real fucking thing.

I want *Clara*. Not an imposter.

Almost on instinct, I pull up the live security feed from the compound to check on her and the kid. It's breakfast time and the cameras in the kitchen show me a sweet moment between mother and daughter over a bowl of fruit Clara pulls from the fridge. It looks like Willow loves strawberries the most—I'll make sure to order extra on the next grocery run.

I keep the feed open a little longer to make sure they're staying put and not making plans to suddenly run for the hills. Not that they would—Clara's not an idiot who would risk her child's safety like that—but I need a reason to justify why I keep pulling up the cameras to check.

Not that anyone's questioning me. They know better.

I just don't want or need Bambi's skeptical eyebrow to pop up as often as it does while we're at work.

Like right now, as she drinks her coffee and stares at me. "So, I'm thinking about organizing a Greco-Roman palace-themed orgy for next Tuesday."

"Huh?" The word "orgy" pulls me out of my own thoughts and I blink at her. "Ah. Yes. Sounds good."

Bambi deadpans her expression as she takes another sip from her mug. "We'll need to order three gallons of olive oil for the event."

She caught me. I actually have no idea what she's talking about. I close the app on my phone and shove it into my pocket so I'm at least marginally paying better attention. "Speaking of events," I segue as a cover, "how's that wedding reception at the hotel going? Everything set up for tonight?"

Part of being a luxury hotel includes providing luxury accommodations to wealthy brides and their even wealthier families. I don't usually involve myself with that end of the business, but it provides enough of a distraction to pull my mental focus back into actual work.

Bambi sighs and checks her notes. "Grigori hasn't sent out an S.O.S. yet, but it'll be worth checking in with him and making an appearance near the ballroom. It's the senator's daughter, after all."

"Fan-fucking-tastic." I make no effort to hide my disdain. I hate politics. I hate politicians. I hate playing their stupid little games most of all. But showing my face as an attentive host bolsters my legitimacy as a businessman and that always comes in handy when suspicions regarding my Bratva are raised. "Have a bottle of champagne sent to their bridal suite, compliments of the house."

"Judge Cartwell is on the guest list."

That catches my full attention. "Oh?" Cartwell has presided over every attempt to re-examine Tolya's case, and he's shot down every single valid argument we've brought to his courtroom. "With his wife?"

Bambi nods. "Looks like. Want extra eyes on him?"

"See what we can dig up on him in the meantime. And when the party starts, keep his glass full. Let's see how loose he and his wife get when the wine flows freely."

"You got it."

I already know Cartwell has a few skeletons in his closet he wouldn't want the missus to know about—like his taste in escorts or the fact that he's high-rolling in the lounge once a week, usually on Thursdays. I'm suspicious that he knows who owns this place and he's counting on my desperation to help Tolya as a sort of safety buffer for his indulgences... but if that's the case, then he's a bigger idiot than I previously thought.

The house always fucking wins.

Thoughts of Tolya darken my mood. I excuse myself into my office for a quick break to clear my head. I left my laptop at home on purpose—minimize temptations, if possible—so there's not much I can do in there other than spin on my chair a full turn and look around the room.

My eyes land on a photo album I haven't pulled out in *years*.

It's something Tolya and I made together back when we were kids. Back when we only had each other, facing down a bleak family life with a beast of a father and a ghost of a mother.

We collected the weirdest shit to stick between the pages next to our grinning faces—napkins from our favorite restaurants, tickets from movies, smooth stones we found on the pavement and thought were cool. If we found joy in something we could stick tape to, we added it to the album. Tolya probably did it more for me; I don't remember seeing him collect anything for his own interests, while I practically had a museum in my room.

He was always like that. Always putting people before himself. Always putting *me* before himself.

And look where it got him.

As I flip through the pages, I feel my resolve build and my focus sharpen. It's been years since Tolya and I have been able to spend time together without the all-seeing eyes of a prison ward.

It's time to put his freedom before my own selfish wants and needs.

I'm lost in my trip down Memory Lane when my phone buzzes in my pocket. It's a text from Raizo, telling me he's almost ready for the auction scheduled for the end of next week. He's been soliciting buyers and has found a few promising options for my "artifact."

I have to think about it for a long moment before I can remember what the hell he's talking about.

Artifact. Clara.

I literally almost forgot: I'm selling Clara.

The thought churns my stomach. But I glance at the scrapbook lying open on my desk and remind myself that this is all for him. For Tolya.

The money, the vengeance... it's all meant to make things right for him.

I text Raizo back confirming that everything sounds good. *We'll be ready.* The ballroom is already reserved for his "event" and several rooms have been blocked for VIP guests, personal use, whatever the fuck Raizo typically needs them for when he's peddling flesh to a greedy—and anonymous— clientele.

This is for Tolya.

I have to put his freedom, his justice, first.

I have to focus on him.

I have to ignore the voice screaming inside me that this is all so fucking wrong.

46

DEMYEN

I don't return back to the compound until late afternoon—and not until after making the briefest appearance possible outside the senator's daughter's reception to "check on things." A single head nod, a perfect smile, and a quick signal to Grigori to start manning the doors as well as the bar to make sure no one gets in or out without us knowing.

With any luck, Cartwright will get inebriated enough to start spilling his guts.

Even better, since it's a political wedding, there's a whole guest list of public officials we'll be able to harvest juicy blackmail fodder from.

It's not extortion if no one reports it.

"Demmy!"

I'm greeted by Willow the moment I walk through the front door of the main house, her little arms extended up for a hug. Without even blinking, I swing her up into a big bear hug and kiss her cheek. "How's my girl doing?"

Because yes, at some point, she became "my girl." She's living in my home and eating my food and, whether she knows it or not, she's helping me figure out things with her mother.

So yes, she's my girl.

"Good." Willow giggles and wraps her arms around my neck. "I helped Mommy clean the sunroom today."

"Did you? Good job!" I feign shock and admiration, fully knowing what her version of "helped" probably means. She more than likely "supervised" while Clara did her best to teach different things like sweeping. It's a habit of hers I've noticed and I kind of admire it.

From afar.

"Wanna help me clean my office?"

"Yeah!"

I tuck Willow into the crook of one arm while I grab my briefcase with my free hand and lead us to my home office. My version of "cleaning" involves letting Willow play with markers or something while I review reports from the daily Bratva dealings. A few of my *vors* have been handling shipments of smuggled antiquities—*actual* antiquities, not anything coded about it—and I need to verify the balance sheets match our expectations.

She's easy to entertain. I set her down inside my office and she immediately skips over to plop herself onto one of the lounge chairs. I expect her to ask me for something, but she only smiles at me and kicks her feet against the cushion to make them bounce. "What do ya wanna clean first?"

Ah. Right. "Here, umm…" I glance around for something she can "clean" with. "How about you help me organize the books? Smallest to biggest." I'm not sure how advanced her reading skills are, so that seems like a safe strategy.

Willow grins and hops back off the chair. "Okay!"

When I see she's being careful with sliding the books out of the lowest shelf and even dusting them with her fingers and shirt, I relax and slide into my desk chair. As expected, the accounting sheets are printed and ready for me on the desk.

It's a bit old school, I know. But it's safer to burn incriminating evidence that it is to delete it.

Pavel did a thorough job ensuring every crate contained exactly what we'd ordered, and by the looks of it, he even negotiated a better price over the shipment of those silly nesting dolls.

The sound of breaking glass and a gasp yanks my attention from the paperwork. Willow's eyes meet mine, then quickly dart away as she drops to the floor and scrambles to pick up the pieces of a picture frame.

"I'm sorry! I'm sorry!" Her little voice wavers, her eyes filling with tears. "I'm sorry!"

I'm not even thinking about the mess—the second I see her picking up broken glass, I rush to her side and crouch down to help her. But when I do, she drops whatever is in her hands and stumbles back on her heels.

"I'm sorry! I didn't mean to! I'm so sorry, Daddy!"

Willow bursts into tears and curls up into herself, wrapping her arms over her head in what is an unmistakable attempt to protect herself.

Normally, I'd be pissed. The picture inside the frame is one of my favorites of Tolya and myself when we were kids. Both of us were sunburnt and scraped, but we were genuinely happy.

But as I look at Willow and see the way she instantly cowers in fear, her body trembling almost violently as she sobs and hiccups through her sobs how sorry she is…

The only person I'm pissed at is Martin.

"Hey." I soften my voice and reach for her. "Hey, it's okay. Come here."

She doesn't want to at first, but I gently pry one arm away from her head. It's enough to peek at her and get her to see my face.

"Come here, sweetheart. It's okay."

Willow sniffs and slowly unfurls, inching her way into my arms.

"Are you hurt?" I make a point to carefully examine her hands. No signs of damage. "Did you cut yourself?"

She slowly shakes her head. "No…"

"That's good. I was worried."

She looks at me, and I see the confusion in her eyes. Confusion that shouldn't be there, along with the fear that no man should have ever instilled in her. "You… you were?" she asks between sniffles.

I nod solemnly. "Glass is very sharp and can hurt you. Next time, just ask a grownup for help, okay?"

Willow looks at the broken frame and starts to breathe faster in panic. "B-but I b-broke y-your—"

I tuck a finger under her chin so she looks me in the eyes. "Things are replaceable, *matryoshka*. But you are not."

Her bottom lip trembles. I'm not sure if she believes me or if she understands. But I want her to know she's safe with me. That I'm nothing like the asshole who haunts her nightmares.

So I do the last thing I'd ever expect of myself: I scoop Willow up into my arms and carry her around the room, slowly rocking her as I hum the melody of a soft lullaby I've long forgotten the words to.

She tucks her head under my chin. She's so small that I can easily cradle her with one arm and stroke her hair back with my free hand. It's something that comes naturally to me, something that just felt right to do.

Which confuses the absolute fuck out of me.

I don't have a paternal bone in my body. And I sure as shit don't have the best examples of healthy parenting from my own mother and father. Mom was too busy sleeping around to spend any time with her own children, while Dad was... well, he was Dad. Overbearing, manipulative, strict as hell, and adamant that women were simply things to collect and use. When he was done using them, or if he'd broken them beyond use, he'd sell them to the highest bidder.

And when he didn't have his "things" to play with, he turned his sick boredom onto Tolya and me.

It shouldn't have been what bonded us, but it was. Tolya always stepped in front of me to take the worst of it. As we grew older and learned more about who Otets was—*what* he was—we secretly plotted our escape out of his world. We didn't want anything to do with his violence, his greed, or his Bratva.

But then everything went sideways. And before I was even legally old enough to vote, I realized that the only way to save Tolya was to step into his shoes as the heir.

It's several minutes absorbed in my thoughts before I realize that Willow is sound asleep in my arms.

I carefully and quietly step over to the overstuffed chair and try to lay her down on the cushion. But her tiny fingers cling to my shirt and she pouts in her sleep, a soft groan of protest purring through her nose.

So I grab my phone from the desk and settle into the chair, leaning back into the cushions so she can sleep more comfortably on my chest.

I can't afford to get emotionally attached to this kid. I know how dangerous that is—for both of us.

But I can do for her what my own father never did for me: I can protect her. I can provide for her. I can chase away the things that go bump in the night and give her the best this world has to offer.

I scroll through the contacts list on my phone until I find the name I need and press **Call**. "It's Demyen. Remember that deal we made? No, no, don't worry about that. Seriously. Yes, I mean it. I have a different way you can pay me back…"

47

CLARA

"Willow? Baby? Rise and shine…"

I open the door to her room, fully expecting a melodramatic performance of groaning at having to wake up before she's ready. Sleepy Willow is sweet and adorable for now. Give it a few more years and I know she'll make me want to rip my hair out.

She must be out cold. Her bed is empty, so I check the hammock she loves to snuggle up in when the night sky is especially pretty to gaze at.

She's not there, either.

"Willow?"

Don't panic. Don't panic. Panic leads to bad decisions.

It's breakfast time, so maybe she wandered off to the kitchen and is eating cereal with Gloria. Even though the head housekeeper is technically my boss, she's slid into our lives and our hearts as a maternal figure and dotes on Willow like she's her granddaughter. It wouldn't be a stretch at all to assume Willow woke up before me and joined Gloria for an early bite.

But when I get to the dining building, both the kitchen and the dining room are completely empty.

Don't panic.

Don't panic.

Panic leads to bad decisions.

My chest grows tight with worry. I rush out of the kitchen to find Gloria, or Bambi, or hell, even Demyen. *Someone* has to have Willow with them. This place is under so much security, which is the one solace keeping me sane. There's no way she could have wandered off into the desert unnoticed.

The thought leads me to the first guard I can find, one of the men who I've seen patrolling the main courtyard and watching over Willow from a distance. He's a gruffly handsome type and the ring on his finger makes me wonder if he's married with kids of his own. I hope so, because that's sympathy I need to soothe my worry.

"Hi!" I instantly realize I sound way too chipper and his cocked brow agrees. "Sorry to bother you. Have you seen Willow?"

"Not yet." He shakes his head. "Just got in." He gives me a quick once-over and must see the panic I'm trying to deny I'm feeling. "Try the greenhouse. I overheard the gardener mention a new batch of flowers. She could have wandered off there."

This place has a greenhouse? Of course it does. I follow the guard's directional nod and run off down the path.

Willow knows better than to go off on her own. I want to scold her for giving me such a scare and I'm writing a speech in my head as I see the glass panes appear around a corner.

But my steps slow as I realize… maybe she didn't disobey my rule.

This isn't some hotel in the city. This is someone's home. The longer we stay here and the more we make friends, this place is becoming *our* home.

I'm not sure where to file that thought. So I let it simmer as a reassurance that Willow is safe here no matter where she wanders.

When I find the greenhouse empty, I chant the thought like a mantra and run back the way I came. She has to be *somewhere*. With *someone*.

Do. Not. Panic.

"Oh, thank God!" I exclaim when I run into Bambi in one of the convertible lounge rooms. She's sipping on an iced coffee and eyes me warily as I approach. "Have you seen Willow?"

Bambi pauses mid-sip. Then: "She's fine."

"Where is she?" I plaster on my best smile and try my hardest to not sound panicked or irritated.

Demyen's assistant, lawyer, whatever she is, fails to hide the eye roll. "Clara. Relax. She's fine. She's safe and she's happy. Now…" She holds her iced coffee up to me. "Care to join me? I can have Alejandro make another one of these. Best wakeup call ever."

Now, my smile definitely feels forced and I'm sure she sees it. "Thanks. But no. I need to find my daughter."

"You really don't."

Who the hell...? "As her *mother*, I beg to differ."

Bambi doesn't even blink at my chilled tone. "And as She-Who-Sees-All here, I promise you, she's fine. Calm down before you overheat. Seriously, this coffee is incredible. He puts this special hazelnut creamer—"

I spin on my heels and storm away before she can finish her attempt to distract me from finding Willow. My heart is pounding too loudly in my ears to hear her anyway.

There's no way in hell Martin snuck in and kidnapped her, right? I wouldn't put it past him, he'd definitely try, but the inevitable gunshots would have alerted me. Demyen's made it exceptionally clear that no one is to get within fifty feet of my baby girl without our express permission—so it goes without saying that any attempts would result in violent chaos.

Plus, I see the way Willow has captured the hearts of our guards. There's no way they'd let Martin get so much as a pinky toe through the front gates.

Another several minutes fly by without sight or sound of my daughter. Now, I'm not just panicking—I'm *pissed*.

I know one person here who should have eyes and ears on her at all times and, judging by the way Bambi dodged my questions, he's the same person who probably told her to keep her mouth shut.

But when I burst into Demyen's office, it's just as empty as everywhere else.

So is his bedroom.

And the gym.

It's when I storm through the garage filled with expensive cars—but not Demyen or Willow—that I get an insane idea.

It's insane, but not for a mother searching for her child.

I dare *anyone* to stand between me and my baby.

I grab the first set of keys my hand reaches off the hanging board and use the fob to unlock the car, the *beep beep* and flashing lights leading me to a breathtaking Ford Mustang. It's by no means the most luxurious car in the garage, but the way it revs sends a surge of adrenaline through my veins and I'm ready to crash through the gates with this beast.

Go time.

I get maybe ten, twenty yards down the long driveway before a group of guards calmly step in my way.

The ferocious maternal instinct within me whispers, *Run them over.*

The normal human being in me decides murder charges aren't worth it. Especially when the guard who was kind enough to help me earlier steps through the line and knocks on my window with a sympathetic smile.

I sigh and lower the window.

"You know we can't let you leave." He leans an arm on the door, but it's not in a threatening way. More like the good cop who wants to let me off easy.

I stifle the snort. There are no such thing as good cops, in my experience.

"I need to find my daughter." The words grind through my teeth. My grip on the steering wheel tightens, but his quick glance down keeps him relaxed. My feet are off the pedals. For now.

"I get it. Really, I do. I've got three of my own and, if I couldn't find any of them, I'd have mowed these jokers down in an instant."

I hate that he's making me smile just a tiny bit.

"But you and I both know the boss would have my head if I let you drive away. In his car. Which, technically, you stole."

Damn. I feel myself deflate a little bit.

"So in the interest of me not getting a bullet to my head and you not getting arrested for grand theft auto, I'm gonna ask you to put this bad boy in reverse."

I shake my head, trying to swallow back the lump in my throat. "I can't. I can't just sit around without knowing—"

"Hang on." He holds a finger up and taps the plastic headphone embedded in his ear. After a few grunts and a nod, he turns his attention back to me. "Alright. Can you at least go back around so you're not blocking the driveway? Envoy is pulling in."

That's not exactly a "no" to me driving off the premises, so I nod. He pats my door with appreciation and waves for the other guards to give me room to do a three-point turn, which I carefully execute while ignoring the tempting whispers in my brain to just floor it and fucking *go*.

When I pull up to the circular drive right in front of the main house, I follow the other guards' casual waves and park off to the side. Apparently, whoever is coming up behind me is important enough to get preferential parking. Probably one of Demyen's underworld buddies.

My heart drops into my stomach when the three cars park, the back door of the middle one opens, and Demyen steps out.

With Willow holding his hand.

48

CLARA

I leap out of the Mustang, almost forgetting to turn it off and grab the keys before I do. My brain struggles to process a billion things at once: Willow being with Demyen, Demyen taking my daughter off the compound *without telling me…*

And the fact that he's in a suit, she's in a dress, and they look like they've just attended a press conference together. And had *fun.*

"Mommy!" Willow squeals with glee and runs over to me, throwing her arms around my legs. The bow in her hair matches her cream-colored sundress and it's almost as big as her face, which is currently beaming up at me.

Demyen eyes the car I've just attempted to steal from him with an arched brow. "Going somewhere?"

I pick up Willow to hold her close—and, I'm somewhat ashamed to admit, to use her as a sweet little shield between me and Demyen's suspicion. "We're out of eggs."

"Tell Gloria to add it to the order. Save the fuel." He casually strolls over to me and discreetly snatches the keys from my fingers. "Willow, why don't you go get changed into your swimsuit and find Bambi? It's going to be a perfect day for the pool."

Willow grins and wriggles her way out of my arms to go do exactly that. "Are you gonna tell Mommy?"

Demyen winks at her. "Promise."

"'Kay!" And, just like a kid who *wasn't* missing for half a day, she runs off into the main house and out of my view.

I brace myself for the full force of Demyen's fury, but it doesn't come.

Mine, however, does.

"What the *fuck* were you doing with my child?!"

Guards and chauffeurs alike pointedly avoid looking at us as they move around Demyen and me, driving the vehicles back to the garage and giving us a wide berth.

I don't blame them. I'm about to skin Demyen alive if he doesn't give me one hell of a good explanation.

Demyen remains unfazed and it's *very* fucking irritating. Maddening. Murderous-thought-inducing, actually. "What were you doing with my car?"

"Trying to find my daughter! Who was *missing*!"

He smirks. He fucking *smirks*. The bastard. "Walk with me." He wraps an arm around my waist and presses his hand to the small of my back. I hate him so much right now, but I hate even more the way a shivering warmth spreads through my body at the way he touches me.

He's steering me toward his office, but not forcefully. Just enough to assert his dominance in this situation, even though we both know I'm about to claw his eyes out.

"First of all, I'm insulted that you think there's any possible way Willow could just suddenly go missing from under my nose."

I refuse to admit I've been thinking the same thing all morning. Instead, I grind my teeth and glare at the floor as we walk.

"Second of all, I know for a fact that Bambi already told you she was safe and sound."

"Bambi didn't tell me shit," I hiss.

Demyen rolls his eyes. "She told you enough. Enough for you to fucking trust me."

I bark out a laugh as we enter his office and he shuts the door behind us. "'Trust you.' That's rich. You kidnapped my daughter!"

It's his turn to laugh and, when he does, I feel the sudden urge to grab something heavy and throw it at his stupid head. "Right. I kidnapped your daughter, changed my mind about halfway through, and brought her right back. To my house. Where I'm constantly surrounded by both of you."

As he sits down in his leather chair and gestures for me to sit in the one facing his desk, I feel my anger dissipate. Just a bit. Enough to at least entertain more reasonable possibilities.

Demyen pulls a thick folder from God-knows-where and slides it across the desk to me. "I got her enrolled for kindergarten. They just needed to meet her and perform a formal evaluation before they approved her admissions. She passed with flying colors. They love her."

My fingers tremble when I start flipping through the flyers and pamphlets stuffed in each side of the folder. "What... *Where* is this?"

He sighs, but he's not irritated. He actually looks amused. "It's a private Montessori elementary school with a high matriculation rate into Ivy-bound prep schools. They're selective and elitist, but Willow really impressed them."

He might as well have been speaking Latin; I've barely processed a single word. I close the folder, set it back on the desk, and stare at it.

And then I stare at *him*. "You didn't consult me about this."

Demyen leans back in his chair. "I don't recall needing to consult you about anything I do."

"I don't recall you being her father."

His jaw sets. The vein tics on one side as he narrows his eyes at me.

But then he blows out a puff of air and relaxes. "I'm certainly not that."

"So why even do it?" I'm seething. I know I should be grateful and some part of me deep down truly is blown away by his generosity and care for my daughter who—as I very bluntly pointed out just now—is *not* his child. "Why go through all this trouble to...to..." I struggle to find the right words that aren't literally *to undermine me as a parent and control me through my daughter*. Even though that's exactly what he's doing. "Just...why?"

"Would you prefer she miss school entirely?"

"I'd prefer for her to not be out there in the open, available for Martin to snatch up with a flash of his badge and a lie—"

Demyen holds a hand up. "I already took that into consideration. Which is why, on top of calling in a favor or two owed to me by the superintendent and headmaster, I made a sizable donation of money and manpower to increase their security. Willow remains under the careful eye of guards she knows and the other children are safer for it, too."

I hate him. I hate him and his stupid... logical... debatably compassionate...

I just hate him, okay?

I hate him. And I hate how he makes me feel.

Because I'm not supposed to feel this *good* with him.

I'm not supposed to feel this relieved or this safe. Or this *trusting.*

"You've got a great kid, Clara. She deserves better than the world has given her."

I open my mouth to protest, to tell him exactly how insulting that is, but again—he holds a hand up to silence me long enough to explain.

"I mean that not as a dig against you," he continues, "but just as a fact. She's too intelligent and too bright to suffer under the thumb of abuse and poverty. You're right: I'm not her father. But I am in charge of her safety and her well-being. Providing her with an education and opportunities you and I both know wouldn't otherwise be within reach is fulfilling my duties as her protector. Something her fucking 'father' never did."

Tears sting my eyes. I have to look away before he sees them.

I hate how so damn relieved I feel because of him. I hate how full my heart is every time I see him dote on Willow the way she should have always been doted on by Martin.

And, even now, sitting in Demyen's office discussing her education and future, I hate myself for having denied her all of this for so long.

And why? Because I was too fucking terrified to stand up for myself. To stand up for *her*.

"Thank you" is all I manage to croak through the lump in my throat.

"Clara. Look at me."

I do. It's hard to do, but I do it anyway.

Demyen tilts his head to one side as he looks back at me like he's trying to decide something. Finally, he sighs. "You and I... Well, let's not even go there. It's a fucking mess. But things don't have to be messy for Willow. And even though you and I have a ton of shit to deal with, none of that is on her. Whatever happens to you—or to me, for that matter—all I'm saying is, Willow's safe. She'll always be safe. I'm giving her the life and the resources I wish I had when I was her age. Let me do that much."

He opened the door, metaphorically speaking. I have to walk through it. "Did you attend a private school?"

A shadow passes over his face. I almost regret asking, but I have to know. He mentioned not having the resources he's giving her and that surprises me. I figured he grew up with a silver spoon in his mouth.

"I did." His voice sounds tense, and he looks away for a moment. "But not because my parents cared about my education. Fuck, I'm pretty sure if my father sent me to boarding school in Tibet, she wouldn't have noticed."

As maddening and confusing I find him, my heart breaks for the child he once was. And as fucked-up as my own childhood was, I can't imagine having a mother who didn't care. So I make the mistake of telling him precisely that.

"I can't imagine what it was like—"

"No, you fucking can't." Demyen goes tense. His eyes are pitch dark as he wades through the memories. "Tolya and I were used to keep up appearances, but a whole lot of good *that* did. Once word got out through the inner circles that my dearest mother was spreading her legs for half the city, well…" He shrugs. "Tolya defended me from the beatings at school until I was old enough to throw my own punches. But by then, our father suspected I wasn't even his, just some bastard of my mother's whoring. So he didn't fucking care if I came home with straight A's or broken ribs."

I want to reach for him. I want to hug him. I want to hug the little boy somewhere deep inside him and tell him it's okay, everything's going to be okay.

But we both know that's a lie.

Everything is fucked-up.

"I'm sorry." I don't know what else to say.

His gaze flickers back to me, hard and accusing. "For what? Throwing a good man, my *brother*, into prison? Or forcing me into the life I once thought I had the chance to escape?"

I freeze.

I never considered that. Not once. The way Demyen swaggers through the days and nights lording his power and prestige over me, over everyone else within a fifty-mile radius, it's easy to assume this is everything he wanted. That it's all by his design, catered to his whim.

I never, not for a single, solitary second, wondered if he actually *wanted* it.

"I'm just sorry."

Demyen narrows his eyes at me. "If you're so fucking sorry, tell me: why did you do it? Why did you testify against Tolya? Why did you *lie*?"

Again, I don't know what to say. Not because I don't have an answer, but because I'm pretty sure it won't be good enough to satisfy him.

"I don't want your fucking pity. I want your answers." Demyen leans forward and stabs a finger onto the desktop. "I want. My brother. Exonerated."

I know what he wants. I know that doing it, going in front of a judge and recanting my testimony, would probably get Tolya out of prison with a nice, fat reparations check for the false imprisonment. Because the more I learn about him through Demyen and the more I look at the photos while I clean or hear snippets of gossip from household staff and men I'm pretty sure have been with the family since he was a baby…

The more I'm seriously doubting Tolya ever intended to harm me, or Michael Little, at all.

But what Demyen doesn't know is that I can't just plop in the witness stand and take back everything I said. Not because I don't want to.

It's because it requires the arresting officer to attend the hearing.

And I can't stomach the thought of challenging my father, the arresting officer in question, after I'd earned a few scars back when I gave my initial statement.

"I'm sorry."

It's all I can say. It's all I can give. I stand up and wait for Demyen to bark an order at me, but he only glares at me. I move to the door, still ready for the barrage of insults and demands… but he doesn't say a word.

So I leave.

My stomach is in knots as I make my way to the main courtyard, where I hear Willow laughing and splashing in the pool. I feel even worse knowing how much she adores Demyen. She doesn't know the real reason why we're here. She doesn't know just how dangerous our situation is.

No. Not 'our' *situation. Just* my *situation.*

Because, whatever Demyen may be, he's a man of his word. I've never once seen him go back on a promise or break a deal.

If he says Willow is safe no matter what, I believe him.

And if he says I'm fucked, I believe him.

49

DEMYEN

Today has turned into a clusterfuck.

I woke up feeling eager to do something *good* for a change. Not something with an ultimatum attached or some sort of quid pro quo string dangling from it.

I took Willow out to breakfast at my favorite Russian teahouse. We ate macarons and honey cake and I taught her how to curse in Russian. It worked out that the interviewing administrators didn't know what she said but were excited that she knows something other than English.

I don't know what I was expecting Clara's reaction to be. Or rather, I don't like what I *wanted* her reaction to be. Because I shouldn't fucking care either way.

And yet here we are. She's stormed off to pout while I'm sulking in my office.

I was supposed to come home with the kid and the papers. Clara was supposed to be overjoyed and excited, and... then what? Show her appreciation by blowing me under my desk?

Fuck. Now, my dick is hard.

All I have to do to tame the beast between my legs is recall the conversation we just had right here in this spot. How she asked one simple question and I just opened up like she's my fucking therapist.

If I'm not more careful around her, I could slip and lose everything.

I'm hitting Pavel's name on my phone before I pull together why I'm calling him in the first place. He answers, of course, so I make something up on the spot.

"Anything new on the digging?"

"Re: Clara?" Pavel's voice sounds like he's shrugging. "Nothing new to report, really. We've been hitting dead ends and people who were talking last week refuse to open their mouths at all now. I don't know if someone made the rounds or if they're just scared of us in general."

"Probably both." I grimace and lean back in my chair.

"There is one thing. It could be nothing, but..."

"Speak."

Pavel hesitates. "It's a note from the stenographer. The one who sat in at Tolya's trial when Clara testified." I can hear him shuffling around on his desk. "She passed it to the judge, but nothing came of it. Which is why I'm not sure—"

"Just tell me what the note said, man."

Another pause. "The stenographer noticed fresh cuts and bruises on Clara's face and arms. Fresh, as in, they weren't there when she did the walkthrough with the lawyer the day before."

"How would they—"

"There were repairs being done to the machine. The stenographer happened to be there returning the machine in preparation for the trial and bumped into Clara, the prosecutor, and Greg Everett."

I swallow. I don't like where this is going. It confirms a suspicion I've long held about Clara and her father…

And it makes me want to do terrible, terrible things on her behalf.

"Any medical reports?"

"None."

Of course there wouldn't be. Greg Everett couldn't risk his precious arrest record or career with suspicion cast over him and his star witness. "Forget Greg for now. What about the mother?"

A nervous laugh comes from Pavel's end. "Oh, you're gonna love this. Jane Everett was, as far as we can tell, unemployed and a stay-at-home wife and mother. And, as far as we can tell, she committed suicide right before Clara graduated high school."

I frown. "Define 'as far as you can tell.'"

"Listen, Dem… Something doesn't smell right. At all. With anything. You know I'm a bloodhound when it comes to digging up dirt on people, but there's a suspicious lack of definitive answers when it comes to the Everett family."

"We were able to get the reports from Clara's teachers, though."

"Yeah, after a *lot* of bribing and promises of security. And now, they won't talk at all. Something has them spooked into silence."

"Or some*one*," I growl.

"My thoughts exactly. I'm gonna be honest—there's a pattern here." He sighs. "And I know you've been counting on Clara's testimony to recant, this is all her fault, she owes you and Tolya her life…"

I pinch my eyes shut. I really don't like where he's sounding like he's heading. "But…?"

"But the pattern is pointing arrows in a different direction." Pavel sucks in a deep breath. "The more I look into this, the less I believe Clara is to blame for anything."

The only reason why I don't slam the phone down is because I can't fault Pavel for doing exactly what I ordered him to. Do some digging, report the information, give me an analysis. That's his job.

He can't control how that analysis makes my fucking pulse race.

"Head back in," I tell him. "I'm going to need you to man the fort while I'm gone."

"Road trip?"

"Something like that." I toss a pen into the air, wishing it would stick to the ceiling just for the satisfaction of stabbing something. "I'm thinking it's time to pay someone a visit."

I wait until Willow's down for her mid-afternoon nap. With the scare I gave Clara this morning, she's been glued to the kid's side. It's easier to pry her away when no one needs their nose blown or lunch made or alphabet sung.

In theory, at least.

The reality is less smooth.

"Where are we going?" Clara asks for the fifth time. I can now officially measure the walk from the solarium to the garage by how many times this woman can ask me the same question—and in how many times I can give the same damn answer.

"Out." I open the door to the Mustang. "Now, get in the car."

I don't have the patience to spell out our itinerary when all we need is for her to plunk her ass into the Mustang. As in, the same Mustang she tried to steal from me. The look on her face is priceless.

At least I am nice enough to open the door for her... and slam it shut after she huffs and slides in.

I'd usually have an entourage of at least one or two other vehicles filled with *vors* to flank us in case of emergencies. But where we're going doesn't look too favorably on mini-militaries rolling up to their gates. It's a risk, but one worth taking.

Clara's knee bounces nervously as we pull away from the compound into the open desert. The farther we drive, the faster it bounces—until my sanity makes me wrap my hand over her thigh to calm her down.

Big mistake.

Now, neither one of us is "calmed down."

I told her to wear something casual, but I wasn't as specific as I should have been. The light linen sundress is plain, but it slides over her skin a little too easily. One move of my fingers bares her skin to my touch and I feel her suck in a breath.

So. Fucking. Tempted.

We have about an hour until we'll arrive at our destination. An hour is enough to work her sweet pussy into a hot, wet frenzy… But I'll only manage to work myself into a hard, aching mass of frustration if I indulge.

And this trip is for business, not pleasure.

I manage to keep my fingers away from the siren song between her legs, but I do keep them on her. I tell myself it's so her nervous tension doesn't drive me insane and distract me from driving. I tell myself the squeeze I give her thigh is a silent expression of power and authority.

I don't know how to explain away my thumb stroking her soft skin.

"I'm sorry… for earlier." Clara's gentle voice suddenly breaks through the silence. She lays her head back against the headrest as she looks at me. "For freaking out like that."

I almost tell her that it's okay, I get it. Her kid was missing. I'd tear the place up and go on a manhunt, too. But then I remember that I'm supposed to be pissed she tried to steal my car and run off, so I just grunt and nod once. I can't let her start thinking I'm negotiable, because I'm not.

Too many people mistake "reasonable" with "negotiable."

"Thank you. For taking care of Willow."

Her hand slowly rests on top of mine. And for one swift moment, I almost turn mine over to lace our fingers together.

What the fuck is that *about?*

I don't hold hands. I keep my distance from the weaker sex. Women are toxic creatures who cause nothing but pain and torment to anyone they latch onto. I should have learned from my mother. I *did* learn—after a while, at least. There was once a part of me that might've believed in shit like love.

That part died years ago.

At least, I thought it did.

I can't entertain the faintest whisper of affection when it comes to Clara. That would be the worst betrayal of them all, and against my own flesh and blood, no less. *Hey, Tolya. How's prison? Meet my new girlfriend, Clara. You remember her, right? She's the one who put you here.*

But I also can't explain why, when she slowly pulls her hand away from me after a long, pensive silence, I quickly grab it back. Something instinctively reacts to her pulling away, in more ways than one, and I won't have it.

She's mine. Whatever the fuck this is, she's *mine*. She doesn't get to pull away from me. Not without a reminder of exactly where she belongs.

My hand tightens around hers when she sees the sign up ahead—and nearly tries to yank away from me.

"Demy—"

I hear the panic in her voice. But I clench my jaw and keep driving toward the dark gray stretch of concrete and barbed wire slowly forming in the distance.

High Desert State Prison.

Clara's breath hitches and she squirms in her seat. "Demyen, what are we doing here?"

It's not until we're through the initial security gate and parked in the visitor's lot that I let go of her hand. I don't answer her questions or look at the sheer panic etched on her face until I walk around and open the passenger door.

My face is an impassive mask of determination when I do finally look at her. "Let's go."

"But—"

"Now."

Clara visibly trembles as she climbs out of the car. Her fingers practically white-knuckle the door, but I usher her away so I can slam it shut behind her. She jumps; her nerves are shot.

Good.

Still, this is a prison. And despite having more than enough loyal connections inside these walls thanks to my brother and my own rise to power, I need to make sure each and every one of these starving men know Clara Everett is off the menu.

That's why I slip my arm around her waist and pull her close to my side. That's why I nuzzle her silky, wild tresses and breathe her in as we walk inside the main building.

"You lied on the stand," I murmur into her ear. "And you choose silence instead of doing the right thing and recanting."

Clara's eyes fly to mine.

"Let's see what you've bought with that pretty mouth of yours."

"Please, Demyen!"

I ignore her whimpered pleas and practically drag her through the security check. Her fear irritates me—it was so easy for her to make up shit on the stand, but now, it's impossible for her to literally face the consequences?

It wasn't her fault, asshole. It wasn't her—

Clara is near tears by the time she shuffles through the metal detector. Her eyes silently beg me to take her away from here, but I'm in no mood for that bullshit.

"I'll do anything you want." Her trembling lips pucker. "Anything, I swear. We can leave right now and I'll do anything."

Fuck. I need her to make this kind of offer when I'm *not* dragging her into an ironclad hell.

"What *I* want?" I force a smile. It's for the benefit of the security guards watching us, not her. "What I want is for you to accept some fucking responsibility for your actions. What

I *want* is for my one and only brother to be free from the life sentence *you* gave him."

This shuts her up. It doesn't stop her from shaking like a leaf, though, so I'm forced to hold her closer and usher her into the Visiting Room like I'm some doting boyfriend supporting his heartbroken lover through a difficult visitation.

Oh, this *will* be difficult. I have no doubt about that.

I put a solid foot of space between us once we sit down at the table. I don't want or need Tolya to get any wrong ideas, especially when they involve Clara Everett.

Only a minute or so passes before my brother is led into the room, flanked by two guards who walk with him to the table and don't leave until he sits down. The table-bench combo sags a bit under his weight. He looks stronger, denser.

But the look in his eyes is what makes me shiver.

"Well," Tolya drawls as he looks between me and Clara. "Isn't this a nice surprise?" His gaze lingers on her face a little longer than I'd allow any other man, but I let this one slide. He's my brother, and hers is one face he deserves to carve into memory.

"*Privet, brat.*" I greet my brother with what little Russian I can stomach tasting on my tongue. Not because I have anything against the language or my heritage, but because—

"You sound more and more like Otets." Tolya smirks. "Won't he be proud?"

"No more than you." I give him a scowl he knows is not as serious as it may look. This is our banter; insulting each other by comparing how close to our monstrous father we might actually come to emulating. "Keep that shadow growing and you might beat him on the beard."

Tolya chuckles as he strokes his stubbled jaw with a conciliatory shrug. But all fun and games end when he turns his attention to Clara.

She, for her part, looks like she's seen a ghost.

"Tol, this is—"

"I know who this is."

I shouldn't be as surprised as I am. Tolya hasn't seen Clara since she was a child, so I figured he'd need a quick introduction to click the two pieces together.

He points a finger at her face. "You may not sound like him, but you look like him."

Ah.

It's always about family. And I hate to admit it, but my brother is right—she does carry some of Greg Everett's features in her face.

Tolya sighs and leans back on the bench. "So, little girl. What can I do for you? I've already given you my whole fucking life, my freedom, any chance of living like a normal goddamn human being. What's left that you want?"

Every word is dripping with the venom any falsely accused man would feel against the prosecution's star witness. I'd probably say the same damn thing in his shoes.

Still… I'm not loving the tone.

"Actually, it's about what she can do for you." I step in after a beat of Clara's silence.

"Oh?" Tolya's brow arches. His gaze slides over her body a little too slowly for my liking.

"And your case."

"Hm." He grunts and folds his arms across his broad chest, finally shifting his gaze to me. I want to ask about the new tattoos darkening his biceps, but now is not the time. "What about my case?"

I nudge Clara under the table so she'd actually speak up for once. But all she does is shiver and lower her wide-eyed stare to the table. I resist the urge to roll my own eyes and lean forward. "We may be able to get an actual appeal for dismissal. Clara can recant her testimony."

Tolya scoffs. "Which part?"

I frown. "All of it."

"Can't lie in an appeal. Perjury and all that."

"She lied when she testified against you." I'm practically leaning across the table; he's not making any fucking sense. "Now that she's on our side—"

"She didn't lie."

I freeze. Partly because I'm not sure I heard what I think I just heard. But mostly because my blood's run cold. "What?"

Tolya stares at Clara without blinking. "You didn't lie. Did you, *malyshka?*"

Clara shivers again. Then, still staring at the table, slowly shakes her head.

"The fuck?" I narrow my eyes first at her, then him. "She said you were in that warehouse where Little was killed. You were nowhere near it."

"That's what my lawyer assumed. And what you assumed." Tolya shrugs a shoulder. "It seemed like a good idea not to correct anyone." Now, he's the one glaring at Clara. "Until *you* showed up."

Clara winces. And, for the first time since we've sat down, she speaks. "I'm sorry."

Tolya barks out a cold laugh. "Sorry? You're sorry? No, no, *malyshka*. I'm the one who's fucking sorry." When she doesn't look up at him, he slams his fist on the table, making her and the guards jump in surprise.

I wave them off before they come over. After a tense moment, they ease and return to their idle watch.

"Look at me," Tolya snarls. "Show some goddamn respect. You owe me that fucking much."

Clara's beyond shivering, but she manages to lift her gaze to meet his.

She deserves this. She deserves every ounce of his wrath. And he deserves to look his accuser in the eye and let her know exactly what she's done to him.

So why do I want to put a stop to this?

"I should have left you in that fucking car." Tolya bites each word in her face. "I tried to do something good for once in my life and what did I get? Hmm? Tell me, Miss Everett, what did you fucking give me for trying to save you?"

Tears brim her lashes, but she doesn't respond.

"See? That." He shakes a finger at her face. "That. Right there. Hear that? *That's* what landed me in this godforsaken shithole."

I'm tired of his riddles and my tolerance is wearing thin the closer he leans toward Clara. "The hell are you talking about, *brat?*"

Tolya doesn't flicker his gaze from her for a second. "She didn't tell you? Fucking figures. She didn't tell the judge, either." He scoffs. "I saw a little girl get snatched from the streets and stuffed into the trunk of some beat-up shitshow. I followed them to the warehouse and waited for him to leave before I went in. And I found her stuffed inside some shipping crate, ready to be sold to some sick bastard."

Fucking hell.

I manage to swallow, despite the dryness in my mouth. "You were there. You were there and you saw who—"

"I didn't see shit. I was too busy hiding behind the crate when I heard voices arguing." He pitches his voice into some sick sing-song. "I didn't want to leave such a sweet little girl all alone."

Tolya swiftly takes her hand. It's not quite a grab, not enough to alert the guards to any trouble. But I see the way he holds her fingers firmly in his… and I feel my own clench into a fist.

"You want to pay me back?" he asks her insincerely. "You want to make up for your silence? For the fact that you made it look and sound like *I* was the one who kidnapped you and hurt you?" He tugs her closer by her hand and lifts her fingers to his mouth. "Get on your knees and put your mouth to good use, for once in your fucking pathetic little life."

"Okay." I pull Clara's hand away from his grasp and shoot my brother a warning look. "That's enough."

Tolya finally looks at me. Then at Clara, and back at me. He leans back with a sudden jolt of surprise, then twists his mouth into an ugly sneer. "No. Not you, Dem. Don't tell me you've beat me to the punch."

As true as that statement may be, I don't like what he's implying. "You have every right to be angry, Tol. I get it and I'm just as pissed as you are."

"The fuck you are!" he roars at me. Again, I wave the guards down. I can take on my own brother. "Was it a rage fuck in my honor? Or did you wait until after you had a taste before realizing this is the bitch who betrayed me?"

"She was ten years old! A *child*, Tol! You can't—"

"I can't what? Try to get what little justice I can against the people who fucked me over?" He turns back to Clara, his grin almost sadistic. "I'll show you what being 'fucked over' really feels like, sweetheart. *That's* what you can do for me."

I've never seen him like this before.

And I've never felt this enraged at him before.

"Shut the fuck up, Tolya."

"Fucking make me, Demyen—"

"Stop." Clara rests a hand on my arm. And, to both our surprise, she looks him in the eyes. "That's enough. Both of you."

Tolya sneers again. "You don't get to tell me what to do, you little whore—"

"You're right. I don't."

She gives him a respectful nod, which does actually manage to ease him back onto the bench. Only now do I realize both of us were halfway climbing across the table to throttle each other.

Clara clears her throat. She's still trembling, but she pushes through. "And you're right. I fucked you over."

He sits and blinks, silent. So do I.

"The truth is…" She slowly shakes her head and runs a frustrated hand through her hair. "The truth is, I don't know what the truth is. I barely remember what I saw or what I heard. And back when I did remember all the details, I kept getting it wrong."

Fuck me and my instincts—like the one that has me pressing a gentle hand to her back to encourage her to keep talking. "What do you mean?"

Clara sniffs and fists her free hand in front of her face. "I had to practice my testimony, for the lawyer and at home. I had to practice what I needed to say, and… and… I kept getting it wrong. I kept—and Daddy… Daddy kept telling me…" She scrubs her face with both hands. "I don't know. I'm sorry. I'm so sorry, Tolya. I just don't know."

I don't move. I'm afraid that if I do, I'll be the one cuffed and thrown behind bars next.

Tolya stares at her for a long, silent moment. Then sighs. "Well, it's a few fucking years too late to 'not know.' You should have said this shit at the trial."

She hiccups and nods. Her bottom lip trembles and she looks away again. This time, the shame on her face is as obvious as her tears.

He clicks his tongue. "Tsk tsk, *malyshka*. You were so brave when you didn't know shit. Why look away now?"

Clara doesn't respond.

Tolya suddenly leaps around the table and grabs her by her face, yanking her to her feet. "Goddammit! Look at me, you treacherous bitch!"

I don't realize I've left my seat until my hands slam into his chest. Tolya stumbles back over the table, caught by the responding guards who quickly drag him to the nearest exit.

He glares at me as they take him, more of that sick madness contorting his face as he laughs and spits on the floor. But they move him out too quickly for him to shout any final words, which is just as well.

I'm pretty sure I don't want to hear them.

It only takes us half the time to leave as it did getting in. The guards are eager to get us out of there and away from the furious Russian mobster we can hear screaming profanities from here.

As we leave, I'm deeply bothered by two things that are certain to keep me up later tonight.

One: Tolya lied. To me, to his lawyer, to everyone. Even by omission, it's still a lie.

And two: I won't hesitate to kick his ass if he ever touches Clara again.

51

CLARA

My sandals catch on the cracks of the cement pavement in the parking lot, but Demyen's firm hold around me keeps me from stumbling.

I wish that was a comforting thing.

As we near the Mustang, I feel like I need to break the silence with my gratitude. "Thanks for stepping in—"

The air is knocked from my lungs when he spins me around and pins me against the side of the car.

"The fuck do you mean, 'you don't remember'?" He grinds the words through clenched teeth, his breath seething.

I need to be afraid. I should be terrified. But the way his hands wrap around my hips, pinning me to the car while pulling me into him at the same time…

One glance over his shoulder clears up the confusion. Technically, we're still on prison grounds. We still have eyes on us, eyes that connect to mouths that speak into the ears of those who hold Tolya's life in their hands.

Demyen is definitely pissed. He just has to make it look like we're having an intense discussion about... *other* things.

"It was years ago," I try to explain. "And what do I... I don't... I can't..."

"Make up your mind!"

"I don't want to fuck it up again!"

Demyen eases back, but only enough for me to see the sudden surprise in his eyes before he shutters it behind his usual suspicion and skepticism.

He doesn't say anything, so I keep going. Either I'm going to dig myself out of this hole or I'm going to dig deeper until I hit rock bottom. "In case you haven't noticed, I actually care about what happens to people. I'm sick to my stomach about what happened to Tolya. What he... he..." I wave a hand toward the prison, unable to find the right words to describe the unhinged madness the man's sunk into.

Because of *me*.

Me and my stupid, stupid memory.

Demyen squints at me. "Tell me what happened. That night, when Michael Little died."

I sigh and lean back against the car. He's still holding me there, but at least I feel like I have a little more breathing room. "I remember walking home from a friend's house. She only lived three blocks away and it was a safe neighborhood. Everyone knew my dad was a cop, so no one caused trouble right in front of him." I purse my lips, puffing out air to cover the scoff. *Oh, the irony.* "Until that evening, when someone grabbed me from behind and threw me into the trunk of their car."

"Did you recognize the car?"

"By the inside of the trunk?"

"You know what I mean."

I never really considered those details before. The rough carpeting, sure, but did I recognize any smells? Clothing stuffed in the corners? "No. My dad drove a Lumina and Mom didn't drive at all—"

Demyen frowns. "Why does it matter what your parents drove?"

"I…" I pause. That… is a solid question. "I don't know. Point of reference, maybe?"

"Hm."

He's not letting me go, so I take that as a sign to continue. "I must have fallen asleep, because the next thing I remember is waking up inside the crate."

"And?"

"And that's when I saw Tolya. He opened the crate to check on me. Asked me if I was okay. Said he'd come back. I think."

Fingers tighten on my hips. "You 'think'?"

My own fingers flutter up over my eyes as I try to push the memories forward. But try as I might, it's all blur and white noise. "That's where it starts going fuzzy, okay? I can't—"

"Did you hear voices? Other than his?"

Maybe? "I don't know. Arguing? I heard… and then…" I shake my head. "I don't know. I don't remember anything clearly after that point."

"So why not tell that to the judge?"

I peer up at him. "What?"

His glare has softened. But he's still just as pissed as he was when we rushed out of the building. "You've had all this time to come clean to the judge. To the appeals council. Hell, write a fucking letter to the D.A. You keep saying you can't remember? That means you can't say without a shadow of a doubt that you physically saw Tolya pull the trigger."

"Oh."

"But you didn't. You haven't. Why not?" Demyen tilts his head to one side like he's staring at something stuck on his shoe. "Because you're too fucking selfish to take the stand."

I suck in a sharp breath. "What?"

"You heard me."

I shove at his chest, but he doesn't move. "How the hell am *I* selfish?! Do you know what would happen to me if I went up there and told everyone, and I mean *everyone*, that I put an innocent man in prison?!"

"A whole lot fucking less than what happened to him."

That one hurts. It sinks into my chest like a dull knife, and the worst part is—he might actually be right.

But it's the "might" that prevents me from actually going through with it. "You don't understand—"

"The fuck I don't." Demyen leans in closer, so close I can almost feel the rumble of his growl through his chest. "I'm not stupid, Clara. You're scared of what Daddy might think if you challenge his report."

I suck in a shaky breath and shake my head. "Not what he'll think. What he'll *do.*"

He stills. I feel him scan me from head to toe, as if he might be able to see the same wounds I carried into the courtroom.

Everyone saw the wounds. But no one said anything. No one acknowledged that they saw what happened to the little girl who couldn't remember things right, not according to the arresting officer.

Demyen was there. He saw them, too. I'm just pretty sure he forgot.

And now, I'm pretty sure he's remembering, because his hands drop from my sides and he takes a slow step back. He stares at me.

I'm too scared to look up at him—I don't want to see the anger etched on his face, even if it is a permanent expression around me—so I find some piece of gravel on the ground to focus on.

He turns. Walks to his side of the car. It's the slam of the driver's side door that jolts me from my withdrawal. I fumble for the passenger handle, open it, and slide in.

We sit there in silence, both of us staring at the dashboard.

And then he turns the engine on and throws the car into reverse.

It's so strange to feel relieved that we're going home. Which is a word I can't believe I'm associating with Demyen's compound. The farther we drive away from the actual prison where his brother is losing his mind, the more I'm feeling like "prison" isn't the best word to describe what Demyen's place is to me now.

"Haven" is more accurate. Especially when Martin can't barge in and threaten to take Willow away.

I just wish the same protection worked against my father.

That's what Demyen doesn't understand: he can't protect me from everyone. Martin is easy. His anger and violence are fueled by his insecurities and inadequacies. He doesn't think before he lashes out and he doesn't go through the trouble of planning his sins before he commits them.

But my father is a different story.

Greg Everett, beloved high-ranking detective of the Las Vegas Police Department, is fueled by greed. By power. By his hunger for more influence, more money, more everything. He never makes a move without calculating it first. He never strikes where it could leave evidence leading back to him.

Unless he needs the jury's sympathy to win his case. Then he plans every sin and commits them with meticulous accuracy so the unknowing but kindhearted people sitting in the stands see an injured little girl and shift their furious gazes to the innocent man in the hot seat.

Martin isn't a threat, because he can't just blindly barge into the compound and demand what he wants. Demyen's men will shoot first, ask questions never.

But my father is the kind of man who no one sees coming. If he knew where I am, and if he knew I challenged his credibility, he wouldn't barge into the compound for vengeance.

He'd wait in the shadows until I'm all alone.

The thought terrifies me. I look to Demyen to pull myself out of my worst imaginings to remind myself that he's right here. He's glaring at the road with one hand on the steering wheel like he's about to break it, but he's here. Next to me.

And the fact that it brings me comfort is almost more terrifying than the thought of being murdered.

His phone vibrates on the magnetic mount, and he answers with the car's internal system. Pavel's name pops up on the console screen. "Yeah?"

"We've got a problem at The Meridian. You're needed onsite."

Demyen frowns. "Send Bambi."

"You're gonna want to handle this one, boss."

"Security breach?"

"More like an uninvited guest. And he refuses to leave until you speak with him in person."

Demyen grumbles something under his breath. "Fine. We're on our way over."

It's another long stretch of silence and one sharp rerouting turn before he says anything to me.

"When we get there, you stay with me. Don't wander off."

I want to make a miserable joke about eloping off into the sunset together, but I get the impression that he won't appreciate it much. So I just say, "Okay."

He grunts and gives me something resembling a nod. I don't push him for anything more.

52

CLARA

The valet takes Demyen's keys without us pausing for a second. Demyen is all business, no time for pleasantries or hesitation. He ushers me to the gilded doors and I have to practically skip just to keep up.

Sometimes, I forget just how powerful he is. How he doesn't just rule the Vegas underworld and half the Sierra Nevada, but also *this*. This world of gold and glitter, of fantasies and indulgent dreams.

Here, people admire him as much as they fear him and it's written all over the faces of the gamblers who recognize him when we walk in.

"… around what time was that?"

I freeze.

No. Please, no.

That all-too-familiar voice makes my stomach turn and my feet glue to the spot—and apparently, it has the same effect on Demyen. He whips his gaze to the bar as quickly as I do and both of us stare at the "casual" interrogation Martin is giving the bartender.

I feel Demyen's arm wrap around me. Next thing I know, he pulls me tight to his side and whirls me around down a side wing that wraps around a cluster of slot machines.

"I need you here." He's talking through his earpiece. "Patterson. No shit. I didn't see him holding a warrant, no."

The smirk that tugs at the corner of his mouth tells me it's probably Bambi on the other end. I don't know what all she does as his right hand, but I've listened to her flay someone alive over the phone before. I can only imagine how she feels about Martin.

"You got it. See you in ten."

Demyen pushes us into a back wall elevator, presses a button, then turns around to face me. He doesn't say anything, but he stands so close I can breathe in his cologne from the patch of skin showing from beneath his undone top buttons.

I dare a peek up at him. I try to hide the soft gasp at seeing he's gazing at me through lowered lashes, and he's not pissed. Not like he was earlier.

I almost think he's going to…

But no. The elevator settles, the panel softly dings, and the doors slide open. Demyen glances over his shoulder, then pulls me close to lead me down a carpeted hallway filled with unmarked doors.

Was he… protecting me?

Is that what he's doing now?

We enter a lavish office that is without a doubt his. It looks like the one he has at home but on steroids.

"Make yourself comfortable," he orders. "But don't leave. And don't open the door for anyone, no matter who they say they are."

"What if—"

"I'll come and get you once this is done."

He hesitates. Or, more like, he doesn't just sweep out of the room as quickly as he ushered me into it. Instead, he takes a step toward me and I swear I see his hand move up from his side like he's about to—

But then he turns on his heel and leaves me there. I hear the door click, then several beeps and another click indicates I'm locked in here until he comes back.

I have no idea what the codes for his security computer screens are and I definitely do not want to try hacking in. But there's also no television and I don't have the patience or amount of calm necessary to just sit down and "be comfortable."

So I pace around the room a few times. Sit on the lavish futon, test its bounciness, hop back up and pace some more. I tell myself he has something to sleep on in here because he's dedicated to his work, not because he entertains dates or trial runs his escorts himself.

Not that it would bother me if he did.

You dirty, rotten liar.

I shake myself clear of those thoughts and lean against his desk, gazing out the floor-to-ceiling windows I don't remember seeing from the main floor of the casino's pit.

It takes me a moment to realize that they're one-way glass. I can see out clearly, but no one can see in.

The office is set just high enough to see everything that goes on in his glistening kingdom of wine, women, and winnings.

It also gives a decent view of the bar, where Demyen confidently strides up to Martin and interrupts the interrogation.

Even at this distance, I don't miss the looks exchanged between the bartender and Demyen, who doesn't waste time and immediately plasters on his best *"How can I help you before I hurt you"* grin. Sharks look more approachable than he does.

Martin seems to wince, just for a second. I almost feel bad for him.

Honestly... I do. I truly do feel bad for him.

In a single night, he lost his girlfriend, his daughter, everything that made home "home" to him. I stole his little girl from him without so much as a written warning. He didn't know where to begin looking for us; he only found the link to Demyen by pure chance. And he's going through so much trouble to find me. He actually seems worried about me.

Shit.

Did I make a mistake?

I bite my lip as the tears start to sting my eyes. I feel terrible. I mean, we did love each other, right? I wouldn't be with him if I didn't...

But then something Demyen says flips the switch. Martin lashes out as much as the law and police regulations will allow him to in a public space, his finger in Demyen's face as spittle sprays from his enraged, twisted mouth.

I step back, my lungs constricting. I'm a floor up and he has no idea I'm here... and yet I'm reacting to that familiar glare as if he's standing right in front of me.

No. I made the best decision for us. For myself and for Willow.

Demyen calmly straightens the sleeves of his jacket as security steps in and respectfully pulls Martin back to a safe distance. I recognize those "security guards." I've heard Demyen refer to them as "*vors*", and while I have no idea what that means, it's clear it involves loyalty and protection even against police detectives.

I let my attention slide across the floor. He's got Martin handled and I don't need to worry about it.

Something in the pits grabs my eye. Someone vaguely familiar laughing and sliding chips across a green velvet table. He nods jovially at something another player says and pulls one of the escorts standing near the table onto his lap. She giggles and playfully smacks his hand, but he grips her ass with that hand while his other reaches up to roll the dice along her cleavage.

I look away. I don't need to see the lechery of Demyen's guests. But I can't resist taking another look.

I *know* him from somewhere.

Is that...?

A pair of men in dark suits approach the table and the man suddenly grows serious. He slides the escort off his lap, nods for one of the concierges to gather his chips, and turns to discuss business with his associates.

That's when I get a better look at him.

That's when I remember.

Raizo.

I suck in a sharp breath and glance over to where Demyen is pointedly avoiding Martin's barrage of questions. He's got that handled, but does he know who else is in his casino? Does he know the Yakuza don is drinking his champagne and gambling with his money?

I'm no expert in organized crime. I can't tell mafia from Bratva and I didn't even know there were so many different terms in the underworld until I started cleaning Demyen's home and overheard snippets of conversations.

But I know about the Yakuza.

And I know Raizo Watanabe.

It was years before I put two and two together. Truth be told, I met Raizo long before I learned about his people and his career choices. I was a little girl and he was a handsome man who exuded power whenever he entered a room. The fact that he would enter my living room or the kitchen, unannounced yet welcomed by my mother, seemed odd but not particularly remarkable.

Nothing flagged my attention as being "off" about him. He was just Uncle Raizo, a man of many secrets who whispered to Mom and slipped me little toys and candies from Japan.

Always while Dad was at work, though. That was the secret Uncle Raizo kept with us. Mom made sure I never breathed a word about our visitor by telling me he was a "secret agent" and we needed to keep him safe. Just like in the movies.

It wasn't until I was in high school that I found out who "Uncle" Raizo actually worked for.

Dad had come home from an afternoon shift in time for dinner, but instead of acknowledging the warm meal Mom painstakingly arranged for us, he threw his paperwork down and complained about the increased violence between territories. *The Yakuza,* he explained, *hate everyone but their own.* He flipped through manila folders angrily, stabbing his finger at stats and photos while he cursed the very existence of "these slimy motherfuckers" who'd recently shot up a rival's nightclub.

Uncle Raizo was in one of those photos. Dad grumbled something about him being an "up-and-comer." I saw the way Mom froze in her seat. Thankfully, Dad didn't, but he still found reason to yell at her for getting gravy on his dossier.

The only time I saw Raizo and my father speak to each other was the day of Mom's funeral. I didn't think much of it; so many people approached Dad to express their condolences and offer support. No one seemed to notice or care that a Japanese antiquities expert attended the funeral and discreetly pulled the grieving widower aside to talk business.

I may have been young, but not *that* young. I could feel the tension between them from where I hid behind a column in the mausoleum. Whatever they spoke about, it had nothing to do with loss or grief or sympathy. Dad looked more pissed than consoled after Raizo left.

It's been several years since. Raizo is older now, with silver streaking through his thick hair, but he's still just as handsome and powerful in the way he moves. His men stand around him and walk with him the same way Demyen's men do. It's obvious "Uncle" Raizo is no longer up-and-coming; he has *arrived*.

Does Demyen know?

Is this about to become a bloodbath?

I step away from the windows to pace around the room some more. I'm not sure if I should risk Demyen's wrath by leaving the office to go warn him that his rivals, enemies, *whatever*, are in his casino and looking like they're up to something.

I'm also not sure how Raizo would react to finding out I'm shacking up with a Bratva boss.

The man in question starts walking away from the table with his men. He doesn't seem to be going anywhere near Demyen. I let out a sigh of relief, even though I don't feel any less anxious.

I need to splash some cold water on my face. Calm down. Regroup and relax until Demyen comes back.

There's a small bathroom nestled in one side of the office. It's just what I need to cool off and tell my reflection to breathe. The water actually does help bring me back to focus and I let the droplets roll over my skin for a moment before I reach for a towel and dab myself dry.

Nothing to worry about. Let Demyen handle all this. Just lie low and be good.

Sounds like a good plan to me.

I flick off the light to the bathroom and step back into the office when I hear the door lock beep and click open. I actually smile, feeling genuinely happy to see Demyen back so quickly—

But it's not Demyen who steps inside and stares at me.

My heart leaps into my throat at the same time my ribcage collapses in on my lungs.

Uncle Raizo doesn't look any less surprised.

53

CLARA

Raizo's gaze never leaves me. His stride is slow, lazy, calculated. When he's within reach, he touches my hair almost reverently.

"Well, well. For a moment, I swore I was looking at a ghost."

I muster a smile through my nervous tension. "It's been a while."

He snorts out a laugh and nods, dropping his hand. "That's putting it lightly." He takes a step back and slowly shakes his head with a sigh. "Little Clara. How you've grown."

The part of me that remembers him from so long ago blushes.

Raizo glances around Demyen's office and chuckles. "I see you really are just like your mother. Beautiful, tempting—and riding the edge of danger."

No idea what he's talking about, but okay, sure. I force my smile to widen and will my hands to stop trembling as I gesture to what looks like a minibar. "Care for a drink?"

"Thank you, but no." Raizo eyes me closely as I grab a bottle of water from the fridge just to have something to do with myself. "I came here on business and already lost myself to distraction."

"Er, right. Well, let me know if you change your mind."

I want to keep things as casual as possible. I want to keep the distance between us as broad as possible, too. Despite what I remember about him from my childhood, I have this distinct feeling that the Uncle Raizo I knew is not the same man who's currently scanning my body from head to toe—and not being one bit discreet about it.

"My god, you are breathtaking." He steps closer to me, ignoring my attempt to keep that distance. I try to casually move toward the futon, but Raizo takes it as an opportunity to grab my wrist and pin the backs of my legs to the cushion. One move and I'll fall back onto it—and the look in his eyes tells me that's what he wants. "I recognized your name on the roster, but I almost didn't believe it. Believe me, I am thrilled to see it's true."

I let out a nervous chuckle. "I don't know what you're talking about."

Raizo tugs my wrist, making me stumble into his chest. He braces a hand against the small of my back, holding me to him, while his other hand combs my hair from my face. I feel his fingers caress my ear, trail down the slope of my neck… and when they linger over the swell of my breast, a rumble of appreciation rolls through his chest.

"A stunning beauty. So warm, so soft…" He smiles. I hate it. "You, my darling girl, are going to make me a very, very wealthy man."

I hate even more how he says that. Like I'm some piece of meat for sale. I pull away from him. I'd rather fall over the futon than let him continue to touch me.

He clicks his tongue and hedges in closer. There's no pretense between us now. He knows I'm trying to get away from him and I know he wants things from me I'm not willing to give.

"Come now, Clara. Be a good girl..."

The office door opens right when Raizo manages to grab my arm. Demyen sweeps in and I'm not sure if I want to breathe a sigh of relief or throw myself at him in a panic.

I choose panic.

I tear myself away from Raizo and practically leap at Demyen before he can take another step into this deathtrap. "I don't know how he got in here, but—"

"I let him in. Gave him the code." Demyen shrugs me off and continues to his desk.

"You what?" I rush behind him, trying to keep my voice low. "Do you know he's Yakuza?"

Raizo chuckles behind me. Demyen just cocks a brow and smirks at me. "I'm well aware. It's why I invited him here."

My attempt to reach for him freezes mid-air. And then I can't back away fast enough. "Wh... what are you talking about?"

I really don't want him to answer that. I don't want to know.

I thought things were bad when I found out who Demyen was. Then they were worse when I realized *what* he is.

But this?

This feels like it's so much worse.

Demyen's Bratva is secretly powerful. Raizo's Yakuza, by reputation alone, is just as powerful and far more publicly feared. Maybe in some alternate universe, I would have stood a chance by grabbing Willow and running for the safety of Raizo's past compassion for me via my mother.

But from the way Demyen sounds and by the way Raizo leers at me, that's not an option in *this* universe.

Which means I'm officially, royally fucked.

"You're in business together." I don't ask it; I'm surprised I even said it aloud.

Again, Demyen smirks. "Gold star to you."

He settles into his leather chair and pulls out a few files from a locked drawer, flipping through them. I expect him to glance up at me to order me around, tell me to sit down, whatever feeds his need for control over me. But he's very engrossed in whatever paperwork he needs to attend to.

Raizo relaxes in one of the overstuffed lounge chairs, unbothered by his colleague's diverted attention. "Mr. Zakrevsky graciously agreed to host one of my antiquities auctions. He's even contributed to this season's collection."

At no point have I ever seen what could qualify as an "antique" in any part of Demyen's home. It must be part of a side business he's got going on. And if it's anything like what my gut suspects it is, I'm better off not asking more about it.

"Come here, beautiful." Raizo gestures to me with his fingers. I glance over at Demyen, who doesn't look up from his papers to stop the man—or me. So I take a few cautious steps closer to the Yakuza boss, who reaches out to lazily glide his fingertips along my thigh.

"I already had the antiquity appraised," Demyen drawls, still not directly looking at us.

Raizo chuckles. "Of course you would. I don't blame you. Such a thing of exquisite beauty is meant to be thoroughly appraised... and *enjoyed*." His fingers slide around to just below my ass, but when I lean away, he calmly grips my thigh and holds me there. "You wouldn't fault an old man for wanting to assure the quality."

Demyen cocks a brow. "I didn't know you like your merchandise to be handled so frequently."

"Perhaps you're right." Raizo pats my ass, then drops his hand to the armrest. "I must be honest: I am more than tempted to make an offer myself."

For some reason, that makes Demyen freeze mid-flip of a folder. He slowly looks up at Raizo, then at me, that vein in his jaw ticcing. Call me crazy, but he looks like that actually pisses him off.

But then he relaxes and scoffs. "You can't resist playing your buyers for the highest bid."

Raizo laughs and nods. "True enough. It is a weakness of mine. But I'm serious, my friend; I may make you an unforgettable offer to—"

Demyen's phone buzzes on the desk. After a quick glance at the screen, he tucks the files away and stands. "You'll have to excuse us. It seems we have an unexpected guest in the pit. Give Bambi a call to reschedule."

The Yakuza lord frowns as he stands. "We have much to discuss—"

"And we will. Later."

Raizo straightens his jacket and doesn't say anything. It may be eons since I last saw him, but I recognize that expression all the same. It's a good thing Demyen has a grip on the situation, because only an idiot with a death wish would stare unblinking into the face of a pissed-off Raizo Watanabe.

The man slides his gaze to me. I wish I could take some comfort in the little smile he offers, but it only makes my skin crawl.

"See you soon, sweet flower."

God, I hope not.

54

CLARA

Demyen is silent in the elevator. He's avoided looking directly at me since the encounter with Raizo. I don't know if I have the energy or the desire to decode his mood swings today, so I just stare at his back and try not to think too much.

He gestures for me to wait at a cocktail table while he checks on something with Bambi, who is over at the bar sipping a martini and reviewing her tablet.

I do as he bids and drum my fingers on the tall tabletop. *Don't think, don't think, don't—*

"Clara."

Shit.

I thought this particular problem of mine was gone. I'm pretty sure Demyen thought so, too.

Guess we both thought wrong.

Martin grabs my arm and spins me around to face him. "I've been looking everywhere for you."

I offer him a tight smile. It's the best I can do while my stomach churns. "I'm sure you have."

"Look. I know I was a jerk. And I'm sorry. I just—"

"Just… what?" I scoff. Now, I really wish I'd ordered a drink just to have something to throw in his face. "Just thought you could treat me like your punching bag? Teach my daughter to hide her face while Mommy gets slapped around?"

His face narrows into a dangerous glare. It used to frighten me, especially when we were alone in his house.

But we're not in his house right now. We're in someone else's.

And that someone, I can see in the corner of my eye, is watching this little conversation very closely.

"*Our* daughter, Clara." Martin's grip on my arm tightens. "And you took her from me."

"You're gonna wanna remove your hand," I warn him icily, nodding in the direction of the security guards nearby. They're watching, though they're not intervening.

Yet.

Martin reluctantly peels his fingers off of my bicep. "I don't like this attitude—"

"And I don't like the way you treat me. Or Willow."

That deflates him. He sighs, slumps a bit, then nods. "Yeah. You're right." He runs a hand through his thin hair and the glare fades into this puppy-dog pleading that used to work on me, once upon a time. "I've been thinking about seeing a therapist. Getting help for this. I want to be a better man for you, Clara. I just… I need you home. I need you and Willow home, with me, supporting me."

I wish I could take a moment to unpack whatever's going on deep inside me. Because I know, if this conversation had happened weeks ago, I would be a sobbing mess in his arms. I would cling to his sweet, empty promises and beg for his forgiveness for ever leaving him, for taking Willow, for making him suffer loneliness.

But it's happening right now. After weeks of living with Demyen, in his world, surrounded by his physical and theoretical protection. Weeks of watching my daughter flourish in ways I've never seen before.

"You need help, Martin. But you need to get it without me."

"I'll be good—"

"You couldn't 'be good' if you had a fucking roadmap!" I seethe, firmly tearing his fingers off my wrist when he grabs me again. "Take the hint and leave. Now."

"Or what?" Martin steps into my space with a snarl. "What are you gonna do, huh? Nothing. You've got nothing because you *are* nothing."

Part of my brain registers that as the blow he intends it to be. I try to hide the wince, but he notices it and he grabs onto it like a leech.

"That's right, baby. You're nothing without me. How can you support raising Willow on minimum wage? Gonna walk the streets? Spread your legs for a quick buck?" Martin tugs me close to him, smiling like this is just any other normal conversation between any other normal couple. "You and I both know I'm the only man who can warm your bed. I'm the only man in this world who will ever want you. I don't care how ugly you got after you had the baby. Getting fat, saggy tits, stretch marks… I don't care. But that's because I love you. Other men, they—"

"Get your fucking hands off my woman."

Martin's eyes widen at the man now standing behind me. Then he narrows into his signature glare—but before he can protest, Demyen rips me out of Martin's grasp and tucks me close to his own side.

"You okay?" Demyen dips his head to nuzzle my hair, murmuring the words in my ear. His thumb traces a slow, lazy circle over my stomach where his hand rests.

I'm gonna need Dramamine for the whiplash this man's mood swings give me.

I nod and give him a meek smile. "We were just talking."

"Hm." Demyen focuses a steady gaze at Martin, which is almost worse than his glare. "I believe my lawyer showed you the exit, Detective."

Martin growls. "And I believe you lied to me, Mr. Zakrevsky. I should arrest you for obstructing justice and impeding an investigation."

"For what?"

"When I questioned you about Clara's whereabouts—"

"Did you file a missing person's report? Open up a formal investigation?"

Martin shuts his mouth. He's fuming. He's fuming because obviously, he didn't. He couldn't. So he shifts his focus back to me, which doesn't help soothe his anger seeing me in

Demyen's arms. "Clara, you need to come home with me. Now."

Demyen laughs. "Take the fucking hint, Detective. She doesn't want you; she doesn't want your shithole of a life. You've been upgraded. Accept it."

Martin stares at me like I've suddenly sprouted three extra heads. "I don't know what lies you've told this son of a bitch, but—"

I don't have the breath of a second to respond. One moment, I'm bracing myself for a barrage of insults from Martin. The next, I'm pressed flush against Demyen's chest, his free hand tangled in my hair at the scalp and holding me in place for the perfect angle for the perfect kiss.

And my God, what a kiss it is.

My toes curl before I can register any sensation other than sheer electricity coursing through my body. His tongue sweeps between my lips and glides over my own, drawing me into him with a low groan. Right when I think he's going to pull away for air, he breaks the kiss—only to adjust the angle and devour me once more.

God help me, I *want* this. I want this so fucking badly that I forget literally everything else hanging between us. My hands smooth over his chest and slide up around his neck. I feed him soft whimpers of need, desire... longing.

I want this. All the time.

I want *him*.

Demyen breaks the kiss again to catch his breath. For a split second, it almost feels like he's just as affected by this as I am. But then he presses another kiss to my temple and smirks at Martin. "As I said, Detective: take the fucking hint."

If Martin was pissed before, he's straight-up *seething* now. He takes a half-step toward me, like he's ready to make a grab for me no matter what the risk.

I'd advise him against that. But Demyen is quicker.

He tucks me behind him and steps into Martin's space until they're practically nose to nose. At this angle, I'm suddenly acutely aware of how accurate Demyen's statement is: I *have* upgraded. By at least a foot and a half.

And, like... five inches in another department. Maybe six.

"Drop the detective act," Demyen growls, "and I'll drop the business owner act. I'm saying this to you, man to man: stay the fuck away from Clara Everett."

Martin puffs up his chest. I almost laugh at the sight. "You can't keep me away from my daughter! Keep the whore, but I'm taking my daughter!"

If it were physically possible, this whole place would drop twenty degrees with the chilling mask of fury suddenly etched on Demyen's face. I wouldn't normally think he'd risk an arrest or charges for attacking a police detective—especially in public.

But right now, it looks like he's on the verge of redecorating the lounge with Martin's blood.

He leans in so close, I'm barely able to hear what he snarls. "Listen to me, and listen well because I'm not going to fucking repeat myself. I don't care if you're a cop. I don't care if you're the goddamned president of the United States. And I sure as shit don't care that, some-fucking-how, you're

Willow's biological sperm donor. If you touch a single hair on that kid's head..."

I see Bambi slide off her barstool, ready to step in. She looks as concerned about the spidersilk-thin thread tethering Demyen to "legally acceptable" as I am.

"... your own cold case will freeze solid long before they ever find your body. Understood?"

Martin's knees actually tremble. They actually fucking *tremble*. It's quick and he recovers himself before it's obvious, but I see it. I see it and I *revel* in it. He's so much shorter than Demyen, he has to practically arch his back just to meet the man's hard stare.

How on earth did I ever find him remotely attractive?

"Are you threatening me, Mr. Zakrevsky?" Even his voice wavers for a second, which he tries to cover by clearing his throat.

Demyen smiles. It's the same smile a cat gives a mouse right before the kill. "Oh, no, Martin. I'm not threatening you at all. I'm making a promise."

"You can't—"

"I think you'll find that I can." Demyen straightens and says this loud and clear for everyone to hear, now that Bambi is standing next to him with her stylus poised over her tablet. "This is my casino. My house. My rules. Everyone inside these walls is under my protection. Everyone and everything in my home is mine. And if you think you have a good idea of how far I'll go to protect what's mine, let me assure you..."

He holds his hand out to me and, when I take it, brings my knuckles to his lips to press a tender kiss there.

"… you have no fucking idea."

Demyen steers us around a stammering Martin, who is now officially being escorted by casino security to the doors. I don't get to see or hear Bambi remind Martin about his warrants because Demyen practically carries me out of the casino to his car. The second the valet sees us approaching the main entrance, he scrambles to quickly retrieve the Mustang and whip it around to the curb.

I don't say a word the whole way, from the bar to the foyer to the car. I don't know what to say and I have a gut feeling that trying to find the right words will only ruin the moment.

And this is a moment I want to savor, even if it's all a charade. Because no man, not in my entire life, has ever stood up for me the way Demyen just did against my ex.

And I've never felt this good, this… *cherished*… by someone claiming me as theirs.

It's a nice change from what I thought I'd always have.

55

DEMYEN

It's silent in the car.

Thank fucking God.

I'm white-knuckling the steering wheel despite the drive being on the flattest, emptiest stretch of road between Vegas and home.

It took every ounce of self-control in my blood cells to hold my fists away from Martin's face. I've never felt such a strong urge to beat a man to a bloody pulp in public, police badge be damned.

Part of me wonders if it's too late to whip this car in reverse and go take care of this urge.

A soft sigh pours from the passenger seat next to me, and I'm reminded why I can't.

"You okay?" I grumble. The intention is nice, but I'm still grinding my teeth too hard to sound like it.

"Yeah."

I'm not convinced, but I say simply, "Good."

More silence. I'm beginning to form a love-hate relationship with the quiet. I love that she's not jumping on my back with a million questions I may or may not have answers to. I hate that I don't know what's going through her head.

I'm confused as to why I even care.

"I think…"

When she doesn't finish her sentence, I glance over and see her leaning heavily on one arm, propped against the door. She's chewing on her thumbnail—a nervous tic I don't think she knows she has. "Think what?"

Clara frowns. "I think my dad screwed up my testimony."

No shit. But I'm curious to know what's brought this revelation on, so I do my best not to scare her off the subject. "What do you mean?"

"I don't know. I mean…" She blows out a heavy breath. "He was the arresting officer, right?"

"Right."

"Why didn't he recuse himself? Since family was involved."

I start to say something, then shut my mouth. She's still going.

"And even if he didn't recuse himself for that reason, his superiors should have made him step down. But they didn't." Clara drums her fingers on the door.

"And you think that's part of it."

"I think that's a flag for something. I don't know what." She sighs again. "I just… I remember how he'd ask me, over and over, what happened that night. And every time I got it wrong, he hit me."

My fingers tighten around the steering wheel. *Focus, man. Nothing you can do about that now.*

Clara suddenly turns to look at me. "How can someone get a memory wrong?" It's a rhetorical question, so I don't answer. Her sigh whistles past her lips as she looks away again. "When I said what he wanted me to say, it stopped hurting. When I didn't, the pain started again."

The ten o'clock side of the steering wheel I'm squeezing to death, in my mind's eye, is Martin's scrawny neck.

The two o'clock side? *Greg fucking Everett's.*

Let's hope I don't snap the wheel in half.

"Do you remember which part got you hurt?"

Clara chews the inside of her cheek for a moment. "Honestly, it's all fuzzy. He hit me in the head a lot. I swear, I'm trying—"

"I know."

She looks at me again, surprised and relieved. "You do?"

"I…" I sigh, just like she did a moment ago. I hate admitting things. It means I was wrong somewhere, at some point, and I hate being wrong. In my life, I can't fucking afford to be wrong. "I remember your face. At the trial. All the cuts and bruises."

"You… you do?"

It was hard to forget. "I kept thinking how fucking stupid everyone was. They wanted to blame Tolya for all those injuries, but they were too fresh."

"It wasn't brought up during questioning."

"It didn't have to be. I saw that jury. So did you. No one had to say a word. All they had to do was look at you. Look at you, listen to the stories, and look at Tolya." I feel the worst kind of laugh bubble up in my chest. "All this time, it was fucking Greg Everett. Honorable public servant Everett, Good Guy Greg, who used his own daughter like a punching bag until she sang the song he wanted her to sing."

Clara picks at her fingernails. "Until I said what he wanted. Which was what I said on the stand."

"Can you remember anything at all? Any specific part that he didn't like in your testimony?"

She's pulling into herself. And away from me. I hate that even more, but I can't just reach over and hold her hand through this.

Actually, I *could*…

No. The last thing either of us needs is more mixed fucking signals.

"I'm sorry." Her voice catches like she's about to cry, but she chokes them back. Whether for my sake or hers, I don't know. "It's like there's just… gaps."

A memory of my mother suddenly flashes unbidden through my mind. She had gaps, too. She'd forget things all the time. But I always chalked that up to her terrible choices in life.

Now, seeing and hearing Clara echo some of Mom's behavior…

I give myself a little shake. *No.* My mother made her bed. She chose to lie in it with dozens of other men, right in front of my father. She didn't care enough about Tolya and me to lift a damn finger to help us.

She's no parent. Not like Clara is to Willow.

"Do you remember seeing anyone else there? Or hearing? Even if you thought you imagined it?" I need to pull myself out of my own thoughts before they get the best of me.

Clara stills. She's silent. Then… "No."

"You're sure?"

More silence. "No. I'm not sure about anything."

I try not to give her a scowl. It's obvious she's not deliberately trying to frustrate the fuck out of me. She's as confused as I am.

"I want to get this right." Clara looks at me again with those big, beautiful eyes and flutters her long lashes. The fact that she definitely doesn't know she has that little habit makes it all the more alluring.

I may have held strong opinions about her—hell, I still do— but I have to give credit where credit is due: Clara Everett is no manufactured beauty. She's one hundred percent genuine.

As is the erection now straining against my pants. It grows even worse when I flick my gaze to those sweet, plump lips that are currently trembling as she searches for the right words.

If I wasn't driving...

Blyat'. It's like all she has to do is breathe and I'm ready to go.

"I don't remember much. Not right now, anyway. But I don't think Tolya killed Michael Little." Clara's serious voice succeeds in pulling me out of the sharp left turn my brain just took. "I do think he was just… wrong place, wrong time. And my dad took full advantage of that."

"The big question is, why?"

"Exactly. Why? Especially when Michael Little was my Dad's partner."

I scrub a hand over my face. "So instead of hunting down the actual killer, your father just landed on whatever, whoever, was convenient and quick. Justice at any cost. I'm no cop, but I don't think that's how the police department is designed to operate."

"No, it's definitely not." Clara peers at me from the corners of her eyes for a moment. Then, to my surprise, she snickers a tiny, broken little laugh. "I'm sorry; this isn't funny at all. I just… I just imagined you with aviators and a mustache and, like, a big highway patrolman's hat."

I should scold her for jumping topics, but I was just imagining her spread wide and moaning in the backseat of the car. Like I am again…right now….

Get a hold of yourself, man.

I clear my throat and manage a wry smirk. "Willow might like the mustache."

"Absolutely not." Clara snorts and shakes her head. "She'd probably shave you in your sleep. With my help."

Something tightens in my chest at how *easy* this is. Her. Me. Us. Easing tension with jokes, talking about our kid…

She must feel the shift inside me, because she returns to her slump against the car door. It's just as well. I'm having a hard time as it is—literally—reminding myself that there's supposed to be a giant wall of hate between us.

There's supposed to be. But as time goes by, it feels less like a wall and more like a chain link fence. Full of holes we keep slipping through again and again.

"I want to help." Clara sighs and rubs the bridge of her nose with one finger. "Really. I can't... I can't sleep right, I can't even *sit* right, knowing that I put an innocent man in prison for the rest of his life. And even worse, knowing that the real killer got away with it. I don't know how to help... But fuck it; I'm going to try. One way or another, I'm going to make this right. For you, for Tolya... and for Willow."

My brow lifts. "Willow?"

Clara fixes her steady gaze on me. It's one of those steady glares that makes her eyes look even brighter and more intense than usual. "She needs to see her mother accept responsibility and do what's right. She needs to see the best example of humanity I can give her. Lord knows she won't get it from her father."

Or from me.

I shouldn't care. I really shouldn't. But for some stupid fucking reason, that final thought still hits like a punch to the gut.

The rest of the drive home is spent with both of us in our respective dark thoughts, my own swirling around with questions I don't have answers to.

And the ones I *can* answer are the ones I most need to ignore.

56

DEMYEN

Clara immediately starts to beeline for Willow's room once we leave the garage, but I grab her arm. "It's late," I remind her. "Willow is already in bed."

"How do you—"

"Bambi texted me. Gloria tucked her in with *Goodnight, Moon.*"

That brings a small smile to Clara's face. "Oh. Well. Okay."

"Come on." I slide my hand down her arm to her fingers and give them a tug. "I don't know about you, but I could use a drink."

I'm wide awake. The sun set hours ago, the stars are scattered across the sky, and most of the household is fast asleep. But I'm wide awake and unable to calm the raging storm of thoughts battering around inside my head.

Who killed Michael Little?

Who kidnapped Clara Everett?

What the fuck was Tolya thinking?

What's Greg Everett's angle in all this?

What is Clara wearing underneath that dress?

I clench my free hand into a fist so hard that my fingernails bite into my skin and snap me back to reality. Unfortunately, it does not have the same effect on my dick, which can't seem to ignore every alluring aspect of the woman walking next to me.

Wasn't I pissed at her just this morning? Didn't I threaten the fuck out of her by dragging her to the prison? Isn't she supposed to be the bane of my goddamn existence?

But then she walks past me into my office and I get a full whiff of my own scent on her skin and in her hair. She's still using my body wash, my shampoo and, *good fucking Lord*, I'm only just realizing she confronted that asshole ex of hers while drenched in my scent and now, I'm officially needing to bend her over that desk—

"Are these… are these the case files on Michael Little?" Clara peers at a stack of folders on my desk that I completely forgot to put away.

"Yeah."

I close the door behind me and head straight for the minibar. I need a drink. I need a whole fucking bottle if I'm going to get any sleep tonight.

There's something else I can do that will definitely relax me enough to get a good night's sleep, but…

As I pull a swig from my stash of bourbon, I watch her face contort into a frown and she slumps into my leather office chair. She's too focused on the case, as she should be.

As *I* should be, instead of standing here debating on whether to carry her sweet ass to bed or just fuck her on my desk.

Either would be good.

Both would be better.

"How did you get these?" She carefully flips through the pages, her eyes never leaving the scrawled notes and highlighted sections. Half those notes are my own. "Aren't these classified?"

"I happen to be very skilled at obtaining things I shouldn't be able to obtain."

"Oh…" Her face falls into a sheepish blush. "I thought you just… I don't know, swindled gamblers and sold drugs or whatever."

She's so fucking adorable. Or this bourbon is strong.

Both can be true at once.

I meander over to the desk and shrug. "That, too. But the casino and my escorts pay most of the bills."

"How charming."

"Guy's gotta have his hobbies."

Clara narrows her eyes at me. In the golden light of the desk lamp, she's fucking mesmerizing. "Is that what you're calling it? Parading your hookers around to drunk tourists is a 'hobby'?"

If I didn't know any better, I'd detect a hint of jealousy in that question.

I lean on the desk and take another swig. "They're escorts, not hookers."

"Oh, wow. Yeah. Such a significant difference." She rolls her eyes.

"There is." I lean in a bit closer, maybe a little too close. But goddamn, I love the way she smells. "I prefer my woman to be willing."

Clara's eyes widen. Then she clears her throat and taps a finger on one of the open files. "So I noticed a discrepancy here in the... ah... *borrowed* police log."

I set the bottle of bourbon down on the desk and angle my head to take a look at where her finger is underlining a section.

It looks like standard clock-in, clock-out shift logs for the officers—in this case, Michael Little. I can't remember why Bambi had this added to the files, but she's always been insanely thorough. I'm pretty sure his dental history is somewhere in the folder, too. "Yeah?"

"On the day he died? He left early."

I frown. "How do you know?"

"He and Dad were partners, right? So they worked the same shifts. Usually until five, maybe seven at the latest. A few graveyard shifts, but this roll call logs him in that morning for their usual day shift. But instead of leaving in the evening, he was out by three."

"So?"

"So it means he was off-duty that night. And had been for a while." Clara sighs. "What was he doing there?"

This entire time, for years, I'd hated the Everetts for fucking up Tolya's life. And, by proxy, mine. So when Clara fell into my lap—a bit too literally—I immediately viewed her as The

Enemy and kept her under my thumb to make sure she couldn't cause any more damage to me or my family.

It never occurred to me how *useful* she could actually be in the investigation. Like, how being the daughter of a cop would actually give her intel we wouldn't otherwise have.

Just add that to the growing list of things I've apparently been wrong about.

If I don't keep this under wraps, Bambi is going to type up every mistake and make me sign it just so she can frame it in my office as a reminder. *No king is infallible.*

"What else do you see?"

"Nothing that jogs my memory." She runs a frustrated hand through her hair. "I don't understand it. Any of it. Uncle Mike was like a second father to me. And he was actually *good*. So why can't I remember...? I just..." Her voice crackles until she breaks into a hiccupped sob.

I slide off the desk and move behind her. My hands rest on her shoulders and I knead my thumbs in slow circles at the base of her neck. "It's okay. We'll figure this out. You've already found something worth looking into. Take the win."

Clara freezes at first, but then I feel her relax into my hands. And soon, a small moan bubbles in her throat when my fingers start to work the tension knots from her collarbone.

I need to distract myself. Quickly.

"Do you remember asking your father about Michael Little? Since you two were so close. And you saw his dead body."

"I don't know. I mean, maybe? I kind of remember asking why..." She raises a hand to touch her cheek. It's a subconscious gesture, one that tells me all I need to know. *It was a question that earned her a blow.* "But I don't think they asked me how I knew him. At the trial, I mean."

A heavy silence passes between us. My hands are still on her shoulders, but I'm not doing much more than just touching her. Because fuck it all, I'm addicted to the way her soft skin feels.

"I'm sorry, Dem." Clara barely mutters the words, but I hear them all the same. "I'm trying and I keep... I keep getting it wrong..."

"Hey." I reach around to cup her face in my hand so she'll look up at me. Tears well in her lashes, and before I can stop myself...

I press a soft kiss to one eye. Then the other. Tasting her tears while brushing them away.

"It'll come back to you. And we'll make this right."

"Dem..."

Blame the bourbon, blame insanity, blame the ache in my pants that refuses to go away. But whatever's at fault, it nudges me closer to Clara until my lips rub across hers.

And when she lets out the softest little whimper of surprise, I sink into the kiss like a starving man.

She tastes so fucking delicious. She tastes like *mine*. Salty tears mixed with sugary lips and a naughty tongue I want to feel over every inch of my body. I slide my hands down along her curves to pluck her up out of the chair and set her sexy ass on the desk exactly where I want her.

Clara doesn't protest. I expected her to at least scold me for not paying attention to the work we're doing, but instead, she wraps her arms around my neck, threads her fingers in my hair, cups my face, smooths her palms over my chest...

She's everywhere at once and kissing me just as hungrily as I am her.

It's when she slides her hands under my shirt and palms my bare skin that I'm brought back to reality. Not that I don't want her touching every fucking part of me, but the sharp need it suddenly spikes deep in my core is almost shocking.

I don't have to press a hand between her legs to know she's hot and wet for me. And I'm sure if I just continued, if I pressed her back on the desk's surface and spread her like the fucking feast her body is to me, she wouldn't utter a single protest. No, she'd beg me for more.

But when I hesitate, something shutters in her eyes. She slowly pulls away, quickly looks away, and just like that, it's over.

The spell is broken.

"I, um..." Clara tucks a strand of hair behind her ear, still pointedly looking at anything but me. "I should go."

The words are barely whispered, but they scream loud in my ears. She slides off the desk, then ducks out of the office before either of us has a chance to say another word.

The fuck just happened?

How the hell did I just let her walk away?

I glance down at the files on my desk, hoping they'll provide something resembling an answer. Like, *you need to focus on this instead of her.* Like, *you shouldn't fraternize with The Enemy.*

But instead, I find tiny little notes she apparently scribbled next to mine while I wasn't paying attention. They're questions, not answers, but still... they're proof that she means it: she's trying.

She's not The Enemy. Not anymore.

And I just let her fucking leave?

Hell no.

I drop the bourbon and go running after her.

57

CLARA

Breathe.

Breathe, Clara.

Just... breathe.

But that's hard to do when Demyen Zakrevsky is sucking the air from my lungs in more ways than one.

I can't believe I fell for it. I can't believe I let him get to me. I don't even know why he's suddenly so... *there.*

I mean, what flipped his switch? Earlier, he was so pissed I thought he was going to chop me up and throw me into some ravine out there in the desert.

You know, like a gangster would. Because *he is one.*

But something shifted in him at the casino. I have no idea what it was or why. All I do know is that he kissed me, right there in front of Martin, and oh my God. What a kiss. Mind-blowing.

At least, I thought that was mind-blowing—until about five minutes ago, when he topped it with whatever *that* was in his office.

A distraction. That's what that was.

I needed to get away from him before I made yet another dangerous mistake. So I fumbled my way out of his arms and out the door and ran to the first unlocked building I could find, which happens to be the laundry facility.

For a household this large, it's practically a laundromat in its own right. But right now, it's a quiet, empty safe haven away from the foggy confusion that Demyen brings to my world.

I just need to breathe. Pull myself together. Remind myself that I'm only working here until I can figure out the next best move.

Until then, I just need to stay far the fuck away from—

The door to the laundry room swings open.

Him.

It should be a crime how quickly my thighs clench whenever that man darkens my doorway. Demyen steps inside and quietly shuts the door behind him, locking it. My heart picks up the pace and I slowly inch my way back against one of the washing machines as he comes closer.

"Listen, Clara, I…" His dark eyes roam over my body. He seems to be arguing with himself for a moment, because he lets out a low growl and takes another step closer. "Fucking hell. I don't know what I'm doing. You're supposed to be my prisoner and I'm supposed to be eternally furious with you for fucking up my family."

There's a "but" in there, somewhere. I hope.

"But…"

Oh, thank God.

Demyen's gaze heats more the longer his eyes roam. "I can't get rid of the image of you making yourself come on your bed. For me."

Shit. I knew it. He doesn't just know what I did—he saw the whole thing.

Which means there are definitely hidden cameras in my bedroom. And I should be enraged at that fact. I should feel violated.

Instead, I'm way too distracted by how close he is now. He lifts a hand to my hair and strokes it back from my face, making me look up at him.

"You know what really pisses me off, though?"

I gulp. "N-no…?"

Demyen rubs his thumb over my lip, his eyes tracing the motion. "The fact that I wasn't there with you."

His mouth crashes over mine and I know, I feel it in every cell in my body, that there's no walking away from him now.

I'm breathless and wanting. I want him. God, I want him so fucking badly. I can't help the whimper of need that escapes my throat, and when he growls in response and nips my bottom lip with his teeth, I almost come right then and there.

His hands rub my thighs under my dress, edging it up more and more as he kneads his fingers into my flesh. When he breaks the kiss, it's only so he can trail his hungry mouth along my jaw and down my neck, sucking on the curve where my shoulder begins.

Demyen sinks his teeth in, not enough to break skin but just enough to make me cry out and surge with warmth between my legs at the same time.

"That's it, baby," he rumbles against my damp skin. "That's what I wanna hear."

Can he hear my heart slamming inside my chest? Does he want that, too? But before I can pull together my thoughts enough to form words, he kisses his way back to my mouth and tangles his tongue with mine once more.

I can't help myself. He tastes so fucking *good*. I suck on his tongue, stroking with my own, which earns me another appreciative growl and his hand suddenly fists in my hair at the nape of my neck, right where he knows I want it.

His other hand rips my flimsy panties apart like they're nothing to him. The quick bite of elastic against my skin only heightens the thrill.

And then he's there, cupping me in his palm. Stroking his fingers along my slit. Pressing, pushing, teasing. I don't hold back the shivering moan he pulls from me and his mouth curves into a wicked smile.

"We were rudely interrupted last time," he murmurs, his mouth hovering inches from mine. "Is that what you were dreaming about?"

I don't know how he figures it out so quickly, but I don't care, either. I only nod. "Yes…"

"Such a good girl." He captures my lips again. This time, his middle finger strokes my swollen slit… and then presses inside me.

I shiver. He smiles. One finger is soon joined by a second, and when I mewl at the slight stretch, he holds me in place with his other hand in my hair.

"Is this what you want, baby?" Demyen presses soothing kisses all the way to my ear. When I gasp and he feels me surge on his fingers, he works them inside me deeper and strokes that glorious spot only he knows how to find.

"Oh, God, Demyen…" I grip his arms, mostly because I don't know what else to grab.

"Good girl. Tell me what you feel." He kisses the skin just below my ear. "Let me hear you sing."

All I can give him is a chorus of whimpers and whines, but that's exactly what he's after. I squeeze my thighs around his wrist and he uses the tension to work his fingers inside me over that one spot that makes my toes curl and my breath quicken from gasps to pants.

Suddenly, he pulls his hand from me. I groan in panicked protest. *What did I do wrong?*

Demyen chuckles and kisses me. Then he uses both hands to tug my dress off over my head and toss it aside. My bra follows without a second thought and, before I have a moment to register what's happening, he grabs me by my waist and lifts me onto the washing machine.

"Now…" He kisses a fiery path between my breasts as his hands return to stroking my thighs. "Wrap these pretty legs around my head, baby."

I don't know if I do as he says or if he just spreads me wide and drapes my legs over his shoulders…but the second his tongue sweeps over my slit, I gasp with surprise and squeeze every muscle in my body.

Demyen growls his approval and holds me in place. The sight of his face buried between my legs is almost too much. And he doesn't just devour me. Not at first, at least. He takes the time to suck, lick, savor. His tongue delves warm and wet inside me, then drags up to flick and circle around my clit. His lips quickly follow, tugging on that bundle of nerves that makes me squeal and moan his name.

He does it again, and again, and again. That deep dive of his tongue, the slow sweep, the warm suckle…

Only this time, he gives my clit another long, deep tug into his mouth the same time his fingers plunge inside me.

Oh.

My.

God.

"Dem…please…" I can barely breathe. At some point, my own fingers tangled in his hair and now, they're tugging at the roots. Any other man would probably complain, but not him. Not Demyen.

The wicked grin on his glistening face tells me he loves every single second of this.

"Are you gonna come for me, princess?" He presses his fingers in and uses the heel of his hand to ground my clit. "Are you gonna be my good girl and make a mess all over my face?"

All I can do is nod pitifully.

But that's not good enough for him—he wants my words. My voice. The nip of his teeth on the inside of my thigh is the kind of scolding that sends molten fire through my veins.

"Uh-huh… yes… yes, Demyen, please…"

He smirks. His fingers slow, then stop. "I can't hear you."

"Yes! God, Demyen, yes!" I cry out, begging, not caring who might hear us. I don't fucking care as long as he doesn't fucking stop. "I'm gonna come! Please, Dem, make me come!"

"There's my good girl."

I don't know why those four words, from his mouth, do it for me. But oh, they do. That spot goes apeshit.

I want to buck away from him—*it's too much, it's so, so, so much*—but Demyen growls into my pussy and yanks me closer with his free hand, wrapping that same arm around my waist so there's nowhere to go but to him.

He milks every single drop my body can give, groaning his own delight and drinking from me like it's the last thing he'll ever taste.

When my shudders subside and I'm no longer spasming so hard, he slowly pulls his fingers from me. But instead of moving away, he uses both hands to grab my ass and hold me to him as he broadly, gently strokes my swollen lips with his tongue. He's careful to move around my over-sensitive nub, focusing instead on cleaning up my juices from every inch his tongue can reach.

I feel that sinful tongue dart lower, to a part of me no man has ever touched, and I yelp with surprise.

Even more surprising? I *like* it.

The grin on Demyen's face is wide enough to split his head in half. "Maybe later. But right now…"

He nips and licks and kisses a glistening trail over my stomach, to my breasts, and fans his breath over a stiff nipple. "Right now, I want to know what the rest of your fantasy was."

What?

My eyes widen and he gives me the sexiest little smirk before kissing my nipple.

"I told you: it pisses me off that I wasn't there. I don't know what made you scream my name and gush all over your fingers." He smolders. "And I don't like being left out."

It occurs to me what this is. It's *trust*. And a power shift. He's not demanding—he's requesting. He's trusting me to give to him the same way he gave to me.

Fuck, if this doesn't make me hot for him all over again...

"Well..." I begin, so softly that he pulls me closer and I have to wrap my legs around his waist. "It was...I mean, *I* was really, really naughty..."

Demyen grins. "Tell me more."

"I asked you to, um..." *Shit. He's gonna make me actually say it out loud.*

"Use your voice, *kiska.*"

"I asked you to fuck me. Hard." I blush bright crimson and glance away. "In front of everyone at the dinner party."

Demyen's expression flatlines. He slowly inches away from me and I'm suddenly filled with nauseating regret.

Shit, that was the wrong thing to say. I should have made something up—

I'm pulled off the washing machine and spun around. His hands grope, fondle, stroke my body while he presses himself firmly against my back. I can feel the solid bulge in his pants rub against me and fuck, he's practically throbbing.

"Oh, sweet Clara." Demyen nips my ear as his hands slide up my stomach to cup my breasts. "All you have to do is ask."

Fuck. Would he...? I mean, *I* wouldn't.

I don't think...

"And then what?" His thumb and forefingers roll my nipples, gently pinching and tugging just to make me gasp. "Did I touch you like this while they watched? Were they jealous? Did they wish they could have you the way I do?"

Something deep within my core quivers with need. As if he knows, Demyen spreads his hand over my lower abdomen and presses. He kisses my neck and uses his other hand to undo his zipper and free his throbbing cock. I feel the heat and weight of it rest along the curve of my ass, and for a moment, I'm suddenly not opposed to him trying out that unexplored part of me.

"You're mine." There's no arguing with him when he says it like that. I'm surprised to realize that I don't actually want to.

I want him to do whatever he wants to do to me.

Demyen presses a hand between my shoulder blades until I'm face-down on the washing machine, the cold metal almost soothing to my nipples until it starts to stimulate them with the chill.

"You're mine. And I'll kill anyone who says otherwise."

That should frighten me. Instead, it only makes me drip down my thighs as he kicks my legs wider apart and lands one, then two, then three stinging smacks on my quivering ass cheeks.

"Say it."

I feel him line himself up to me, but he holds back. The tip rubs against my clit and it sends shivers of pleasure to my fingertips, but he still holds back from giving me what I want —what I *need*.

"Say it, Clara."

"I'm yours." I arch my ass up more just to prove it. Because, heaven help me, I actually mean every word. "I'm yours, Demyen. Only yours."

"Mine."

He pushes inside me, hard, and it sends the breath flying from my lungs. I barely have time to suck in a gasp when he tightens his grip and surges deeper, harder.

"Mine."

Oh fuck, he's filling me. He's filling me and stretching me around him and God help me, I want more. I want more. "Please," I whimper.

"Please, what?" Demyen growls with pleasure, his palms smoothing from my hips to my waist as he works his cock deeper. Only when his balls are nestled against my clit, every thick, throbbing inch of his shaft buried inside me, does he slow his pace. Instead of thrusting, he grinds, and I can't hold back the guttural groan of pleasure.

"Please, Dem, fuck me."

I can't see it, but I can definitely hear the wicked grin on his face. "Fuck you *how*?"

Oh, goddamn him! I need him to stop playing his fucking games and just fucking *fuck* me already! I whimper, I whine, and I roll my hips until I'm shamelessly working myself on his cock without him moving.

Just like in my fantasy.

Fuck...

"Demyen, please!"

He answers with a firm smack to my ass, which makes my pussy spasm on his shaft. "Good, baby. Give it to me. Give me that sweet pussy. Work for me. That's it."

I give him what he wants and fuck, it's what I want, too. I angle my hips so he rubs exactly where I need him to rub; I push back and pull off and push back at the speed I'm aching for him to give me.

Demyen's hands smooth over my back, caressing the dip of my waist, the sides of my breasts, up into my hair. He strokes the tousled waves over one shoulder and leans over me until I feel his bare chest pressed to my back. At some point, he managed to work his shirt open and his pants all the way down and now it's him and me, skin to skin.

"What if I want to fuck you in front of him?" he muses.

He doesn't actually need me to answer. The way I suddenly shudder and surge around his cock is answer enough.

"What if..." Demyen slips a hand between my breasts, up until it's wrapped around my throat. Not squeezing, just pressing. Holding me firm against him, even as I keep trying to fuck myself on his dick. "What if I make him watch us, just like this?"

"You did." I turn my head enough so he can see I'm telling the truth. "In my fantasy, when you watched me finger myself… that's exactly what you did. I begged you to."

His smirk broadens. "Good. Fucking. Girl."

Whatever response I might have had is thrown out the window with the way he devours me in a searing kiss the same time he finally, *finally* thrusts into me.

Hard.

Fast.

Deep.

I'm clawing at the washing machine, but the way he's holding me against him gives him leverage to pull me away from it so I have no choice but to take him.

I don't even realize my eyes are rolling back into my head until he eases his grip on my throat and I gasp. Air rushes into my lungs and I scream as another orgasm rips through my body without warning.

"That's it, baby." Demyen holds me there. His voice is starting to fray and break apart as he gets closer. "Scream my name. Tell him who you belong to."

"Dem… Demyen… fuck, Demyen…"

"Yeah, baby. That's right." He grunts, pushing into me harder and deeper than before. Long, solid, sure strokes that make me grunt. "I've got you. I'm right here. Take it."

He keeps one hand on my throat and slides the other down to where we're joined between my legs. I cry out when I feel his fingers circle my clit, then shudder and squeal when he begins to rub faster and faster.

"I'm not fucking done with you, Clara. Not yet."

I'm gonna pass out. It's too much. Darkness creeps in around the edges and, just when I think I'm about to blackout, I feel him surge inside me. Once, twice, bottoming out the third time as heat suddenly pours into me.

He bites my shoulder hard as he groans, grunts, then murmurs my name over and over until he starts to soften inside me.

"Clara. Goddamn. Fuck."

I don't know how long we both stand there, slumped against the washing machine, panting and clinging to each other as we try to regain some semblance of consciousness. Even when he eases out of me, Demyen still holds me close, his face buried in my neck.

I slowly turn to face him. I don't want him to let go and I don't want to lose this rare moment of actually being allowed to touch him. For a few blissful seconds, our brows press together and we almost, almost share an exhausted kiss.

But for some reason, we don't.

I can't put my finger on what exactly it is that settles between us. But whatever it is, I hate it.

Demyen slowly pulls away and looks around the room. He finds my dress and hands it to me, looking away as I slide my bra back on and toss my torn panties into the lint bin. I watch him tug his pants back on and grab the shirt that he threw off to the side at one point.

And still, he doesn't look at me.

The silence is so deep that I almost jump when he finally speaks. "You okay?" It looks like it takes a world of effort to drag his gaze to me.

I almost laugh. Almost. *I am way, way more than okay,* I want to tell him. But the way his face seems so stoic and taut keeps me quiet.

So I simply nod. "Yeah."

He nods. "That, ah…" He clears his throat and finds something fascinating to stare at on the far wall. "That was a one-time thing."

I shouldn't be surprised. And I shouldn't feel as dejected—or rejected—as I do. "Hit it and quit it. I get it."

Demyen actually flinches like the words themselves slapped him. But he nods again. "Something like that."

And then he walks out of the laundry room and into the midnight air.

I shouldn't feel so disappointed.

I shouldn't feel like I could cry.

But I can't understand how it's possible to be so full and so empty at the same time.

58

DEMYEN

Well, *that* was a colossal mistake.

A fucking delicious, mind-blowing, toe-curling, dick-draining mistake.

One that I definitely don't regret making.

Except now, I'm distracted from actual work and responsibilities by the constant thought of *What if we do it again?* Or what if I just moved Clara into my bedroom and we make it a nightly occurrence? Shit, why just the night? My libido doesn't give a fuck what time of day it is.

I almost sleep straight through both my alarms the morning after. When I do finally wake up, I feel more refreshed than I have in months.

"Oh no, no, no. Tell me you didn't." Bambi scowls at me as she answers her own unasked question. "Tell me it was one of the escorts and not—"

"Shit, who cares who it was?" Pavel grins at me over his mug of coffee as he joins her side. "Let's just give thanks where thanks is due."

I narrow my eyes at him. "I'm not that—"

"Yes, you are." They declare it in unison, totally deadpan. Like it's been obvious to everyone but me.

Pavel shrugs. "I mean, we all go through our slumps. Yours just happens to last a decade and results in more missing persons than it should."

Bambi rolls her eyes but I notice she doesn't exactly disagree with him. "Just be careful. Things are difficult enough on Willow as it is. I'm not sure introducing a new family dynamic is the best for her—"

"Enough." I hold a hand up to stop them both in their tracks. "You're making a hell of a lot of assumptions, there."

"Am I, though?"

I glare venomously until they leave shortly after. I spend the next who-the-fuck-knows-how-long staring at the wall of my office, trying to figure shit out.

My phone buzzes on the desk and yanks me from my thoughts. *Thank God.*

At least, that's what I think—until I see who's texting me.

RAIZO: *I've narrowed the list of interested buyers down. Each of those who made the cut agreed to cash on delivery. Very eager to acquire your artifact. Should bring an exceptional price.*

There's no ignoring the nausea that suddenly grips my stomach.

This is what I wanted. Everything is going according to plan. I found the person responsible for Tolya's hell; I captured her; I struck a great bargain with Raizo; he's pulling through on his end. I just don't have the time or the energy to focus on trivial details like vetted buyers, payment processing, blah blah blah.

What's troubling is that I also don't seem to have the *willpower*.

It's not just the sex. It's the way she... fuck, the way she *everything*. The way she walks, talks, breathes. Blinks. Giggles at the stupidest jokes and fawns over exotic flowers. Reads bedtime stories with the voices and sings lullabies that damn near knock down every last one of my walls.

The way she steals glances at me when she thinks I'm not looking and, when she does, it's not hate or fear in her eyes.

It's...

... something I can't afford to acknowledge.

Because regardless of whatever comes to light, Clara Everett is still the reason why my desk is covered in police files and investigation notes.

I stare at the time logs of Michael Little's last day alive. Just as Clara pointed out, it shows he left the precinct early that afternoon, but there's no notes as to why or where he went. For all we know, he left to get a fucking haircut.

The irony is, that could be exactly why he left. Something so simple, so mundane.

The idea doesn't feel so farfetched, so I make a note to have Pavel run intel on local businesses near the precinct as well as around Little's old house. If we're able to pull purchase records, receipts, anything...

I sigh. Once again, it feels like I'm not just trying to find a needle in a haystack—I'm trying to find the world's smallest needle in a field full of haystacks.

The easiest solution would be to just burn it all to the ground and pick up what's left. Theoretically, of course. In reality, the duality of my worlds provides mutual safety nets. Should I lose the Bratva for whatever godforsaken reason, I need my legal front to catch me. And if the casino suddenly detonates tomorrow, the Bratva is here to rebuild.

I can't risk losing my mind and burning it all down just to figure out what the hell Michael Little was doing at 3 P.M. on a Tuesday thirteen years ago.

Overtime? No family—lived alone. No kids. Ex-wife moved to Reno.

Clara's scribbled handwriting catches my eye. It seems she wants to know, too.

Who called him?

That's the Big Question. Who called Michael Little to bring him to the warehouse? The whole scenario was undoubtedly orchestrated. Things happened a little too perfectly in the killer's favor for it all to be sheer coincidence. The fact that we're nowhere near close to finding out who pulled the trigger is proof enough of that.

I don't like admitting when I've made mistakes because, again, I can't afford to make them.

But as I study Clara's notes in the margins, her doodled arrows and subconsciously-drawn flowers, I'm realizing I've been putting blame on her as if *she* was the murderer.

She was just a scared kid traumatized out of her mind.

Now, she's a grown woman with even more trauma seared into her brain—yours truly included—and yet she's still trying to help me. She's forcing herself through memory loss and terror just to make things right for Tolya, who made it clear during our visit that he's not going to be forgiving her anytime soon.

And she still pushes forward anyway.

She's still determined to figure this out.

Pairing this with the memory of last night and all the sights and sounds of Clara coming on my cock, her exhales heating that laundry room until they coalesced as sweat on our skin…

Fuck, I need more coffee. Preferably along with something alcoholic to make the rest of the day bearable. Whatever will help me ignore the feeling in my chest I don't want growing there.

59

DEMYEN

If I thought I was going to get any reprieve from Clara haunting my every waking moment, I was sorely mistaken.

She's scrubbing one of the ovens in the kitchen, on her hands and knees with that perfectly juicy ass rocking back and forth. It doesn't help at all that her uniform happens to be a fairly short gray dress just barely covering where her thighs meet her ass.

Those thighs, wrapped around my head...

I only clear my throat because my mouth is suddenly dry as hell. Clara startles and glances over her shoulder, sees me, then returns to scrubbing the oven.

"Good morning," I mutter, heading to the coffee bar to make a fresh pot of cold brew.

"Morning." Her head is still ducked inside the oven. She only pulls out to rinse her sponge. Still, she doesn't look up at me.

I focus on filling a thermos with ice to give myself something to do. She's cleaning, doing the job I hired her to do; I can't stand around being butthurt that she's not gazing at me with those long, dark lashes fluttering in my face.

"Sleep well?"

"Mhm." Clara rocks back onto her heels, does a final check of the glass front, then closes the oven. She pulls off the rubber gloves and carefully drapes them in the supply bucket, smooths down her uniform, then heads to the fridge.

I watch her grab a tumbler, take a long sip, then put it back and return to her work. And even though she's facing me during her short break, not once does she look up at me.

It's starting to feel more than a little insulting. Especially after she practically went hoarse screaming my name last night.

"Something on your mind?" I blurt before I can stop myself.

Clara offers a small smile with her eyes locked downcast. "Doing great. You?"

"Can't complain."

Actually, yes, I can. And I'm going to. Because I'm a selfish bastard who wants what he wants and gets what he wants and right now, I want her to fucking *look at me.*

I hear her suck in a sharp breath when I cage her in at the kitchen island. She's just turned to grab something from the cleaning bucket and I make my move so she's got nowhere to slink off to. My hips press hers against the drawers.

And, God help me, I can't resist wrapping my arms around her waist. It's too fucking intimate but damn it all, it's what I want right now.

It's what I seem to be wanting a lot lately.

I bury my face in her hair and breathe her in. *Fuck*, she took a shower and her wild waves give me a hit of my own scent. My arms tighten around her out of sheer instinct and my fingers can't help but flex and stroke her soft curves where they rest.

Clara sucks in a shivering breath. "I thought…"

"I know." I can't fault her for it. I was pretty damn clear when I left her alone in that laundry room after fucking her brains out. "I'm not supposed to want you. But fuck, Clara, you make it impossible."

I feel her swallow back a whimpering moan when I move my mouth to press a kiss over her racing pulse. At the same time, I slide a hand down and under her uniform, under the waistband of her panties. If I can't shake her, I'm sure as hell not going to let her shake me.

"You said it was a one-time thing," she whispers in protest.

"I did." I press my teeth to her skin, just enough for her to feel it, as my fingers find her slit. *Fuck yes*, she's already damp for me. "I lied."

"But—"

"Tell me it wasn't good. Tell me it wasn't fucking incredible. Tell me you're not addicted." Beneath my fingertips, I feel her going from damp to dripping in a matter of seconds. "You can't. And neither can I."

"Dem—"

"Clara." I know I sound possessive when I growl her name. Protective. *Mine.* "I want you. In my bed. Every fucking night and every fucking morning so I can make you scream my name."

She shivers and I feel the effect my words have on my fingers. I tease her opening and, when she rocks against my hand, I'm so tempted to plunge inside her. But I hold out, just long enough to really make her beg for it.

I want her to.

I need her to.

Because goddamn, hearing her beg for me is a fucking *high*.

"That's... *suchabadidea...*" Her words come out rushed and breathless, with no pauses in between.

"Of course it is. But I want it anyway. And I always get what I want." I swipe my thumb over her clit just to underline the truth of that statement, and she bites her plump bottom lip with a whimper. "Tell me what *you* want, Clara."

She doesn't even hesitate. "You. Fuck, Demyen. I want you."

I turn her face and capture her lips with mine. I want to taste her gasp, her moan, when I push my fingers inside her. She's so sweet and I can't get enough of the way her tongue flicks along my own while she's taking me. My fingers or tongue or dick, it doesn't matter which—she takes me so well.

One hand buried between her legs, the other tangled in her messy bun, I have her right where I want her. In my arms, melting into me. Gasping, whimpering, trembling.

I could just fuck her right here. Lock the door, check the blinds, and then just spread her on the counter and make her scream and come on my cock just like before. The idea is so fucking tempting that I have to grind my bulge into her soft ass just to ease the almost-painful tension.

But part of me really wants her to feel, to know—to *embrace* —the fact that I can make her orgasm any way I want. I don't need to impale her just to get her off. I want her to make her scream for me just by touching her where she needs to be touched and whispering the words she needs to hear.

"You're mine," I breathe between searing, possessive kisses that make her sweet lips swell and pinken. "You're fucking *mine*. And if I tell you to get in my bed, you'll fucking do it."

I curl my fingers over her G-spot and immediately feel her legs buckle. She lets out a sweet little mewl, a shuddering gasp of pleasure, and her eyes flutter close.

"If I tell you to spread your legs and give me this sweet fucking pussy, you'll do it. You'll do it because we both know you want it."

Clara nods. Or at least she tries, given my hand fisting her hair. She rocks and bucks and grinds on my hand, riding my fingers like the hot little vixen I'm determined to bring out in her. "Fuck! Yes, Demyen! Yes! I want it... God, I want it..."

I smile because fuck, she's so perfect like this. "Earn it, baby. Be my good girl and earn it." I know it's a bit mean, maybe even cruel, to make demands while I'm working her wet pussy with my fingers.

But that's something I've noticed about her that I think she's starting to notice about herself, too: Clara has a submissive streak. A strong, deeply-ingrained submissive streak that, when I play it up just right, hits every pleasure center in her brain.

And mine.

"Please, Demyen..." Clara pants my name between moans. "Please, I need... I want..."

I kiss her throat. There's a soft bruise where I bit her last night and the sight almost makes me unload in my pants. "Tell me, baby. Be my good girl and ask nicely."

She's panting, clinging to my arms, pulsing around my fingers. But then her brow furrows and she grows frustrated; her bottom lip sucks into her teeth with a groan.

I release her hair, guiding her head to lay back on my shoulder. She's so pliant and eager to obey; it takes no effort for her to slump against me. I move my hand around to cup her breast.

But that's just the warm-up. I slide my hand further up her body, until my arm is braced between her luscious breasts and pinning her back to my chest, my hand banded across her throat.

And just like last night, she practically melts into a shivering, gushing, mindless release.

"That's what you need, baby?" I tease her softly, cooing in her ear between nibbles as I work her spasming pussy without stopping or slowing. "You need to feel owned. Claimed. Mine."

Clara cries out. *Music to my ears.*

"It's okay. I've got you. You're mine."

I kiss her deeply as she rides out the final tremors. Only when she completely slumps against me do I ease my hand to a slow massage of her soaked pussy.

A gentleman would offer to fetch her a clean pair of panties since she is, technically, working... but I've never been a gentleman a day in my life. The second she's able to stand without collapsing, I'm stuffing that ruined pair into my pocket and she'll have to work the rest of the day commando.

Fuck. I should make that a new requirement. Just for her.

This time, when Clara slowly turns in my arms, I take the time to kiss her. I know she's still buzzing, but I need her to understand that I'm insatiable. I need her to understand that this is not a "one-time thing."

And it's her fucking fault.

I lift my hands to cup her face, but stop when I realize one of them is still wet with her juices.

But to my surprise, Clara looks me in the eye with a devilish smirk, grabs my hand, and sucks my middle finger into her mouth.

The only thought in my brain is more like a wordless growl mixed with a groan... and I don't realize I actually made that sound out loud until she giggles and slowly, *sofuckingslowly*, pulls her lips and tongue off with a wet slurp.

She does the same to my other finger, her warm tongue swirling and stroking in ways I really, really need to feel in other places.

Fortunately, she doesn't stop there.

Without ever looking away from my eyes, Clara drags my pants down along with my boxers, slowly easing herself down to kneel before me. *What a fucking view.* I can't help myself. I reach for her hair and tug her bun loose, growling my appreciation as her long, thick hair tumbles down her shoulders.

She's so goddamn beautiful. It's a fucking curse. I don't know how I ever thought I stood a chance against this woman.

Not now that I have the image of her soft, plump lips tracing my shaft permanently etched into my mind.

Clara seems unsure of herself, even though she didn't hesitate to wrap her fingers around my cock and stroke it a few times before nuzzling it. It's like she knows what she wants, but she's scared to go for it.

Given what I know about her history, it makes sense.

Time to rewrite.

I stroke her hair back from her face. "Go ahead," I encourage her. "You know what to do."

What I expect is for Clara to wrap her sugary lips around the head and give it a few sucks.

What I don't expect is for her to stroke my shaft, lift it, and wrap her lips around my sack.

FUCK.

She tugs on one side and the moan is ripped involuntarily out through my chest. I don't know how long she spends there, sucking and swirling my ballsack, one side and then the other. I've lost all sense of time. My mouth is dry from hanging open and gasping; my head rolled back on the first suck and I haven't had the wherewithal to right myself.

I've slept with women. Many of them.

This is different.

Clara eases off my balls with a wet slurp, humming her delight as she moves her lips to the base of my shaft. She kisses the skin there, then gently sucks between her teeth so her tongue can swirl and rub. And she does this, again, and again, and again, taking her sweet time with every inch of me.

By the time she leans back on her heels to look up at me, I'm hard as steel.

She doesn't stop stroking me with her hand; long, smooth, firm strokes that coax precum to the tip that she eyes while licking her lips. But before she does what we both want her to do, she reaches up with her free hand and quickly unbuttons her uniform.

It may be a plain, gray dress with a white collar just like every other maid's uniform, but there's nothing plain about what she's wearing underneath it. The soft pink, lace bra does very little to hide her puckering nipples.

"Goddamn, *kiska*..." I don't bother hiding my awe. She needs to know how fucking sexy she looks. I reach down to trace a finger along one cup and, to my delight, she shivers with pleasure and her nipples pucker even more. "Wearing this for me?"

A sudden blush colors her cheeks. "Um..." She glances away shyly. "... Maybe..."

Fuck.

"Such a good girl."

Clara basks in my praise. I can see her gaze light up, her face glowing. With her eyes lifted to mine, she parts her lips and wraps them around the tip of my cock and *fuck*, she pulses them in time with the flicking of her tongue. Her eyes roll back a bit and I feel myself swell with pride as much as pleasure knowing she's getting off on this as much as I am.

"That's it. Just like that, baby. Show me what you can do with that pretty mouth."

I scoop her hair up with both my hands, taking the time to stroke and massage her scalp as I gather up the silky strands. That makes her moan, which opens her mouth more, which means my cock gets to sink a few more inches into that warm, wet heaven.

"That's it, baby. Moan for me. Be my good girl and moan on my cock."

I keep her hair in one hand and slide the other down to play with her breast. She hisses a gasp through her nose when my fingertips flick over her nipple, and the throaty moan she gives me when I pinch it lets my cock sink deeper past her lips.

"Let's see if you can take it all."

I don't know if she can, but she seems willing to try. I hold her head in place, pushing in deeper, inch by inch, while teasing and massaging her sensitive breast. Whenever she starts to gag, I ease back, even though the muscle spasm feels fucking incredible. I let her catch her breath and then she's back at it, sucking and slurping and doing her damned best to swallow me down her throat.

Now, it's my turn for my knees to buckle.

"Fuck, Clara... just like that. Goddamn, baby." I let her breast go so I can hold her thick hair with both hands because *my fucking God*, she's gonna suck my soul through my dick.

It's wet, it's sloppy, and it's the best fucking blowjob I've had in a *long* time.

She starts moaning again, her eyes fluttering close. Her arms press her breasts together in the best fucking way possible, and that's when I realize what she's doing.

"Fuck. Yes. Baby. Touch yourself for me." My chest rumbles with each word. "Look at me, baby. Look at me while you touch yourself. Let me see those beautiful eyes."

Clara gazes up at me with lust and longing; it's a struggle for her to keep them open while her fingers work her clit and my cock plunges deeper. I'm fucking her face, holding her head in place so I can control the speed and depth because heaven knows I'm about to lose what little control I have left.

"Good girl. *My* good girl..." I smile with pride, with lust, petting her hair back as I stretch her lips wide around my shaft. "So good at being so fucking bad. Just imagine what your father would think... a cop's daughter sucking Bratva cock..."

That hits a chord buried somewhere deep inside her psyche. Clara's eyes roll back and she shudders, her fingers working her clit in a blur. Her moans travel up my shaft and vibe in the best way through my limbs.

"That's right, baby. Open that pretty throat for me."

She's close to coming; I can tell by the way her breath staggers and her fingers start to spasm between her legs. I pull my cock from her mouth and fist it, tugging her hair back enough to make her gaze up at me no matter how far her pleasure takes her.

"Look at me, Clara. That's right. Give me those pretty eyes and come for me."

I don't know what comes over me. I don't know where the sudden urge comes from, but I follow it without a second thought. Clara arches her back, her thighs quiver, and I pull her up by my fist in her hair to taste her cries of pleasure.

It's so fucking intimate.

I want it like I want air.

She slumps back down to her knees. Right where I need her. Part of me doesn't fucking care what happens to her next as long as I unload the ache she created—but an ever-growing part of me wants her to want it as much as I do.

"I'm gonna come, baby…" I cup her face in one hand while my other furiously fists my slick shaft. I practically have to grind the words through gritted teeth; I'm that fucking close to the edge.

She understands what I'm asking. And, to my surprise and fucking delight, she bats my hand away from my cock to take it in her own, her mouth not far behind.

This time, she has no trouble gazing up at me. This time, her eyes are filled with daring determination, like she's demanding I give her what she wants.

This time, *she's* the one taking.

Inch by inch, she sucks harder and as far as she can take. The sight of her being damn near balls deep, her glistening eyes blinking up at me, is what shoves me over the edge.

The added sight, and sound, of her throat gulping down my load is what makes me come so fucking hard, I actually worry about passing out.

I'm vaguely aware of my back hitting the island countertop at some point. I'm far more aware of the burning in my lungs as I gasp for air—apparently, I forgot to breathe.

I can't feel the bottom half of my body. I think she sucked it clean off me.

When I finally pull myself together, I lean on my elbows and watch Clara self-consciously try to do the same with her uniform. She's blushing, very obviously trying to look at anything anywhere that isn't me.

I tug my pants back in place and reach for her. She's reluctant, but only for a moment. The second my arms wrap around her, she sighs into me.

I shouldn't like that as much as I do.

But fuck it all... I'm doing, and liking, a *lot* of things I shouldn't.

"I gotta get back to work," she mutters.

"I know." I rest my chin on top of her head. "I hear your boss is a real asshole. You don't want him finding out what you do on your breaks."

She snorts and shakes her head. When she tries to slip her panties back on, I quickly snatch them and stuff them into my pocket.

"Dem!" she gasps. "I have to work!"

"I know. But I'm keeping these."

Clara spins around, clearly ready to glare at me and scold me for being such a perv. But all she does is press a hand to my bare chest and sigh. "Let me guess. One-time thing?"

My answer should be "yes." I should reaffirm the barrier between us, brick up the wall that's supposed to be there, and remind her of all the reasons why whatever the hell this is can't continue.

But while I may be many things, a liar isn't one of them.

And if I'm going to be honest with myself... that chain link fence is crumbling away pretty damn fast.

At the core of it all, I'm a gambler. So I take a steep gamble and hold her face in my hands, look into her eyes, then press a solid kiss to her sweet lips. It's supposed to be one-and-done, but like I said before: she makes me insatiable.

It's not long before we have to pull away, breathless and wanting, my hands firmly gripping her bare ass under her dress.

I can't think of anything clever to say. The only things that come to mind are words that should never, ever be uttered, especially not by me. Things only idiots who have nothing to lose whisper to women who can't afford to believe them.

So I do the next best thing and let her get back to work.

At least this time, she doesn't look like I just crushed her heart under my foot. Instead, Clara blushes again, twists her hair back up into a messy bun, and sprays down the countertop.

She's back to work.

I need to do the same.

This time, I don't feel any regrets at all.

60

CLARA

I think I'd have an easier time pinning a tail on a donkey, blindfolded, drunk, with one hand, in a wind tunnel, than I am trying to tie ribbons in Willow's hair.

She's a bouncing ball of pure excitement. She has been since 4 A.M., when she thought it was time to get up for her first day of school. Now, she's hopping from foot to foot, whining that I'm not moving fast enough.

"We're gonna be late, Mommy!" Willow tugs on the straps of her sparkling unicorn backpack which is, as she verified during this morning's third, fourth, and fifth repacking sessions, filled with matching unicorn school supplies.

"If you would hold still, this would go much faster."

She sighs but does her best to contain her energy. The second she feels me finish adjusting the purple bow in her curls, she flies out of her room toward the main entrance.

"Willow!" I call after her, grabbing my purse from my room as quickly as possible so I don't lose track of where she is. "Honey, we gotta go find Pavel!"

I sigh out my frustration while I'm still alone so it doesn't taint her first day of kindergarten. Truth be told, I'm an emotional wreck. She's growing up too fast and, even though I've been chanting to myself that this is just another day, she's just starting kindergarten, she's still my sweet little baby girl…

Breathe. Pull yourself together. You still have twelve whole years before college.

The garage is in the opposite direction of the main house, but Willow didn't wait for me to tell her where we actually needed to go. So now, I'm rushing through the back archway into the main entrance and—

Demyen's standing there, holding Willow in one arm and her backpack on the other. He smiles at me and leans in to loudly whisper to her, "See? Mommies are always late. Tsk tsk."

Willow giggles and shakes a playful finger at me. "Don't be late, Mommy!"

I missed something. Somewhere, somehow, I overlooked a memo.

"Ready?" He arches a brow and opens the door for me. "If we leave now, we'll have enough time to grab breakfast on the way."

"Can we get donuts?" Willow squeals excitedly.

He exaggerates his eyeroll and scoffs. "I don't know how you'd start the day any other way."

I let my feet carry my dumbfounded self to the car on autopilot. Demyen helps Willow buckle into her booster seat, carefully avoiding bumping her bows. "We don't want to mess up your beautiful hair, okay? We want to look our best when we roll up in style."

As if on cue, Willow whips out a pair of pink glittery sunglasses from her backpack and slides them on. "I'm ready!"

"Yeah, you are." He chuckles. "Let's go show them who runs the playground."

And then we're driving down the desert road, turning onto the main highway, and heading into the city limits.

Like it's normal.

Like we're a *family*.

Demyen turns on the radio. It's a song that apparently both he and Willow know. She sings it loud, and he does his best to hide his face from me, but I don't miss him humming a note or two under his breath.

I stare at him like he's possessed. Because he is. He has to be. That's the only logical explanation.

"Oh, no…!" Willow whines suddenly from the backseat. "I forgot to brush my teeth."

Wordlessly, Demyen pops the central console compartment open and holds up a pack of dental gum. "But wait until after we eat. Mint and orange juice do not go well together."

"Okay!"

He glances at me, then does a double-take. "What?"

I wish I had a good response. Something cohesive to say. Other than, "Who are you? And where's Demyen?"

He smirks. "You'd think you'd be way happier this morning. It's a beautiful day, it's Willow's first day of kindergarten, and... well, you know..."

"I'm very happy!" I realize that folding my arms and huffing in protest doesn't exactly prove my point. "I just... you're acting weird."

"I'm acting like a man who got laid."

"What's 'laid'?" Willow's small voice asks innocently.

Demyen's eyes widen. *Serves him right.* I should be pissed, but honestly, I'm way more entertained by his panic and backpedaling. "It's, ah... you know how you feel so much better after a nice, long nap?"

"Yeah?"

"It's that. You lie down, you take a nap. And then you feel very, very happy and relaxed. Like you can conquer the world."

"'Kay." She thinks for a moment, stroking the rainbow mane of the unicorn stitched onto her backpack. "Do you think they'll have me get laid at school?"

I facepalm hard enough to hear the smack of my hand against my forehead. But damn it, I can't stop laughing. "Um, sweetheart? Let's just call it 'taking a nap'." I press my lips together to hold back the laughter and try my best to shoot Demyen a pointed look. "That means you, too."

"Right." Demyen clears his throat and shifts in his seat. "I just took a very good nap. A very, very thorough—"

"Where do we want to get the donuts?" I cut him off before he digs us another parenting hole. The last thing either of us needs is a letter home from the teacher about Willow's "expanded vocabulary."

"Can we go to Cake Castle?" she asks.

"Oh, honey, that's—"

"A perfect idea." It's Demyen's turn to give me a look that says, *Chill.* "Let me guess. Unicorn donut?"

"With rainbow sprinkles."

"Well, of course. What kind of unicorn donut doesn't have rainbow sprinkles?"

"Mommy eats plain donuts." She makes it sound like I commit war crimes. "No frosting or anything."

That little snitch!

Demyen smirks. "I'm pretty sure she loves the ones with cream filling."

That big asshole!

No one is on my side anymore.

I don't know if I want to slap him, scold him, or kiss him. He's confusing the ever-living fuck out of me while simultaneously pushing my maternal buttons.

But... in a good way. Because hardened mob boss, crime lord, whatever he is—he's also everything I've ever wished Willow could have in a father. Someone who laughs with her, gets silly with her, treats her seriously enough to let her into his world. Someone who protects her with every fiber of his being and doesn't act like she's bothering him even when she almost certainly is.

Someone who still makes mistakes as a parent but does his best to get it right, even when he doesn't know what the fuck he's doing.

Demyen's everything I could ever want for Willow.

I just can't figure out who or what he is for *me*.

One minute, he's romancing me with sweet words and promises and treating me like a goddess in his bed. The next, I'm the scum of the earth, the bane of his existence. But then I'm someone he cares for again. At least, until I'm someone he can use and abuse in front of his colleagues, which only lasts until I'm suddenly so valuable that he might actually kill a cop for me.

And then I'm a servant. Until I'm his partner, then his commodity, and then his girlfriend?

But I'm not, because it was a "one-time thing."

Until it wasn't.

And even then, he swerved back and forth between treating me like I'm the air he needs to breathe and treating me like I'm just one of his escorts "servicing" him.

The fucked-up part is how much I enjoyed it.

Yeah. *Confusing* doesn't even begin to cover it.

I'm buried deep in my thoughts while they order at the drive-thru. I only come back to reality in time to request a latte and old-fashioned. Demyen mutters, "Are you sure you don't want something thick and creamy?"

To which I respond coolly, "Yeah. I'll get that at home."

The way he suddenly freezes makes my whole morning.

I make sure to request extra napkins. My maternal anxiety is in full swing and I turn in my seat to arrange several spread napkins over Willow's lap. "Try not to get sprinkles everywhere," I caution her.

"It's fine. I'll have it detailed when we get back," Demyen assures me.

When the cashier hands us our donuts, my eyes bug out of my head. That unicorn confection is more frosting than donut. "Oh, Willow, sweetie, that's going to get all over your face!"

Demyen hands me my latte and donut. "Here. Drink this. Calm down. Let the kid enjoy her special day. There are wet naps in the console."

"But—"

"Clara." His voice lowers into the *don't argue with me* tone that somehow manages to make me obedient and wet at the same time. "It's fine. Trust me. We only get one first day of kindergarten."

Dammit. Here come the waterworks. And I was doing so good, too.

"I know. I just… I…"

He reaches for my hand and strokes his thumb over my fingers. Even though he's driving, he glances at me a few times and squeezes my hand whenever he sees the tears. "Hey. You got this. We'll pull up, take a few pictures, embarrass her with smothering hugs and kisses, and then you can cry your heart out all the way back home. Okay?"

I sniffle and nod. "Okay."

Something in my gut says the optimal route between Cake Castle and the Montessori school is much shorter than the one we actually end up taking, but I don't say anything. Demyen keeps glancing in the rearview mirror and only when Willow's licking up the last bits of frosting from her fingers does he turn down a road that actually leads to the school.

My heart hurts. I don't know if I can handle this. Between Willow starting school and Demyen being *this*, my heart hurts so much. All I want to do is cry until I crash.

61

CLARA

We finally pull up to the school. It's all I can do not to gape in awe.

It's one of those high-security, intricate wrought-iron gated institutions that looks like a cross between a manor and a luxury spa but decorated with rainbow handprints and crayons.

You know, the kind of school I used to drive past without a glance because there's no way in hell I'd ever be able to afford the tuition.

We're sitting in a long line of cars waiting to pass through the security checkpoint. Guards in police-looking uniforms with grim, serious expressions check their clipboards against IDs the parents hold out for them.

I blow out a sigh. At least this means Martin can't just traipse in and grab Willow. Demyen would never put him in the paperwork as a contact, not even for emergencies.

My heart suddenly squeezes at the realization that Demyen himself is probably the emergency contact listed in the school's records.

We're only four cars behind now and Willow can't stop wiggling in her seat. Demyen flashes her a grin. "Excited?"

"Did you see the playground?" She points over his shoulder to a fenced area between two of the buildings. "It's huge!"

One car to go now. My stomach twists.

Breathe. It's just like any other day.

Demyen pulls us up to the checkpoint and nods at the guard. "Morning."

The guard peers at us through his aviator sunglasses, then looks at his clipboard. "Name?"

"Zakrevsky."

I knew it. And now that my uterus knows it, there's no stopping the sudden rush of heat through my body. *Focus, woman. My God.*

Again, the guard slowly stares at us, then the clipboard. Something crackles on his radio and he switches it to his earpiece. Then frowns. "I'm gonna need to see your license. Both of you."

The heat is doused by an icy feeling. Something isn't right. We didn't see any of the vehicles in front of us show two cards or take this long to check a piece of paper.

Demyen acts unfazed, but I hear the slight downshift in his voice. "One second, lemme grab those for you."

"And while you're at it, go ahead and roll down the back window."

I freeze. So does Demyen, who was mid-reach for the glovebox. He looks at me and I give him the same expression.

Something is definitely wrong.

He slowly eases back to his window and sighs. "Sure. Here…"

I watch him press the button for Willow's window, but it doesn't go down. He does it again, but still nothing.

And that's when I realize—he's pressing the "Up" button. *On purpose.* But there's no way for the guard to clearly see that.

"Damn. Just bought this thing, too." Demyen acts real *aw-shucks* frustrated as he sighs. "Sorry, man. I'm gonna need to take this in and get that fixed."

The guard grunts but nods. "Okay. Go ahead and pull over to that section with the dashed lines. Someone will meet you for orientation."

"Thank you!" I try not to sound overly cheerful. My heart is throbbing in my throat.

Demyen rolls his window back up and grips the steering wheel. We're still stuck in the line of cars dropping off kids and trying to find parking, so we inch our way toward the section the guard indicated.

"I don't like this," he mutters.

"Yeah." I scan the crowd, looking for any clear signs of trouble. Like Martin waving his badge, or worse—my father waving *his* badge.

Then sirens pierce the air.

It's one heart-stopping moment before we both realize it's an alert screaming from our phones, his smartwatch, the car's phone system, even the tablet in the backseat meant to keep Willow entertained.

Demyen hisses a curse when he sees the dashboard.

Me? I feel like I'm going to throw up.

AMBER Alert: Las Vegas, NV. Child Abduction—5-year-old female, dark hair, hazel eyes. Suspect: Clara Everett. Early twenties. Presumed armed and dangerous.

"He actually did it." The words tumble from my numb mouth. Everything feels numb. Drained. Hopeless. "He actually did it."

The line clears up enough for us to pull into the reserved section, where we can see a small group of official-looking school administrators slowly gather. They smile at us as we drive closer, but those smiles feel as fake as the one Demyen's suddenly plastered on his face.

He smiles at them and gives a little wave. The one who looks like she's in charge responds with a polite nod, her hand gripping a walkie-talkie as she waits for us to approach.

Which we don't.

Because Demyen keeps driving.

He doesn't hit the gas; we're still in a school driveway. But he also doesn't pull into the orientation parking, or any other parking. He just… keeps driving.

"Dem?" I grab the doorframe. I don't want to startle Willow, but I'm watching the faces of the administrators shift from fake geniality to confusion to concern.

"I know." He taps the gas a little. We're almost to the exit gate where another guard is stopping each car to verify whatever the hell needs so much oversight. "Almost there."

We're two cars behind.

People are walking faster toward the car. The guard at the exit gate listens to something in his earpiece and whips his gaze to us.

Shit.

Shit. Shit. Shit.

I can't believe Martin pulled this stunt. If he gets Willow, I can't afford the attorney or court costs—

"Hey, Wills?" Demyen glances at her through the rearview mirror.

"Yeah?"

"You buckled up?"

We hear a click. Then another. "Now, I am!"

I feel sick. She was so excited, so ready to just leap out of the car for her first day…

"Great. We're gonna play pretend, okay? Pretend we're on a rollercoaster." Demyen grips the steering wheel tighter. "So I need you to hang on tight, okay? Just like on a rollercoaster."

"Okay!"

I whip my wide-eyed stare to him. "Dem…"

He meets my gaze. Then grabs my hand and squeezes it. "I told you, babe. You're mine."

And that's when he floors it.

62

CLARA

"It's fucking bullshit." Demyen grinds his teeth and listens to whatever Bambi's saying on the other end. "Yeah, I know. But it's still bullshit, and you know it. No, listen: I don't care if he hand-carved her from marble and gave her the Breath of Life. He fucking lied and I need you to make him undo it."

The mechanics working around us pretend to not hear their boss lose his absolute shit. I'm not doing such a good job of pretending.

When he hangs up, Demyen looks like he's about to throw his phone across the garage. But he manages to stop himself and shoves it back into his pocket instead. "Bambi says her hands are tied. Martin pulled strings as a cop and for all anyone knows, you're a dangerous drug user on the run with his daughter."

I feel blood drain from my face. "But he's not a custodial parent."

Demyen nods. "She is working that angle. Right now, he's acting as a detective with information about a missing child."

Said "missing child" calmly sips the juice box one of the mechanics gave her shortly after we arrived at the garage. It's on the outer edge of the city limits, near a salvage yard most people try to avoid—including the police. Demyen drove us in, unannounced, and the second the men saw who was driving the Tesla, they literally dropped everything and locked the doors behind us.

And the second they saw Willow climb out of the back seat, at least half the men melted into the equivalent of doting uncles who have been making sure she's comfortable and calm ever since.

Now that the initial panic is settled, I take a moment to look around the garage. A car is elevated on one of the platforms with half its body missing; another sits beneath a tarp in the corner. Along the far wall is a neatly organized storage system of boxes, some as small as a stapler and others large enough to ship an engine in.

Which, come to think of it… "Is this a chop shop?"

Demyen glances at me. "I told you: I'm a smuggler. This happens to be part of what I smuggle—luxury car parts. Sometimes full builds, but only for the best customer."

"What's a smuggler?" Willow asks between sips.

A few of the mechanics snicker while they pretend to focus on their work. I shoot Demyen a look. Yes, Willow is supposed to be learning a lot today, but at *school.* Things like sight-reading and abstract shapes.

Not the ins and outs of criminal enterprise.

Demyen thinks about it for a second. "Do you know what a pirate is?"

She lights up. "Like Captain Hook? And Smee?"

"That. Smuggling is that."

Willow's eyes widen and her mouth drops open in awe. "You're a pirate?"

"Close enough."

"Are you friends with Captain Hook?"

One of the mechanics swoops in on a creeper, brandishing a suspension hook and squinting at her with one eye while snarling, "Arrrgh!" Willow shrieks in surprise, then laughter, and darts away to the safety of Demyen's protective shadow.

The men chuckle, and "Captain Hook" gives her a playful wink before returning to work.

I sidle over to Demyen's side as well, keeping my voice low. "I gotta admit, your world seems to be more... family-friendly?... than what I expected."

He shrugs a shoulder. "Do you know what 'Bratva' means?"

I shake my head.

"*Brotherhood*. We're not a gang; we're family. Literally, for the most part. Half the guys you see here are cousins to some degree. And most are married with kids of their own. They treat Willow the same as they treat their children."

"Family" is not a concept I've had good experiences with. Except for my mother, up until she died. "That actually sounds... nice. And not at all criminal."

"The things we do pay the bills."

I level my gaze at him. "Come on. That's such a lame excuse."

"Is it? Tell me: how much did you make as a cocktail waitress, working full-time, *with* tips?"

I blush. Not enough for me to even bother to vocalize.

He nods. "That's what I thought. Now, what if someone came along and told you you could make an entire month's paycheck with one sale? And not even of yourself; it could be a new pharmaceutical not widely available, or a car part someone's spent half their life searching for."

I hate that I'm starting to see the appeal. But still… "You have the casino. The hotel. You don't need all this."

"Whatever the casino makes in a month, my Bratva quadruples in a week."

Well… shit.

Just doing some back-of-the-envelope math based on what I know about casinos, if what he's saying is true, then Demyen could use hundred-dollar bills to blow his nose and it wouldn't make a dent in his bank account.

Me? Finding four quarters in the couch means it's a good day.

We live in different worlds.

Demyen beckons one of the mechanics over. "How's it looking?"

The guy rubs the back of his neck. "I mean, it's a Tesla. Like workin' on a fuckin' spaceship. We can remove the plates, give it a paint job, switch the leather, but that's about it."

"Do it. Have it brought to me whenever you're done. In the meantime, we'll take whatever's under the tarp."

I've never ridden in a Firebird before.

We roar down the desert highway. Demyen is clearly enjoying the drive and, I have to admit, so am I. The purr of the engine is so much louder than the silence of the Tesla that there's no way we're able to hold a decent conversation over the noise.

Which is fine by me. I'm too busy panicking to talk.

Martin's pulled some shit before, but nothing like this. I knew he wouldn't give up on his hunt, but I never imagined he'd have me publicly labeled as a kidnapper. A drug-wasted, child-endangering kidnapper. A criminal at large.

The fact that my father let it happen only makes the stone in my gut sink lower. Does he know? He has to know. There's no way Martin could get this past him without his knowledge or his blessing. My father may be many things, but he'd never misuse police resources on fake kidnapping charges.

Unless...

Unless he doesn't think it's fake.

I'm glad for the loud engine—it drowns out the whimper of fear I feel in my throat. If this seat would let me sink any lower, I would.

My only comfort, my only relief, is seeing Willow happily comb her unicorn backpack's mane while she sings to herself. She's happy, she's safe, and she's with me. That's all I can ask for right now.

When we pull through the gates onto Demyen's long driveway, the guards leap into action and immediately lock up behind us. The compound is buzzing with activity, from uniformed patrol doing extra-thorough checks to men I recognize as *vors* calmly but sternly strolling the walkways and peering out windows.

It's like they're expecting an attack.

And maybe they should be. Clearly, Martin has no problem misusing police resources for his own gain. I wouldn't put it past him to show up with a full SWAT team.

I wouldn't put it past Demyen to come ready with a team of his own, either.

Guards and *vors* alike greet us with nods and gestures that say, so far, everything is in the clear. Demyen nods his approval and drives us into the garage, pulling into one of the few empty spaces flanked by luxury cars I don't know the names of.

He doesn't get out right away, so neither do I.

"Hey, Wills." He turns in his seat to smile at her. It's tense, but he's doing his best to keep her oblivious to the danger surrounding us. "Bambi just texted me. Gloria's gonna put a movie on in the sunroom and make you some popcorn. Sound good?"

Usually, Willow would scream with excitement at that, but not this time. She pouts and hugs her backpack to her chest. "But what about school?"

I choke on the sob I won't let her see. My heart is breaking for her at the same time the anger is welling up. None of this is fair, least of all for her.

She didn't deserve to have her day ruined by the asshole who claims to be her father.

"I forgot some papers." Demyen scrunches his face. "Sorry, Wills. That's my fault. Can I make it up to you later?"

She squints at him. Then: "I want ice cream."

"Well—"

"For breakfast. Tomorrow. Before school."

Okay. I might be laughing just a bit. I know Demyen hears my hiccupped laugh because he very quickly side-eyes me before facing down his little negotiator.

"One scoop," he concedes.

Willow narrows her eyes. "With sprinkles."

He makes it seem like a tough bargain. "Fine. You win. Now, go find Gloria, you little juicer."

I take my time sliding out of the Firebird. Demyen helps Willow out of her booster and shoos her to the main house with a pat on the head. The sight should make me happy, but it only twists the knife in my anxiety.

She deserves so much better than I've been able to give her.

She deserves to have the life Demyen's building for her.

And I know Martin won't let her have it. Not without a fight —and he fights dirty.

My thoughts are interrupted by hands suddenly spinning me around and pressing me against the car. Demyen's mouth devours mine before I can blink. I moan—I can't help myself. He tastes like coffee and confidence, two things I really need right now. His hands thread through my hair and his tongue sweeps over mine, coaxing and comforting all at once.

When he finally pulls away, it's only enough for us to catch our breaths. I feel a little thrill travel through my veins at seeing the way he's just as breathless as I am.

I *do that to* him?

"Clara." Demyen rumbles my name. I love the way it tastes on his lips. "Clara, look at me."

I do. It's hard to look him in the eyes when he's all fire and fury mixed with lust and desire, but I manage to meet his gaze without flinching. On the outside.

"I'm not going to let anything happen to Willow. Or you." His nose touches mine for the briefest of moments. *Is he...* nuzzling *me?* "Understood?"

"Dem..." I know he means well, but this is no small arms deal. This is an AMBER Alert, a manhunt for me and my child. Sanctioned by the police, led by my ex and supported by my father.

We don't stand a chance.

"No matter what happens. You, me, whatever this is... No matter what happens, Martin will never get his hands on Willow. You have my word."

Demyen is practically swearing a blood oath to me. I know he means every bit of it. So I muster a small smile and reach for him. "Thank you."

I just wish I could believe him.

63

CLARA

Demyen leads me into his office and quickly shuts the door behind us. He rummages through his desk drawers and then, suddenly, I'm holding my cell phone.

"If we can get his confession recorded—" Demyen starts, but I cut him off with an eager head nod. I know exactly what he's going for and it's a brilliant idea: work Martin into a careless rage so he'll admit this is all a bunch of lies he made up just to spite me.

And we'll record every word.

Even my father won't be able to deny that.

I've got several missed calls from Martin. No surprise there. I also have a bunch of texts from him that I don't recognize but are marked as Read—I quickly glance up at Demyen, then back down at my phone. I'm not going to get upset and surprisingly, I'm really not.

Dad tried calling. That's... odd. We're not exactly what anyone could call "close." He doesn't call me other than to remind me about his birthday dinner or to reinforce his stance with Martin after I've done something to warrant complaints.

He sure as shit never calls me just to see how I'm doing.

The timestamp says he called shortly after the AMBER Alert went out.

And so did Roxy. Who, in my book, gets preferential treatment.

I tap her name and quickly show Demyen the screen so he knows it's not Martin. I'm ready for him to get frustrated or blow up at me, but he only nods and pulls up a chair for me to sit in, then settles into his own. I keep the call on speaker; I want Demyen to see he can trust me in times like this.

"Oh, thank God," Roxy rasps when she picks up.

I wince. "I take it you heard the alert."

"Me and every person from Vegas to Reno. The hell happened?"

"Martin—"

"That son of a bitch. I'll kill him." Something rattles around in the background of Roxy's call. "I am officially going to kill him."

I can't help but smile a bit at my best friend's protectiveness. "I just wanted to call and let you know I'm going to be off the grid for a while, until this all clears up." I glance at Demyen, wondering how true that statement actually is. But his face doesn't give away any indication either way. "Martin lied to get the AMBER Alert sent out—"

"Yeah, no shit."

I realize now, in this exact moment, that I've been afraid she would actually believe the alert. It doesn't fully occur to me until a heavy sigh of relief leaves my body. "You know I'd never kidnap Willow."

"'Kidnap'? From who? The asshole didn't even sign the birth certificate, remember?"

Demyen shoots me a shocked and perplexed look. I, for one, completely forgot about that detail until now. I actually laugh a little. "Roxy, I fucking love you. No, I actually forgot about that."

"Just tell me you're safe, Clara. You and Willow, you both good?"

"We're fine. She's upset she had to miss her first day of school, but we're making up for it."

"Can't blame her." A pause. Then, "Wait. Are you... are you with that super-hot guy we met at my apartment?"

I blanch. Demyen smirks.

"I... uh..." I clear my throat. "I'm safe. We're safe. And we're just gonna be—"

"You *are*. You're totally shacking up with Hotty McHotterson. *Gurl.*" I don't have to look at her to know her face is breaking into a shit-eating grin. "Take your time. Seriously. Do what you gotta do and get what you gotta get—"

"I'm hanging up now."

"Am I on speaker?" Roxy gasps. "I *am*! He's right there, isn't he? Hey, Hot Stuff!" She yells like she's calling him from across a field. I immediately want to die in this chair and puddle onto the floor.

Demyen, to his credit, actually seems wholly amused by this. "Yes?"

"Knew it. You got a gun? Oh, what am I talking about? Of course you do."

That smirk only widens. "I might have one somewhere."

"Uh-huh. I get it. This call may be recorded for quality assurance and all that shit. I know your game. So listen up. You take care of my girls, okay? And if Martin shows up, you put a bullet between his eyes. Got it?"

Demyen arches a brow. "Killing an officer of the law is a federal crime."

"And probably the least illegal thing you've done so far. Am I right?"

He looks at me. Then shrugs. "Hypothetically."

"I work in the crime lab. I can make things very easy for you or I can make things increasingly difficult for you and your little enterprise. So you're gonna protect my Clara and Willow, understood?"

I love my best friend, but she's going to get us all killed. "Oh my God, Roxy, you can't just—"

"I can and I will, Clara Everett. I don't care if he's fucking Don Corleone—yeah, I picked up on your vibe real quick, sir, so don't even try to deny it. It's one thing for a dirty cop to go missing. But a crime lab tech? Good luck making *that* look like an accident."

Demyen actually seems impressed. He's trying not to laugh, but he gives her a concessional nod she can't see. "Alright. We have an agreement. I'll protect your girls and you'll owe me a favor or two down the line when I'm... shall we say, 'stuck'?"

Roxy falls quiet. I'm about to tell her she doesn't have to make deals with the devil when her voice cuts back in. "Done."

"Roxy—" I begin to protest.

"Clara, I love you, but shut it. I'd rather lose my job protecting his ass than lose you or Willow." Her voice suddenly cracks with emotion. "I couldn't live with myself if anything happened to you." She clears her throat. "Besides, better for him to pull the trigger than me. I'm better at cleaning up messes than making them."

I sigh. She has a point. "I love you, Rox."

"Ditto, Clara. Give Silly Willy big hugs from me, okay?"

We say our goodbyes and hang up. When I glance at him, I see that Demyen's brow still hasn't descended. "Your friend—"

"She didn't mean anything by it, I swear!" I nearly leap out of my chair to placate him. I'll deepthroat his soul through his dick if it'll keep him away from harming Roxy.

But he quickly holds a hand up to stop me. "I have no beef with her. It's good to know you've got someone out there who cares about you."

I... was not expecting that.

We sit there in silence for a moment. Then he nods down at the phone in my hand. "It's time."

I sigh. "Yeah." But instead of Martin, I pull up Dad's number and hit Dial. I place it on the desk for Demyen to see. He frowns, but pulls out his own phone and starts recording.

"Clara! Oh, thank God."

Now, I'm frowning. It's not like Dad to sound so concerned. "Hey, Dad." I don't know what to say; he's the one who called me. "What's up?"

"'What's up'? Clara, what the hell is going on? You're all over the news and the precinct—"

I sigh. "I know. It's a… a terrible misunderstanding, is all."

"Why did you kidnap Willow?"

I freeze. "What?"

Dad scoffs. "I don't understand, Clar-Bear. I thought you two were good. And now, Martin's saying you up and left him in the middle of the night? And you kidnapped Willow—"

"Dad! Dad," I immediately drop my voice. He hates it when I shout. Or when I talk back to him. Or whenever I generally disagree with him. "That's not what happened. At all."

He pauses. "Okay. Okay. Tell me what happened."

"Martin…" I look up at Demyen. He sits there, stoic. But he nods for me to continue. "He hit me, Dad. A lot. Martin hit me that night, too, and I just—"

"Well, what did you do?"

Again, I freeze. I try to swallow back the sudden lump in my throat. "I didn't do anything."

"Well, obviously you did *something*, Clar-Bear." He sounds so sympathetic, but his words curdle in my stomach. "You know how Martin is. He runs a tight ship. And you know how you are…"

I see Demyen's fingers tighten around the arms of his chair. For some reason, that actually bolsters my confidence. "No, tell me: how *am* I, Dad?"

He sighs. "Now, we don't have to get into this—"

"I think we do. How am I? How do I deserve to be treated like Martin's punching bag?"

Or yours, for that matter?

"That's not what I meant and you know it." Dad sighs yet again. "We're just worried about Willow, okay? You can't blame Martin for being worried about his own daughter."

I can blame Martin for a lot of things, but that isn't one of them. He'd have to actually *be* worried about her, which we all know he isn't. Not really.

"She's safe. *We're* safe. Okay?"

Dad doesn't respond for a long, tense moment. I look up at Demyen again, who meets my gaze with fury glazing over his eyes. I know he's got a history with my father and a score to settle…

But this is something different.

I flatten my palms on the desk to contain my own growing frustration. "Willow is *my* daughter and I'm going to do whatever it takes to protect her. Even when—no, *especially* when I have to protect her from Martin. I don't care if he's her father; he doesn't have the right to hurt her or scare her."

I don't realize I'm shaking until I feel Demyen's hand cover mine. He doesn't grab me, just presses his fingers on mine and makes me look at him.

Look at me and don't look away.

I'm saying things I've been wanting to say for years. For a lifetime. And I'm horrified at the reality that I'm having to say them for the sake of my child rather than myself because history is so close to repeating itself.

But as I keep my gaze locked with Demyen's, I also realize that history changed the moment we ran into each other at his casino. Maybe even earlier than that.

Because with Demyen in the picture... just like he said, no matter what happens between us, Willow is safe. Protected. Cherished.

Everything I needed to be when I was her age.

"Let's meet up. For coffee." Dad's voice breaks the tense silence. "My treat."

"I don't know if that's—"

"You'll be fine, Clar-Bear. I promise. I just want to see you. You're my daughter and I need to make sure you're safe, too." He clears his throat as if he was about to get emotional. I'm so used to him putting on fronts, but part of me really wants to believe he cares. "How about tonight? Six o'clock?"

I gently scoff. "A bit late for coffee, don't you think?"

"You're right. I'm still on night shift cycles sometimes. Tomorrow morning then? Breakfast?"

Now, Demyen squeezes my fingers, but in warning. I choose to ignore him. "Sounds great. Your usual?"

"You got it. Oh, and Clara?"

I still. *Here comes the backlash...* "Yeah, Dad?"

"Give my grandbaby hugs and kisses for me. I miss her."

The strange thing is, I don't doubt that. He's not winning Father of the Year awards anytime soon, but he's always been a doting grandfather to Willow. Whenever he's around, that is, which isn't as often as one would expect. But not once has he ever raised his voice, or his hand, to my baby girl. In a weird sort of way, he's the kind of grandfather I needed him to be as my father.

It doesn't make sense—but since when did my life ever make sense?

"I will."

The second he hangs up, Demyen stops the recording app. "I don't like it."

I furrow my brow. "Which part?"

"All of it. I don't want you to meet with him."

I scoff. "Excuse me?"

Demyen braces his hands on the desk and leans in. "It's a trap, Clara. An obvious one."

"How could you—"

"You're going to look me in the eye and tell me that nothing seems suspicious to you? That your father, who can't be bothered to check in on you any other time, suddenly wants to meet up for fucking pancakes?"

That cuts me. Deep. But I don't know if it's the fact that Demyen's trying to prevent me from seeing my own father or that he's pointing out facts I don't want to look at. "He's my father, Dem. He wouldn't trap me—"

"Are you listening to yourself?" Demyen's voice goes raspy with disbelief. "Did you hear anything he just said? He doesn't care about you or your well-being—"

"And you do?"

The room falls silent. I instantly regret lashing out at him like that, with those words in particular.

Demyen straightens. I almost think he's about to storm out, but instead, he grinds his teeth until the muscle in his jaw pulses.

When he barks out a breathy laugh, it's filled with sarcasm. "A lot more than he does, that's for fucking sure."

Again, I don't know what to do with that information.

He collapses back into his chair and glares at me. Not in the way that makes me feel like he wants to hurt me, but more... well, how I'm feeling right now, too. Frustrated and afraid all at once.

"If you go, Willow stays."

"Absolutely." I'm ignoring the way my heart thumps at his unwavering protectiveness over my daughter. "I wouldn't bring her regardless."

"Because you don't trust him."

I don't answer. I can't answer, because I know exactly where he'll go with it.

Which he does anyway. "You don't trust him with your daughter, but you'll trust him *as* his daughter?" Demyen curls his lip in a sneer. "Make that make sense."

"It's just better to not be seen in public with her, don't you think? With the alert up and all."

"Sure. Whatever you need to tell yourself."

"Besides..." I stare at my fingers, which are now tugging at each other's nails and flicking invisible dirt from the cuticles.

A nervous habit of mine. "She's safer here with you than anywhere else."

Demyen doesn't say anything. I don't know what else there is to discuss. I sure as shit don't know when that happened— when I stopped *fearing* him and started *trusting* him. With my life, yes—but more importantly, with Willow's.

I'm just not sure if I'm actually safe...

Or if I escaped a bear by running into a lion's den.

64

DEMYEN

The punching bag swings away from me, but it still doesn't feel like I've hit it hard enough.

I want to send it through the fucking wall.

She never.

Punch.

Fucking.

Punch.

Listens!

I swing a roundhouse kick just to feel the satisfaction of the blow reverberating through the heavyweight bag. The chain links suspending the bag creak and spin. I won't be mad if they break and the whole thing crashes to the ground.

In fact, I'd probably feel better.

Clara Everett has a death wish. She has to—there's no other logical explanation for why she eagerly walks into danger again and fucking again.

She knows how dirty and underhanded her father is. She knows he's buddies with her ex; hell, we both heard him stand up for the douchebag and try to shift blame onto her.

I damn near smashed the phone when he said those things.

I always knew Greg Everett was a dirty cop—I just never fathomed how deep his corruption sank or how far he'd go.

And for... what? His interests are so fucking vague. It's one of the reasons why we've struggled to pin anything to do with Michael Little's murder on him.

I *know* he's dirty.

I *know* he's involved somehow.

I *know* he's going to trap Clara and sell her over to Martin.

She knows all that shit, too. But instead of acting like a smart person who values her life, she's pulling a dumbass cartwheel right into the jaws of a deathtrap.

I want to chalk it up to family loyalty. I'd meet with Tolya regardless of a trap, right?

But he would never do that to me. He may be losing his goddamn mind behind bars, but he's still my brother. My big brother who always looked out for me, even at his own expense.

It's one of the biggest reasons why I couldn't accept the murder charges, even with the evidence stacked against him. DNA or no, fingerprints or no, there's no way Tolya pulled the trigger.

I wanted to believe he wasn't even there. So did a lot of people. That one was a lie of omission I'm still processing. But regardless, he's always been the kind of guy who would sooner give someone the shirt off his back than put a bullet through their head.

Our father *hated* that about him.

I aspired to be just like him.

I laugh. I laugh like I've lost my fucking mind because I feel like I have, and there's no one around to hear me.

I wanted to be like Tolya? *Mission fucking failed.*

I splash some water on my face and stare at myself in the floor-to-ceiling mirrors lining one wall. Stubble darkens my jaw and I'm overdue for a haircut. I'm letting myself fray at the edges in a way I've never done before. Visual evidence of how I'm crossing all the lines I drew in the sand for myself years ago.

My phone buzzes nearby. One of the overnight guards is alerting me that we have an unexpected guest in the middle of the night. I suck in a sharp breath and brace myself for the worst.

I might actually have to kill a cop.

So fucking be it.

∼

"Oh. It's just you."

Raizo turns around from where he's reading a plaque in the study and chuckles. "Expecting someone more entertaining?"

Visions of knifing Martin between the eyes fade from my head. "No. Someone more irritating."

Raizo chuckles again. "Well, I'll cut to the chase then." He shakes his head when I gesture to an empty lounge chair, which I'm thankful for. I don't particularly want him to stay.

"You've been avoiding me." His eyes narrow at me. "I don't like being ignored."

I shrug. "I've been busy."

"I know." He trails a finger along the bookshelf. "You've been busy playing house."

My pulse pounds in my ears. What all does he know?

Raizo rubs his forefinger and thumb together as he turns around and paces across the room. "Don't think I didn't see your little chat with LVPD the other day."

Martin. Of course. "Belligerent house guests tend to stir up trouble." *In more ways than one...* "Being a public figure like I am, I have to deal with LVPD on a fairly regular basis. You understand."

"I understand how easy it would be for you to arrange the auction as a, shall we say, 'public performance.'" He turns on his heel to face me. "You are not reconsidering our deal, are you?"

"Of course not."

"Good. Because let me make something exceptionally clear to you, Mr. Zakrevsky." Raizo remains calm, but his fury crackles in the air as he offers a wolfish smile. "If you fuck me over in this, we won't just be through as business partners. I will rain down upon you the full fury of the Yakuza until all that remains of you and your precious

Bratva are distant memories collecting dust in the police archives."

I cock a brow. "You seem to forget where you are, Mr. Watanabe."

His smile widens as he sweeps an arm around us. "Home base. I know. Which is why I am here, to give you the full sincerity of my words. I do not threaten someone within their own home; I make promises I fully intend to keep."

"The Yakuza—"

"Has been eyeing Las Vegas for many years now. My sector, small as it is, has been extremely profitable, most especially with the skin trade. Do you think any of the other clans will allow some Russian bastard and his band of bleeding hearts to stand in their way?"

I scoff. And then, on second thought, I outright laugh. "Come, Raizo. All this from what, bad timing?" I usher him toward the back door of the study, the one that leads to a direct path to the secondary courtyard. The one that nobody, least of all Clara or Willow, ever visits. "I think we both need a good drink. This auction has us on edge."

Raizo is not as easily misdirected. He peers at me, seems to think something over, then follows me with a terse nod.

I send a quick text to the household group chat for a bartender to be ready and waiting by the entertainment pool. I don't care who it is; I just need to get Raizo tipsy enough to ease off and fuck off.

"Let's talk details. I just confirmed this morning that the entire hotel has been reserved for the event. The last thing either of us needs is some honeymooning couple crashing the wrong room, right?"

I wanted to grind my teeth to powder when Bambi ran the numbers for the hotel accommodations for Raizo's auction. Hundreds of rooms that ought to be going for thousands per night means millions of dollars that won't end up in my pocket. And that's just the hotel fees; I don't even want to think about the ballroom rental, catering, waitstaff, decor…

"What's your average selling rate per artifact?" I casually ask Raizo as we settle into the outdoor bar.

He chuckles as he gestures to the bartender to bring him an imported beer. "Don't worry, my friend; I'll make sure you're more than compensated for your efforts."

"Call me curious." I nod to Gary, the bartender on duty, to just bring me the whole bottle of bourbon and a glass of ice. I'm going to need it.

Raizo snorts. "You should. Average sale per woman is anywhere from one point five to seven. *Million.*"

Figures like that should have me excited. Curious for a taste, even.

I don't know why the liquor suddenly turns to ash in my stomach.

"Times how many per auction?"

"Depends on the reaping and culling." He sees my swift, sharp glance at him and he holds up a hand. "My elite clientele buys the cream of the crop. The others, we sell at a discount price and they end up… well, you've seen the edge of town."

I have. I prefer to avoid those areas: the outer rim, the backside of the Strip, the Red Light District. It's not a place you go for a repeat trip.

Raizo studies my face. "If you're concerned about your particular contribution to the auction, don't be."

I'm not. I tell myself I'm not every time his texts pop up on my phone. So I repeat the mantra out loud for both our benefits. "Why would I be concerned? You're doing me a favor."

"Am I?"

I take a long, deep swig of bourbon. "If you think I'm going to blow up our treaty over some whiny, petulant woman I can't wait to get rid of... well, my friend, you're out of your damn mind."

Raizo doesn't join my laughter nor does he stop peering at me over his bottle. "She didn't tell you, did she?"

I pause. Something sinks inside me, but I don't let him see how his words get to me. "You're going to have to be more specific."

He thinks about it. Then sighs with a nod. "Fair enough. I don't imagine anyone would want to brag about their ties to the Yakuza."

The only reason why I don't choke on my next sip is sheer willpower.

Raizo stares at me before he breaks into a genuine laugh. "Oh my God, Zakrevsky, you should see your face. Clara Everett is Detective Greg Everett's daughter. Everyone knows that. *I* know that. I've dealt with her father many times before over the past few decades." He leans in closer. "Which is how I know 'whiny' and 'petulant' are things she is not."

I should be taking this in stride. I should be grateful to be so close to avenging Tolya. I should be laughing at his jokes and playing the good host for the sake of our treaty.

But I'm just not feeling it.

"If you know her so well, how is it easy to just throw her to the wolves?"

Raizo shrugs. "Money. Is there anything more seductive?"

I can think of a few things. All of them are attached to Clara. "Must be a pretty high price—"

"Twenty million."

Excuse me?

He sets the bottle on the counter with a decisive thunk. "Twenty million dollars, starting bid. And as I've said before, the selective bidders all agreed to bring cash on site."

I don't have a fucking clue how he managed to manipulate the market around Clara. And I'm quickly realizing I don't want to know.

"I hope we're sticking to our agreement," I say instead.

"Of course. You get half of her proceeds and twenty percent of the rest."

I freeze. "The original agreement was for thirty."

Raizo clicks his tongue at me. "Now, now. Don't get greedy on me. You stand to make a baseline of ten million from one sale alone. What's a minor adjustment going to do for your books, hm?"

I set my glass down and discreetly signal for the bartender to leave. After a quick wipedown of the counter, he does, and I slide off the bar stool with all the collective calm I can muster.

"It's one thing for you to arrive unannounced to my home." I force a smile that he does not mistake as being genuine or happy. "Unarmed and unguarded, except for your driver. Don't worry—we've been making sure he stays comfortable."

Raizo stands and opens his mouth to retort, but I hold a hand up to stop him.

"It's an entirely different level of disrespect to threaten me in my own house, then turn around and try to cheat me out of ten percent. Give me one very good reason why I shouldn't have you gunned down on your way out."

He doesn't seem fazed, but everyone has their tell. His is in the way he quickly wets his lips—they get dry when he's nervous.

Then he pulls out his cell phone and holds it up to me. "I saw the alert. Seemed as good a time as any to have a chat and clarify a few details. You can't afford to have the cops sniffing around here, especially when you're harboring Miss Everett and her brat."

Ice shoots through my veins. "Excuse me?"

Raizo pockets his phone and nods. "I saw the toys on my way in. The children's books in the study—"

"You mean Gloria's grandkids?" I laugh and shake my head. "Really, Raizo. Do I look like the babysitting type?" I clap a hand on his shoulder and steer him back down the side pathway we took here. "Half my staff lives on site. Of course we're going to have kids visit now and then, especially for my head housekeeper. She's got more grandchildren than you have skeletons in your closet."

I usher him out the front door to his waiting car.

"I'll settle on twenty-five percent or the deal's off. Including the event."

Raizo turns to me, his voice low. "Throw in the kid and you can have seventy."

I pretend to not know what the hell he's talking about. I shove my hands into my pockets so he doesn't see my fists clench.

"Think about it, Demyen," he suggests when I don't answer. "If you think Clara's bringing in a good price, you should see how much the other side pays." Raizo glances over my shoulder at the compound, his eyes calculating.

But then he gives me one final nod and slides into his car.

The only reason why I don't give the order to gun him and his vintage Rolls Royce down is because he's right—now is the worst time to draw attention from the police.

What has me on edge is the sudden realization that I don't know Raizo as well as I thought I did—and I sure as hell never fathomed how far his greed would go.

There are many things I've done and will probably do in my life. Terrible things. Unforgivable things.

But my God, there are limits even for men like me.

And the fact that Raizo doesn't have them makes him far more dangerous than any of us can afford to fuck with.

65

DEMYEN

"Double up security. Pull in guards from each location and set a rotation for every half hour."

Bambi scrambles to keep up with me, both physically and on her tablet. She met me at the door after Raizo left and now, she's tripping over her sandals to match my furious pace. "I take it that went well."

"He's a sick fuck." I'm doing my best to not vomit the bourbon every time his final words echo in my head. "And he's unpredictable. Those two things are a deadly combination."

The first place I beeline for is Willow's room. She's sound asleep in her bed, curled around her doll with a storybook spread face-down on the floor. Clara isn't in there, which means bedtime went well and Willow must have snuck in one last book before falling asleep.

I can't help but smile.

And then instantly feel sick to my stomach when Raizo's "offer" bubbles up in my head again.

"Get a second room set up for her, just in case." I slowly, silently test the door handle and frown. "And add a better lock on here. Make sure the second room is close enough to get her in within ninety seconds."

"Want it set up like a panic room? Bolted doors and security feeds and all that?"

I know she's trying to lighten the mood by being facetious, but I also know she wasn't there to hear Raizo Watanabe's disgusting threat. "Yes. Exactly like that. But comfortable and familiar enough that she won't be too scared."

Bambi frowns and lowers her stylus. "Dem... what's going on?"

We're too close to Clara's room to have this discussion. Even if she is asleep, one mention of Willow's name will undoubtedly wake her up.

So I gesture for Bambi to continue walking with me until we're out of earshot. "Raizo threatened Willow."

Bambi sucks in a sharp breath. "He doesn't think she's here, does he?"

"It's that fucking AMBER Alert. And he saw the toys, the books..." I want to rip my hair out. "I passed it off as Gloria's grandkids visiting, but he knows."

I'm going to murder Martin. Slowly. Painfully. If anything happens to that little girl, I'm going to make him wish for death long before I give it to him.

"So..."

"So he offered to sell her."

Even in the sliver of moonlight, I can see the blood drain from Bambi's face. "No. He wouldn't."

Every word tastes like bile on my tongue. "He would and he will if he gets an opportunity to grab her. Apparently, there's no market off-limits to him."

She thinks on this for a long, tense moment. By the way her own fury and disgust twists her face with each passing second, I'm getting the impression all I need to do is hand her a gun. Raizo won't stand a chance.

"So what about Clara?"

I hesitate. That's something I'm not wanting to delve into. "What about her?"

Bambi focuses her glare on her tablet screen as she makes notes of the new panic room specifications. "You're gonna let her go to that meeting? Even with all these threats?"

I clench my fist. "She wants to go."

"So stop her."

I roll my eyes. "You think I didn't try? She won't listen—"

"So tie her up and throw her into your bedroom until she does!" Bambi throws her hands into the air, exasperated. "You and I both know it's a trap. They'll arrest her faster than they'll brew the coffee."

"So what if it is? Maybe she'll be better off in prison."

"Wow." She laughs and shakes her head. "I've watched you make some interesting decisions, but this one takes the cake."

Bambi is walking a very fine line between honesty and insubordination. "Careful," I warn.

"Or what? You'll punish me for doing you a favor and telling you the truth?" I don't respond. So she continues, "None of it makes sense. But I see the way you are with her. Hell, I see the way you are with Willow. Are you going to stand there, look me in the eye, and tell me that you're totally okay with Clara getting cuffed and thrown behind bars for trying to protect her baby girl?"

Fuck no, I'm not okay with it. But I don't say that out loud.

"And what about Willow?" Bambi tilts her head to one side. "Hmm? You're not her biological father or her legal guardian. The second Clara's arrested for child endangerment and kidnapping, they'll interrogate her until she's forced to reveal the location of her child. And then where will Willow go, after this place gets raided by the police and they inevitably find her?"

She's speaking as my attorney as much as my friend. I know that. I don't have to like it, though. In fact, I hate where she's going with this.

"Think about it, Dem. Think about Martin just waltzing in here and taking Willow away to go live with him. Unsupervised, away from her mother. The one parent who actually loves her."

My fists clench tighter. My jaw does, too.

She digs that theoretical knife in deeper. "You and I both know Martin is dirty. He's dirty and he's greedy. Greg Everett is even worse." Her face contorts like it sickens her to even say it. "What's going to happen if Raizo gives either of them the same offer?"

When I still don't respond, she sighs, shakes her head, and walks away. I hear her muttering something about wallpaper for the panic room, but other than that, she leaves me to my frustrated internal debates.

I was ready to let Clara do whatever the fuck she wants. But I can't, I *won't*, let Martin get his hands on her ever again.

And I won't let her out of my sight now that I know the disgusting ends Raizo will go to just to make himself more money.

I have to protect my family.

66

CLARA

The doorbell jingles above my head as I'm greeted with the signature smell of Happy's Hotcakes fresh off the griddle.

It's been Dad's favorite place for coffee and a quick bite to eat between shifts for years. It's quiet, cozy, and pretty good comfort food. I have to admit, I was actually looking forward to this.

Not anymore. My excitement drains from my body the moment I see the back of Martin's head sitting in the same booth as Dad.

Who, much to my bad luck, immediately spots me and waves me over.

I slide into Dad's side of the booth and pointedly avoid looking up at Martin. But I see enough of him in my peripheral vision to note the patronizing smile on his face.

"Isn't this nice?" Dad cheerfully quips as he flags down a waitress for a refill. "Get what you want, honey. It's on me."

What I *want* is to slap the smile off Martin's face.

What I *want* is to just go home and be with my child.

What I *want* is for all of this to just go away and leave me alone so Demyen and I—

I stop myself from delving into those thoughts. It's bad enough I'm calling his home my home as well. I shouldn't be thinking about him in a "we" sense.

I mutter an order of hotcakes to the waitress, despite not really feeling hungry. I know that if I don't eat something, Dad will needle me with questions and criticisms until I do.

"So, Clar-Bear," Dad starts with his best *I'm-only-thinking-of-you* voice, "Martin's told me all about his side. Now, I want to hear yours. And he's promised to let you finish before jumping in. Right, Martin?"

Martin nods and sips his coffee. I'm struck with the notion that I've always hated his mustache; it just never stuck out to me until now. Now, while I watch the cream-filled coffee soak his facial hair, I just...

Ew. I kissed that?!

"Well, let's see." I stir the lemon wedge in my ice water, gathering my thoughts as much as my courage. "I was tired of being Martin's punching bag. And I feared for my daughter's safety. So I left."

Dad slowly rolls his wrist, waving for me to continue. To elaborate.

I look at him, confused. "What more is there to say? He hit me, Dad. All the time. Thank God he never did that while I was pregnant! Slapping me around and pulling my hair and forcing me to—" I stop myself. We're in a public place, after all.

"Forcing you to what?" Dad gently asks.

Suddenly, those hotcakes sound like a terrible idea. I might end up puking them right back onto the table. "Honestly? That shouldn't matter. It should be enough for you that he hit me. Martin *hit* your child."

Dad scoffs. "You're hardly a child, Clara. Don't be so dramatic."

But right when I'm ready to climb back out of the booth and leave this fucking diner, he surprises me. "Still, these are pretty serious accusations I know you wouldn't make lightly."

Hope blooms in my chest. Does he... does Dad actually believe me?

He levels his hard stare at Martin. "Well? Is this true? Did you abuse my daughter?"

The way he says it makes that hope burst wide open. He sounds angry. He sounds like he's ready to arrest Martin for domestic assault and child endangerment. He sounds like the protective father I need him to be.

Martin balks. "What kind of question is that? Really, Greg, I thought you knew me better."

Dad sips his own coffee and doesn't look away once. "I thought I did, too. But now, my Clar-Bear is telling me some very disturbing things about you and how you treat her. What am I supposed to think?"

Finally. He's finally on my side.

"What are you—" Martin scoffs and leans back in his seat. When he looks at me, it's all fake sympathy as he slowly shakes his head. "God, Clara... I am so sorry. I should have been there for you more. I should have… God, I should have been more careful."

I have no idea what he's talking about. And neither does Dad, who squints at him.

Martin holds a hand out to me. "I know it's been stressful, being home alone with our daughter. And I haven't always been there for you. That's my fault and yeah, I'm gonna own it."

"What are you—"

"Fuck, Greg, you remember that case over in Summerlin?" He turns to Dad, sadness etched all over his face like a cheap mask. "That woman and her mental break?"

Dad heaves a heavy sigh. "I'll never be able to forget that one." He stirs another sugar packet into his coffee, only glancing up at me once. "Mother of four. Stayed at home, lost her mind. Drowned all her kids before she tried killing herself. Terrible."

Martin solemnly nods. "Absolutely terrible. And I'm gonna say it right now: I should have learned from that and spent more time with Clara and the baby."

"The baby." She has a fucking name, asshole.

"Is that what's going on, honey?" Dad rests his hand on my shoulder. "We can get you help—"

"I don't need 'help.'" I bite the words so I don't burst into tears. "What I *need* is for Martin to get the fuck out of my life and away from my daughter!"

Martin simply looks at me, fake empathy in his eyes as he slowly shakes his head. "I didn't know it'd gotten this bad. When I saw the drug cabinet go empty, I just… Honestly, I don't know what I thought. Clearly, I should have paid more attention to you and I'm so sorry."

Dad rubs my back. "When did you start using, honey? It's okay—no one is going to arrest you. We just want to help you."

I can't breathe. I can't breathe. My ribcage is folding in and my lungs are squeezing so tight...

"Clara? Are you okay?"

Martin clicks his tongue. "She must be going through withdrawal. Baby, I'm here—"

I almost stab his hand with a fork when he reaches for me. *Almost*, as in, it's definitely in my hand. And I definitely slammed down on top of his outstretched hand. I just had the stupid, merciful thought to cover the prongs before taking the plunge.

"Don't. Touch. Me."

I don't know where this is coming from. I've never let my rage simmer over and burst out of me in their faces. I've always been too scared of their retaliation.

Now? I don't fucking care what they do.

And it.

Feels.

Phenomenal.

Martin pulls his hand back, eyes wide with surprise. He swallows, hard.

Dad tries to grab my hand. "Clara—"

"You, too." I turn on him, literally as well as figuratively. I grit my teeth and keep my voice low, but there's no mistaking my fury for anything else. "Get. Your hands. Off. Me."

For a moment, I don't think he actually will. But then I see him glance around us and I'm suddenly aware of the eyes flicking our way as this scene unfolds. A man sits in one corner, casually reading a newspaper. A tired nurse, still in her scrubs, pokes at a stack of pancakes at the counter. The waitress freshens up the coffeemaker but keeps glancing our way.

Neither Dad nor Martin are in uniform. For all anyone knows, they're a couple of guys seriously stressing out a lone woman.

So Dad removes his hand from my shoulder and sarcastically lifts both of his in mock surrender. "Alright, Clara. You're calling the shots."

I'd feel like I've finally accomplished something, if it weren't for the fact that I know that exact jargon from his years in the force. He's not conceding—he's starting hostage negotiations.

Demyen was right: this was a trap. No one wants to hear me out or actually help me; they just want me to play Good Girl and do exactly what they want, whenever they want.

Fuck me, right? As long as Martin gets his dick wet and can lord his claim over my daughter.

And as long as Dad gets to feel like he's actually doing something good for a change. Fuck if he actually does. I needed him, now more than ever, and he dangled that carrot in front of me without blinking.

I slap my palms on the table and start to slide out of the booth. "Well, this has been hell. I'm out."

"You can't just leave—"

"I can and I will." I stare Martin dead in the eyes. "I did it before, didn't I? At least now you'll be able to watch me leave."

"Clara." Dad lifts a hand again, as if I'm about to bite his head off again. "We just want to know you and Willow are safe."

"She is. We are."

"Where is she?"

"With a friend." *A friend with a whole fucking army.* The thought makes my lips tug up in a tiny smile.

Dad narrows his eyes. "Who? I already checked with Roxy."

Martin's whole countenance shifts. I feel it before I see it; it happened so often back when I was dumb and naive enough to stick around for his twisted games. The air around him grows colder. His posture stiffens.

He glares at me. He knows exactly where Willow is, who she's with, and it pisses him off.

So he stares daggers at me.

And then he slides out of the booth and grabs my arm. "Clara Everett, you are under arrest for kidnapping and child endangerment—"

I'm suddenly bent over the table with both arms forcefully twisted behind my back. "What? No! *No!* Get off me!"

I hear the clicking of his cuffs as he pulls them from his pocket. "You have the right to remain silent. Anything you say or do—"

Gunshots.

Screams.

Oh, God.

But it's not inside the diner. It's outside, only a block away. People are screaming and running into the streets, ducking for cover and frantically trying to dial their loved ones.

Dad springs into action. He may be off-duty, but he's still a cop. "Forget it, Martin. We need to go."

"But—"

"*Now!*"

My father is already out the door. Martin growls with frustration, then pockets his cuffs and pulls out a zip tie instead. "This is some timing, don't you think?" He snarls in my ear as he tightens the plastic around my wrists.

I don't know what to think. I just don't want to get shot by a stray bullet through the window.

Martin yanks me to my feet and shoves me to the door, one hand braced against my back while the other holds the tie. He curses under his breath the whole way and even louder once we're outside.

"I know this has something to do with your new boyfriend," he continues to snarl. He yanks open the back door of his squad car and shoves me onto the hard seat. "So is it just him you're fucking? Or do you let the whole goddamn gang get a taste?"

More gunshots, then a small explosion. Now, Martin seems to be taking the attack seriously, because he flinches and ducks behind the door for a moment.

"Stay here," he barks at me. Then he slams the door shut, hitting my shins with the sidebar.

Like I'm going anywhere...

I can't. I can't breathe. I can't move. I can't stop shaking.

I don't wanna die.

I don't wanna go to jail, either.

I want to just be able to get up and walk away from here. But I can't because I can't breathe and I can't move and I can't *think...*

Spots blur my vision. I hear more than feel my lungs wheeze for every gasping breath.

I'm having a full-blown panic attack.

Tears roll down my face as I struggle to breathe, or even move beyond the violent shaking in my limbs. I'm so fucking scared and the worst part is, I'm not sure which outcome terrifies me more: getting shot in some streetside attack, getting arrested and thrown in jail, or going back to Martin.

I think I'm gonna throw up.

Someone yanks the back door open.

And the panic swallows me whole.

TO BE CONTINUED

Demyen and Clara's story continues in Book 2 of the Zakrevsky Bratva trilogy, SONATA OF LIES.

Printed in Great Britain
by Amazon